QUEEN OF DIAMONDS

HIGH ROLLER OMEGAS

MARIE MACKAY

Everly Yours Cover Design

Thank you to Nika for sensitivity reading, and Jayla Jacobs for looking over scenes that referenced to Knight's locs to ensure they were culturally accurate and appropriate.

Thank you to my amazing alpha readers and ARC readers for keeping up with the chaos!

SWEET KNIGHTS
GLADE
KYAN
QUEEN OF DIAMONDS
MARIE MACKAY
ART BY @LUCIELART

THE HIGH ROLLERS

Welcome to the High Roller Omegas, a shared Omegaverse universe.
Our world adheres to many classic Omegaverse rules, but to stay true to each author's inspiration, we have kept them as broad as possible. Scent matching, for example, occurs with preformed packs, individuals—and there are even soul matches. In addition, we have both omega-centric packs (biting the omega to bond) and alpha-centric packs (pre-established).
The four High Roller books all spend time in the High Roller, a Las Vegas club, and we hope you enjoy your stay!

Glade's book is also followed by another duet from me, Psycho Alphas, which follows characters that are introduced in this book!

CONTENT

Anything I should know about before I start!

Yes! There is bully romance for about half the book with one guys on the her side always. There's gun and knife violence, poison; torture, murder + dismemberment (bad guys). A near death experience with discussion of CPR. Extended emotionally + physically abusive captivity of FMC prior to book start.

Other woman trigger: MMC taunts FMC mentioning prior sexual experiences + threatens to bring another omega in to make her jealous. Threat is not followed through with (+ she learns he's a big fat liar).

Anything else?

In passing mentions: the torture of Omegas via isolation during heats, extreme + psychological mistreatment of an Omega within a scent match. Discussions of suicide attempt (not followed through with), mental health struggles + oppressive upbringings.

There's also spicy group scenes, sub/dom dynamics, and CNC (undiscussed on page) primal MM. This list is non extensive.

Oh, and I write in British English (Realize/realise).

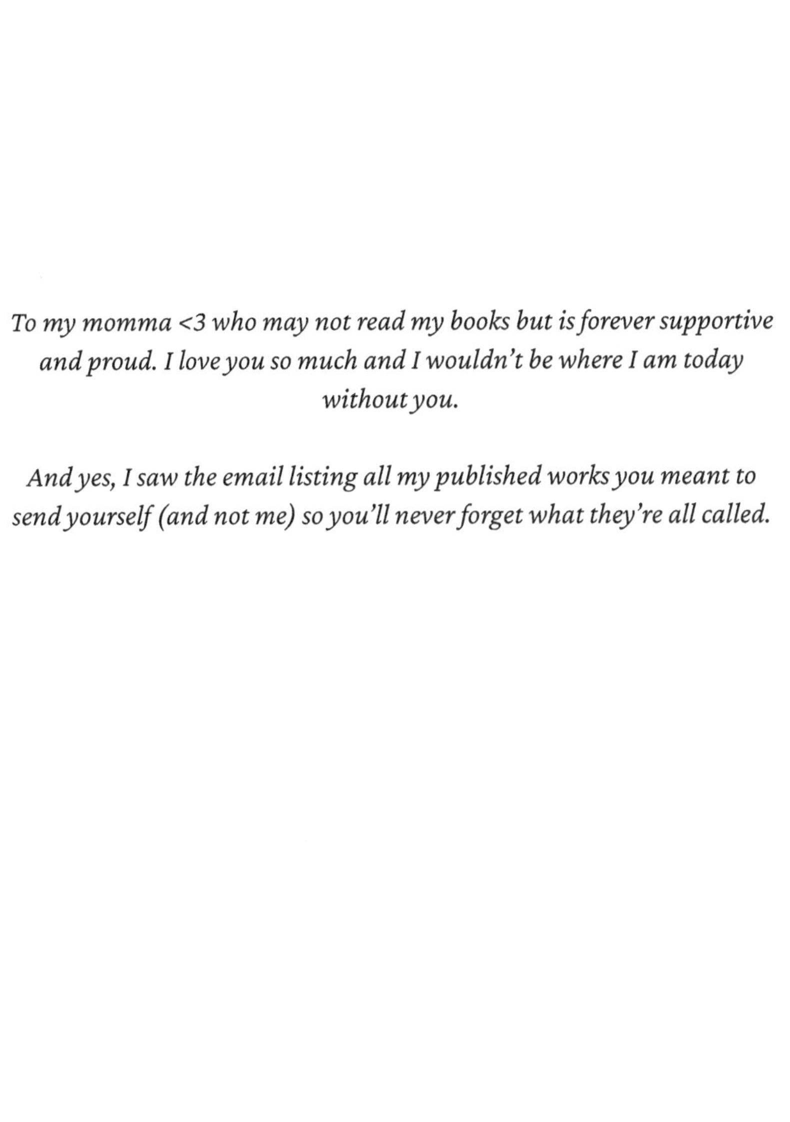

To my momma <3 who may not read my books but is forever supportive and proud. I love you so much and I wouldn't be where I am today without you.

And yes, I saw the email listing all my published works you meant to send yourself (and not me) so you'll never forget what they're all called.

1

Black coffee was a shot of adrenaline to sleepless veins.

The first sip was as bitter as it was necessary as I peered down through the broad breakroom window. Below me was an opulent club with the spotlights that lit up a dance stage.

I was a bartender at the High Roller where rich patrons came to watch Omegas dance—Omegas with a thousand times more confidence than me. But that didn't stop me from admiring them from my little table in the breakroom that overlooked the floor.

The building was nothing to scoff at. It was cavernous, with lavish velvet drapes lining the walls, and gleaming fixtures that cast golden pools on the kingdom below. The floor was busy with wealthy guests of all kinds who were milling at bars and casino tables, but in the centre was a massive stage, and Jade drew the eyes of the whole room as she began to dance.

This place was more than just a job to me; the High Roller was my home. Literally—since I lived in suite four beneath the club—

but there was far more to it than that. The people here were the only family I had.

Tallow, the other bartender tonight, was covering for me—which delighted him, since one of his favourite packs was here, and lavishing him with all the attention he absolutely didn't need.

He could keep the tips.

I needed caffeine.

I always settled here to watch the floor on my breaks, not just to admire the dancers, but I was proud of what they had claimed.

Something I never would.

The Omegas here were all breathtaking. With every movement it was as if I watched them reclaim something from this world—and so many of the women who worked here deserved that.

I couldn't catch her scent from here, but by the state of the Alphas in the firing line (who were leaning forward and practically drooling on their shirts), she was wielding it with as much skill as her dance. That's what the Omegas here were like: world-stoppingly beautiful and able to command a room full of Alphas with such authority that packs might step out of this club and be shocked to find there were other Omegas left on the planet.

But that wasn't the part that made me envious—not that I would ever admit to that; it wasn't a good look. I loved everyone who worked here, even if some of them kept their distance. I wasn't good at showing people I liked them, never had been. I'd been trained to walk and talk like a mafia princess, as lonely as she was deadly. It was a protection I couldn't shake, but sometimes that put people off.

But Jade... I could see it in her eyes. In her smile that lit in the brief seconds that the music lulled. I think she loved dancing as much as the Alphas loved to watch. I was so fucking proud of what she'd done for herself here. I knew, because she was a talk-out-loud kind, and would chat my ear off at the bar without the slightest concern that I'd never quite figured out how to act like friends were supposed to.

But that was the true secret to how she drew every eye—the reason it could never be me, no matter how long the club left the offer on the table. No matter if I sometimes came back to the room below after the doors shut. Even if I sat on the edge of the stage in the dark, staring up at vacant lights, empty casino tables, and shadows of huge drapes.

I would never have the confidence the others had.

"So. How did the date go?"

I contained my wince as a drink was set at the table beside me, ripping me ungracefully from my self-pity. I think it was the years of dancing that gave Leisha the uncanny ability to sneak up on people with such ease.

Shit.

"Date," I said with a side eye, "Is a strong word."

Her dirty blond hair was loose, long enough to frame both her pretty face and generous cleavage. *She* was unbelievable on the stage and she had a presence that made me think she was a female Alpha in another life. I might struggle to get close to people, but from the first time Leisha had smiled at me, I felt like she was the older sister I'd never had. It was impossible not to trust her.

She sipped on her drink, waiting quietly.

"It went well," I lied, glancing down at my nails. They were mismatched, one painted with a muted lilac I had on hand instead of the silver I'd got at the salon. I'd patched it after it had snapped last night.

· · ·

I'd arrived early to the restaurant.

The bustle of servers and fellow diners was nothing but white noise as I stared at the Alpha dressed in a smart suit three tables down. I hadn't realised how hard I was clutching my handbag until a nail snapped against it.

I shook it off, focusing instead on the Alpha waiting for me—Kent Warner.

Except, when I'd walked up to the table, I'd panicked and hurried on by, dropping into this seat instead, grateful it wasn't a reservations only kind of place.

What if he wanted to come home with me?

I mean, he would. He'd been told I was looking for a decent meal and a hookup. But he didn't know what I looked like—I'd asked Leisha to keep that part quiet.

I was done up my best, my makeup was pristine, nails were salon-fresh, and my usual studded earrings were in. 'Omega goddess' was the term Leisha had used when she'd finished adjusting my dress straps. The scars on my upper back ached beneath this thin silk, but the fabric covered them well.

Would he think I was hot, though?

Did I want him to?

"You're beautiful, Glade. You haunt the dreams of every Alpha here." I heard the ghost of a whisper as if he were next to me. The voice was Ace's, curdling with nightmares in the blink of an eye.

Still, I was staring at Kent from afar, fingers digging into my purse for dear life.

All I had to do was approach him.

Leisha had set me up well. Her texts were clear. She'd told him I was a sexy Omega bartender not looking for commitment, and that my resting bitch face wasn't real. Couldn't ask for a better wing-woman.

"Kent was charming," I said, taking another sip of my horrible coffee. "And just as pretty as you promised."

I'd had this whole plan in my head for the date, like I was sixteen again, and my stomach turned at the idea of a kiss.

We would eat, there would be small talk. It didn't have to come up that I was a mafia princess sold for an alliance the moment I'd turned eighteen. That I had left three scent matches who'd loved me on their knees, staring down the barrel of rejection and exile. Or that—after everything—I'd fled two years later, and now I was on the run from one of the most powerful men in the state. That there was a trail of destruction in my wake, a wreckage that haunted me every second I couldn't keep it away.

Instead, I could lie and be whoever I wanted: as confident as Jade, as sweet as Elena, or as cunning as Annika.

I'd planned to tell him mundane, normal stuff—like how I liked sweet potato fries over truffle fries, and maybe we'd discuss hobbies—like I had any normal ones, cold night sweats driving me to kickboxing in my living room didn't sound quite as simple as 'I enjoy crime TV'.

And after, maybe we would go to his place. If I did, I could leave at any moment I needed to. Only he was an Alpha. The apartment would smell like him.

His territory...

And when he touched me, maybe he would have had enough drinks not to notice how broken I was? The touch of an Alpha was like a hot iron for me, making me shiver, and turning my brain foggy with a need I was afraid of. For years my hormones were worn thin, tortured and twisted so far beyond what was natural it left me vulnerable. It's why I stayed alone, though I wish I could blame it on only that. It wasn't like I'd dated betas, either.

So, naturally, I'd chickened out, yet the plan was still spiralling in my head again as I clutched my coffee mug. Like telling myself this lie would make it easier to tell Leisha.

What would have happened next, though?

Well, next, I'd put on an oversized night robe, we'd watch Netflix all night, and he'd cuddle me.

Like... we'd actually watch Netflix, and nothing else would happen.

Okay.

I knew that last part was stupid.

Somehow, after ages in that restaurant, I'd found the courage to stand from my chair, knowing I had to try to make this work.

It would be fun.

One piece of myself at a time, I'd clawed back, and this was next. Why shouldn't I enjoy a nice dinner and the knot of a sweet Alpha? Well... not too sweet. Gentle was a taunt, silk laced with poison designed to make me suffer.

I shoved the thought away. Ace's games would never leave. They were the last thing I had never faced. But tonight, I'd rid myself of him forever.

Only, as I'd stood, Kent shifted, reaching down and setting something long and slender on the table.

A wrapped rose.

The gesture was common, romantic, and innocent. But a thousand games flooded back. A thousand nightmares, and that alone was enough to send me fleeing.

I'd spent the next twenty minutes in the restaurant bathroom retching up stomach acid.

"Decent in bed," I told Leisha with a grin. "Well—he kept up."

Leisha's eyes slid to me for only the briefest flicker, as if trying to work out what was happening.

That meant she knew.

Of course she knew. I'd never replied. I'd switched my phone off and ran. Kent was from one of her (many) social circles, and the Omega she'd set him up with last night had bailed with no warning.

Still, without flinching, Leisha took another sip of her drink. "Ex-military," she said. "Was told he had stamina."

My smile widened as she played along.

"Kept me busy until the morning," I said.

I'd fled the date to do the only thing that made me feel better.

The recoil of the shot struck me to the bones. Goosebumps rose across my body. The gun range wasn't well insulated, and I hadn't changed. The brush of the black dress Leisha had helped me choose was cool against my skin.

I shifted my gun again toward the forehead of a faceless poster.

Never faceless.

Not to me.

Dorian, the beta who ran the range, never asked me to leave and never said a word when I slipped by him at one a.m., two hours after it should have closed.

At home, I stood at the foot of my bed, hugging myself, broken nail tapping anxiously at my waist as I stared at my pillows in the dim room.

Paranoid.

"Roses are normal," I chided. "Get a grip."

Still, I knew if I lay my head down on those pillows, they would swallow me into the late hours of the morning, trapping me in night-mares I couldn't escape.

I'd turned the late night news on and began drills I'd long committed to memory on the heavy punching bag that hung from the ceiling in my room. Sweat glistened across my skin in the morning light before I'd dared pass to my blaring TV, feeling safe

*that no broadcast had whispered the name of the Brotherhood in the
area.*

"You were right," I said, watching the club below as the music
finally came to an end. "A night like that was exactly what I needed." I wasn't expecting the burn in my eyes as those words struggled out of my mouth. I shoved the tears back, horrified. I was at
work.

I couldn't cry at fucking work.

But maybe… maybe that date *was* exactly what I needed.

What if Kent really had been nice? What if we'd spent the
night together, and I'd panicked when I reached for the hem of
my dress, and he had been okay cuddling me in my oversized
bathrobe while we watched Netflix?

I was fooling myself about all of this.

I was a shell.

A lonely, broken coward.

Three years, and Ace was still stealing from me with every
breath I took.

I sat beside Leisha for a while in silence. She was watching the
floor below with a half smile on her lips, she was the mother hen
to all the girls here.

When my break was over, I took the last sip of my coffee with
a sigh. Two hours of sleep wasn't enough for a night as busy as
tonight, and I was fully committed to never trying that date
debacle again.

I didn't need an Alpha. I didn't even want one.

Not Kent, anyway.

There were things I'd claimed back. It had taken such a long
time, but I had. At first, I hated what was stolen. I hated the shell
I'd become. But in the years since, I'd seen the gift on the other
side of that coin.

I'd discovered the things in life I wanted for no one but me.

I'd been raised a seductress, reared like a sheep for sale at a market, no better than livestock. A role that would gain my mafia father the most for his only Omega daughter. But I hadn't been prepared for what had happened next. No one could have been trained for that, and the Omega who'd stumbled from that nightmare years later was a husk.

I'd been broken down into rubble.

Everything I had now, everything that lifted my spirits or made me smile, was something I'd fought for. And in that was the gift.

Like the moment I realised I could get my nails done, and that was safe. I loved doing them for me, and it had nothing to do with Ace—or anyone else. Seeing the trigger of a gun between long nails was just... sexy, and *I* liked it. Even if the stupid things broke at inconvenient moments.

I only wished this gift was ready to start dealing out as many highs as it did lows.

When had I fought enough?

I was so tired of being fragile. I wanted normal. Instead, it felt that with every day I regressed. The last few weeks had been the worst. I'd seen threats around every corner, felt like I was being followed each time I left the High Roller. I'd even ordered groceries to my doorstep so I didn't have to go out.

And the roses?

I saw them everywhere. Petals tumbling in the wind until I blinked to find it was drifting garbage. A bundle of thorns like a bouquet with the flower heads ripped off—but there were some weirdos around here, and they could have been any flowers.

I wanted to be like Leisha, in her fierce claim on her own life. But for me, weakness was the default, and strength was something I had to fight to get a glimpse of.

My fault. All of it.

I was an Omega who'd rejected her own scent matches. I'd thrown away a connection that should have meant happiness and love. I'd given up a pack that wanted to love and protect me.

There was no one left in this world who would truly look out for me—no one but me. And this is what my life looks like now.

Three years of fighting to get on my feet, only to be destroyed by a rose.

2

"Rose Royale." Tallow's voice snapped me to the present.

"What?" My voice was dry as I spun on him, almost knocking over a row of flutes.

It was the next evening, and I was thoroughly wrecked. I'd been haunted by nightmares and, once more, barely got a wink of sleep. I usually loved when my shift came around—especially on days I worked with Tallow, but today, the goal was to survive to the next caffeine infusion.

Tallow frowned. "Guy at the end wants a Rose Royale, Kir Royale with a—"

"I know what it is." We'd done them far too much last Valentine's.

But I was getting whiplash.

Roses—again?

I stared at the Alpha at the end of the bar. He looked normal enough, I supposed. Neat suit, buzzed hair. There was a tattoo creeping just up above his collar, but that wasn't unusual. The bar's mahogany surface reflected the soft, ambient lighting, upon which he was quietly playing a game of solitaire, laying his cards out before him one by one.

He wasn't looking at me as he waited.

Right.

It meant nothing.

"You don't want him?" I asked.

"He's your type, Ice Queen," Tallow said with a grin. We played a bit of a good cop, bad cop scenario, covering the bases of clients who liked the fun-loving male Omega energy Tallow brought to the table, or the much cooler energy I gave out. "Besides, I've got gossip to hear from over there." He nodded his head toward a pack in the corner. They were regulars, and very up in the know with High Roller politics. "Apparently, a mob guy... Forbes? I think, commandeered Spades for the night, brought his full security team and all. Bet Travis is fuming."

I raised my eyebrows, the news catching me off guard a little. Private security wasn't usually allowed in the club. It explained why there were less of the guys up here—they were probably making it a pissing match.

"It's Spades. Don't care if he's mob, no way he stands a chance against Annika," Tallow scoffed.

I snorted. He wasn't wrong. Annika was one of the Omegas who worked here, and Spades—one of the private card rooms— was hers. She was a no bullshit type—spotting card counters a mile off, and I was also convinced she had secrets just like I did. I couldn't be sure, but something about the way she held herself felt like looking at a reflection. Especially if she'd been recruited just like I had. I had a suspicion the manager, Travis, was a little more in the know of the city's underbelly than he let on. I don't think I was the only Omega who had found refuge in this place.

I tried to pull myself together and not think too hard about the Rose Royale order, even as I made it, then took a breath, steadying my nerves as I glanced back at the Alpha and his solitaire game.

None of it meant anything. I had gossip waiting for me when Tallow returned from that pack—that was much more worth focusing on.

I forced a smile on my face as I reached him, the clink of the crystal glass sliding across the bar was nearly drowned out by the music and hum of conversation around us. "No petals right now," I told him. "Come back in February, I'll do you up a proper one." Thank God my voice was steady.

There was a curve at the edge of his lips as he took it, and I didn't like the way his eyes lingered on me, dark as charcoal and far too intense.

Alarm bells were going off like sirens, and goosebumps pricked my skin. "Here with a pack?" I asked, swallowing back panic. I was paranoid—that was all. But the sounds of the club were distant, as if muffled through water. I couldn't help glancing down at his wrist, but it was covered by a white cuff.

His gaze followed mine to his wrist for a moment, then flicked to the balcony that overlooked the main casino below. "At the tables."

"Not for you?" Bartenders weren't the primary entertainment of patrons, but packs sometimes had an Alpha or two who felt 'dragged along', and they sometimes enjoyed their time at the bar.

Was that all this was?

He let out an amused breath. "I don't have a poker face good enough to salvage luck *that* bad."

"Sorry to hear that."

"Doesn't look to have turned up quite yet," he mused, peering at his cards. I could see he'd only revealed three of the four starting suits in the game, missing a stack for diamonds. "Soon, perhaps." Still, his eyes held mine curiously.

I nodded, stepping back and forcing myself to turn from his unnerving smile to replace the Glenmorangie to the mirrored shelf it came from. When I drew my hand away, I could see my fingers trembling.

But I was tired.

Seeing things.

The drink meant nothing.

When we'd caught up enough behind the bar, I gave Tallow a heads up and took my break.

Two sleepless nights in a row had put my paranoia through the roof.

On my next break, I sat alone in silence. No coffee—not when I was jumping at shadows. It had been over an hour, and the Alpha at the bar never left. It was like I could feel his eyes on me with everything I did.

"Get a grip," I breathed to myself again as I pulled out my deck of cards. It wasn't like the cards on the tables below, with fresh packs for every game. These were mine.

Broken and beaten up, shuffled to oblivion. Bent and faded.

A deck of forty-eight.

"There are no roses," I whispered again. The soft sound of my cards sliding together mixed with the distant clatter of cocktail glasses being stacked—just not enough to ground me.

"Why don't we play a game?"

Ace's taunt echoed in memory. "A rose for every night you try to escape, and for every event in which you think you can undermine me."

And with that promise, I would step into my room to find a rose on my pillow, and a card that read, 'A rose for a queen'.

· · ·

I shivered, shoving the memory away.

It was a stupid drink.

I began shuffling my deck quicker as I watched the dancer below.

I had taken time to scent these cards. A perfect blend, so painfully faint in the air as I shifted them between my fingers. They were the only scents in the universe that brought me absolute calm—or as close to them as I could get.

Pear grove ... *Like being drawn into the arms of a bear, he held me close, his crisp and comforting scent whispering me to sleep...*

The rain and wind in a lightning storm... *Static in the air, crackling between us as his fingers tangled in mine, squeezing as if he would never let go...*

Snow santal ... *A cool winter forest, reminding of a time when I knew if I stumbled, he would catch me. Every time. No matter what it cost...*

Forbidden. A million miles out of reach. But... once mine.

It was working. My nerves were settling. A million flashes of what should have been a sad song shoving away my nightmares.

There was no sign at all that anything was truly—

"Glade?" I jumped violently when Leisha poked her head through the break room door. "Travis says there's a pack in Bluff asking for you."

"What?" I froze, my blood turning to ice, cards freezing in my hands. I didn't do private sessions with clients. "By name?"

"Nope. Asked for the hot bartender on floor two."

My panic mellowed as I gathered myself. "Tallow's... hot," I said stupidly.

"With 'big hair to the waist'."

Ah.

Okay. Well. "I don't take clients."

Bluff was one of the penthouse rooms on the top floor reserved for private meetings. Anyone who came to the High

Roller had to be a member, but frequent fliers knew the Ice Queen absolutely did not do private showings.

"That's what Travis told them. They paid a premium to sit up there on the off chance."

"Well. They can enjoy the evening alone—and tell Travis I won't be taking drinks up there, either." Tallow could. I did deliver up there sometimes, but if some pack had it in their head they could buy my evening, I'd steer clear.

Leisha added. "They're *really* good looking."

"*Travis* said that?" I laughed.

"*I* did. And he said they were very respectful," Leisha added, shooting me a side eye.

"If they weren't, they'd be out on their ass."

She snorted, but left me to my cards, alone in the small break room.

I checked my phone. I had what? Another fifteen before Tallow would get pissed.

I needed every second to still my frayed nerves.

Shuffling my deck, I tried to focus on the dancer below. She was mesmerising and beautiful. I wanted to pretend that today, my biggest fear was never having that much confidence in myself.

I paused, glancing down.

Something felt wrong with my deck. The cards' edges were rough, softer than average, but...

I frowned, turning the cards and sifting through them.

A perfect 48.

But that wasn't true.

My blood chilled.

There was one that didn't belong. It had a black back instead of the faded red, and it was brand new.

I reached for it, blood roaring in my ears. For every small clue of paranoia, the Rose Royale, the headless bundle of thorns on the side of the road, I'd convinced myself over and over that I was seeing ghosts.

Overreacting.

Paranoid.

And in one heart-stopping moment, I felt an incongruous, chilling relief as I looked at the black card. I hadn't been seeing things at all.

Until the truth of what that meant hit me like a freight train. Until the tremor in my hands left half the deck spilling from my grip. Before I turned the card and saw what was on the other side.

One of the four that I'd removed from my perfect 48.

That I'd ripped to pieces and burned.

Because on the other side was an ace of diamonds.

3

I dropped the card as if it had burned me, frozen in terror.

They'd found me at last, playing games and sending taunts just like Ace. But *he* never sent those until he was sure he'd won the hunt, and neither would the men outside.

Ace Maverick didn't often get his hands dirty. Instead, he made it a game—offering rewards to the Brotherhood to catch me. And one pack, it seemed, had finally caught up. I didn't recognise the Alpha at the bar, either. New to the Brotherhood, perhaps? Trying to make a name for themselves?

But he was all I'd seen. The others—they could be anywhere.

How many were here?

My mind flashed to the pack waiting for me on the third floor. Could that be them?

But... Why would they be on the third floor? Unless they just wanted to get me alone. To whisper blackmail I couldn't ignore.

My mind was spinning.

The club didn't allow weapons, but those checks weren't enough to truly keep a determined Brotherhood member down, just like it didn't stop me from wearing knives beneath my dress.

But if I made a scene, people could get hurt, and the moment I tried to leave, they'd be there.

What the fuck was I going to do?

"You all right?" Tallow's voice had me spinning on my heel.

Shit.

How long had I been in here frozen like a trapped mouse?

"Sorry..." I could barely focus. All I knew was that I couldn't panic him. Not him, not security. No one could get involved.

In a nightmare, Ace's hand closed around mine. Crimson glistened in the dim light of the mansion hallway, blood dripping from the dagger I held with his hand closed around mine so I couldn't let it go.

His words tickled my neck as the tang of iron curdled with the stomach-turning scent of redwood and roses. "You thought he could help?"

"Glade?" Tallow was waving a hand in my face, a slight frown on his.

"I'm fine." I swallowed. "I just need—"

"Girl. I brought drinks up. That pack waiting for you is fucking hot. Look, Molly's extra tonight..." He gave me a meaningful look. "If you *did* want to—"

"How many?" I cleared my throat, fighting with everything I had to keep my voice steady.

"Huh?"

"Upstairs—the pack asking after me. How many?"

Tallow gave me a sly look. "Three."

Three.

Could I deal with three if I was good enough? I'd be giving them what they wanted, going to them.

Brotherhood packs typically ran between three and six. If I'd identified one out there, if I could neutralise three, would that give me a shot?

But there could be more. That last time I'd had to flee, it had only been two packs. All Alphas, happy to split the obscene reward I knew Ace must have offered. Greed was the only thing on my side. The more packs, the more they'd have to split.

"Tried asking me about you six different ways," Tallow was saying. "They're *obsessed*."

"You didn't notice any... flower tattoos on them, did you?"

He shrugged. "They did have ink, but I didn't notice any flowers. A dragon, skulls, stuff like that."

"Okay..." I made the decision in a split second. "I'm going up."

Tallow's expression lit up. "Excellent!"

I had one choice.

Ace's men had found me and I was stuck in the High Roller. My home, filled with the only people I could call family.

The card was a taunt, which meant they knew where I was. If I wanted to get out, it would have to be without their notice. If they cornered me, if they threatened anyone here—it was over. I would cave in a heartbeat.

The one thing I knew about Ace's men was that they weren't sloppy. The card meant they had been tracking me for a while, and that meant they knew my habits.

If I was right, then they would know I never saw packs.

That meant on the small off chance the pack upstairs weren't Ace's men, a pack could be my only way out without notice.

My decision was made.

"I need a favour," I told Tallow. "The Rose Royale Alpha. If he asks after me, tell him I'm serving downstairs."

"But you just—"

"Please, please, please. No questions."

"Fine." Tallow grinned, zipping his mouth with a nod. I forced myself to roll my eyes as if adrenaline wasn't scorching my veins and terror making it impossible to think.

"Thank you," I said. I waited until he was gone, then I snatched up my purse, slinging it over my shoulder, and backed up to the back door of the breakroom. From here was a back staircase that led to the third floor. But more importantly, in the storage rooms back here was exactly what I needed.

It took me minutes to tear through the boxes and find what I was looking for.

The gun was just small enough to fit in the thigh holster already home to a small blade. There was no way I'd be able to sneak in a weapon like this daily. Once was all I'd needed, because a part of me had always known this day was coming.

I reached the door to Bluff, one of the upstairs rooms, plush carpet of the quieter third floor muffling my footsteps.

If the Alphas within were Brotherhood members, I was ready. If they weren't, then I needed them to get me out of the building. Then I could run. Well, figure out how to get Lucy—then run.

I took a breath and turned the door handle, praying that if they weren't enemies, then whatever had made them ask for me was enough to convince them of what I needed.

I had to swallow my insecurities, channel my inner Omega, and use the skills my tutors had taught me. Mafia princess and seductress.

I pushed open the door, slipping in quietly, gun in hand but tucked behind my back.

Their scents found me first.

Impossible. And yet... pear grove, snow santal, and a fresh lightning storm weren't something I would ever mistake.

My heart tripped, soaring for the briefest moment before the crash. Instinct igniting first and filling my heart with more hope than I'd had in years.

That was before I saw them and reality caught up, a shadow

swallowing that flash of joy whole. They were on the couches, each looking up at me in surprise.

I realised I'd lifted the gun, shock getting the better of me even if the Alphas I was looking at were my mates.

Kyan, Knight, and Zed. The pack who'd got on their knees to ask for a bond.

The pack I had left rejected.

And the only three Alphas in the world I could never ask to save me from Ace.

4

I stared at the three Alphas in the room, trying desperately to pick my jaw off the floor. *What were my mates doing here?*

There were people after me—men sent by Ace. So how was his brother lounging on the couch in Bluff, head cocked like he didn't have a worry in the world—*despite* the gun I was levelling at him?

Zed Maverick was everything I remembered: lean, with shaggy silver hair and an obscene amount of tattoos across his body. He was pack lead, and as stubborn as I was, with a vengeful streak, and petty as fuck when pushed. Kyan perched on the couch arm, while Knight had frozen on Zed's other side, a drink halfway to his lips.

I stared between them, pulse erratic as I tried to understand what was going on.

"*You...* brought them here?" I asked.

I realised how stupid the question was the moment it came out of my mouth.

"Brought who here?" Knight asked.

My gaze slid to him. His brow was cocked, head tilted as he watched me.

How were they more beautiful than I remembered?

Knight was a huge guy, over a foot taller than me and made of solid muscle. He wore the same locs I'd always loved, and they reached just above his waist now. He had ebony skin, a strong nose, and a devastating jawline. His intense midnight eyes still had a way of making me feel like we were the only ones left in the universe when they were fixed on me.

Used to.

Now they were cold, as if I was the last person he wanted to be looking at.

"I…" I shook myself.

They didn't know? How could they not know?

This had to be a trick. But they were exiled—completely and irrevocably exiled from the Brotherhood. I had seen to that.

But that meant their presence here the same night Ace's Brotherhood thugs were looking for them, left them in dire danger.

Kyan was the first to his feet, his jade eyes drinking me in like he couldn't get enough. He crossed to me as if there wasn't a gun pointing in his direction at all.

"Don't." I lifted it.

I couldn't do this. Not now.

But he didn't stop. He was… well. The one I'd fallen for first and hardest, with the scent of a lightning storm that had turned my world upside down. Equal parts passionate and mad, saying Kyan was my weak spot would be an understatement.

I loved him. More, now that I was looking at him again, with the same snake tattoos winding around his wrists, and accompanied by a few beaded bracelets. The same wild, dark hair tied up in a ponytail with an undercut, and a few strands that were flying loose. He wore a thick chain necklace made of gold that complimented his olive tan skin. And his smile was as wild as I remembered, boyish and wide, with pointed canines. From the first second I'd caught his scent like a summer storm, I'd known he was mine.

Mine...?

Nothing is yours. You gave them up.

I swallowed as Kyan reached me, unable to break his gaze. Meeting those beautiful eyes as I hadn't been able to do the day I rejected him. Zed and Knight, I'd met their eyes and seen their hatred, but Kyan... I hadn't thought I would see hatred if I looked at him, and that was worse.

He had changed, though. There had always been a spark of mania in his eyes, but that spark had lit to an inferno. A flame his father had fanned, no matter how it destroyed the boy I'd once fallen for. Exile had come too little too late for my mate. That madness was a vicious torrent, drowning everything else that he'd once been.

He stepped right up to the gun levelled at his chest, ignoring it completely. My lungs were tight as he moved closer still, staring down. I jumped as his touch found my waist. It was hard to suppress the low whine that desperately wanted to escape. Not just the touch of an Alpha to my damaged body, but his. Static and lightning, a promise of safety like nothing else in this world.

"My Oasis," he whispered.

Tombs of stone built from years of fear cracked. The snake that had been slowly constricting my heart with every day that had passed without them slackened for the first time in memory. My grip weakened on the gun, and I couldn't take my eyes from his.

My mate.

I was in danger, and he was here, just like he always promised to be. Everything was as it should be. I almost closed the gap between us, dropping the gun and letting his touch veil this world in darkness.

In the safety of the scent of a lightning storm.

Almost.

"Double or nothing. That's the deal."

Ace's voice in my head was enough for me to return my conviction. I shoved the gun harder into his chest, choking down my spike of fear. Kyan's grin widened, and he sidestepped the gun, slipping behind me before I could react. He didn't let go of my waist, and I could feel the heat of his body against mine, chest against my back with a closeness still begging me to melt against him.

I'd been touch starved for too long...

"I... have to go," I stammered.

The others were watching from where they sat. Zed's expression was stiff. "Who did you think we were?" His gaze was fixed on the gun.

I couldn't answer that.

"It doesn't matter." I'd figure this out... somehow. But not like this.

I tried to step away from Kyan, but Zed's eyes flashed, and Kyan's grip turned to iron. "*Who* did you think we were?" Zed asked again.

"I don't have time for this." They didn't understand, and I couldn't explain it to them.

There was a nasty sneer on Zed's face as he leaned back. "Haven't changed one bit—our charming little scent match. We didn't come here so you could blow us off again."

"Why *did* you come?" I asked, and I saw Knight's gaze slide to Zed for a moment, as if wondering what he would say.

"You aren't going anywhere until you answer. We have all evening," he said, ignoring my question completely. "Do *you*?"

The gun might as well have been a prop for all the fucks they seemed to give about it. No matter what had changed, no one in this room believed I would actually use it.

"Let me go. Stay up here, and I'll be out of your hair." This time I'd have to be better at hiding. I don't know if I could even stay in the country.

"You expect us to hang out up here, when we've just found out what a damsel in distress our own scent match is?"

Fuck him.

"That isn't what's happening here."

"You certainly seem a little... distressed." I jumped as Kyan's teeth grazed my ear.

Lord help me.

With a growl, I spun, unsheathing the blade from beneath my dress hem. In seconds, the gun was jammed against his rib cage and the blade against his throat.

Instead of flinching, Kyan Quinn Beaumont gave me the wickedest grin.

His pupils blew, and I saw, at last, a true echo of everything I remembered. When he tugged me closer, a pinprick of blood beaded on the edge of my knife as it cut his skin.

And... *shit.*

The faintest rattle of a purr rumbled to life in his chest. Vibrations that unwound that coiled serpent in my chest just a little more.

I gritted my teeth.

"That's enough. I'm leaving. You're going to stay here and pretend you didn't see me. Wait a few hours if you know what's best for you." I scowled as I heard one of them stand behind me. I made to shift, but Kyan wouldn't let me go.

I'd hoped, rather stupidly, that the knife might help convince them I was serious.

My heart rate climbed to hummingbird speed as I caught the deadly cool of Zed's snow santal behind me. I couldn't let him get this close. I could barely handle being this close to Kyan, but he was holding me too tightly. With any more force, I'd slit his throat.

Another whimper *almost* destroyed the last of my composure as Zed's fingers curled around my neck.

These fucking touch-starved, over-drugged goddamned hormones.

I was trapped between them. This wasn't the faintest whisper of a memory like shuffling my old cards brought.

This was real.

They were right here.

The only men I'd ever loved.

"If the plan was to leave," Zed growled. "You shouldn't be flirting with Kyan like that."

His grip might be impossible to fight, but I did manage to shift my gun hand enough that I could jam the barrel up against his jaw. "You aren't taking me seriously."

"You don't believe my offer was serious?" he asked. "I didn't come here for a corpse."

Why *had* he come here? Was this truly a coincidence? Worst coincidence of my life, if so.

"Let me go."

There was a long pause, and then, to my surprise, he did. His touch was gone, along with the toxic proximity of his snow santal.

"You can't be fucking—"

"*Kyan.*" Zed cut him off.

There was a long pause, and the air felt like static with the tension in it, but finally, Kyan let me go.

It might have been the hardest thing I'd ever done, stepping away from him. I took a breath, glancing back up at Zed. I could see the frigid viciousness in his eyes. I needed that from him. Again, like the coward I was, I didn't look at Kyan. I couldn't even manage Knight.

I had to go now and never look back. Seeing them—even once —it was never supposed to happen.

I forced myself toward the door, tucking my knife away, but keeping hold of my gun. I'd barely opened it for a second before I was tugging it closed but for a crack, stifling a curse.

There was a man in a black suit in the hallway beyond.

He fit in at the High Roller and could even be a bouncer for the way he was standing, palm clasped over wrist by the stairs. But we didn't have security that waited there like that. He wasn't facing in my direction, and I watched as he adjusted his cuff absently. Beneath the sleeve was a flash of black.

I couldn't see the details from here, but I knew what it was all the same.

The slender tattoo of a rose.

5

I pressed the door shut silently, heart in my throat.

I'd been gone too long and the men after me were getting antsy.

There was one bit of good news. If he was waiting like that, blending into the High Roller staff and patrons, they still wanted to avoid making a scene.

Whether it was because Travis's security posed a threat, or they didn't want to tread on the toes of whoever had caused a scene around Spades, I wasn't sure, but I'd take it.

Or perhaps they wanted to avoid it until they had me.

No member of the Brotherhood I knew of cared if bystanders got hurt.

"Change your mind?" Zed's voice made me jump, and I turned back to him.

"No…" I trailed off, staring around the room for answers. I crossed to the window, grabbing the latch and trying to wrench it open. Of course, it was sealed. The side of the building wasn't easily scalable anyway. From the outside it was all tall, decorated walls and sealed windows.

"Fuck."

Fuck fuck fuck.

What had made me think going *up* a floor was a better idea? I was even more screwed.

A thousand useless options crossed my mind. I could pull the fire alarm, but they'd know it was me. They might lash out at the attempt. If they were smart, this whole place would be surrounded.

The police were out of the question. Ace had them in his pocket—and this was clearly premeditated.

I'd seen Brotherhood members secure delays in police response to areas for hours, sometimes completely.

"What's the problem?" Zed walked back to the table and picked up his glass before sitting back down on the couch. "Seems like you're in some trouble."

I tried to ignore him.

Plan...

I needed a fucking plan.

"Someone's after her," Kyan said at my side. He looked rather pleased. "That's my guess. But Glade doesn't want a mess."

"Is that right?" Zed asked. "The people downstairs must be important. Almost like family?"

I stared at him, knowing what he meant by that.

His family was what he'd given up—what he'd had ripped from him—because of me.

"They're innocent."

Knight let out a breath, expression twisted. "And what were we?"

Is that what this was? They'd found me and now they wanted to ask questions I couldn't give them answers to.

"Who are you running from?" Zed watched me with narrowed eyes.

"Just…" I couldn't tell him. If he knew I was fleeing his brother, what might he do? "Ended up on the bad side of a drug dealer."

Knight frowned, and I didn't get the impression he believed a word I was saying. "This about product, or a pissed-off ex?"

"Not your business."

There was a long silence, and I saw Zed exchange a look with Knight. "They're looking for a bartender, not a pack," Zed said finally.

I stared at him, every insecurity colliding like nuclear fission in my brain all at once.

They were offering to help?

"I left you."

I'd rejected them. Temptress. Siren. Betrayer. Those were titles etched into my soul, on display for the world to see.

Zed was the oldest son of the Maverick family; he had been first in line to run the entire Brotherhood—a powerful gang with reach across the east coast. But when his father died, there was a power struggle. Ace, his younger brother, had staked a claim for what should have been Zed's.

But, Zed not only had a stronger claim, he had something else that secured him that position beyond a shadow of a doubt. The daughter of one of the heads of the Romano Mafia had scent matched his pack. I was the perfect catalyst to an alliance the Brotherhood needed.

I'd always known my role. Always known I was destined to be traded by my father for politics, but I'd never imagined it would be with a pack I fell in love with.

Only when Zed had dropped to his knees before the Brotherhood and offered a bond, I'd done something no one had seen coming. I stepped past him—past Knight and Kyan—leaving them in the dust, and I had chosen Ace Maverick instead.

The younger brother.

My choice empowered his claim, and Zed's pack had been exiled.

That was the story the way they knew it, and it was the only way they, and any of the world, *could* ever know it.

But the fissure through my heart from that moment had never closed. I remembered every second. The look of shock on Zed's face as I stepped back. His silver hair messy across blue eyes exactly like it was right now. Eyes that were wide with shock as he heard the words that sealed his fate.

"I reject you, Zed Maverick."

"Time's ticking, Little Devil." His words and the old nickname—that now carried a heavier meaning than it ever had—ripped me from my thoughts. "If you don't ask, we can't help."

"I need to get out of the building." That was all. I couldn't accept more. And if we were masked, no one would know.

How long did I have before they burst into the break room to find me there? How many would get hurt?

I had to assume they'd know I wouldn't want to see the club devastated. That meant I was in a cage full of hostages, ones I would cave to protect, and Zed was right: I was running out of time.

"Fine." I seized my hair, fists balling wildly for a moment. *"Fine."*

"Disappointing."

I glared as Zed spread his arms, lounging back on the seat like he had all the time in the world.

"You're taking it back?" I asked.

"No. I just think you can do a better job of convincing me."

"Fuck you." People were at risk here, and I could feel my panic clawing up my throat, trying to get the better of me.

The man outside this door meant they were already creeping around the whole place to cover their bases. Ace and his men liked games, but not more than winning. And with the bounty on my head, it was worth far more to burn this place to the ground. Any second, the men outside could call it on the subtleties and bang the doors down looking for me.

Zed grinned, tongue pressing against his canine like he was enjoying my tantrum.

"What do you want?" I asked, teeth gritted.

He cocked his head, eyes sliding to the floor before him.

I worked to contain my snarl. "*Right* fucking now?"

Zed Maverick might be more balanced than his brother, but that was a low bar. I fully believed that he'd refuse help until his petty vindication was satisfied.

"Your words, right?" he asked. "We're not going to have time for it later."

He didn't say what it was. He didn't have to. I *knew*. The only thing he'd really be here for. And it was so very Zed.

But my options were dwindling.

Years living beneath Ace had left my pride a fatally wounded creature that I was working hard to nurse back to life, but in this case, it was a benefit.

If that's what he wanted? Fine. Let him have it.

I approached, trying to keep my expression as neutral as possible as I sank to my knees before him.

"Ask me nicely."

Perhaps I'd done a better job at nursing my pride than I thought, because my mouth was dry. I cleared my throat, ignoring his obvious enjoyment of my struggle.

I glared, irritation spitting like an overflowing hotpot in my chest. This wasn't what he thought it was. I clung to that. He didn't know the truth and he never could.

They could bust that door down any second.

One spark, and this gas-doused fire heap was ready to erupt into an inferno with everyone I loved inside—*actually*, everyone, now that this fucking pack was here.

"I..." I trailed off, steeling myself. "I need your help to get out of the building without getting caught."

He said nothing, leaning forward and taking my chin in his hand, eyes twinkling with malice. His touch was like a brand, turning the world hazy, and I drowned in the cool scent of a snow santal. I swear he flinched, too. I knew how broken I was, I didn't touch Alphas that often at all, but I always wondered if they felt the same draw to me as I did them—a need to patch up something long shattered. Or maybe it was because we were mates.

I forced a bitter smile to my face. *"Please."*

"Good girl."

My blood went hot, and not with rage this time. Memories flickered to life in my brain. The good ones. The ones that I usually rejected. But right now, that was impossible as I felt the hard ground beneath my knees with him before me, repeating words I'd heard exactly like this.

The humour in his eyes told me he was thinking the same thing. That, and the other part—something he couldn't control—that left me with slick pooling under my dress in possibly one of the most inappropriate moments of my life. Because his pupils definitely dilated as he looked down at me.

Well.

Fuck him. He'd sorely underestimated quite how pathetic his scent match was. He had no idea I'd spent years pining after Alphas I could never have. I might take something away from this, too.

He still wanted me.

I didn't *dare* look at Knight.

Seeing that reaction in Kyan, and now the lead of the pack I should have been in, was already setting me back years.

"What's the best way out?" Zed asked, dropping his hand and leaning back. I hated the little twist of sadness in my stomach as his touch vanished.

I took a breath. "There's a guest on the first floor drawing security attention which will make it easier, and we can blend in." The High Roller catered to a variety of desires. There was something for every occasion in this room, and mystery, masked Alphas and Omegas were included in that.

It would have to do.

"Golden robe and masks in the closet—" I made to stand, but Zed stopped me, hand cupping my neck. "Knight will get it."

I gritted my teeth as Knight got to his feet and crossed to the closet I'd nodded to. It didn't take him long to find what we needed.

The golden masks would get us out as long as I could divert questions as to why we were out of the private top floor rooms while wearing them.

Knight dropped the robe and a mask before me, then tossed one to Kyan and Zed. I noticed he didn't meet my eyes. Kyan, on the other hand, couldn't seem to look anywhere but at me. I avoided thinking too hard about that.

"Can I move now?" I asked, heavy sarcasm in my voice.

Zed just flashed me a grin, placing the mask carefully over his blue eyes. Then he picked up my mask and robe before I could grab it.

I could feel his attention on me like lead weights as I stood. It was one of those sheer night robes that were translucent under certain lights. A thousand times I'd seen an Omega on stage shrug it off, leaving it pooled on the ground like water as they revealed something much more mesmerising in its wake.

"I don't get the impression the gown is supposed to have so much fabric beneath," Zed said.

"My dress stays," I snapped. Again, I felt the scars on my back ache.

Absolutely not.

"Shame. We did pay a lot of money to come see you." His smile was cold as he handed me the mask, which I fit on my face, ignoring him.

But I couldn't ignore the fragile, long crushed part of my soul that blinked awake.

He was my mate.

Prick or not, hearing him suggest that was like feeling a puzzle piece slot into place; something returning home. I ripped it back out and did away with it, knowing I had no room for those sorts of thoughts.

He would help me get out of here, then we'd part ways.

And for how long would I mourn them?

That failed date with another Alpha felt a million years away now. I tugged the golden silk gown on and pushed the thought away, making sure my purse was tucked away. I didn't have much in there, but it would have to do. Phone, keys, lipstick, a few spare pens, and my knives. But I'd need to loop back around the moment we'd drawn them away to grab Lucy.

For now, all we needed to do was get past that Alpha without drawing too much attention, then we'd blend in with the other packs and Omegas.

If they'd been watching me as long as I thought they had, they'd believe—quite rightfully—that I was a fucking loner. I never took clients.

"All right," Zed stood and stretched. "We're going to make this look convincing." He glanced over at the hulking Alpha at his side. "Knight? You're up."

6

KNIGHT

I'd known from the moment Kyan had brought up finding her that this was the stupidest plan Zed had made to date.

Zed and his fucking ego.

And sure enough, here we were, stuck with her. She was in trouble, because of course she was—and worse, she was a thousand times more captivating than any memory would have me believe. A fragment of our past, a dark shard that ached with every step forward—never letting go of the hold she had on us.

Why was she so *goddamned* beautiful, too?

That just wasn't fair—especially in a dress that showed off her incredible curves. Her wavy black hair was loose, she wore thigh high boots with heels and the outfit was topped with pretty diamond stud earrings that flashed with extra contrast against her bronze skin.

Stubborn, fierce, and an absolute goddess with that dark cream cardamom scent that I'd *thought* I remembered in my dreams. I realised now they'd never been comparable to the real thing.

If only she wasn't a snake—one that had left us bleeding out.

I understood Zed's bone-deep reaction not to leave her for dead—instincts howling because she was more than just an Omega in danger.

She was ours.

Our girl. A dream once upon a time. A dream she had crushed beneath her selfish mafia princess heels. We would get her out then dump her on the side of the road for good.

I'd convince Zed to move to a new city because there was no way in hell Kyan would survive now he knew where she was. We could barely control him as things were.

He'd taken what she'd done harder than any of us. It had split his already unstable mind in two, and I didn't like how he was looking at her. He was made of pure instincts—rutting more often than any Alpha I knew.

When we found a place to dump her, I'd be checking our rear view for a literal straw man to make sure he hadn't bundled her into the trunk so he could keep her in the basement or something.

He would, too—I could literally picture him making a Glade scarecrow *just* for that.

And then she'd gut him to escape, and Zed would have to put a bullet in her skull.

Nope.

No scarecrow Omegas.

And no fucking keeping her—not under *any* goddamned circumstances.

We were going to make sure our scent match didn't die because we weren't fucking monsters. That was all she got from us—and she didn't even deserve that.

I couldn't help the part of me that thought it seemed really, really obscene to commit to *only* this when she was currently slung over my shoulder with her biteable ass about an inch from my canines.

But we'd done it, because like this, she just looked like a sack of Omega and not the single bartender these fuckers were looking for—whoever *they* were. I didn't buy her drug dealer story for a second. I'd already eyed a few Alphas I thought looked suspicious. She'd also had to hiss at one of the bouncers to leave us be, since this behaviour might be a little low class for this kind of club.

By how tense she was, I could feel her irritation at our chosen method for extraction.

At least it was pleasant for me.

We reached the second floor back hallway that led to the stairs and heard a commotion. I turned my head before remembering it landed me a pleasant face full of Glade peach.

She was a real piece of work, but I'd loved her once. And that sweet, sweet ass.

I felt a sharp prick of pain up my side, reminding me again of who she truly was.

"Knight!" I heard her hiss as Zed spoke to the bouncer who'd been on his way up the stairs.

Right.

Mafia princesses and the spikes they carried everywhere.

I grinned with unexpected playfulness, clapping her on the ass to a wriggle and snarl of derision. "Go on, Princess, dig those claws in, see what happens."

We were saving her.

I could give her a nip and she couldn't complain. Really, *really* tempting. Especially since I could feel the slightest trickle of blood down my shirt where she'd nicked me.

Damn. I'd forgotten how hot she was.

Zed managed to redirect the bouncer and then took the back stairwell to check ahead. He was back in a second, catching my eye with a look that told me it was bad news.

Shit.

Whoever was after her must be past there and by Zed's urgency through the bond—they were coming up.

Slinging her over my shoulder was good for a crowded room, but in the quiet stairwell, if they wanted to stop and check who she was, they could. And we would both be in a poor position to fight. Counting Glade out as an asset if this came to blows was a rookie move—even if Zed had her gun right now.

So I dropped her from my shoulder with as little grace as I could manage, then caught her and set her straight before I could stop myself.

She was trying to rip her hair from her face when I caged her against the wall, hearing footsteps echoing up the stairs.

"Gives us a reason to growl if they look too hard," I told her. Her lips drew back for a second as she glared up at me. Then her eyes darted between me, Kyan—who was blocking her from view of the staircase, and Zed, who had just reached us.

With one haughty look at me, she grabbed Kyan by the cheeks and drew him into a kiss.

Whatever.

Whoever Zed had spotted was scaling the stairs, and we needed to be in one apparent horny tangled mess if we wanted them to pass us without stopping.

Except...

Fuck me.

I did *not* like Kyan's response. I felt a rather unnerving thrill down the bond from him. My relationship with him might be unconventional, but I knew what that meant.

This would undo years of work.

Before I knew it, I had Kyan's hair in my fist and I dragged him back, slamming him against the wall. Glade was panting, eyes darting from Zed, to me, and then to Zed's chest, behind which we could hear the footsteps approaching. Without another moment's hesitation, she launched herself at me—the only one in reach—her lips finding mine for the first time in years. Dark cream cardamom rose in the air, subtle through fading scent dampeners, but enough for a million memories to collide with my hindbrain.

Lying on a field at midnight, mapping stars.

Forbidden evenings when she'd climbed our balcony.

Stolen moments among sunlit trees.

The way her scent had tangled with ours, completing us in a way we'd never been.

The kiss was so primal I didn't have time to prepare. Not for the shocking softness of her lips, or my body's reaction.

I almost let go of Kyan, though from the indignance down the bond, he was at risk of knocking me flat. Her legs tangled around my waist as I crushed her against the wall, my other fist in her hair. Her tongue drove into my mouth and dark lust shot through my veins like lava.

Kyan threw his weight against mine and I felt his fury like it was mine.

Okay.

Given the laundry list of kinks that Alpha had, this *possibly* wasn't the best option for settling him.

But this was just an act, I told myself.

Zed's growl joined Kyan's, though his was directed at the passersby.

This was an act. They'd be gone and that would be it. We'd drop her off and drive away.

Forever.

What had we been thinking, coming here? Trying to meet her? For what—closure? To tell her we were over her?

Over her?

Were we mad?

My rock-hard cock (which she could one hundred percent feel) disagreed en-fucking-tirely.

And Zed's grip was now closed on my shirt, clearly telling me the danger had passed, yet my tongue was still lodged halfway down her throat.

Disengage.

Dis. En. Gage.

Fuck.

Me.

We were such idiots.

When I managed, at last, to shut down my hindbrain and drag myself from the kiss, it was to find a pair of blown pupils through the golden mask.

Glade was catching her breath, eyes fixed on me, plush lips parted in shock.

I couldn't look away. Well, not until I heard the click of a gun at my side and glanced to see Zed readying it.

Okay.

Life and death first. Giving the sweetest-tasting Omega on the whole planet the most mind-blowing orgasm of her whole life later.

No.

That wasn't the plan.

We were supposed to drop her off with a scarecrow or something.

I blinked.

What?

"Are you... rutting, dude?" Kyan's words were the equivalent of a bucket of ice water being dumped on my head. I glanced at him and saw genuine concern on his face.

Was I...?

Oh. Shit.

Shit shit shit.

Kyan rutted.

Not me.

But I could feel the boiling surge of hormones in my bloodstream, a warning that one might not really be far off.

"You"—Zed snarled, shoving the gun against my chest—"go ahead. I'll deal with the goddamned Omega."

The goddamned... what? *That* was our scent match?

I almost pounced at him.

Reel it in.

With difficulty, I shook it off, tearing the gun from his fist and —with more self-control than I knew I possessed—let go of her to take the stairs, violence like white hot lava streaking through my veins.

7

GLADE

We were almost free of the building.

We'd taken the back way, through the dressing rooms and hallway with cleaning supplies and extra stock. Knight was in front, Kyan just before me, and Zed was at my back, never more than a step away.

We were on the main floor now, and my heart raced uncomfortably, both from the tenseness of the situation and the adrenaline from the kiss. Knight's lips against mine had been electric. For a flash, we were both one, scents tangling, and my heart was open like I was letting him in.

Of the three, he had always been the pillar. Kyan was a firecracker, Zed hot-headed, but Knight was their grounding, with a sense of honour and loyalty I'd never seen matched. And this man, closed off to so much of the world, had opened up to me.

It's why I knew he carried more hatred than the others. But for those few seconds, when our lips had touched, it was like everything after my rejection had vanished.

I was the one he'd let in, and we'd found, in each other, a

mirror we'd never expected. We were both raised to fit in a box, to become the perfect image our parents wanted to see painted.

I really needed to get my head on straight. We weren't even close to out of the woods. Tallow had been right, at least. A lot of security had been diverted to Spades, which meant it was easier to spot Ace's men.

I couldn't allow myself to consider what might happen if we were all caught.

If I ended up on my knees before Ace with my mates at my side.

Don't think about it.

My knife was in my hand and tucked beneath the sheer robe, even if Knight had my gun right now. Kyan had also produced a gun, and I had no idea how he'd snuck that in.

If we had two guns between us, the men after me couldn't have more than that—not if they were inside the club.

Travis would never put the Betas, Omegas, and Alphas working in this club in danger, not for any amount.

"Front doors," I hissed as Knight tried to take a turn to the back exit. Knight scowled, but tucked his gun out of sight as he took the door toward the main room.

My mind was racing with terror of the consequences of what would happen if we got caught, but I didn't have time to lose it now.

At the back of the club was an exit with a keypad and security cameras, but I'd seen another thug with a flash of a wrist tattoo loitering at the door that led down to the basement—and my home. The front doors were public—but if there were more people waiting for me, they'd expect me to run to the quieter exit.

The good news was that they still weren't desperate enough to make a scene.

I was momentarily so relieved for the High Roller. Of all the places to make my home, it was safe. A safer place than I'd ever had.

Even Ace's thugs weren't having an easy time staking it out, and I knew for a fact there wasn't anything they could do to bring hell down on their own heads, more than trying to get down to the Omega's rooms below.

"Glade?" I could hear the surprise in Roger's voice as we reached the front door. He was squinting at me, but he knew everyone here well enough to know it was me behind the mask. If we were going the main route out, that included passing the massive doorman who was always looking out for us.

"Oh…" Well, this was awkward. I looked down at the golden sheer gown wrapped around my waist.

"Are you sure you want to leave?" Roger was eyeing Zed, Knight, and Kyan suspiciously.

"It's not—Tallow kicked me off the clock for the evening." I nodded to the others meaningfully, hoping that would be all I needed.

"If you take them off-premise, well, it's not as…" He glanced at them again. "Regulated."

"I want to go to the Painted Dragon. Feeling Chinese."

"Like a date?" he asked, surprised.

Wow. Okay, so my Ice Queen reputation was more widespread than I thought.

I swallowed, glancing back at them, knowing I had to get out of this fast, before one of Ace's guys spotted us. We were exposed. "We, uh… scent matched," I said, stepping back into Kyan's arms.

Roger's eyes almost bulged out of his head. "Oh… *Well…*" He looked a little lost for words, then he nodded, gaze less damning as he glanced back at the others. "I guess… go have a good night." He stepped back.

Kyan's fingers wound into mine as he tugged me through the great doors and onto the golden statues and broad steps beyond.

The familiar Las Vegas air was dry in my lungs, a faint, cool wind enough to make me shiver in the thin fabric I wore.

"You're taking the masks?" Roger asked as we reached the steps.

"They're *fun*." I grinned, glancing back, fingers still curled in Kyan's. I waved at Roger. "Travis can bill me."

Past him, I saw another patron within. He was tall, with salt and pepper hair, hands clasped as he stared at me. Our eyes locked, and my instincts went haywire. I was wearing a mask; he didn't *know* it was me. Only, his cuff was covering his wrist, and I couldn't tell if there was a rose there. Yet, as I turned back, hurrying down the steps, my stomach twisted uncomfortably.

I didn't dare look back. If I did, and he wasn't sure, he would be then.

The High Roller was located on The Strip and we needed to get far away. I needed a way to get out of sight, and off the main roads. As we stepped into the evening crowds and bright lights, I noticed Knight had his hand beneath his jacket where I was sure my gun was gripped tight. I wasn't much different, with my hand firmly closed around my knife beneath the robe.

The Strip lights were bright, huge buildings towering above us, and enough crowds we should be able to disappear, but my anxiety didn't wane.

Finally, after a good ten minutes of walking in awkward quiet, trying not to be too obvious about throwing my gaze over my shoulder, Kyan tugged me around the corner of an alley.

"Why here?" I asked. We'd been walking in the direction of the quieter part of the strip, and the world here had suddenly become far too quiet.

It was late, and between the two buildings it was dim enough we could barely make out the shadows stretching ahead. No one was stupid enough to pull out their phone for light, and I cursed my heeled boots for being too loud upon the concrete.

Had that man from beyond the doors come out after us, or were we clear?

I cursed as I almost stumbled into the gutter. They were thigh high boots with obscenely thin heels, but the gaps in metal grates were persistent enemies. Zed was the one who steadied me, though he let go all too fast, a scowl on his face.

"I have to keep moving," I said. I didn't know what their plan was. None were showing signs of leaving.

"You know we're not going anywhere until you're clear of them," Kyan said as I tugged my hand from his.

"I asked you to get me out of the building. I'm out. You're free."

I'd have to leave for good, but I wasn't focusing on that. Or the fact that I might have just seen my last night in the High Roller.

And my friends.

I would go back for Lucy, but I think we were safe for now. For a second I reached for my purse, knowing I might be able to text Elana or Jade to get her out of my room.

I stopped, mind flashing to the black ace in my deck.

How much did Ace's men know? How long had they been watching me?

I couldn't put anyone in danger. Even tipping off Ace's men to who at the High Roller I was friendly with could be a death sentence.

I would get Lucy. Later tonight—I couldn't risk waiting long, just enough that they'd think I was long gone.

"We are not alone," Knight murmured. "Two at the end. One behind."

My blood chilled.

How far had they been following us? The Strip traffic wasn't easy to navigate, but if they had some on foot, they could have been directing their friends on where to turn.

"And..." Kyan's fingers tangled in mine again as if we were on a date, but I saw him nod his head upward. I didn't look straight away, but scanned the building's lower levels. There were metal railings all the way up.

Shit.

We'd been in this alley mere minutes, and we might already be surrounded.

"This drug dealer of yours, he isn't messing around is he?" Knight asked. He didn't look at me, but his tone was heavy with scepticism.

"How about you give me my gun and fuck off?" I asked.

Knight ignored me entirely, turning his back to me. Kyan grinned at my expression.

Did I feel confident taking on a bunch of Ace's guys at once? I might be good with a gun, but my odds weren't great. And still, I'd rather take my chances than end up in the mess that was barrelling full steam toward me with no brakes.

I needed them gone, and that meant I needed my goddamn gun.

"I could use a spare blade." Zed's eyes flicked to me as I walked.

I glared at him as Kyan shifted closer to my side.

Fuck.

They weren't going anywhere. Stubborn fucking Alphas.

But I didn't have time to argue, so I slipped him the blade and tugged out the one fixed to the inside of my purse. Not really a big enough blade for a fight like this, but it would have to do.

Knight, at least, was tricky with a gun, better than I'd ever been able to match even if he'd never come close to Kyan.

If things hadn't changed too much...

Three years...

Kyan dropped my hand, instead sliding his arm around my waist, pulling me close.

"What are you doing?" I asked, stifling the shot of warmth coiling in my tummy at his touch.

"Do you think they know, yet?" he breathed. "Pretend we're just a pack in love. Throw them off."

I don't think Kyan was stupid enough to believe we weren't way past that, but he didn't seem to care. Again, I fought the comfort his scent brought. Fought the desperate creature deep within me who wondered if, after so many years of taking care of myself, I was finally complete.

Mafia princess, I might be, but I was still an Omega. A pack creature—shattered beneath years of loneliness as much as I pretended otherwise. And that creature was so touch-starved, she was making it hard to focus on the brink of a literal gun fight.

We were nearly at the end of the alley. On the other side were a few mini back-end parking lots and an abandoned building.

"Still four?" Zed asked.

"Yup." Kyan sounded so fucking confident, even though he'd barely turned. Even in the dim light, and through the golden mask, I could see his jade eyes burning with pure thrill.

"The car's up ahead. Put four down and we're out."

"Wait—you *parked* down there?" I hissed.

An old lot in the back end of fucking nowhere? How goddamned easy would it be for someone to hide a body in this place?

Cheap fucks.

Zed turned on me. "Do you have any idea how much that club of yours charges for parking?" he demanded. "You'd think locals would be able to catch a fucking break."

"How much did you pay for Bluff?" I asked. That room they'd waited in for me was expensive.

"Would you lot shut the fuck up." Knight spun on us. "There's still a chance we can deal with this without too much attention."

I narrowed my eyes. "I want my gun back," I hissed. I needed them gone, and wouldn't blame them for ditching me, but if they did, I'd need the gun.

Knight sneered. "Too bad, Princess——"

Bang!

The gunshot blew my eardrums, setting every sense on high alert.

I drew to a halt, looking around wildly, all my training kicking in only to see Kyan had spun, gun over forearm, one eye shut as he raised it to the dark metal above us.

There was a creak as a shadow of a body slumped in the metal siding I could only just make out.

"You fucking *idiot*," Zed spat.

"Eh." Kyan shrugged. "They knew the whole time. The old prick through the doors called in our location the moment we left."

"You *saw*——?" I was cut off by another gunshot aimed our way followed by a shout.

Knight was covering the front end, but Kyan, grinning like the maniac he was, held out his hand at a clatter of metal on metal over our heads. With barely a flicker of his eyes, he caught a gun that tumbled from the dead man above.

Zed and I both flinched as he almost fumbled the catch with no idea if the safety was on. But then Kyan flipped it in his grip and held it out to me, looking maniacally proud of himself—an image that was bolstered by a huge glob of blood that chose that moment to splatter across his mask from above.

"She wanted a gun." He shrugged. "Plus, we got the best spot in the alley."

I snatched the weapon before Zed could, side-stepping him to get a glimpse past the wooden pallets that were giving us cover. Kyan wasn't wrong. A stack of pallets and a dumpster were the best we were getting. I ducked back at another bang.

"Three there," I said. "More coming."

"Two in front," Knight muttered.

How many more could they pull in?

I checked it and was relieved to find it was loaded. "They want me alive," I added. That was good information for them to have. Changed everything.

"Pissed ex, then." Knight grunted, as if that explained everything.

Technically, not untrue.

I tried to find a good angle through the wooden pallets. They were closing in on us, but they were being careful about it. I jumped as I felt a warm hand at my waist and the dry air and rank smell of the dumpster behind vanished for a lightning storm. Kyan rested his free hand with the gun between a gap in pallets with a far more casual motion than he was actually ready for.

My Kyan.

We were going to be fine. I was safe with them. I'd forgotten how easy that was to believe when their scents were so close.

"This is *not* a date," Zed ground out from my other side. I could see the edge of fury as his ice-blue gaze jumped between our weapons. He wasn't the kind of Alpha who dealt well with being the useless one.

"Go fuck yourself," Kyan sung, drawing me closer and brushing teeth along my neck.

I shivered, trying to focus on the figures ahead.

Through the dimness, I spotted a flicker of light, like a phone screen coming to life. Kyan pulled his trigger before I could move. I heard a grunt and the muffled sound of a dropping body, then silence.

"Sweet Oasis, you're losing." His voice was playful.

Fuck that.

I caught the shift of a shadow behind what I thought was a broken wood pallet. An easy squeeze of a lilac nail upon a trigger and another *bang*.

Then another, but that one I missed.

The world was a blur of action, and adrenaline burned my veins. It was a feeling I hadn't had in forever. For far too long, enemies had been so much more than villains lurking in alley shadows, ended by the right aim of a gun.

This was simple. Thrilling, even, with my pack at my side.

I shoved that thought away in shock.

Not yours.

Never yours.

Behind us, Knight took another down. I didn't realise more men had arrived on his side until I heard a struggle. I turned to see Zed past the dumpster. He had a figure in a headlock while Knight aimed for another who was backing up now. A gun tumbled from the man's wrist, going off in a wild direction. To my horror, the man managed to get an elbow in Zed's face, knocking his mask straight off. There was a nasty gurgle as knife found flesh, then the man went limp. Zed grabbed the weapon as my terror dialled to an eleven. His mask...

It was dark.

No one would see him.

Kyan cursed at my side. "Aw, *shit.*"

I turned back around to see him aiming, but the last guy in the alley turned the corner before Kyan could get a clear shot.

Gone.

Quiet descended on the alley, broken only by the faint hum of traffic and occasional shout in the Las Vegas night.

Had we done it?

That felt too quick. Why had they left?

Was it, perhaps, because he'd seen Zed and known he had to get back to Ace?

"Time to go. Police won't be long."

Right... *if* these men hadn't warned them off.

There was a strange tightness in my chest, a fear I couldn't shake.

Zed's mask...

But then the body Kyan had shot first finally slid from the metal railing above. It landed with a sickening crunch in a heap on the wooden pallets before us. It was twisted at a horrible angle, leaving his arm sticking out. Even in the darkness, the thin rose tattoo across his wrist was stark.

Oh shit.

An eerie silence fell as all gazes landed on it. I shut my eyes.

"Well." Knight was the first to speak. "*Fuck.*"

8

"That was the *Brotherhood?*" Zed's eyes were wide as he stared at me.

I couldn't rip my gaze from him, knowing we were both reaching the same conclusion.

Ace might know by the time the night was out. Zed's mask had come off. But that would mean...

My breath caught, a whine almost escaping. This wasn't how this was supposed to go.

How the hell was this supposed to go, actually?

It had been a mess from the start. There'd been no good option, not from the first second I'd opened the door to the private room, and found my goddamned mates waiting for me.

"It's over," I said, voice weak. "I'm gone. That's what you want."

That was the best I could do now.

I tried to take a step away, but Zed snarled, grabbing me and shoving me against the wall by my neck. "You set us against our own fucking family?"

I flipped my knife in one easy motion, meaning to deter him, but Knight reacted in an instant, grabbing my wrist and pinning it to the wall.

"No more games." Knight snarled.

"What the fuck have you just brought down on our heads?" Zed sounded more angry than I'd heard him yet.

Me?

What the hell had *they* been doing at the High Roller on the same night Ace had found me?

I opened my mouth, about to lash back, to accuse them of bringing Ace here.

But that was a lie.

It had to be a lie.

This feeling of being watched, it had been lingering for weeks now. The paranoia that wasn't paranoia.

Unless this was a test. Ace played games upon games. What if he'd known they were coming tonight? What if it was all a plan to see—

"You're done, Glade," Zed growled, ripping me from my panic. "You needed our help. Now it's on our terms."

"What the fuck does that mean—?" I cut off as he shoved me to my front, trapping my arms behind my back and easily dragging me down the alley in stumbling steps. "Zed—wait!" I began, but he ignored me.

"Cuffs. Knight. Now," he snarled.

"Cuffs?" Knight sounded as dumbfounded as I felt as he followed us.

"*What?*" I tried to pull from Zed's grip, but he renewed it with both arms, hauling me closer.

"You wanted our help, sweetheart," he hissed. "This is what it looks like." He turned from me as we reached a beat up truck. "Get me the fucking cuffs."

"Zed." Knight caught us up. "Think about—"

"*Before* she takes my eye out."

I twisted in his grip enough to see it was a rather delighted looking Kyan who reached into the truck and tugged out a pair of police cuffs that looked strong enough to hold an Alpha.

"They want *me!*" I snarled. "Take me, and it just means—"

"In-fucking-surance. That's what it means," Zed growled as he tugged my arm behind my back and I felt the cuffs close around them.

"No." They couldn't do this. This was too dangerous. "You *don't* understand—"

"Oh, now you know what's going on?" he demanded.

I heard the clink of keys. "Knight, you're driving, unless you think you're going into a rut—"

"I won't if we don't bring the *literal goddamned siren* in the car."

"Does Kyan seriously need to drive?" Zed asked.

"I can fucking drive." Knight sounded furious as the front door was ripped open.

Then Zed was dragging me back by my arms. My mind was spinning. Everything was changing too fast.

They were actually taking me?

That buried creature stirred, something relieved flipping my stomach.

They didn't... hate me? But that was obviously not true, and I had bigger problems as Zed climbed into the truck, before dragging me behind him.

He was so close, and my pulse was racing. It was hard to think straight as Kyan ducked in after us.

"*Wait, wait, wait!*" I was trying to catch my breath, speaking through the mouthful of hair I couldn't rid myself of. "*Lucy...* please, just let me get Lucy." My voice was shaking but I had no room to be embarrassed. What if that hadn't been all of them. What if they raided my room... My blood chilled at the thought.

Ace would take anything from me that he could.

"Who the fuck is Lucy?" Zed asked.

"Please... she's in my place." I hated begging but they'd leave her otherwise. I scrambled for a way to convince them. "She's... she's only two. I can't—"

"Two?" Knight sounded startled, turning in the driver's seat to stare, eyes wide with shock.

"You have to let me get her. My room is under the club."

"You're lying so I un-cuff you—"

"I'm not. I swear, I'll do anything if you get her." I could see the distrust on Zed's face. Please let there be something of the Alpha I'd fallen for in there.

Please.

"Fine."

"Thank you—!"

But he was rooting in my purse for my keys. "You," he snarled, "are not going back into that place."

9

KYAN

We had our Omega back.

There was no way we were giving her up. I didn't care what the others said.

A two-year-old was definitely unexpected, but I could pivot. *Really* unexpected.

I was the one who'd found Glade. I thought I'd known the deal.

My instincts were at war as I took the outer stairs to the basement of the huge High Roller building, gun tucked into my belt at the back. On one hand, someone had fucked my mate, so... a hunt. On the other there was a two-year-old, so... Well. With a kid involved, that seemed a little fucked up.

Could I just catch him and put him in a cage somewhere? Just in case we needed bio-dad for some reason.

Unless he was a deadbeat. Then it would be fine to gut him—right? Even Zed would be on board for that.

She'd told me her room number was right next to a back basement exit. It was still a bit of a pain to slip past security to the backdoor—it was a damn good thing they were preoccupied with Forbes tonight.

The Brotherhood members seemed to have mostly cleared out. If any were lingering here, they weren't watching the back entrance of Glade's place.

Only, when I opened the door with Glade's key, I didn't see any immediate signs of a two-year-old at all.

I peered around her room. It was a nice space, if small, with a punching bag hanging from the ceiling. Looked a bit like a dorm room, which meant they probably shared a common space.

No sign of a nest though. I shoved that back, focusing.

Shouldn't there be signs of like… a small human in here?

But the bathroom looked normal. It was full of scattered makeup and far more bottles of soap than any human could sanely use, but no diapers or potty.

I frowned, upturning her bedding like a giggling kid was going to tumble out.

Where the fuck were we going to put a two-year-old in our warehouse? How big were they on average?

The lighting in our place was crap except we needed new curtains. No kid was going to sleep with all that. Maybe those big, old cupboards we didn't use in the kitchen? A kid could fit in one of those, right? Like a wall-mounted bassinet or something… We'd have to lock it in case they rolled, but I could stuff it with extra blankets. Cut holes… Hmm… No. That was a nest.

I was thinking of Omegas. Or birds, maybe.

It'd be fine.

Glade would figure it out.

I drew myself up from peering under the bed to re-assess.

Where the hell was she keeping her kid?

Something was wrong. I got to my feet, examining the room again. I was good in a fight, not a baby hunt. Maybe Knight should have come.

Being in this amazing smelling home would definitely not help how close he was to a rut. The shoot-out had helped, but he needed a little more. Possibly, *if* I was a brat enough, I could be that little more.

As I glanced around again, I spotted a fluffy brown cat poking its head up from beneath the bed.

We stared at each other for a long moment before it padded over.

"Hi," I said. "I'm looking for Lucy." The cat rolled on its back and let out a meow. "Actually, I'm in a bit of a hurry—"

Oh.

Oooohhhhh.

"Lucy?"

A… cat?

Oh, thank God.

No one had fucked my mate—and cats were cheaper, anyway.

I reached down to pick it up, but it straightened lightning fast and took a swipe at me.

Dammit.

I lunged, trying to grab it up, but for something so round, it was certainly fast, darting out of my way and diving back under the bed.

I ducked down to see a pair of white orbs reflecting back at me from the dark. I swiped for it, but it—*she*—backed up. I could upturn the bed but she was quick.

"Why are you being so difficult?" I sighed, sitting back and scratching my head before coming to the only rational solution. "Look. I'm sorry. Not personal. Really."

I tugged the metal vial from my back pocket, pulled the top, then tossed it under the couch.

The gas was invisible and odourless, nothing a cat would be alert for.

I'd be fine. Had no effect on me, I laced a bit into my joints at least once a week now—though it had been more frequent when I'd started. I just got a bit of a high.

Grinning stupidly, I lowered my head. No more glowing orbs. Thank God it had worked. Though… come to think of it. After I'd dragged Lucy out, I poked her, trying to find a pulse, which proved difficult with so much fur. I breathed a sigh of relief as I heard a purr rumble to life in her chest.

Perfect.

Glade might have killed me.

She might have a bit of a kitty headache, but it was nothing compared to what would happen if the Brotherhood found her in Glade's apartment.

I didn't put cat cruelty past Ace at all.

I went back to her room to grab her gym bag and stuff it full of clothes—who knew how long she'd be staying, then I scooped Lucy back up in my arms and made for the sliding door.

I'd never had a pet, but she was kind of cute: caramel coloured, with an obscene amount of fluff, and a big bushy tail. And she was kind of big for a cat. That was a good thing. If I did have one, I preferred a pet big enough to hug.

Good call from Glade, really. Lucy would be a perfect addition to our family.

I know Zed and Knight were furious about what we'd just got tangled in, but I wasn't. Our pack was tied to the Brotherhood. Couldn't help it. The question wasn't if Ace would come for us, it was when.

Zed might deny it, Knight might tell me not to waste my time worrying about shit that I wasn't sure about, but that was the thing.

I *was* sure.

Knight cared all too much about me, but there were parts even he couldn't reach. Parts that knew Ace would never truly leave Zed behind because Ace and I, we weren't that different.

Two sides of the same coin. Same people, different paths.

I supposed I did have Knight to thank for that. Without him, I'd have never packed up. Without him, I might be as lonely as Ace.

Re-adjusting Lucy in my arm and readying my gun in my other, I hurried up the steps toward the new spot we'd parked, still grinning stupidly and trying to stay alert for watching eyes.

Come to think of it, I'd be even less lonely now and even further from Ace, because I had my girl back.

10

"A cat?" Zed was absolutely livid. "You almost got Kyan killed for a fucking cat?"

I could barely hear him as lights from Vegas streets flashed in the window. "Why isn't she moving?"

"She's fine." Kyan sounded defensive. He scratched her head and I heard a low purr rumble to life.

Oh, thank God.

"This isn't a fucking joke," Zed snarled.

"We scared them off." Kyan sounded unperturbed as he drew Lucy closer, examining her carefully. "Was a cinch."

"Kyan—oh for fuck's sake. You can't—" Zed tried to snatch Lucy from Kyan's arms, but Kyan growled, drawing his jaw along her fur. His lightning storm scent filled the car like a scent bomb —to me, anyway. I knew that to everyone that wasn't me, Kyan smelled like autumn persimmon. That was just how it had always been.

"Did you just scent-mark a cat?" Knight demanded as Kyan drew her close enough that Zed couldn't wrangle her away.

"Don't hurt her!" I snapped.

"She's gonna love me."

"You knocked her out," I hissed. "She won't."

"You'll eat those words."

"Stop *talking* to her," Knight growled from the front, levelling a death glare through the rear view at me.

We finally came to a stop at a huge warehouse, which, it turned out, was their home, though only after Kyan had demanded they stop on the way for 'cat stuff'. Knight had been the one to go into the store, since he was the only one mostly blood free.

Reality was slowly sinking in, though, and the relief of getting Lucy back wasn't near enough to fix the mess I was in.

Zed, it seemed, was completely serious about not letting me go, and clearly dragging me here had nothing to do with affection. He'd grabbed a shirt from the seat beside me, shredded it with my own knife, and tied it around my mouth as a gag when I hadn't stopped demanding Kyan give me Lucy.

It was still tight around my mouth when the truck stopped, and he showed no sign of removing it. I'd forgotten what a fucking cunt he was.

Where they lived was apparently an old warehouse which suited them entirely. It was messy, with a huge main space, and a faded wall of graffiti on the far end.

Cuffs and gag still firmly in place, Zed led me past a huge open space with a scattered gym and graffiti wall, into a more insulated living room that still spanned at least five of my High Roller rooms. There was a makeshift kitchen on one wall, a cove of couches and TV on another, an old wooden dining table, and other rather randomly scattered items of furniture. There was also what looked like a woodworking bench in a far corner, and doors that I assumed led to bedrooms. But they were like... box rooms, how offices sometimes were in warehouses, where the flat roof only reached halfway up the roof of the outer space.

This was where my mates made their home?

How many times had I wondered what living with them would look like? What my life would have looked like?

And the answer wasn't at all what I'd thought. Nor was it... bad, somehow.

"You going to deal with Kyan?" Zed asked, gracelessly tossing me onto the couch. I let out a snarl of derision, struggling upright with the cuffs, but neither Alpha was paying me attention.

Knight was looking at Zed with a raised eyebrow.

"I'll deal with Kyan if I don't have to go near her."

Kyan, who'd already placed a box of litter and was running water into a dish, glanced back at us all. He set it down, then folded his arms. "I don't need dealing with."

"You scent marked her fucking cat," Zed snorted. "If I tell you not to go near her, will you listen?"

"Don't go—*what?*" Kyan spluttered a laugh like Zed was joking.

Zed gave Knight a 'told you so' look, but Knight was already crossing the room toward Kyan. Kyan's reaction surprised me. He backed up a pace then turned, leaping onto the kitchen counter, reaching for a metal grate attached to the wall.

"Oh no you don't," Knight growled, pouncing after him in a second. Kyan managed to get his second hand on the grate before Knight had his fist in his hair and began dragging him back down rather ruthlessly.

I straightened, eyes wide as the grate groaned. With a growl of fury, Kyan released it, tumbling back into Knight's grip. Knight barely stumbled. Kyan was tall and ripped as fuck—feeling pretty big next to me, but he wasn't in Knight's weight class, and all it took was a hand clamped around Kyan's neck and nothing Kyan did seemed to matter.

"Tell me you'll listen to Zed?" Knight growled. "Or we'll do it right fucking here."

Kyan spluttered another laugh.

"You won't touch her." Zed's voice echoed around the bones of this strange home that we'd just entered. "You won't go near her. Is that fucking clear?"

Kyan raised his eyebrows with a smile, eyes sliding to me. He pressed his tongue into his canine, grin widening, but didn't answer.

"Kyan!" Knight growled. "*Say* it."

He wrinkled his nose, cocking his head as he stared at Knight. "Nope." He popped the 'p' arrogantly, just like I remember him doing when we were younger.

There was a struggle as Knight dragged Kyan toward the scratched up table that was bright with spray paint. Knight pinned him over the table in moments.

Holy. Shit.

Things had definitely changed since I'd last been around them.

Kyan struggled, muscles taut, a snarl on his lips, but Knight's fist curled in his hair and he slammed Kyan down hard enough to make me jump.

What the fuck were they doing?

"Zed gets to touch her, why don't I?" Kyan snarled.

Zed laughed, reaching for the gun still holstered at Kyan's hip and removing it. I saw Kyan tense for a moment, the briefest flash of irritation in his eyes. Then Zed tapped the barrel against Kyan's temple.

"Say it. I'm not letting you get her in your obsessed little sights."

Kyan let out a manic laugh. "*Fuck* you!" He struggled again, palms flat against the table, but this time Zed took over fisting his hair and holding his cheek against the surface, shifting real close and pressing the gun between his eyes.

I tensed, suddenly on high alert.

Knight took the opportunity to readjust his position, and I swear he... wait, what *was* he doing?

Mother above...

Knight was tugging out his cock, and I had to fight my own perfume hitting the space as I saw it. Kyan snarled as Knight easily shoved the back of his shirt up and—*Woah!* Was he about to do what I thought he was?

Zed cocked the gun, and panic burned my veins. All eyes snapped to me. I froze, catching the low whine as it rose up my throat, not forming anything coherent through my gag.

Shit, shit, shit.

Kyan's pupils were blown wide as he stared at me, lip caught in his teeth. Zed turned his gaze back to Kyan, tapping him on the head with the gun.

"Say you won't fucking touch her," Knight growled.

There was a wild grin on Kyan's face. He dragged his hand to his mouth, made a V with two fingers, and slid his tongue through the gap in a vulgar sign, never taking his blown pupils from me.

I shivered, trying to stifle the crazy fucking response my body was having to that.

Zed sneered, taking a few paces back and letting Knight take over the grip on Kyan's hair.

"Say it, you filthy rat," Knight snarled. "Or you won't walk straight tomorrow."

Kyan wasn't fighting Knight, though, or paying attention to the gun pointed at him. He was just staring at me. I would be lying if I said it wasn't making my blood hot.

Kyan didn't seem to even notice as Knight unhooked the chain from his belt, attached it to a cuff on his wrist, and latched it instead on matching metal on Kyan's necklace—well, collar, actually. If I hadn't been gagged, my mouth might have dropped open.

But no. Kyan was staring at me without a care in the world for the two insane Alphas around him about to—

My eyes caught the movement of Zed shifting his finger on the trigger, and my heart skipped a beat. Another terrified sound of shock tore from my chest through the gag, but when he pulled the trigger nothing happened but for a small click.

The chamber was empty.

I only had a split second to process that, or the brief delight on Kyan's face as he saw my terror, because then Knight slammed into him without prep or warning. A strangled growl loosed from Kyan and his eyes shut only for a moment, a twisted expression on his face. His whole body arched, struggling against the death grip Knight had on him. Then he was panting, low whines slipping from his throat as Knight bent over him and set a brutal pace.

"He emptied his clip for you," Zed muttered as he set the gun down beside me. "How fucking precious." He dropped onto the couch at my side.

I struggled away from him, eyes still fixed on Kyan, heart racing a million miles a second. I heard his breath of a laugh beside me and then he was dragging me onto his lap. "You should watch, Little Devil, or how will you sleep tonight knowing he might come in at any time?"

It was an unnecessary command. I couldn't have taken my eyes from Kyan and Knight if I'd tried. The sounds Kyan was making, half wounded, half wild... and he *still* hadn't taken his eyes from me.

"Your scent is giving you away," Zed murmured, sounding far too pleased. "Once, we wanted you and you didn't want us. And now..." Fingers closed around my throat as he drew me tighter against him, letting the silence finish the sentence for him.

I warred with my reaction to the feeling of his touch around me—even the one at my neck. Hostile as it was, it was filling a void that had been left to scab and rot. It was easier to keep my attention on Kyan than it was to consider how pathetic that made me.

Knight's grip was closed around Kyan's wrist, the other dragging his head back by the chain now wrapped in his fist, leaving him to scramble with his one free hand to find a hold, a low growl ripping from his throat.

"You're never ready to take me, Rat," Knight taunted. "But you always bait me, anyway."

The sounds Kyan was making were getting more desperate, despite the snarl on his face.

"This is the part he hates," Zed murmured, sounding amused. "Every fucking time."

I didn't move, unable to look away, not understanding what I was watching. "If he gets there before Knight, he'll do what we want," Zed breathed.

Kyan let out a low whine, his breaths short and sharp, his cheeks hot.

Fuck.

I clenched my legs together, but it was far too late for that. I felt every Alpha's gaze snap to me. Knight even paused for a moment, a snarl curling his lips as he took me in.

It didn't matter.

Kyan groaned, teeth bared as he inhaled the perfume I'd just released into the space. I could see the moment the orgasm took him, clenched fist trembling, and a feral sound sliced through the momentary silence.

I felt Zed's scent shift from derision to fury, and he was on his feet in a moment. "Right. Show's over." He gripped me by the neck as he dragged me to my feet and into another room.

11

Inside was a small space with a bathroom attached, and on the floor a single beat up mattress. Zed slammed the door behind us, then he ripped the gag from me, and I heard the sliding metal sound of a key before there was pressure on the cuffs around my wrists. They were free in moments.

"On your knees. Strip." He'd changed. Before he'd been taunting me. Now he just seemed pissed.

"Go fuck yourself."

"You just brought the Brotherhood down on my pack's head," he said, lips drawing back in a snarl. "Please, Glade. Be difficult. Find out what happens."

"We can be *civil*."

I needed that as a baseline. They *had* bailed me out and saved Lucy. That was something. He sneered. "You're not here because we like you, sweetheart. You're here because my brother wants you. Don't think I've forgotten who you are, and all the weapons you're carrying. I'm not above pinning you like a dog and searching you myself."

I had to work to control my breathing.

"Boots. Toss them."

I knew the look on his face, and how little he was fucking around when he was in this mood. Zed Maverick rarely fucked around.

I tugged them off and threw them at him with as much force as I could muster. He caught them easily, dropping them to the floor at his feet.

"Socks and robe."

He tapped his knife against his wrist impatiently. Scowling, I shrugged off the robe, and tugged my socks off, trying to ignore his expression when one of my switchblades tumbled out.

It was small. Not my smallest, but still. The satisfaction twinkling in his eyes made me want to scream.

"Dress."

"No." The word came out too fast, carrying with it a bit of panic.

He didn't understand. I couldn't.

He raised an eyebrow, but I gritted my teeth, beating back my fear. I didn't want him to see it, or he might force it on principle.

But if he saw the marks across my back... I swallowed, not wanting to imagine.

Everything I'd ever sacrificed for...

I'd lose it.

He would know the truth he could never know.

"You don't understand. You *have* to let me go."

He ignored me, waiting quietly.

I took a breath, forcing a snarl on my face as I reached for the clasp of my bra and unhooked it. If he wanted to see the weapons, we could do that without losing the dress. He raised an eyebrow as I fought to get it off. I threw it at him too, holding my head high as another folded blade bounced across the mattress. A little part of me calculated going for it, but there was no way Zed wasn't waiting for exactly that. And then what? Put a knife to his throat to escape.

"Shit." His eyes were fixed on my tits, which were on full display through the dress.

My lips drew in a snarl.

"Never found a set quite as good, you know? Would it go to your head if I said I missed them?"

My mind battled with that. *Never found?*

How many Omegas had they been with since I'd left them?

"Trip on your fucking knife," I spat.

His grin was wide.

"Am I reading that right—are you jealous?"

"I hope it lands right on your dick."

He stepped toward me, eyes twinkling dangerously. "Oh, the arrogance."

"*Me?*"

"Tell me what you think of that, sweetheart? That we've banged more Omegas than I can name since you left."

A wounded growl rose in my chest born of instinct and nothing else. I tried to stop it, but I couldn't, years of agony, of nightmares, catching up to me in one moment. Zed had me by the throat, pinning me to the wall.

"You betrayed us," he hissed. "You don't get a claim."

I shut my eyes, trying to find safety, solace. Trying to calm my breathing. His cool scent of snow santal made it impossible.

"Do you understand me?"

I didn't answer.

"I'll bring an Omega home tonight and make you watch," he threatened.

I buried every instinct deep, buried the pain at the thought, and swallowed every bit of pride I'd so desperately clawed back in the years since I'd escaped Ace.

"I understand," I hissed.

No claim.

I couldn't love them.

Even if that love had been the pillar of my survival for years.

Still was, a little voice whispered.

And he could never know that.

"So. That's all?" he asked.

"All what?"

"All of your spikes?"

"Yes."

"Say it for me, Little Devil. *'That's every weapon I have on me.'*"

"Get fucked you piece of Maverick trash."

He sneered. "Glade. If I go searching and you're a filthy liar, you'll sleep chained to the foot of my bed."

I clenched my jaw. "You wouldn't."

He raised his eyebrows with such an incredulous look that I cracked. "Fucking—fine. Just let me—" I tried to pull away to the bathroom, but he pressed me against the wall by my neck harder.

"*Right. Here.* Little Devil."

I hated him.

I fucking hated him.

It was a task, with him pinning me against the wall by my neck, but at least he didn't get a view. The last weapon was slim with a soft case, and roughly the size of a tampon.

There was a nasty smirk spreading on his face the whole time.

"Better," he said, when I had it clutched in my fist. He plucked it from my grip. Then he collected the rest of them up and opened the door, tossing them out before he turned back to me. "Now. Get in the shower."

"What?"

"You smell like blood and sex, sweetheart. Get in the fucking shower."

"*Sex?*"

I hadn't perfumed that badly, had I?

"You want to get horny for the Alphas you rejected, you'll have a cold shower every time."

His pack might have saved my ass today, but Zed was out of mercy. He dragged me to the bathroom and forced me to my knees in the shower. When he turned the water on I gasped. It was frigid. When I tried to scramble out, he shoved me back with his foot.

"Fight me again, I'll take the dress myself."

That stilled me, terror made of colder ice than the water running through my hair. That terror seeped to my marrow, a secret I could never give up.

So I remained, shivering on my knees as he sprayed me with the shower like I was an animal.

"Does this get you off?" I asked. "Seeing me like this?"

He barked a laugh like it was a stupid question. "You took our entire life and crumpled it in your self-serving, spoiled Omega fist —and for what?" He looked truly disgusted as he stared down at me. "Status? Pride? Or did you just want to feel powerful?" He crouched, the shower head still in his fist. The jet caught me in the face and I was forced to look away. "I don't just want you on your knees, I want you to suffer, and I want you to know it's because of me. You asked why I came tonight? I wanted to find a way to see this."

I couldn't answer that, trying to control my breathing. This cold, it was nothing. Not really. I'd faced worse.

His fury was absolute. He was an Alpha who put his pack first no matter what, and I had betrayed him. *Them.* I had betrayed him the same moment he had been about to extend that protection to me. I didn't have the strength to contemplate, again, how my life would have looked if I'd said yes to that offer. My chance stolen. I hadn't known that day how much more could be ripped away.

Hearing his fury, borne of the protection for the very pack I'd damned, though, it was hard not to let those time worn dreams creep back.

"Nothing to say?" he asked.

I remained silent.

I'd endured worse.

I told myself that as I shivered, counting the seconds like I used to do to stay afloat.

Finally, he turned the water off, seeming satisfied.

"Get up."

I staggered to my feet, needing this to be over. Needing him to be done. His hatred saturated his scent, making it impossible to escape.

He looked me up and down, eyes snagging on my chest where my dress clung for dear life over my tits. He stepped closer and his proximity triggered a cascade of confusing reactions in my half functional Omega brain. Torment crumbled for comfort, as if being close to him might fix everything.

He was my mate, after all.

He'd brought me here to protect me—just like he was supposed to.

I shoved that away much too late.

"You want to know the part that brings me the most satisfaction?" he asked, cupping my chin and forcing me to look at him.

My hair stuck to my face, dripping down my body, and my shivers wracked me head to toe. I jumped as I felt his hand brush the underside of my breast, trailing up just slightly.

Heat speared my core and I stifled a whimper. Traitorous. Desperate. Fucking foolish. He was *everything* I'd dreamed of through heat after heat. A desperation I'd come to resent.

"I *almost* believe that if I offered my touch..." His finger circled my nipple through the thin fabric. "...You might just beg."

I clenched my teeth to fight my whine.

"Why is that, after everything?" he asked. "The scent match? Or maybe I remind you of my brother?"

I flinched back, bile rising in my throat. I reacted in a flash of rage, and struck him across the cheek before I could catch myself.

He went deathly still, head turned, pupils constricted. The cool santal of his scent turning to ice.

"I was going to let you have a visitor—even though you almost got my pack mate killed for her today, but now—"

"What...?" My voice shook.

Lucy?

He was going to let Lucy in?

I needed to see her.

I shoved the tears back. I'd endured worse, I told myself again. So, so much worse without tears, and yet it was harder to fight them now than ever before.

He was my mate.

He was one third of the tiny slice of comfort I'd used for years as a crutch, and that crutch, flimsy, desperate and weak as it was, was dissolving at last.

A trickle of blood trailed down Zed's cheek from where my nails had made contact.

He drew his finger along the scratch, examining the drop of blood, a cruel smile on his face.

He pressed his thumb to my lips and I tasted the tang of iron on my tongue. "Kiss it better, Glade. Apologise. Get on your knees and beg me. I *might* change my mind."

He was taunting me.

He wouldn't change his mind.

I could do all of those things, and he would never let Lucy visit. I recognised the wounded pride of a Maverick with deadly clarity. That same look had cost me over and over. That look alone was almost enough to turn me back into the shell I'd once been.

"No?" He took a step back. "Shame. I'd have taken a photo. Would have kept me nice and warm tonight."

"Fuck yourself."

His grin widened as he placed a hand on the doorknob.

"Wait—" Shit. He was really leaving? "I n-need a fucking towel."

I was shivering. The mattress had the thinnest of blankets, and it was freezing in here.

"You aren't getting shit." He was opening the door.

He *had* to be joking.

I threw myself after him just too late.

"If you don't give me a towel, I'll get sick and then you'll have to deal with—!" My voice raised to a screech but he slammed the door in my face.

12

She was as dangerous as Knight had warned. I realised that far too late.

Not just because of what she'd just dragged me into, but because I had been wrong. I hadn't been ready to see her.

I'd only ever been in love with one person in my entire life. When I'd loved, I'd opened up every door in my whole world, so when she'd set fire to it, there had been nowhere it hadn't spread.

I hated her.

I hated her, and I loved her all at once and it was twisting me up.

Never in my life, had I ever experienced being so angry and so... fucking hurt at the same time. Not until today, when I'd seen her again, in those first few moments.

I sat down on the couch alone, staring at the gym bag Kyan had grabbed from her room.

She'd get what was inside.

As fucking pissed as I was at this mess, making the imprisoned Omega sick was not on the agenda. But she could curl up believing it for another few minutes.

We'd solved a few problems, even if entirely un-ideally. First off, I didn't think Knight was near a rut anymore. If a regular fuck was enough, Kyan would never rut. But you needed an Omega for a rut, or a massive outlet. Of course, Glade had gone and perfumed—her scent was still filling the space—and none of us wanted to admit it, but it might have settled him.

And then there was Kyan. Another thing Knight had been right about.

He was obsessed with her—*again.*

Which wasn't fucking good.

But he'd listen to Knight and stay away from her—well, as long as Kyan decided the dominance play lasted. We should have a few days at least.

The two of them were in Knight's room right now and would be for a bit longer. Knight didn't fuck Kyan like that and not deal with it after—even if he had to be as forceful in the aftercare. I had no idea what that looked like, but I was sure it was just as wild as the sex.

Somehow, it worked between them. Kyan snarled and fought, and then he was just... happy afterward. Yet their strange love was as absolute and consistent as anything I'd seen.

It was extra impressive because getting close to Kyan was like a minefield in a desert. The terrain was rough, and any step that looked right was a mirage that might blow up in your face. I got by, but Knight had managed to figure it out somehow—*properly* figure it out. I'd never been a part of their relationship outside of being pack lead. I called the shots, Knight enforced them.

Well, I watched sometimes. Kyan never cared—actually, I think he loved it—and I'd never complained, so it was up to Knight if he put on a show. It was kind of comforting. I didn't have to want to fuck Kyan to be a part of the bond.

There was something intimate about watching, and I was sorely lacking on anything on the intimacy front.

I'd lied through my teeth about screwing other Omegas. It wasn't *just* Omegas. I hadn't banged anyone in my life except Glade. Which meant my only goddamned source material was shivering in the locked room behind me. I wrinkled my nose, grabbing the bag, a towel, and a proper blanket from the cupboard and tossed them into the room.

I tried not to look, but it was so fucking hard.

Furious chestnut eyes met mine from where she was curled on the mattress.

Her scent was intoxicating. Dark cream cardamom. Dangerous, cool, earthy, with an edge that suited Glade perfectly. A flawless scent for the most beautiful woman in the world. I'd had to learn the hard way that beauty couldn't be trusted.

Neither could scent matches.

"Please check on Lucy?" Her voice was harrowingly fragile, and for a moment, through the drops of water still running from her hair, I wasn't sure if she'd been crying.

I considered ignoring her.

I mean, Lucy was fine. I'd even looked it up on my phone in the car ride here if that gas was damaging. Not because of her, but since Kyan had done it and I was pack lead, it was sort of my responsibility.

And I *might* be a cat person.

The drug wouldn't hurt her cat—who was actually stupid cute. Lucy was already poking around the kitchen rather drunkenly and had found her litter box.

"She's okay," I said.

Glade nodded, shivering, clutching her bag as she remained curled up.

I forced myself to shut the door, reminding myself that she deserved everything that she was getting. When she'd rejected us that day, she'd torn us from our family. Taken everything that had ever mattered.

She deserved this.

Less than this even, because by bringing her here I was offering my pack's protection from the Brotherhood, and no matter how much I hated her, that was something I took seriously.

I returned to the couch, watching as Lucy sniffed at the TV stand, then stumbled a little on her way over to the couch.

Knight appeared from his room as I leaned down to scratch her, and found myself rather irritated that I didn't get the purr Kyan had.

Was he actually onto something with the scent marking?

"This," Knight said, sitting down on the couch beside me with a beer. "Is the stupidest thing we've ever done."

I couldn't argue like I had earlier—before we'd decided to visit the High Roller.

"What's the worst that could happen?" I'd asked. I *needed* this. I would tell her to her face that we were over her. I was a prideful, arrogant idiot, and I'd eaten my fucking words.

Getting in Ace's crossfire was not a direction I'd thought the night might take.

My silence was damning enough.

Knight snorted. "She's going to leave us for dead first chance she gets—just like last time," he went on. "Just asking to get kicked in the nuts again."

I took a sip of my beer but it was tasteless.

Had she been crying? I wondered. Was she, right now? How could I hate her this much and still care? If she was crying, it was probably because of me for fuck's sake.

"We meet her again and what's the first thing she does?" Knight went on. "She fucking lies. And now we're caught in a Brotherhood feud."

She *had* lied. I knew that. But there was more to it.

She'd been angry when I mentioned Ace. She tried to control it but there was a cut on my face in testament to that fury. Fury and… something else I'd seen in her eyes when I'd brought my brother up.

"I think she's scared," I said. I realised how true it was the moment it came out of my mouth. Glade and fear weren't words I'd easily throw together in a sentence. "Way more than she's letting on. If she lied about the Brotherhood, it's because she didn't think we'd save her if we knew."

"Zed." Knight looked at me incredulously. "She didn't seem dead set on our help in the first place."

"I don't get it."

"You don't get why she doesn't want to be around us? After she left—"

"If she's running from the Brotherhood then no," I snapped. "I don't get why she doesn't want our help."

"You're blind. She wanted to go, but what did you do? Tied her up and dragged her here against her will."

"Something's not right." I couldn't shake that. "And besides, if she'd told us, would it have changed anything?" I asked.

A strange silence followed that question and Knight's lip curled. Fuck the answer we were both thinking.

The last intel we'd got said Ace had dropped her. She'd cheated on him and he'd curbed her. Exiled, just like we'd been— only it hadn't blown up his relationship with the Romano Mafia she'd come from. I guess her dad thought her behaviour was shitty enough to keep the alliance.

Well, no. That wasn't why.

It's because the alliance had become useful to them both.

I was a prideful fucker, and being afraid of my baby brother wasn't something I'd admit to lightly. But I wasn't a fool. Ace had turned out smarter than I'd even known. Both on taking my place from me, and what he'd done with it since. I hated him, but I couldn't deny he'd picked the Brotherhood up off the floor and made it into something unstoppable.

But the point was, she was exiled, which meant... "If she's on Ace's radar now, it's not good," I said.

Knight was silent. We both knew the only time they came knocking after they sent you packing was for one thing.

"She hasn't told us why," Knight muttered. "It's dangerous. We've never bothered him, and he's never bothered us. So what did she do to get back in his sights?"

I took another drink of my beer, feeling a chill creep up my spine.

"If she's lying, even now," Knight said. "Whatever she's hiding, I just hope it doesn't put one of us—or all of us—in a grave."

13

"*Another game...*"

Ace's voice was the first I heard when I finally succumbed to sleep on the old mattress. I was instantly stolen by the same nightmare that was haunting my every waking moment.

A memory. And the moment, of every one I'd lived, that had truly broken me.

"What do you want?" I asked him.

The dark marble of his mansion was icy beneath my shins, a coldness that rose from the floor itself, chilling me in the thin nightdress I wore, as if the soul of this place had turned to ice long ago to match its owner.

"Last week, the trick with the maid. I was... impressed."

I dared glance up to the Alpha lounging on the armchair before me. We were in his rooms, the place to which he had summoned me in the middle of the night.

"You almost escaped," he said. Dark hair swept over skin as pale as Zed's, but the only other things that they shared was the electric blue eye colour and the slight crook on their nose. His lips were rich red in contrast to his skin, stretching over his teeth in a cruel smile. "It doesn't seem to matter how hard I try. I can't seem to crush you. It makes me jealous, you know?" he asked. "Thistle is long broken—perfect obedience, and rather fucking dull. The universe promised her to me, yet saw fit to promise an Omega like you to my brother, instead?"

I was silent as I waited.

It had been days since I'd almost reached freedom. He hadn't said anything after, the punishment had been exacted instantly, far more than anything he could think up in the aftermath. And then he'd joined me in my bed each night since, delighting in the nightmares that consumed me, wanting to be there each time I woke.

That was enough for him. I paid.

Or so I'd thought.

"I would be a fool to dismiss your mind," he said. "Or your determination to be free of this place."

I took a breath, still kneeling before him, holding his gaze with a blank expression he knew, by now, was a mask.

"Do you disagree?" he asked.

I blinked, considering that. I didn't lie to Ace, not unless there was no choice, and certainly not when he'd know. "No."

"I propose a game." He smiled, something malicious dancing in his blue eyes. "Double or nothing. I think it would be amiss to assume that one day you might win—for a time. One day, you might get free, and this dance will shift from this mansion, and into the greater world."

I felt goosebumps rise on my skin from far more than the cold air and marble.

I tried to reject what he was saying. With such ease, he moved the goalposts. He promised that, should I ever escape, this wouldn't be over. His games would always go on, no matter how far I ran.

Still, I was silent, holding his gaze with perfect neutrality I'd trained myself for.

"So. If you do find yourself on the other side of these mansion walls, our deal holds."

My lips parted in shock for a moment, a reaction I couldn't contain. I saw a flash of delight on his face as he saw it.

Our deal?

The one that had landed me with this fate.

"You gave up so much that day—all in the name of their protection. I won't waste that. Unless... I see, even once, even for a second, any Alpha in my brother's pack protecting you. Then, I will hunt them down alongside you, and they will die like that maid this week."

Ice-cold dread slid through my veins. Dozens of images crossed my mind. Ace was ruthless, cruel, and merciless.

How many had I watched die by his hand?

He knew how much I feared it, so he made sure I was there every time. And when it was my fault? I almost shut my eyes at the thought.

The bodyguard who'd taken pity on me. The maid who'd slipped me a key and her own clothes so that I might get free.

They hadn't died like the others.

Instead, the gun shook in my own hands. Ace was at my back, chest crushing the scars he'd so recently opened. He held me still. The barrel aimed.

My finger was numb. I didn't feel the trigger. With the last of my courage I'd shifted the aim. I'd shot a gun enough times to easily land the bullet right between the eyes.

Mercy.

Everything I would never have.

He could have stopped me. He always could have stopped me.

But he never did. He loved watching me defy him so he had reasons to torture me more. He was far, far more obsessed with me than he ever was with his compliant scent match.

"Double or nothing. That's the deal." Ace said into the silence, a smile playing on his lips as he watched me work through the threat.

Those words sunk in.

For a moment, that gun was in my hands, but it wasn't the maid before it, it was Kyan. Knight. Zed.

Double, or nothing.

Pack and freedom. Or neither. Forever.

And it would all come down to whether or not I trusted Zed and his pack could match Ace and the resources he held as leader of the Brotherhood.

I didn't know if it was his plan, but that night he finally found the thing that would kill my fight. The last thing that gave me hope. The final lantern I followed, snuffed out at last.

Because I believed him, and after everything I'd given up to keep them safe, I would never risk it.

Ace had won.

Even if I did escape one day, somehow, the final dream waiting for me on the other side was dead.

14

KNIGHT

Glade was...? I frowned. *Was she showering?*

It was the next day, and I'd spent the night tossing and turning about the stupid-ass situation Zed had got us into.

And now, Glade was apparently showering, which didn't make sense because there was no hot water in that room. Zed was in his bedroom, and Kyan was in the warehouse—which was what we called the massive multi-purpose space beyond what we used as the main living room.

I dug my key from my pocket—I had one and Zed had one—and approached her door, expecting a trick. I opened the first door, peering around to see the bathroom one shut, but the sound of the shower was louder from here.

"Glade?" I asked, knocking.

Nothing.

At least... I thought it was nothing. I pressed my ear to the door with a frown.

Was she... crying?

In a cold shower?

No. The hairs on my body stood on end, instincts dragging a growl to my throat, hand closing on the doorknob in an instant. Through the door I could definitely hear the low, desperate whines of my mate.

Was she hurt?

I paused a second longer, then shoved the door open, holding onto the meagre threads of sanity I had left.

What was...?

Shit.

She was on the shower floor, curled up and panting as she clutched her stomach.

I crossed toward her, but her eyes snapped open, finding me, and she shoved back, crashing against the shower wall.

"What's wrong?" I barely noticed the frigid water streaming over my back.

She shook her head, eyes wide with terror, another low whine slipping out. In this small space I was drowning in her scent, dark cream cardamom like an...

Shit.

Her scent was an aphrodisiac. It was impossible not to notice she was wearing nothing but an oversized T-shirt, the beautiful brown of her smooth legs on full display.

"Heat?" My voice was hoarse.

Fucking *heat?*

Right now?

What the hell were we going to do?

My mind went blank as another low moan tore from her and she doubled over. I almost reached out, but caught myself. I hadn't lost myself completely, probably because of the icy water washing her scent down the drain.

Oh no. This was bad.

And it had started... *could* we stop heat after it started?

"What do we do?" I asked stupidly.

We couldn't *fuck* her—right? I'd almost rutted from a kiss. We *couldn't*. And she didn't want us—that truth smashed into me. She'd chosen an ice shower over telling us.

She *didn't* want us.

"Sh-shut the door." Her voice shook. "Just k-keep them out for a few days."

"Are you joking?" That would be agony.

"Knight—" She reached out to me, trembling fingers, seizing my shirt. "P-please. I can't—" She broke off with another moan of pain. Tears were streaking down her cheeks, chestnut eyes glistening. "I'm scared..."

My mind was foggy with panic.

"If you don't want us, there are drugs..." Fuck. It had already started. I was sure that made them a whole lot less effective. "They'll shorten it..."

What was I saying?

She was *still* going to be in agony.

"Is there..." I almost winced at the words that were coming out of my own fucking mouth. "Is there someone we can call?"

Right.

Invite another Alpha over to our pad, so he could fuck our mate senseless while we tried to drown out the sound of *literal heat.*

There was a beat as her gaze snapped to mine, shock so complete that it seemed to wipe her mind of the pain for a moment.

Her lips parted like she didn't know how to answer. Then she swallowed, shaking her head.

"No one?" I demanded.

What? As screwed up as the idea was, it had kind of been the solution. And I was still fucked in the head enough I had to stamp down little embers of relief that flitted to life in my chest.

"Just... go." Her tears were back.

I... *Shit.*

I needed help.

Zed would know what to do.

I was on my feet in a moment, backing out. Leaving the bathroom and her intoxicating scent sent shivers of panic down my spine, my hindbrain screaming that it was unnatural to leave.

I reached Zed's door in seconds, ripping it open and finding him in his bed, laptop open.

"What?" he said, glancing at me. He set the laptop down the second he caught my expression. Oh. I'd forgotten how hard I'd locked down my end of the bond. He had no idea I was panicking.

"Glade," I hissed. "She's in heat."

"She can't be." He scoffed, getting to his feet. "I saw her last night—"

"She's in *heat*," I spat, crossing to him and jabbing him in the chest. It was his stupid fucking idea to bring her here. "In *agony*. Right fucking now—and she doesn't want anyone to fuck her."

"She doesn't what? That's stupid—"

"There are meds, right? Please tell me we aren't too late—at least to make it shorter, or... or pain control."

"Are you out of your fucking mind?" he asked. "That's not a solution—"

My hand snapped out, fist closing in Zed's shirt. "We're not fucking her if she doesn't want us." Even if it wouldn't scramble our brains for good, I'd seen the terror on her face. He had been right. There was something else going on.

Zed peeled my hand from his shirt, stepping past me. "I wasn't saying we should," he snapped.

I followed him as he made for the spare room Glade was in. I shouldn't have left the door open. Her heat hormones would be in the whole space before we knew it.

I didn't dare follow him in, though, not sure I could take

seeing her like that again. I was just wringing the water from my locs when Zed appeared in the doorway, expression deadly.

"Knight," he snarled. "You're a fucking idiot."

"What?"

But Zed was tugging his gun from his belt, eyes scanning the room.

No...

Oh, *no*—there was no way she was faking it.

It took me half a second to cross the little room with the old mattress and into the bathroom. The shower was running, but sure enough, Glade was gone.

I backed out, mind racing. "That was... real. She was *crying*—"

Zed spat a curse back at me as he crossed toward the cracked door that led to the rest of the warehouse.

I was after him in an instant, wildly trying to catch up.

I reached the large open warehouse space just behind Zed and scanned it.

"Kyan!" Zed spotted him just before I did. He was standing at the graffiti wall, mask in place, can of spray paint halfway to the spot with the skull he'd designed last week. He lowered it, turning to us.

"Glade," Zed snarled. "She's gone."

Kyan said something as we approached, but it was incomprehensible through the mask.

"What?"

He tugged it off, a smile on his face. He looked high as fuck. "She was just here—you know, I forgot how sexy those thighs are. I want her like..." He narrowed his eyes, lifting his hands around his face, one still holding his spray paint, "... right here. She can crack my skull any day of the week."

Zed seized him by the shirt. "Why didn't you stop her?"

Kyan shrugged, voice dropping low as he mocked me. *"'Not allowed to touch her.'"*

"You little shit!" Zed hissed.

Kyan just grinned.

"Which way did she go?"

"Uh…" Kyan looked around, then nodded in toward one of the doors. "That door."

Zed released him, already making for it.

"*Wait—!*" Kyan called out. "—Might have been that one." He waved his can at the other side of the warehouse. "Can't remember. She's too pretty."

"I thought you *wanted* her here?" I demanded.

"I believe in you." He clapped me on the shoulder, then returned his mask to his face.

Resisting the urge to strangle him, I glanced to Zed. He looked ready to murder Kyan, but he made for the far door, while I went for the nearer.

15

GLADE

Why the fuck did they live in a *warehouse* district?

Instead of there being a dozen busy Vegas city streets for me to vanish into, I was hemmed in by mile-long industrial buildings and a scattering of cars. In my fist was a kitchen knife and a pair of cuffs.

Not ideal, but they were the only things I'd been able to reliably grab without wasting time. The knife had been planned, but I'd spotted the cuffs still on the couch from last night.

Despite my feet burning from the hot concrete against my soles, I was shivering. Not in heat—luckily, though Knight had bought that faster than I'd imagined.

Every breath burned my lungs, having sprinted my hardest down a road that looked exactly like the last in a soaking wet shirt.

It had been what—five minutes, maybe?

When the fuck would this district end?

I froze at the sound of a car at my back, then spun, trying to find something to duck behind. When I found nothing, I stilled instead, praying the car was just a passerby who wouldn't notice a half-dressed Omega wandering in a place like this.

Why had I decided to take off my sweats?

I'd thought maybe the more skin, the more likely to scramble the brain of whichever mate walked in. Now, I was regretting it—Knight's brain had scrambled so fast I could have probably been dressed like a beekeeper and I'd still be free right now.

Ah, fuck.

My heart sank as I saw a beat-up black truck pull past the intersection behind me. I didn't wait to see which of my mates was behind the wheel. I took off, the sound of an engine revving behind me, but when I turned my next corner, it was to meet a dead end with two industrial doors and a van.

Shit.

I didn't have time to change my mind. I tried the doors, but found them locked, and instead ducked behind the black van, chest heaving, stupid kitchen knife clutched in my fist.

I heard the truck stop and a door slam, then the crunch of boots on gravel.

Only one of them? Good. I held my breath through a pause.

"Glade?"

Knight.

Okay, Knight, I could work with.

"You don't want me here," I called back. "Let me go. Tell Zed you never found me."

Silence.

Come on. *Please.*

The quiet went on for too long. Finally, I heard his voice from the right of the van. "That's not how this pack works."

I ducked to the left around the car.

Fuck me—he'd left the keys in the ignition? It was still running. I glanced behind me, hearing something scrape concrete on the other side.

This was it. My only chance.

I made a break for it, heart in my chest.

If I could get the door shut and locked in time—

A strangled sound of shock tore from my chest as Knight's huge fist closed on my hair. I reacted on instinct, knife whipping out, and he snarled in pain as I caught him on the forearm with a shallow cut, but didn't let me go.

"Glade—!"

Fuck him. I shoved the open cuffs between my teeth to free my hand and threw myself to the side, using the back of the van for purchase with my foot and launched myself behind him. My free arm circled his neck as I swung around, ending up on his back. My movement forced his wrist at such an angle that I could rip my hair free. He staggered back, reaching for me with a growl, but I shifted, pulse thready, and managed to secure the knife at his neck.

He froze, fist trying to close around my wrist until I dug the knife deeper.

"You're going to let me go," I hissed through the metal between my teeth.

"I can't do that. Zed's orders."

I tried to lower myself down, to get my feet on the ground and have more control. I reached out with my foot and found nothing but air. He was so cursedly tall. If I dropped to the ground, I'd lose my advantage. I could hold the knife to his neck at the front, sure, but that might leave me toe to toe with his strength, and I couldn't match that.

"Crouch!" I demanded.

"No."

"Knight." My voice was a warning.

"You aren't going to—" He cut off with a hiss of pain as, in a flash of movement, I shifted the blade, cutting it across his shoulder. I returned it to his neck in a second.

He *had* to let me go.

None of them understood. I let the cuffs drop, able to reach them with the hand not holding the knife. They hadn't locked shut, thank god.

"Go to the wall," I said instead.

"What?"

"The dumpster." I tried to use my elbow to direct him to the dumpster that was just around the corner of the dead end. "Now." I pressed the knife harder and he tensed.

"Okay. All right . I'm going."

He took a tentative step toward it, and I could practically see the cogs turning in his mind as he tried to find a way out. He flinched, and I dug the knife in harder.

"Don't try anything," I snarled.

He did as I said, closing the gap to the dumpster, if slowly.

"Okay. Give me your wrist."

"What?"

"Now."

He lifted his arm, and I hooked the cuff around his wrist. "Secure it to the bar."

"No way—"

"Do it, Knight!" I failed to keep the tremor from my voice, which probably made me sound more crazy, because he did what I said and lowered his arm. Wasn't this what I wanted... To leave them?

Again?

I was shaking; the blade pressed so hard against his flesh I worried I was already drawing blood. "Try anything..." *Fuck*, I was almost sobbing. "I swear to God—"

"Okay." Knight's voice was deathly calm. He did what I said, and next thing I knew, he was cuffed to the bar.

I slipped from his back instantly, stepping away, trying not to think about what I'd just done.

The trick I'd set up, bottling up my hormones as best I could to convince them I was in heat, had been designed on the assumption that they'd let me out to help it *pass*. I was their mate, after all. It would make sense.

I'd told him to leave me in that room to seem more afraid, but he'd thought I was saying I didn't want them. And then—at the slightest hint I didn't—he'd left to get help. He'd thought I was going into heat—his own mate—and he'd been willing to listen to me. To find drugs to help me. He'd even offered to... to *call* someone.

Another sob almost broke from my chest.

I had to go, now.

But there was such a lost look on his face as he stared at me, as if he didn't know what he was seeing. Not his mate. Not the woman he'd once loved.

I'd changed—*Ace* had changed me. I could never escape that, no matter how many years or miles I put between us. Tears stung my eyes, but I blinked them away.

I took another step back, his scent of pear grove fading, and tried to forget that it was the last time it would ever truly be with me.

I had to vanish completely—go somewhere so far away neither them, nor Ace, would ever find me.

"Glade..." For a moment, Knight was so much more than the Alpha who'd argued with Zed not to keep me. Who was just angry that I was here—angry at me. Those beautiful dark brown eyes flashed with desperation far beyond the fury I'd just seen. His chest heaved, voice low and wounded as he threw his weight against the cuffs holding him. *"Don't."*

Don't leave...

I could almost hear those words.

Don't leave like before...

"It's best for you, I promise." My voice was thick. "For all of us." That last part. That was a lie. This had never been better for me, but I'd never had a choice.

I forced myself another step back, bracing to do it again. To leave them, and this time, forever.

But then I hit something solid and warm—some*one* that, should I not have been so panicked, I might have sensed was near. A hand closed over my mouth, covered with... something.

A... *cloth?*

I struggled briefly, inhaling something sharp and sweet, but then the world went fuzzy.

"...I'm sorry, my Sweet Oasis..." I heard Kyan's breath in my ear, drifting away as the world went black. "After everything, I won't let you go."

16

ZED

I caught up to the truck to find Glade, Kyan, and Knight all there.

Glade was unconscious.

A wave of relief slammed into me with shocking magnitude.

She hadn't managed to escape.

I hadn't realised, until now, how much larger than life she always seemed. It was easy to forget, beneath the blaze of her fierce chestnut eyes, that she was shorter than us by a foot. Kyan had her scooped up like a princess, and she looked oddly small, cheek against his chest, eyes shut. Her bare legs hung limply over his arm, bronze skin shining in the daylight above. Her thick, black waves tumbled over his arm, damp hair still dripping as Kyan carried her to the truck.

I'd rarely seen him so tender as when he set her down on the seat, adjusting her carefully in place.

"Do we need to cuff her?" I asked.

"Nah. She'll be out for hours." He turned back to me, looking rather proud.

"You helped," I said flatly.

He grinned as he hopped from the truck. "Knight lost, I won. I can touch her now."

"You will absolutely fucking not."

"Can someone get the goddamned key?" Knight asked from behind me.

I turned back to him, taking him in fully. He was cuffed to a dumpster, though he'd done a number on the metal holding him; it wasn't broken but it looked pretty mangled. There was a faint trickle of blood trailing from two shallow cuts across the corded muscle of his upper arms. I opened my mouth to ask how that had happened, but then saw the glint of a kitchen knife on the ground.

Right.

Glade was not to be fucked with when it came to sharp objects.

If Kyan had seen the knife when she'd run by, and failed to mention it—actually, I was happier not asking.

"Where's your shoe?" I asked, noting he was missing one.

"Kicked it to the other side of the van, gave me a chance to grab her."

"Yet," Kyan said, fetching the boot that had been tossed across the concrete. "You still fucked it up."

We took Glade back to the warehouse where Kyan tucked her in before I made sure her cell was firmly locked, and Knight began angrily frying up cold takeout from last night.

"No one talks to her except me," I growled.

"Can I get this straight?" Kyan straddled one of the dining room chairs. "She tricked Knight into thinking she was in heat, then ran?"

"She's a fucking snake." Knight didn't look at either of us as the cap of the soy sauce flew off as he violently shook it, dumping half the bottle onto his meal. He growled, slamming the pan down and tossing the spatula at the wall. "When it all goes up in flames, that's on you."

One-upped by our mate or not, he was too angry—for him especially—and his side of the bond was locked down tight. "She's a scent match," he muttered. "She can fuck with our brains."

"What about what she said when I got there?" Kyan asked mildly.

"What did she say?" I asked.

Knight scowled, taking a breath before he spoke. "She said she had to leave. It would be better for all of us."

I paused.

What did *that* mean?

That she cared about us? After all of this? My mind rejected it. "She's lied since she got here," I said slowly.

"She was free. I was cuffed." He wrinkled his nose distastefully as he emptied his ruined meal into the garbage and then stomped over to his room. "No reason for her to lie," he said, before slamming the door on us both.

I sighed, looking back at Kyan as he stood and stretched. "Well. I'm going to go and put a bit more work into our Brotherhood tracking." He was doing a deep dive into their movements, trying to figure out where they were, so we'd know if they got close. This warehouse was secure for now, but we hadn't had Brotherhood eyes searching for us like we knew they would be now.

"You won't go near her," I said again.

He just flashed me a grin.

"Before she wakes, can you go out?" I asked, glancing back at the mangled cuffs I'd tossed on the table. They weren't broken, but they weren't something I trusted to hold her anymore. Not when she'd proven so intent on getting away. "I need another." He'd got the last pair, and I didn't know where from.

Kyan brightened. "You want me to buy her bondage?"

I rolled my eyes. "I want something that will hold her, preferably before she wakes up. I need options if the cell isn't one."

"All right," he said, looking far too mischievous as he got to his feet and made his way toward the metal steps up to his room. "I'll go later."

"What do you think she meant when she said it's better for us all?" I asked.

He peered back at me, closing one eye like he was genuinely considering that. "That's a great question," he said. "I have no idea."

I didn't buy it. I might not be able to read Kyan quite as well as Knight, but I knew when he was hiding something.

"Any update on the Brotherhood?" I asked. We were on the back foot. It was far easier for us to track Brotherhood movement than it was for us to know if we'd been found.

"Nothing yet," he said. "Been monitoring the district cameras, haven't seen anything suspicious."

I nodded with a sigh, picking up my own laptop and slumping onto the couch as Kyan's footfalls echoed across the open living space and he climbed up toward his room. It was a small bunk upon the roof of Glade's cell, and was surrounded by spray-painted designs and the remains of the huge metal cage he'd dismantled to fit his bed in.

When we'd first arrived here, it had been an abandoned gym that had hosted rut fighting. There were still remnants of that in the wall of the metal cage that reached to the ceiling beside Kyan's pad, or the climbing wall that spanned the whole place.

The steps were old and beaten up, and the last stretch was just a precarious wooden ladder that Kyan always climbed with far too much confidence.

I mindlessly opened up my usual work tabs but couldn't focus on them. Using my foot, I nudged the coffee table door open, spotting the gun stashed within. It had been years since I'd been this paranoid, but with Glade in our home, I hadn't been more than six feet from a weapon—if I wasn't outright carrying. And it wasn't a response to the threat she might pose to us. If the Brotherhood discovered us, would they negotiate? Try to take her? Or just come in guns blazing?

I wished I could say I knew my brother well enough, but the truth was, I didn't. I never had. When we were children, he'd been... different. It was hard to put my finger on, but as we'd entered teenage years, I thought he'd grown out of it. Until the day our dad had died, and he'd taken everything.

My place in the Brotherhood, my home, and my scent match.

That was when I realised my brother had never changed. He'd just become better at wearing a mask. Glade had chosen him for power, and I doubted it took her long to realise he could never offer anything more than that.

Not like we could.

But she'd shown us all her priorities, and apparently even the power wasn't enough in the end.

I made an effort to focus on my screen. I had a few jobs to do, and Glade wouldn't be awake for hours. Until Kyan gave me something to do regarding the Brotherhood, I was stuck.

We made our money in cybersecurity. One of the generous gifts my family left me with was the foundational knowledge on how to manage dirty money. I was an expert at laundering, untraceable wiring, and setting up offshore accounts. Kyan did the crazy shit with computers, but Knight and I worked with clients who needed simpler expertise. We located missing or stolen money, or tested a trail to make sure it would be impossible to follow.

I picked through my latest job list absently, unable to stop my mind from crawling back to the Omega in the room behind me, like the desperate prick I was.

She'd just been so damn beautiful in Kyan's arms. Peaceful and protected... The glow of her skin in the sunlight, the flutter of her thick lashes brushing her cheek.

A glimmer of the reality we might have had.

I couldn't help dragging up more distant memories... Her smile beneath the stars on a cloudless night. The feel of her lips against mine... She'd kissed Kyan and Knight, but not me. Not since she'd left.

Was I *jealous*?

How many times had I stayed up, remembering the way her body fit so perfectly against mine, the touch of her fingers at my cheek, and the dazed look in her eyes as I claimed her? There had never been anyone else.

I hated that I felt the urge to make sure she knew that.

I hated myself for dreaming of those moments.

I hated myself for thinking of them now when she was here, and we had bigger problems to deal with.

I did need to find out when her heat actually was because we needed a plan for when it came.

Maybe Knight was right, and we should just let her go... But what if we did, and they caught up to her? A Brotherhood hunt wasn't a joke—even less now that Ace was in charge. If she got caught by herself—a low growl rose in my chest and I stifled it, viciously rubbing my face in my hands.

Fuck me.

I could barely remember the original plan. We'd taken her for leverage, *not* to protect her. But if she was in my brother's sights —and *not* in a good way... She'd cheated on him and he'd let her walk—what the hell had she done to provoke him this time?

Every glimpse of her was like driving a knife into an old wound, drawing fresh blood each time, but that didn't mean I could stomach the idea of her alone, facing shit odds.

The idea of her lifeless body, abandoned in a Las Vegas alley, the bronze of her skin fading to grey, those bright eyes dull and lifeless...

A shiver ran up my spine, a tremor in my heart, and I shoved the image away.

No.

I slammed the laptop, running a hand through my hair as I got to my feet and crossed halfway to the door to her cell before I'd caught myself.

For what?

The compulsion to go in was overwhelming. I needed to look in there just to see the rise and fall of her chest... The life of an Omega who'd haunted me for years. Who'd broken me. Who I'd come to believe I would never see again.

She couldn't die.

I couldn't... I couldn't hate a dead woman, and I was nothing if not hateful.

I took another step toward her door, but saw a flash of fluff at my feet, and lost my balance as I tried not to step on it.

"Fuck!" I crashed to my ass, turning in time to see Lucy diving under the couch.

"Did you kick her cat?" Kyan's voice sounded from up in his pad, and his head poked up and over the railing.

"She tripped *me,"* I snarled.

A pair of white orbs flashed from the small gap beneath the couch.

Oh...

"I'm sorry, Lucy." She might have been the one trying to kill me, but I had been wearing my boots. I crossed back toward the couch and knelt beside it, but Lucy backed up, then darted from beneath it. I poked my head up in time to see her leaping up the mismatched metal stairs to Kyan's pad.

Well, she clearly wasn't hurt—not like my pride as I caught Kyan's smug expression and Lucy vanished into his pad. Suck up.

I glanced back to Glade's cell. My nerves had dissipated, and I didn't feel such a pull to check on her.

Probably for the best. So far, no interaction with Glade *hadn't* gone to shit. Even last night, holding her in the shower and forcing her on her knees... I'd stayed up all night, resenting that it didn't bring me the peace I knew it should.

I'd never struggled with vengeance before now, but it just... hadn't felt good. It should have. I wasn't a nice person, but every second I was around her unsettled me, a whisper just out of my vision, nagging that something wasn't quite right—that hating her was a mistake.

I shook it off, returning to the couch to finish a job just so I could prove to myself she wasn't getting to me.

Knight was right. She was a snake, and since I was the only one of us who could be trusted to speak to her, I had to be careful.

17

GLADE

I woke to the ghost of arms around my waist.

"Tell me," Ace whispered in my ear. The sharp scent of redwood and roses lifted in the air.

Being the face of my nightmares wasn't enough for Ace. How many times had he been there when I woke? Dragging me from one nightmare to the next, distorting reality so I could never escape.

Sometimes my dreams would cycle. I would wake to his arms around my waist, the brush of his breath on my neck, only for it to begin again. I woke over and over, never sure what was real and what wasn't.

I focused on my surroundings, trying to find something to hold on to.

The filthy, bony mattress dug into my body, leaving me aching. The lights from the bathroom were on. I'd left them that way, and now, in the dim light, I stared at the wall. Concrete covered in cracked paint that might have once been a pleasant cream was now aged, dull, and grimy.

The room smelled dusty with a faint, damp scent from the bathroom, where I could hear the drip, drip, drip of the leaky shower. Their scents were here, too. Fainter than in the warehouse beyond, which told me this wasn't a room they used much, but they *were* here.

A tangle of a lightning storm, of snow, and pear trees. Not enough to contend with redwood and rose that clogged my airway like a cruel promise.

"Tell me," Ace asked again, his hand curling around my throat ever so gently.

I shut my eyes.

This wasn't real.

He couldn't be here.

There is nowhere he can't be... Not even in the home of your mates. If you believed they were beyond his reach, you would have told them the truth. You wouldn't be fleeing their protection.

But to answer his question, I might be handing a dream the power to be forever. If I didn't, and if he *was* real...? Then I would pay.

My breathing caught as I cycled through my options. My breath hitched as Ace's hand closed tighter around my throat.

Make a choice.

Real or dream?

"You," I whispered, my voice weak. I wished I was strong enough to fight it, but after yesterday? He'd caught up to me, almost within reach.

But I knew it was the wrong choice the moment I'd spoken.

"Good." His voice was a low purr that vibrated down my spine.

Tell me who you belong to.

I hated that demand.

It always came, becoming more terrifying every day after I'd escaped.

Another trap, designed to cage me in fears while it threatened the freedom and confidence I fought for every day. I always answered wrong, and when I woke, I'd spend the day a shell of myself. No matter if I was out for a night on the town with the girls, or working the bar with Tallow, as if I'd given up the right to the life I stepped back into.

Ace dragged me closer, teeth grazing my neck—a gesture of dominance more than anything—as he'd never truly intended a bond.

I shook, trying to find the courage to take it back, to deny him, knowing I would fail.

My eyes traced the cracks in the wall. It was so real. He was here. He was really here, and if I didn't answer, he would—

"Glade!"

I jerked violently, eyes snapping open. The same cracked walls swam in teary vision. I turned, confused by the scents around me. Redwood and roses had vanished, and in their void, violence was a shot of adrenaline ripping me from sanity. I had a body pinned in a flash, and Ace's blue eyes stared back at me.

I blinked, panic shredding my lungs to ribbons, a fist squeezing my throat.

Real.

It had been real, like I'd always known it would be one—

I froze.

Silver hair. Messy silver waves swept across those blue eyes, not flutters of black. Tattoos, detailed shards and thorns and leaves, beautiful in how they reached up his neck, scattering almost delicately across his chin and cheek, emphasising a razor sharp jaw.

I blinked.

"Zed?"

Still, my heart thundered in my chest. Ace had one tattoo, no more.

My breathing eased slightly.

Not real. Not this time.

"What are you doing?" I asked.

"I brought dinner," he said coolly. "Wasn't expecting to be mounted."

I loosened the fist at his shirt.

Once, ice-blue eyes had been a reminder of Zed, but Ace had become so much larger than life, and now my mate was an echo of a monster, instead.

"...I want to be more to you than they ever were..."

I shook the whisper away, looking around. There was a plated sandwich on the floor by the door, along with a bottle of water.

"Why were you... down here?" He could have just dropped the plate off and left. Instead, he'd been crouched at my side.

"You were whining like a wounded puppy. It was pitiful to watch."

"I'm fine," I lied.

He raised an eyebrow. "Do you plan on dismounting?"

"We have to talk."

"Is that what this is?"

I swallowed, pushing back off him and staggering to my feet, grabbing my wrist with my other hand so he didn't see the lingering tremors from the nightmare. I looked at the door, but it was shut. Was it locked from the inside? Did I dare try? I glanced back to Zed, and a faint smirk curved his lips as I scanned him.

"Checking me out?"

"Looking for keys," I told him flatly. "You know, people are going to start asking after me."

"I got into your phone and let slip to…" He frowned. "…Leisha, I think? That you eloped."

I sneered. "She won't believe that."

"You kindly told the doorman that you scent matched us. I think we'll get away with it. Love can do funny things to Omegas and all that." He waved a hand.

I glared at him, wondering how much of it Leisha would buy. She knew I wasn't the eloping type. But he was right about the scent match changing things.

"Plus," he added. "Since you nearly got Kyan killed getting Lucy, your cat is gone. I'm sure that made you look much more committed."

I scowled, but honestly, it was good. I didn't want anyone asking after me.

"Is she doing okay?" I asked. She was my comfort, always there when I woke to my infinite visions of Ace, sweating and terrified that he was truly here. Lucy would curl up on my chest and let me hug her, the faint vibrations of her purr settling me.

Zed shrugged. "She's obsessed with me."

I narrowed my eyes, but didn't reply. I would be having stern words with Lucy if he was telling the truth. She was not allowed to bond with them.

"How did you convince Knight you were going into heat?" he asked. "He said it really felt like you were."

"Uh…" I blinked at him like he was stupid. "How do you think?" All I'd really needed was to make him think I was aroused, and my panic had done the rest.

He just stared at me blankly for a moment before his eyebrows shot up.

I gave him a fake smile. "Five times, and if you want all the details, I find it easy to get off to thoughts about—"

"That's fine, Sweetheart." His voice was cold as he got to his feet. "I really don't care."

I found that a little hard to believe, not missing the subtle dilation of his pupils.

Still, he'd saved me from a lie, since there was no way I'd admit to a living soul it had been easy to bring myself to climax that many times just at the very recent memory of him closing cuffs around my wrists and pinning me to the wall.

The reality had been horrifying, but in hindsight... Well, who was I to waste a good turn on?

"Kyan's still looking into the Brotherhood situation," he was saying. "It would be a lot easier if you told us why they're after you. Could speed things up, get you out of here quicker."

I didn't answer him, trying to control the bitterness on my face as my mood instantly soured.

"No?" he asked, when I didn't reply, and I could see a flicker of irritation. "Then we won't bother keeping you updated."

"So, what?" I asked. "You'll just keep me in here forever, like a fucking—?" I cut off, unable to find the words.

"Pet?" Zed supplied, folding his arms and resting a shoulder against the wall as he peered down at me. "Our little Omega pet." There was malice twinkling in those ice blue eyes. "Has a ring to it."

"For how long?" I asked, mouth dry, thinking back to my nightmares. How many more of those did I have in me before I went mad? I needed outlets. "I can't just stay in here."

He picked at a nail. "My brother might have spoiled you, but that title you used to trample my pack holds no weight around here." He looked up from his nails for half a moment with a curious gaze. "Quite the opposite."

I took a breath, steadying myself at the mention of Ace. I'd reacted last night, but I couldn't afford to again. I couldn't afford to draw any particular attention to Ace at all. Yet, it was hard to shake the distinct impression that, despite his apparent interest in his nail, the mention of Ace was no accident.

He was much too tense for someone acting so casually.

"My title has nothing to do with it," I forced myself to say. "You can't keep me in this room. Not unless you intend to splash out on some expensive drugs."

Finally, he reacted, eyes jumping to me. There was a long pause, and he looked stiff. "When's your heat due? Your *real* heat."

"A month, but trapping me in a tiny room with nothing to do isn't exactly asking for regular behaviour."

That was a slight lie. It was a *bit* less, but I planned on being far from here before two weeks was up.

And I wasn't wrong; stress, fear, a complete lack of outlets—this heat was barrelling toward me at high speed.

"What do you usually do?" Zed asked, cocking his head and tensing like he was bracing for the answer. "We don't have heat auctions set up—"

"Sedation," I said before he could make a joke of it. It was getting increasingly hard to keep the panic out of my voice.

"Partial, or the numbing—"

"Total." I knew some Omegas used suppressants, but my hormones weren't stable enough, having been pushed to the edge one too many times.

His eyebrows rose. "That's some good coverage, even for a club like that."

I stared at him.

I didn't have coverage like that. Instead, over a third of my income went to covering the cost of complete sedation every three months—more frequently if I was stressed.

But it was the only way I felt comfortable riding out my heats. The High Roller had ways to set them up safely, to vet the Alphas involved, but it didn't matter. It wasn't about the safety. I was never more vulnerable than when I was in heat. I couldn't ensure

I wouldn't lose myself entirely, and reveal my scars to Alphas I didn't know—not well, anyway. Not *enough*.

There *was* no *enough*, no amount of trust I would ever feel with an Alpha, that would make me comfortable letting them see what was carved on my back. Least of all the one staring at me now, with his messy sweep of silver hair and eyes as blue as his brother's.

No.

It was sedation, or agony.

At the High Roller, Jade would check on me when I was on the heat drugs. I would be passed out, or almost entirely out of it, if I did wake. Even then, I was more vulnerable in that state than I'd ever dare be outside the care of the High Roller.

I gritted my teeth, not showing any tears to Zed.

I was never going to see them again.

Shoving the thought away, I scrambled for a solution. This was bad timing. Even if I escaped them, I couldn't access my bank. Ace might be watching. The rest of my money was hidden back in my room, which might be being watched. And if, by some miracle, I managed to escape here and get hold of the drugs, what then?

Find a safe hole to crawl into and pray no side effects hit—ones Jade would treat if they came up—heat fever or SRS were no joke. *Fever* I might be able to ride out, but unmanaged Sedation Rejection Syndrome could kill me if I was more than halfway through the heat. Those sorts of things were rare, though. Were they rare enough that I could risk it once?

"They might be tracking you," Zed said at last into the tense silence. "But I can get Kyan to put an insurance claim through without tripping any—"

"Can he get my money from my bank?" I asked.

"Not easily, not if they are watching. Insurance will be safer—"

"There is no insurance." I winced when the words tumbled out.

I desperately ran my fingers through my hair, then realised how crazy it made me look. He narrowed his eyes, and I hated the million calculations that flashed across his expression as he digested that.

Another silence stretched, and I felt more vulnerable than I ever had—like he was seeing through everything and looking right at who I really was. The broken, lonely, terrified Omega who'd stumbled from Ace's mansion all those years ago, still feeling the aftershocks of what my body had suffered in that place.

"We'll get the meds," he said.

I frowned at him, unsure if I was relieved or pissed that he was offering to bail me out. But there was one thing that made me pause, that made it impossible for me to take my gaze from him. First, it had been Knight, now Zed; the truth was unavoidable.

My mates wouldn't abuse my heat.

I took a breath, finally forcing out a bitter laugh so I wouldn't burst into tears. The universe played some twisted jokes, sometimes. "You parked your beat-up old truck in murder-alley, I don't think—"

"Parking is a matter of *principle*," he snapped. "We can afford the fucking meds." He dropped his folded arms and took a step back to the door. "Eat and get dressed. I'll be back."

"Back?"

"You said you needed to get out of this room."

"What does that mean?"

He just gave me a cold smile, before he slammed the door behind him.

18

ZED

I returned later that evening, slipping into Glade's cell to find she hadn't got dressed at all. Still wearing no pants, she'd reduced her outfit to a lacy tank-top-like thing with cups that pressed her full breasts into obscene cleavage. Other than that, she wore a pair of black panties and a thin silk night robe.

I tried really hard not to stare as she peered up at me from the mattress with an icy smile on her face.

"*Why* are you dressed like that?" I asked.

"These are my only nightclothes," she said, as if it were obvious. "Usually, I dress down, but Kyan packed my bag, so…" She shrugged. "If you plan on taking me out somewhere, you might draw a bit of attention."

"Fit right in on The Strip," I said coolly.

"Are we going to The Strip?" she asked.

I laughed. She'd sorely misunderstood the meaning of my earlier statement. My issue was that I didn't trust Kyan one bit, and the spare key to this room was predictably missing.

"Get up," I said.

She looked like she was considering ignoring me, but finally got to her feet.

I stepped toward her, acutely aware of the way she tensed, pupils narrowing as she watched my movements. Too alert, almost nervous—if I were to put my finger on it. Looking for an opening for a fight? Or afraid I would hurt her?

Strangely, I wasn't sure.

The more time I spent with her, the more convinced I was that she was hiding a lot of fear.

Still, if she was looking for a fight, I was ready. She might have one-upped Knight, but he hadn't had a weapon. If she wanted to try to bring it to blows, I wasn't too worried.

"Hands out," I told her, stopping before her and looking down into defiant chestnut eyes.

Again, she paused a beat, considering, before lifting her wrists to me.

I tugged out the cuffs Kyan had brought, keeping my expression painfully neutral as she saw what I had.

"What the fuck?"

"You broke our last pair. These will have to do."

True to his bratty fucking word, he'd gone and found a pair of leather and fake fur cuffs. They definitely looked like bedroom toys, though Kyan had sworn they'd hold her. Alpha grade, he'd said. I tested them, too—trying to break the chains—but they'd held.

"Is this a joke?" she asked, tugging her wrist away as I moved to fasten the first cuff.

"For your comfort," I replied, like this was my idea.

Fucking prick.

"One mention of heat, and you pull out your toys?" she asked, disgust twisting her expression. "Are they used?"

I cocked my head, watching the feral flash in her eyes.

There it was again. A territorial claim she didn't have a right to. She thought I was bringing her a sex toy I'd used with another woman?

Damn.

Well, if she wanted to make her own life harder.

"Wrists."

Those perfect round lips pursed in rage and her chest heaved. It was almost impossible for me to keep my eyes on hers with the way that top cupped her breasts, and her scent of cream cardamom became deadly at that moment.

For a second, all I could think of was sliding my hand around that pretty neck and pressing my lips to hers.

Both of my pack mates had. I was the only one who—

No.

Focus.

Knight couldn't handle her, and Kyan would blow up all the progress he'd made in the last few years if I let him at her. But for me, this wasn't even the beginning—not even the tip of the iceberg. I couldn't be losing myself right now.

"I *will* pin you down," I said with absolute calm, as if the visual didn't send boiling hot lava through my veins.

Word choice.

With absolute fury, she lifted her hands and let me fix the cuffs on. Unlike regular sex toys, these didn't have belt latches. They locked like regular cuffs. And I had my key tucked into my pillowcase.

I turned from her, happy to avoid looking at her as much as possible as I tugged her to the door, unlocking it. I made sure to keep her on my left side so Knight and Kyan would not have a view of what she'd chosen to wear as I led her across the living room.

In a wild moment, I couldn't believe I was doing this. How had this become the best option?

"Where are we going?" she hissed as I opened my door and pushed her in. I didn't answer, slamming the door behind me.

"Zed." She spun on me, clearly realising we were in my bedroom. "What the hell?"

"I can't control Kyan," I told her.

"*This* is your solution?"

"Would you like him creeping into your cell in the middle of the night?" I asked, fist still tight around the chain as I dragged her to my bed.

"More than I want to be cuffed with you like some kind of—"

"*Don't* flatter yourself," I snorted, not looking her way as I reached down to find the thick wire loop secured with a number lock attached to the frame. "Besides, I told you, if you fucked around you'd sleep chained to the foot of my bed." Well, this was the head, not the foot, but I needed her in eyesight. Though, having her in eyesight had been the plan before I'd seen the insane outfit she'd decided to wear. Now, I was rethinking it.

Clearly realising what I was about to do, she threw her weight against me viciously. "This is stupid," she hissed.

"You trying to escape by pretending to be in heat was stupid."

"Fuck you—!" she snarled as I dragged her toward the headboard. "Wait. What...?" She seemed to be scrambling wildly for an out. "What if I need to pee?"

"Do you?"

"No."

I flashed her a smile before throwing my weight into dragging the chain to the wire. "Then you'll have to wake me up, Little Devil." I almost winced, regretting the nickname the moment I'd used it. Too familiar. But she was so pissed she didn't seem to notice.

"No, just—*Fuck*!" She let out a hiss of fury as I closed the lock around the metal chain.

I let go of her at last, straightening to examine my work. A huge mistake, since I'd dragged her curvy-as-fuck Omega body into a position that kind of resembled presentation.

Well. There went any hope of unsinful dreams for the next goddamned year.

Luckily, she turned quickly, snuffing out the flash of lust by kicking out and almost catching my nuts before I jumped back.

I grinned. "Good luck getting out of that."

"Good luck sleeping," she spat.

"Bed's big enough," I said with a shrug, heading for the bathroom to brush my teeth and get ready for sleep.

By the time I was done, my brain must have reset, because walking out and seeing her lying on my sheets, arms trapped above her head, chest heaving and eyes flashing with hatred was like being hit with a truck.

Why was she so goddamned hot?

I saw Omegas all the time—we lived in Vegas, for fuck's sake. There was no shortage of sexy women.

I never even noticed *them*, though. She was like a brand, burned into my brain, a bright outline in the pitch black.

Fucking scent matches should not be this potent.

My skin was even reacting, palms prickling from where I'd brushed her, like she was calling to me. As if every touch was made of a million whispers waiting to follow me all the way to my dreams.

I slipped under my blankets, ignoring her furious-cute little growl as I did. She shifted, trying to kick me, but only managed to brush me with her toes. "Too short," I chuckled, shutting my lamp off, and trying to ignore how thick the air was with dark cream cardamom.

19

I felt a flash of victory when Zed rolled over, fast asleep, putting himself unknowingly within kicking reach. I was preparing myself to wake him, going for the most pain I could manage. When he shifted again, it was his pale hand reaching out in the darkness and curling around my waist.

I froze, goosebumps rising across my body as I felt his touch slide lower, to the place where waist met hips and my top ended.

His skin on mine was like a shot of relief I wasn't expecting. My heart rate slowed, my breathing coming easier, rage draining away.

The pain of old scars and aching wounds, ones I'd carried so long it was hard to imagine a world without them, now dulled. Instincts, warped and desperate, dissipated at the touch of an Alpha. Not just any Alpha. It mattered that he was my mate.

I knew that as surely as I hated it.

He shifted again, a frown creasing his face in the almost non-existent light my eyes had adjusted to. His hand curled around my waist possessively, as if... as if he wanted to hold me.

I lay still for a long time, half my mind drowning in a long buried want, the other trying to gather the strength to give him that kick he sorely deserved.

My breath caught as he shifted again, hand closing tighter as if he was trying to tug me toward him. Well, his cuffs meant I wouldn't be budging.

Fucker.

Only, instead, he shifted again on the bed, and—to my shock —drew closer, both arms adjusting to pull me into what felt like... oh. Shit.

Was he trying to *hug* me?

I froze, mind spiralling, panic taking hold. I didn't even know why. He shifted closer again, and suddenly I was in his arms.

This was... I swallowed. This was great. He was exactly where I wanted him. I would make sure he woke up to *agony* (and the news he would never have kids).

Instead, tears burned my eyes, and I had to bite down on my lip to try to stop them.

Fuck.

I had to get a grip, but the low forest scent of snow santal unwinding my sanity without mercy.

I needed to—

My thought died a sudden death at the vibration that rumbled through him. I frowned, but with his next exhale, a purr as loud as a motorbike rumbled to life, sending shockwaves down my spine. It was like he'd just reached into my chest and swaddled my heart in cotton wool.

I tried to claw back hot, wet escapees from my eyelashes, because Zed *fucking* Maverick could not be the one to free them with the flick of a stupid Alpha-purring switch.

I sniffled, trying to figure out what to do, but then he drew me tighter to his chest and—to my horror—I melted against him with a little whine.

If I wasn't cuffed, I'd have clamped a hand over my mouth, silently screaming into it with frustration.

No.

My Omega side needed to sort herself out.

Heat was two weeks away, right?

Two.

Two weeks.

Not *tonight*.

It wasn't until Zed buried his face in my neck that I realised my distress was making this worse. Actually, it was possible my distress was the cause in the first place. The more frustrated I got, the more he reacted.

Now he was purring, and I was unwinding beneath him with disgusting speed.

I took a breath, trying to calm myself. Well, *uncalm* myself since *he* was calming me. He wasn't allowed to calm me.

Fuck.

I tried to wriggle away, but his purr shifted to a growl and his arms clamped around me like a vice.

Okay.

We were getting aggressive with the cuddles.

I needed to stop moving. It was like when the seat belt stops unrolling, so you have to feed it back to make it shift again, but instead you trap yourself against the seat tighter and tighter.

Zed, I reminded myself, was a *very* possessive, *very* primal Alpha. Definitely the faultiest seatbelt in the history of seatbelts, and I was his scent match.

For a second, another little whine rose, but I shoved it down.

His snow santal scent was like a fog, smothering my last brain cells to death. For a moment I shut my eyes, and I was stepping through a winter forest where the warm lights of santal cabins glowed ahead. Warm and comforting, a fire crackled in a deep winter night...

I'd slept half the day, but it hadn't been restful. I was... tired, my eyelids heavy. Zed's arms were warm around me, a blanket of protection, threatening to seal shut wounds I never thought would heal.

He was asleep, though. He wouldn't know I'd given into this, that I sank against his chest, vanishing into a dream I knew I could never truly have.

And if *he* didn't even know, Ace certainly never would... That... That was how it worked, right?

"Do you want to get out of here?"

My eyes flew open from a deep slumber at the sound of Kyan's voice, a faint breath in my ear.

I froze, blinking up at him, trying to make out his shape in the shadows. He waited for my reply, knuckle lingering on my chin, and it was like static leaped between us. It took me a long time to orient myself, but then I nodded.

That was right, I thought. I *wanted* to get out of here.

But was Kyan a good alternative? I thought Zed might be right to worry about what Kyan could handle, but—Oh, my God. I was still in his arms. I definitely couldn't face him waking like this— knowing he'd hate what he'd done.

"Is he... cuddling you?" Kyan asked, a frown in his whisper.

I nodded again.

"That complicates things," he said.

He vanished for a moment; he could move in silence far too well.

Then he was back, pressing a pillow to my face. "Scent mark it," he breathed.

I did as he asked, drawing my chin along the pillow.

"Shhh, shhh, shhh," Kyan breathed as he slipped it past my back—to Zed, I assume. His grip was much weaker than it had been before I'd gone to sleep, and he was no longer purring. It took a little while, but Kyan managed to get me free of Zed's aggressive cuddles.

How would he undo the cuffs?

Only then, I saw what he'd brought.

Bolt cutters?

Right. Obviously.

I opened my mouth when I saw him lining up the bolt cutters with the wire that Zed had attached to his bed instead of my cuffs, but then I knew Kyan hadn't come here in order to *free* me.

I'd still take it over this non-nightmare-nightmare that was whining pathetically as the mate who despised me cuddled me while he slept.

The cut was clean and silent, and the next thing I knew, Kyan had his arm around my waist as he tugged me to my feet. In the darkness, his smile flashed, then he swept me up in his arms, rushing me from the room.

He froze through the doorway and I twisted my head to see Knight on the couch, bowl of popcorn in his arm as he watched what looked to be a cop show on TV.

Kyan was careful as he padded by, still frighteningly quiet. We got across the room to the strangely unsafe looking metal steps that led up to what seemed like a second-floor room. Or... something like that.

Kyan took the first step, metal creaking, and I tensed. Then another, and another, his steps sounding casual enough.

"What's with the boxes?"

Both Kyan and I froze dead still at the sound of Knight's voice. I glanced over; he was still facing the TV, settled in for the night, a black silk wrap around his locs, wearing sweatpants and a thin bathrobe that hung open.

Kyan took another step, clearly trying to stay casual. "Pillows. Building her a nest," he replied, continuing up the steps.

Knight snorted, still not turning. "Where?"

"In my pad."

"You think Zed's gonna let you take her up to—" Knight cut off as he turned his head, incredulous expression on his face, mouth full of popcorn.

There was a long, long silence, where Knight stared at us, and we him.

Then he leapt to his feet, growl (and popcorn) suddenly filling the air.

Kyan ran, and I flung my chained wrists over his neck, holding on for dear life.

"NO!" I could see Knight scrambling hands and feet behind us as Kyan clambered up the steps along the wall, boots clanging with each step. My eyes flicked down to the floor for half a second, trying not to think about what would happen if Kyan made even one slip up. There was no safety barrier.

That was before we reached the fucking ladder.

"Kyan!" I gasped, as he released me with one hand—with far too much ease and balance—to carry me up. He reached the top, where he set me down, then turned in a flash and ripped the ladder back.

Knight was seconds behind, but had enough momentum to leap across the now empty gap. I let out a breath of shock as he missed, but his fingers curled over the platform. With a grunt of effort, Knight managed to drag himself up, elbows over the edge, eyes lit with fury.

Kyan reacted quickly, skidding on his knees before Knight. "Let go," he snapped.

"No."

"Last warning."

"Kyan!"

Kyan grabbed Knight's arms dramatically, leaning close as he whispered, *"Long live the king."*

Knight, rather smartly, let go before Kyan could actually shove him off and I heard a thump and then a curse from below.

Kyan whooped with joy, to turn and find me bent double in stitches of laughter. Laughter like I hadn't experienced in as long as I could remember.

For a moment, the last few years melted away entirely. Tears streamed down my face as Kyan's arms wound around my waist, just holding me close, the wind of a lightning storm sweeping me away.

From the ridiculous thrill of that chase—and the stupidity of hearing my mate quote the fucking *Lion King* in the name of my defense—the world had flipped in an instant. Why wasn't I mad? Or anxious? Or... anything. Instead, he was just... perfect and beautiful.

"This space is for you," he said, looking around. I followed, seeing we were on a wide metal platform with a huge inset bed. "I got pillows. Omegas like pillows."

There *were*... so many pillows. Everywhere. Against the metal bars that made up the walls, piled onto the bed, crowding before the wall mounted TV. Not to be cliche or anything, but I swear slick pooled between my thighs at the sight of them all. "And snacks and water," he was saying. I spied two boxes full of every snack under the sun. "And the bathroom's over there."

"There's a bathroom?" I asked, peering around the corner to see a door that led to a small room.

"I paid a lot for the plumbing," he told me rather proudly. "And even the metal around here." He clapped the bar set up like a boxing ring that circled the whole thing. "Can't spy through here, so no bugs. Basically, it's safe, and it's yours. You can stay as long as you like. I'll even walk the plank if you—"

"*No.*" I grabbed him.

And... shit. I was crying again, and laughter was no excuse this time.

He cupped my chin, leaning close and licking the tear from my face because... well, because he was Kyan, but it made me giggle. And cry more.

"What the hell?" Zed's voice from below gave me an irrationally giddy shot of adrenaline. Both Kyan and I scrambled to the edge of his pad. "Where is—?" He cut off, eyes finding us. "Absolutely fucking not," he snarled. *"Knight—!"*

"No." Knight had a broom in hand and was sweeping up his popcorn with a stoney expression. "You want to try and get up there?" he spat. "I won't. Last time—"

"I took his fucking tasers—"

"Like he hasn't got two more?" Knight demanded. "I quit. I quit this whole Omega bullshit."

"You can't *quit—*"

"I can. If you and Kyan want to fight over her, go for it. She can do what she wants."

"There, see," Kyan breathed, tugging me back to the bed and already arranging pillows around us. "Up here you're safe. This is *your* Oasis."

The sounds of Knight's TV, and a hissed argument between the other two was faint in the background. The TV was comforting. I always liked sleeping with one on, and here my mate's scents were everywhere.

"Why?" I asked, peering up at him as he finished with his pillow arrangement.

I'd... *left* him.

"You were my first Oasis," he whispered. "When I was about to break, you gave me more to live for." He drew me close. "I've always believed in you."

I swallowed, suddenly terrified of what he was saying. Of what it meant. "What if it was dangerous for you to... to be with me?"

"I would rather die than leave you behind," he said, as if it was the easiest thing in the world. "How long has it been since you've had one?" Kyan asked.

"One... what?"

"A place you knew you were safe?" I clenched my jaw, eyes burning, curling up tighter. He wound his arms around my waist, and it was the most comforting thing I'd ever felt, down the feeling of his bracelets brushing my skin.

I let out a squeak of surprise as a tentative paw pressed up against my hip, followed by a whole chunky, fluffy cat.

"Lucy?" I asked, blinking through the dim light.

Her purr got louder at the sound of my voice and she dug her way into the blankets at my side. A sob broke from my chest as I hugged her close.

"Oh," Kyan chuckled. "She loves it up here. Now." He pressed a gentle kiss to my temple. "Sleep, Baby. It's still nighttime."

20

I woke to Glade lying peacefully in my arms, which was exactly where she should be. I knew, by how it smoothed every shard of the Alpha instincts that had, for years, been lodging deeper and deeper into my soul.

For far too long, I'd ached for this. Being apart from her had been unnatural, but *this* completed me: having her in my arms, *knowing* she was safe and alive. Feeling it from the warmth of her skin and hearing the slow rhythm of her breaths.

My pack was half of me, and she was the other half. She had been since the first moment I'd laid eyes on her.

That moment had been something like this, with her dark lashes brushing her cheeks, a faint pinch between her brows as she slept, hair tumbling around her in a huge bed.

She'd been hugging a pillow close then, instead of a cat, and she was covered by nothing but a silk sheet draped over her like liquid. The summer air had been warm, even this late, and the moonlight filtered through her window, reflecting silver pools along each curve of her perfect figure.

Her scent turned the world upside down. It was a lightning storm, heavy in the air; a drug trickling bone deep, halting me in my tracks and changing everything forever.

I knew, to the others, she smelled like cardamom (whatever the hell that smelled like), but to me, she was static in the air, rain in the wind, a clap of thunder in the distance.

I'd been awake with her in my arms for a while now, and below us the smells of breakfast cooking wafted up. The TV was always on down there, but I heard one of the others flicking through channels. It ended up on boxing, which meant it was Zed who was awake.

Still, Glade slept, which I took as a great sign. I was safe for her.

She smelled like me, and I loved it. A few times in the night I'd been woken to nails digging into my arms, her body tense and eyes squeezed tight shut. I'd purred, holding her closer and marking her with my scent until she relaxed.

Finally, nearing midday, she woke, rubbing her face and peering around blearily.

"Morning," I breathed, nipping her ear.

Pretty chestnut eyes blinked up at me as she turned, disturbing Lucy, who was sprawled out beside her, fluffy belly up and paws curled.

Glade seemed, for a moment, lost for words, lips parted, a faint frown creasing her face as if she couldn't figure out what was going on.

"This isn't a dream," she said faintly.

"No." I grinned. "I've claimed and captured you. You're mine."

Pushing herself up into a sitting position, she stretched as best she could with the cuffs still on her wrists. My gaze snagged on the flashes of her body visible as the robe parted. She was wearing pretty black panties with what might have been a normal tank top if it wasn't made to hug her breasts so tight.

I wanted to pounce on her right now, but I'd let her settle in a bit.

"Bag in the bathroom should have everything you need—toothbrush, hairbrush, and all that."

"No one came up?" she asked as she got to her feet and peered over the side of my room.

"I'm sure they're plotting," I snorted. "But I can keep them out."

Zed was wrong. I had way more than two tasers up here.

While she was gone, I peeked at my phone, and sure enough it was blown up by texts and calls from Zed. He'd given up last night, going back to sleep, but I knew he'd be trying to get her back down before long.

I got to my feet, peering over the side of my pad that overlooked the rest of the living space.

Zed was on the couch, laptop beside him, while Knight was eating an early lunch at the table. Knight's eyes flickered up at the movement, but he dropped his gaze instantly, clearly set on ignoring me completely. Oh boy, that meant I was in trouble.

"You're so fucked when you come back down here," Zed growled up at me.

"I'm stocked for days," I told him.

He scowled, but deliberately turned his attention back to the TV as if I wasn't worth his time.

I turned as I heard the bathroom door open.

Glade was stepping out, glossy thick waves looking freshly brushed.

"What are we gonna do about the cuffs?" she asked, glancing down at them and then back to me.

"Bolt cutters are down there," I said, nodding toward the rest of the warehouse as I stepped toward her.

"Was that on purpose?"

"I do like the cuffs," I admitted, hands brushing her waist

before I drew her close. I loved how her lips parted, chest heaving all of a sudden. "Does that get you hot?" I asked, hooking my grip around the chain and tugging her hands above her head as I stepped closer. "Thinking about all the things I could do with you at my mercy."

Her pupils dilated as I stepped us both back and pressed her wrists against the wall, caging her in.

"I want you," I breathed. "Say I can, Sweet Oasis, or I'm gonna die of thirst."

She let out the sweetest bubble of a laugh. "We... shouldn't. I'm not staying—"

I clamped my hand over her mouth, a low growl in my chest. "You think I'd ever let you go?" Never. Not now that I had her back.

Her eyes were wide, and for a moment, glassy. I knew she didn't believe in safety. One day soon, I'd fix that, but until then, we'd make do.

"Pretend, while you're up here, that none of those nightmares are chasing you." I dropped my hand from her mouth, taking her chin and tilting her face toward me. "It's just me and you and no one else."

I wasn't stupid. I knew what those nightmares were made of —*who* they were made of.

The last loose thread I could now tie up.

Now I'd seen her, I had my answers. I'd known she wanted us from the moment we'd caught up to her.

"Take a chance with me," I murmured. "I'm going to keep you safe."

For a second, those beautiful chestnut eyes were vulnerable as her brows furrowed. I saw a flicker of defiance, and her voice was breathy. "Okay."

There she was. My girl.

I swept her off her feet and set her down on the bed, hooking the cuffs over one of the metal railings fixed to the wall.

"You set this all up?" she asked, eyebrow cocked as she peered up at me, but because she was so fucking perfect, she didn't even try to get away.

"Maybe."

"This isn't exactly private. The others—"

"Are losers," I purred. "Forget them. Now, rules, Oasis? Or I'll ruin you my way."

She swallowed, chewing on her lip. "The shirt stays."

I frowned, trying to figure out the significance of that, but shrugged. "That's all?"

Dangerous.

But she said nothing else, instead letting out a low moan as I ran my teeth along her thigh. She was not to be underestimated when she was all heels and curves, muscle and weapons, but *here* she was mine, chained up, with that sweet body at my mercy.

I slipped my finger beneath her panties, nudging them aside to an outrageous amount of slick. "When was the last time you were this wet for an Alpha?"

I shouldn't have asked that. There was a distinct possibility I was adding an innocent to a hit list, but her back arched, chestnut eyes fixed on me as she let out the cutest little moan.

She didn't answer, and I didn't push it.

Fuck, she was stunning as she wriggled against my touch, scent rising catching fire as I added a second finger and lowered my lips to her centre.

I worked her, hand clamped over her stomach, right up until she was shivering, body tense, the addictive taste of her cunt sending me to fucking heaven.

This was years of dreams condensed into a cluster of seconds that I didn't think would last long enough.

"Kyan—*oh!*" She gasped, thighs clamping around my ears just like I dreamed of. I didn't stop. Loving the noises she made—and the sharp spike of irritation and lust from both Knight and Zed down the bond.

They could hear everything, loud and clear, and even Glade grinned, breathless, as the volume of boxing suddenly turned up to deafening levels.

That wouldn't fucking do.

I drew back, tense, and she let out a low growl of derision.

Right.

I'd stopped just before the best part.

But I was unhooking the cuffs and tugging her up.

If my brothers thought, for one second, they could get out of being a part of this, they had something else coming.

"Kyan," she hissed. "What are you doing?" she asked as I drew her into my arms.

"I want you screaming for them, too."

21

"*K*yan!" My voice flipped from breathless to shrill in a heartbeat.

We were at the edge of his raised bedroom, one low bar of metal keeping me from tumbling over the edge, and Kyan was lifting my cuffs. Below, the world spun. I could see Zed on the couch and Knight washing a dish at the sink below. Both were frozen, staring up at me.

"*No—!*" Shit. I tried to throw my weight backward, but with way too much ease, Kyan hooked my cuffs over a metal bar that served as a hook. "Kyan, you fucking—*shit!*" The last word was half groan as he slipped his fingers back between my legs, driving up into that perfect spot.

The world went fuzzy, lust drowning everything else as I felt him at my back.

My mate wanted me.

"*Kyan!*" That was Knight, but he didn't sound like he could find any words, and my blood ran hot at the sound of his voice.

Hormones and years of loneliness made it hard to reject him, even if I was strung up on display for the whole fucking warehouse as Kyan dragged his teeth along my outer thigh. His two fingers worked me as slick dripped down my legs. I bit my lip, fighting a tidal wave of pleasure as I tried *really* hard not to meet Zed's eyes, but he was staring at me in shock, lips parted.

Kyan's touch drove me to the edge of an orgasm. I was panting, trying to catch my breath and not look back at Zed as Kyan removed his fingers and instead began circling my clit. I let out a moan, wriggling back against him, needing more.

"Sweet Oasis, relax. The show's only just started," he growled in my ear, speeding up his fingers as he pressed his lips to my neck. His other hand ran up my waist, squeezing my breast as I tensed. I whimpered as he tugged my nipple free of the top, pinching it roughly, gaze sweeping below before I could help it, this time landing on Knight.

Meeting his eyes was a mistake. Another orgasm rushed in, my blood far too hot with the tangle of Alpha scents in the room, and before I knew it, I was panting once more, goosebumps alight on my skin.

"Good girl," Kyan breathed, his touch withdrawing from my clit, my panties out of place, revealing the obscene amount of slick coating my thighs.

Okay.

Climaxing in front of my mates wasn't the end of the world. I could live this down. Somehow.

I let out a squeak of surprise as Kyan twisted my nipple again, another rush of heat spearing my core.

We weren't done.

I had to calm the fuck down.

Only, Kyan shifted at my back, adjusting my hips back as he pressed up against me. I let out a shameless moan as I felt his cock, which was hard in his pants, press against me from behind. At the sound, he released my breast, fingers tangling in my hair as he arched my neck back, and then I felt his fingers at my lips.

"Taste yourself, Sweetness," he breathed, fingers pressing past my lips before I could react. I jerked against him, a growl in my chest, but his grip on my hair made it useless. "See how turned on you are?"

I let out another whimper as he withdrew his finger and then tugged at my nipple again. With his other hand, he released my hair, finding my other breast.

"Kyan," I whimpered. "You can't—" I cut off with a whine as he freed my other breast, twisting both my nipples between his fingers.

The rising, frustrated edge of snow santal and pear grove in the room told me everything I needed to know about the attention from below.

"You don't have to be shy," he told me. "They're going to hear you begging for me by the time we're done."

I shivered, squeezing my eyes shut as he rolled my nipples between his fingers. I was getting way too hot from just that, knowing that I was still on full display, tits out, thighs soaked with my own juices as Zed and Knight watched.

"*Mmmm...*" I felt a spike of lust as Kyan ground his hard on against me again, pinching hard on my nipples.

"Can you come just like this, Oasis?" he asked. "Are you hot enough for us?"

I tried to clench my thighs together, but he growled, knee jamming between my legs so I couldn't. "No. They get to see all of you. You belong to us, baby. Our pretty little Omega, coming just from the idea of us all watching." I moaned again as he flicked my nipple.

Fuck.

"They want you too, baby. I can feel them in the bond. They wish they were up here, playing with you like this."

I was shivering, eyes still squeezed shut.

"My perfect mate," he growled. "So turned on, I can make you finish just like this."

He found a perfect balance of rolling my nipples between his fingers and squeezing them. "Imagine how hard you'd cum if I was doing this while you were trapped between them," he breathed. "Zed claiming that tight throat," he went on.

No, no, no.

"And Knight knotting you so good."

That was it. The whimper of a sound I made was, frankly, embarrassing. Kyan growled, so pleased as I shook with the orgasm.

"I can't," I whined, all dignity forgotten, as Kyan returned his fingers to my clit.

"You can, Baby. We're going to give them a show like no other."

He wasn't lying. Despite my desperate sounds, he pushed me over the edge of another climax. My brain was full of cotton balls, and I could barely think straight until he adjusted himself and I felt the tip of his cock at my entrance.

I arched back against him, tugging against the hook, lips parted as a whine rose in my chest.

"You want me, Oasis?" he breathed, nudging his tip in.

"Mmhmm."

I was completely incapable of caring any longer.

He slid in and I let out a moan as I stretched over his girth. He edged in so slowly, fingers trailing down my stomach until they found my clit again. I jerked against him, a pathetic mewl in my chest as he stilled, impaling me half way and circling my clit aggressively.

I was so overwhelmed that I sagged, hair tumbling about my face, lip caught in my teeth as I relaxed around him, contented sounds escaping me as I clenched over his length.

"You're so perfect," he purred, squeezing my breasts, getting another shudder from me as he drove in deeper.

"Do you want me to fuck you properly?"

"Yes, Alpha," I whispered, the wrong words coming to my lips.

His grip on my breasts became punishing once more. "I want them to hear."

"Fuck me, Alpha."

"I love you so fucking much, Oasis," he growled and I let out a groan of shock as he drew back and then drove into me.

I hadn't been fucked in forever, and I was a mess from the things he said.

"You're so pretty, Baby, taking me so well," he said as he pressed in again. "Not one of your mates can take their eyes away."

I dared a glance down from where I'd fixed it on the ceiling.

Both Knight and Zed looked primed to flee. Knight was at his bedroom door, and Zed was backing toward the door that led to the outer warehouse. It was like someone had pressed pause on a tape, though, because neither were actively taking a step, but they were both staring like deer in headlights.

"Zed hasn't been honest with you, Oasis," Kyan said, loud enough for everyone in the room to hear as his hands ran up my waist. "He told you he'd fucked all those Omegas, didn't he?"

I tensed, unable to control my spike of fear at those words. Zed's expression furious, hand still on the door.

"Wait, he... *ugh*"—I gritted my teeth as Kyan drove his length right to the knot—"he lied?" My whine was too desperate.

"Kyan!" Zed's voice was a warning, but I couldn't take my eyes from him.

"He's the crowned Ice King," Kyan laughed, hand dropping between my legs and circling my clit.

Zed took a step toward us, lips drawn back. "Keep your mouth *shut!*" He had his gun in his hand out of what looked like pure instinct, though didn't seem to know what he was doing with it.

Kyan barked a laugh. "Hasn't touched a soul since you left, Oasis"—Zed ripped the door open to leave, backing through it "—you are his one and only."

Zed halted halfway through the doorway, the gun still useless in his fist as I cried out, orgasm slamming into me viciously.

Even with the distance between us, I couldn't break his ice-blue gaze, seeing the collision of fury and shock as he watched my climax sweep me away.

"That was *so* beautiful," Kyan breathed in my ear. "But they've already seen more than they deserve." He reached up, unhooking my cuffs and drawing me into his arms where I still shivered from the climax.

He lay me on my back and my dazed sigh was content as he slid his length back into me, this time rocking his knot against my entrance, stretching me around it. I let out a low moan from deep in my chest.

"Good girl," he told me, thumb returning to my clit, circling until I arched against him, lip caught in my teeth, another wave of bliss streaking through my veins.

"Kyan..." My protest was weak as he rocked into me, gripping my hips and rutting me gently. "I don't think..." I was hot from the number of orgasms I'd already had, and another was building. An impossible mountain to scale with how sensitive I was.

"Keep going, Baby," he purred and the world beyond his beautiful jade eyes vanished as he rocked into me, finger working my clit again, teeth finding my nipple until he'd pushed me past the edge.

Then again, and again until the scent of fresh storms wiped out everything else in the world, a breeze, wrapping me in a feeling of security that no memory could compare to. A bubble was closing around us, and in it, there was nothing but me and him.

No danger I was running from.

No guilt or fear for falling for Alphas I knew in the end I could never have.

Not the fact that when I surfaced next, I would have to run, and the vulnerability Kyan was offering me here was the greatest tool I had.

No ever present lingering threat of Ace, and what might happen when he caught up.

Those things fell away in a way they never had. Instead, it was just my mate's purr sending vibrations up my spine as he wrapped his arms around me and his teeth grazed my ear. "You're so perfect, Sweet Oasis."

22

KNIGHT

Fucking Kyan might have diverted rut number one, but the stupid fuck was out to ruin me. I couldn't imagine Zed was holding out well, either.

Kyan had been banging our Omega, loudly, all fucking day, and they were making our home a swamp of sex hormones.

It was late now, and I'd been lying on the stack of mats we used for the gym for hours, tossing and turning, unable to sleep. I didn't dare go to my room. Proximity was a problem.

Dark cream cardamom and autumn persimmon, two scents designed to burrow deep into my head and torch every last functioning brain cell, were thick in the air.

If Kyan ever climbed back down from that pad, I was going to ruin him.

And *her?*

Oh, it was a dangerous game to place Glade and punishment in the same line of thought.

There was no way I was ready to face the desperation I'd felt when she'd chained me up and backed away, ready to take our truck and ran.

For a second, it was like she was ripping my heart out again.

She shouldn't have that power. I wanted to say it was biology, but I'd seen something else in her eyes. I shut mine, shoving the memory away.

How many times had I circled back to this thought?

Sighing, I sat up, rubbing my eyes and trying to dispel the millionth hard on since seeing Kyan and Glade fuck. Sleep wasn't going to happen, and this rut was fast incoming if I didn't sort myself out. I got up and grabbed the hand wraps from the training bin.

I'd just finished wrapping my fists when I heard a faint thump, the clink of chains, then silence.

I narrowed my eyes, quietly stepping around the gym and reaching the open door to the inner living space. Sure enough, Glade was picking herself from the floor where she'd clearly just dropped down from Kyan's pad.

I rolled my eyes, ducking behind the door and waiting until she arrived.

When she edged through, it was all too easy, with the cuffs, to snag the chain on her wrists.

"Fuck!" she hissed, but I had her pinned against the wall in seconds. Her eyes were wide as she took me in. "Do you not sleep?" she hissed, throwing her weight against me, but I didn't shift. She might be a good fighter, but she was small and chained up.

"How did you get away from Kyan?" There was no way he hadn't anticipated her running.

She eyed me for a moment as if unsure if she should reply. "You were right about the tasers."

I almost laughed.

Served him fucking right.

"So you were going to run away in the middle of the night like that? You wouldn't survive ten minutes."

Her lips drew back in a snarl. "I can find myself some goddamned clothes."

"I wasn't talking about the clothes," I snorted. "You're like a walking hormone beacon, demanding to be fucked."

"I am *not*."

I raised my eyebrows, but stepped back, dragging her with me.

She absolutely *was*.

I knew because even being this close to her was soothing the edges of the brewing Alpha storm that was struggling to get out. A little part of me wanted to do exactly what Kyan had. *Not* doing so was making this all so much harder.

Actually... I had an idea.

"What are you doing?" she asked as I easily picked her up and tossed her over my shoulder.

I didn't answer, carrying her back past Kyan's graffiti wall to the gym.

"You know what we can't afford?" I asked. "The Brotherhood coming down on our heads when I'm in a fucking rut."

"So... what?" she asked, looking startled as I grabbed one of the cords from the huge climbing structure and hooked it at the top—far out of her reach.

"What is this?"

"You're going to sit tight while I sweat this rut out."

"You can't sweat a rut out."

"I can if you keep giving off those..." I waved my hands vaguely. "Siren *pheromones* or whatever they are." I adjusted the hand wrap that hadn't been secured.

She shifted back, satisfyingly affronted. "You *cannot* use me like some Omega hormone *Pez* dispenser."

I felt a smile tug at my lips as I tangled my hand in her hair.

"You sure?" I asked, tugging her neck back briefly. "Seems to be working just fine."

The more pissed she was, the more her hormones were leaching into the space. And *fuck me*—she was horny—even if she had been trying to run.

Horny and angry.

That's what I needed—the stronger the better. Well, that's what I convinced myself of as I leaned down, pulling her neck into a sharper arch and drawing my jaw along hers.

The low whine that rose from her stilled me, chest suddenly tight. Before I knew it, she shifted closer. Her bright chestnut eyes found me in the dim light from the lamp I'd set up beside my makeshift bed.

I couldn't move. Couldn't take my eyes from her, and I knew she could feel my reaction to her body, pressed against mine like it was.

It had to be the scent match, but touching her was like taking a shock to my heart. I'd never experienced anything like it. I was drawn to her, unable to shake the feeling that she was made of a million cracks, and with each brush of my skin on hers, I was closing them.

Was that... normal, even between scent matches?

"There are better ways to get rid of that rut," she breathed.

My fingers dug into her hips. I didn't know when my hands had moved, but I was enveloped by her entirely for a second, imagining how easy it would be to hold her like this and make her cry my name like she had for him.

"Why...?" The word was rough, struggling on its way out of my mouth, every instinct demanding I claim her without question. "Why do you want us after *you* left?"

For just the briefest flicker, I saw a shadow cross her eyes, a moment of something pained. She was vulnerable. Wounded.

My girl.

The one Omega that biology had wired me to protect.

To fix or heal.

I'd reached up without realising, palm cupping her cheek, feeling my own energy shift to something gentle.

Then the flash of pain was gone, and her expression hardened. "It's logical," she said quietly. "You're near a rut, I could crash into heat if I'm any more pent up—"

She cut off at the hostile growl that rose in my throat, fury surging at the idea that this was just... business to her.

Kyan had fucked her.

Kyan, who I'd almost lost after she left.

Her lips parted slightly as she felt the vibration of my fury rolling slowly through me. Her whole body went still in response. The slow rise and fall of her chest came to a halt, and her eyes darted between mine for a moment as she calculated what that growl meant.

No longer a moment between rejected mates.

We were Alpha and prey.

I didn't know what it was I wanted in response. Fear? backtracking? Just... anything to show an ounce of vulnerability, a crack in her mask.

"Don't bait me, Glade," I breathed. "You don't want what's on the other side."

She shivered, then delivered me exactly what I wanted just in time to realise that it was far too much for me to handle. She tilted her head, lifting her chin and revealing her neck to me, eyes dropping. It was the most primal thing I'd ever witnessed, and my rut-fogged brain almost cracked.

My mate.

The Omega I loved, who'd thrown me away like I was trash.

Who'd ruined us.

And she was giving me everything. *Permission* to ruin her. I wanted to rip the cuffs apart just so when I fucked her she'd have a chance of fighting back.

Instead, I let her go.

"Knight..." Her pupils were blown, and her voice had a little edge of a whine—just like it had when she was getting railed by Kyan.

I shook away the intrusive thoughts. "No."

With more self-control than I was aware I had, I stepped back.

Kyan.

I had to remind myself of him. Of what she'd done to him. My smile was bitter. "You're going to sit there, bundle of steaming Omega rage, and settle me down *just like that.*"

"Fuck you," she muttered, but she seemed somewhat resigned to the fact we kept catching her, because it didn't take her long to settle down, cross-legged, glare fixed on me. She had a very cute little fight with the rope she was hooked to, in order to get low enough for her to relax.

I tried not to think about how much it *should* make me angry —that she wanted us after all she'd done. But if she was nearing heat, she just wanted Alphas.

That was all.

I landed my first punch on the bag, blood boiling in my veins.

And with each hit after another, I tried to sweat this attraction to her into the ground, so it couldn't come back.

There was nothing between us, I told myself. *Nothing but hormones and biology.*

23

I was forced, cuffed to workout apparatus, to watch as Knight turned from sexy hunk of topless Alpha, to *glistening* sexy hunk of topless Alpha, as if that was going to help me get my head on straight.

Kyan had sent my fragile hormones completely haywire, and I would be lying if I said I was crossing my legs so tight because I was cold. I'd *bared* my neck to Knight, like a desperate Omega in heat. I'd never done that to an alpha in my life.

But *boxing* in front of me? This was getting out of hand.

I needed to get out of here.

I watched with a scowl as Zed appeared. He stopped in the living area doorframe, narrowed eyes fixed on me, then crossed to Knight like he was on a mission.

I wrinkled my nose as they argued—clearly about me, since they were hissing under their breaths like angry snakes.

As I watched, Knight threw up his arms, no longer lowering his voice. "I *would* say this is a bad plan, but I'm starting to wonder if you know what those words mean when they come out of my mouth."

"She's right about the heat," Zed said. "Lock her up and she'll go into it instantly. Kyan's using it as an excuse to go behind her back—"

"It's gonna fuck with our heads a million times more if she's wandering about like this is her home."

Uh... what? I glanced between them. "You could just... let me go—"

"No!" both of them snapped at the same time, glaring at me with furious expressions.

"Put her in the fucking room, lock the door, and take all the keys away from Kyan."

Zed was shaking his head.

"Did you forget what she did?" Knight demanded.

"As if I could—"

"What about Kyan—you know what she did to him."

Zed paused, jaw ticking as he stared at Knight, and I saw a shadow cross his face.

"What?" I asked.

Silence hung between them, neither looking at me.

"What happened—?"

"Don't." Knight's voice was more dangerous than I'd ever heard it. He still wouldn't look at me.

I got to my feet, staring at him.

"Knight," Zed hissed. "None of this gets better if she goes into heat. We can't actually keep her in that cell."

Silence followed, and Zed stepped toward me, reaching up and unhooking the rope that was keeping me here. I tugged it free around the cuffs, still looking at Knight, whose jaw was firmly clenched.

Zed nodded his head in a *'follow me'* motion and stepped away.

Right. Okay, I guess I was just expected to do what I was told at this point.

With a scowl, I listened because the alternative was him dragging me by the damned cuffs.

He led me back to the room, grabbing something black and small from the counter on the way, but I couldn't see what it was.

"Here's the deal," he said once we were in. He tossed the black thing at me, then dug in his pocket and produced a key. "You can come out of this room, but *only* if you wear this." I frowned, trying to understand what I was looking at as he undid my cuffs at last.

"A... collar?"

"Perimeter spans the warehouse."

"Perimeter?" I asked. Like a... I blinked, mouth going dry. "A *shock* collar?"

Zed shrugged. "We use it for Kyan's ruts if we have to be out. If it works for him, I can be damned sure you won't be going anywhere."

"Is this a joke?"

"You can always stay in here." He shrugged, folding his arms as he watched my expression with a little too much satisfaction. "I'm not forcing you."

I stared at him, entirely lost for words. "You're just trapping me in a tiny room—"

"Nope." He snorted. "We're not doing this whole thing where you pretend you didn't get us involved with Brotherhood shit without telling us. Pout all you want. *That*"—he pointed at the collar—"is your call. Knock on this door if you decide you want out." With that, he vanished, shutting the door behind him.

I looked down at the collar in my hands. It was black, and made of leather, with a little device attached at the front. It looked like as soon as it closed it would need a key to undo it.

This was... well, it was madness.

I touched my neck, trying to unclench my jaw as I stared at it.

It wasn't just madness... It was kind of... a claim, as twisted as that was.

Oh.

I needed to get a grip. So did my body. At the thought of it, slick was pooling between my thighs.

I really needed help.

KNIGHT

It took her less than a day.

Less than a fucking day for her to knock on that door to be let out.

It was midmorning when it happened, and I glared at Zed as he crossed toward it, wanting to stab him for the little spike of smugness that shot through the pack bond.

When she stepped out, I couldn't help but stare, every Alpha instinct going rabid.

Our house. Our collar. *Our* fucking Omega.

Zed knew I had a thing for collars, dammit. It's why Kyan wore the golden choker everywhere—and I always had a chain on my belt.

Fuck.

Me.

She looked nervous as she stepped out, as if she were looking at a whole new home.

I found it endlessly frustrating that despite her spiky exterior, I would occasionally catch glimpses of vulnerability that looked so real. Like there was another person beneath the crazy Omega cunt who'd left us in the dust.

I didn't just hate that I sometimes—for the slightest flicker— believed in that side of her. I hated that I *wanted* to.

Her eyes found mine, and she examined me. I was frozen, a spoon of cereal halfway to my mouth. She was so stupidly pretty, even in black sweatpants, a simple tank top and hoodie, sleeves to her knuckles, and thick hair tied up in a messy bun.

Great.

What was there to worry about? It was only the hottest Omega on the whole fucking planet, wearing our collar, about to flit around our home and make it hers.

Would she start nesting?

I mean, if she did, I had a lot of pillows—not like Zed. Maybe, would she want—?

No.

Goddammit.

I torched the thought with a flamethrower.

If Glade started nesting in our home, I would lose all of my self-control. Even now, as she stepped out in her fluffy socks covered in... I squinted... was that a bunny pattern? How infuriatingly cute. I just wanted to scoop her up and cuddle her. Or bend her over the table. It was really hard to decide which called to me more, actually.

She wasn't nearly as innocent as her bunny socks would let on, not inside the bedroom or out. Half my dreams were filled with memories of banging her, and damn if she didn't like it rough with my teeth at her neck while I made her beg for me... She liked that, too... being made to beg while I held out...

Real-life collar-and-bunny-socks Glade, cocked an eyebrow.

I lowered my spoon to my bowl, scowling as I realised I'd been staring at her like a maniac for fuck knew how long. My pupils were probably blown, my scent giving me away.

I cleared my throat. "The collar's a fucking stupid plan," I muttered, mostly to Zed, who was also staring like an idiot from the kitchen where he'd returned to his eggs.

They were burning by the smell of it.

Glade's smile was dazzling, her fingers trailing the stupid black piece on her neck.

Lovely.

I'd forgotten what a brat she was, too. Almost as bad as Kyan. The plan was to ignore her. No nesting. No pillows. No nothing. She wasn't here to stay.

How long *was* she going to be here?

If this was a Brotherhood issue? Well, there wasn't a clock on that… We were pretty well hidden from them. We'd worked hard to keep our heads low.

But things were different. She all but had a bounty on her head.

"Oasis?" Kyan's voice carried from up in his pad. He was staring down at her, eyes wide.

Fuck.

It took him seconds to slip down and hurry over to her.

"You tasered me," he said, hands weaving around her waist as he drew her close.

She shifted uncomfortably, meeting my eyes for a moment like she wasn't sure what to say.

"You're so fucking perfect," he breathed, nudging her chin up. I found myself irritated that she didn't fight him, letting him draw her into an intense kiss which ended with his hand cupping her throat. "You're wearing our collar?" he asked when he drew away. "That's the hottest thing I've ever seen."

I swear her pupils blew as she looked up at him.

Nope, scratch that, they definitely did, because her cream cardamon scent hit the air like a sex drug.

I got to my feet, scowling, but Kyan didn't seem to notice. He'd picked her up, getting a cute little squeak from her, and then dropped them both onto the couch. Kyan was beneath her, and lifting her easily until—

"Fuck, dude," I growled, stepping back.

I met Zed's eyes, but he winced, looking back at them.

Could Kyan give us a break?

Apparently not, because he was tugging her sweatpants down and dragging her hips right over his face.

I groaned for a very different reason than she did, backing toward the outer room. It was hard—the hardest thing I'd ever done—shutting the door on her desperate little whines as Kyan dragged that all-too-sexy tongue ring of his across her centre.

I hated them all.

GLADE

A very odd day went by in which I lived in the home of my mates. Not locked in a room, but... with them?

Despite Kyan's penchant for dispelling my nerves via rather pushy orgasms at random times of the day, I was an anxious bundle, constantly torn between curling up on the couch with Lucy and trying to pretend I wasn't there, and attempting to start normal(ish) conversations with my mates.

I dared edge over to Knight while he was cooking that evening, silently joining him in the kitchen as he made mac and cheese.

That was my favourite. He... he knew that, didn't he?

Why was he making it?

Maybe he just had a craving.

Plus, I wasn't expecting them to cook for me, so I'd begun my own meal. The plan, awkwardly, had been Kraft Dinner...

I stirred my pot, dissolving powder in butter rather nervously, trying not to glance up at the hulking Alpha to my left as he checked on his real-pasta-mac-and-cheese.

It looked and smelled delicious. Like, I wasn't one to turn my nose up at Kraft Dinner, but Knight could make a good fucking mac and cheese.

Lucy wound around our legs as we cooked, seeming to have

taken to all of my Alphas—the Alphas—quickly, which was surprising because she was a nervous thing.

I served myself up my Kraft and made for my table. Before I could take a step, though, Knight had plucked the bowl from my hand, opened the garbage with his foot and dumped my whole meal in there.

I stared at it, lips parted in shock.

I was really fucking hungry.

A little hiss of fury rose in my throat before I saw him set the bowl down beside the three others he was serving into.

He didn't look at me once, but my bowl did end up on the table with a really tasty meal in it—and he gave me an extra large portion, which I was really ashamed to admit, made me tear up as I stared at it.

I didn't look at any of them while I ate, knowing I might crack if I did. Kyan's arm was around my waist, though, a slight joyful edge to his lightning storm scent as we all ate in silence.

After we were done, I washed my dish, trying and failing to fight my instincts. Carefully, I snuck it into my room and tucked it inside the cupboard in the bathroom.

Knight had given me that bowl and spoon. *And* made me food. I stared at the objects for a long time, pleading with myself to just take it back to the fucking kitchen like a normal person. Instead, when I picked it up to do just that, I found myself nuzzling it with a scent mark instead.

Fuck me.

I had to close the door on it after that. No choice. But if they went looking, then they'd find it, and then what?

They'd make fun of me.

My lip trembled. I didn't know if I could handle that. But I was nearing heat, and my nesting instincts were getting out of hand, so I shut it away, my heart settling as I returned to the living room.

They'd given me a collar. Twisted as that was, it was a claim, and it was making me possessive over this place.

That was all.

Nothing else.

Over the next few hours I slipped one of Kyan's bracelets off his wrist without him noticing, and snuck into Zed's room to grab a ring from his drawer. He loved his rings so much.

I placed them beneath the sink in the bathroom with the bowl, something loosening in my chest as I closed the door on them once more.

It was balanced and even. All of them were in there. Safe and mine.

24

Zed was a genius.

The collar meant we could keep her. Like—properly, actually keep her as we should. Locking her in a room was doing none of us any good.

After dinner, I had to go up to my room to make sure we were still safe. I had a pretty good grip on Brotherhood movements, but I had a few blind spots.

Ace hadn't been on my radar until Glade had chosen him, but ever since I'd watched closely. Taking the lead of the Brotherhood had shown a side of him I'd never seen before, and for so long, I'd believed it had been what drew Glade to him.

She was an Omega; it was in her nature to select a partner that could protect her. If she'd seen, before we had, the Alpha he'd revealed himself to be after he became head of the Brotherhood, it wasn't inconceivable that she'd chosen him. Scent match or not, he was one of the most predatory Alphas I had ever witnessed, and she had been raised the same way we had.

Merciless and cruel were the traits we were taught, and that

Omegas were taught to seek. When we'd fallen for her, we'd shown a softer side to us than we'd ever shown anyone, and for a long time, I'd grappled with if it was the right choice.

I knew I was drawn to her far more than I should be, but I was never normal... I'd convinced myself it meant more to me than it had to her.

When I'd gone through my list of checks, satisfied we were safe, I reappeared to find she'd fallen asleep on the couch. Naturally, I went to find her blankets from all of our rooms so she could sleep in our scents—as she should.

Knight caught me and tried to refuse, which made him more of a fool. I waited until he was asleep, then snuck into his room with the blanket she'd been buried in (after swapping them for mine and Zed's), and held it near his face.

Even deep asleep, he frowned, reaching out and drawing it close. I only meant to get him to hold it for a while, but a rare purr had rumbled to life in his chest, and the next thing I knew, he'd scent-marked it.

Ha.

And the idiot thought we were going to be able to get rid of her? Not a goddamned chance. I hadn't heard Knight purr since she'd left.

I was rewarded by the most beautiful smile on Glade's face when I tucked her in with the last of the three blankets.

"What are you doing?" Zed's voice drew me up, right as I was lifting my foot to clamber in behind her.

He was staring at us both.

"Tucking her in," I said, like that was obvious.

"Are you giving her our scents?"

"She likes them." I glanced down at her, then did a double take. She more than *liked* them, she'd almost vanished, the sweetest little hum of contentment sounding from the pile. I scrambled in behind her. She was burrowing without me?

Absolutely not.

I heard Zed's footsteps approaching.

"You're getting too close."

"Uh… no. I'm not close enough." That was obvious. Glade really liked it when our skin touched—I'd cottoned onto that when she was sleeping up in my bunk with me. Before I'd been tasered, she had snuggled close, breath hitching if contact between us ended for even a second.

To prove my point, I slipped beneath the first blanket.

Glade's dainty hand surfaced from her burrow, finding my face, then my neck, and drawing me closer.

I smiled smugly.

Of course I was right.

"I'm coming, Oasis," I told her, slipping beneath the blankets further and letting out a breath of relief as I felt her palms drop to my chest. I drew her into my arms, feeling her breathing slow as she curled up into my embrace.

"Her heat can't be far," I murmured, popping my head up and over the blankets to check Zed's expression. He looked appropriately stunned as he watched us, and through the bond, I could feel his frustration keep cresting pitifully before it drowned to the much more potent envy that was eating him alive.

"She's ours," I said.

"She left us."

"And now, she can't." What was hard about this?

We were Alphas, she was our Omega. We'd claimed her. Like I'd said, the collar was genius. They could stop being butthurt about the whole rejection thing.

Bump in the road, really.

"We can't keep her collared forever."

"Why not?" I asked. "It stops you and Knight from panicking every time she glances at the door—and she wants it."

"Wants it?" Zed spluttered, loud enough that Glade visibly

stirred, eyes blinking for a moment as she tilted her head toward the gap in the blankets around us. We both froze, keeping silent until she settled, relaxing back against me. Zed lowered his voice. "She does not."

"Are you blind?"

Earlier I'd noticed she'd been unable to stop looking at my silver bracelet decorated with little leaves. There was such intensity in her gaze, pupils expanding, scent shifting to something possessive.

I tested my theory as we sat on the couch, flicking through channels, and tucked my hand in my pocket. The little growl she let out was swiftly covered with a cough, and Lucy, who was curled up on her lap, startled awake.

So, next I went to the bathroom and scent-marked in private. To my delight, she snuggled next to me on the couch when I'd returned.

She didn't think I noticed as she slowly eased it off my wrist and stuffed it into her bra.

Bless.

After, she'd darted back to the cell under the guise of using the bathroom, and was almost glowing when she returned to burrow under my arm.

That was definitely nesting...

"Kyan." Zed dragged me out of the pleasant memory. "She doesn't want us."

"She fucking well does," I snorted.

I dared tug the top blanket down a little as I cupped her neck and collar from behind, thumb stroking her jaw. She whined, arms circling my chest and drawing me closer. "Good girl," I murmured. "You're ours, Baby, we're not letting you go."

I thought, if Omegas could purr, she would have—I mean, it was stupid they couldn't. It would be so cute. But her beautiful stormy scent hit the air like a lightning strike, and she nuzzled closer to me, a very out of character whine slipping from her chest.

I brushed a knuckle along her cheek, my own purr rumbling to life. With each breath, I inhaled fresh rain, cool billowing wind, and my skin on hers was a spark of electricity. "You want us, don't you, Oasis?" I whispered. "You just don't know how to say it."

I was missing a piece of the puzzle, still. I thought... Well, I had believed she'd *chosen* to leave us behind, but that was making less and less sense by the day.

Something was wrong... I had to find out what it was.

"You're fucking delusional." Zed's tight expression was offset by the fact that his snow santal scent was almost as thick as hers.

I just flipped him off, though that made Glade whine, because it meant taking my hand from her neck. I replaced it, then tugged the blankets back over us so my fool of a pack leader didn't get any more visual gifts he was yet to deserve.

Tonight was ours.

My purr began again as she nuzzled her head beneath my chin, and I felt the way she melted against me.

"No nightmares tonight, beautiful," I whispered, closing my eyes in the darkness of the blankets.

He was wrong, it wasn't me. Not this time.

Zed was the delusional one.

25

Kyan had packed me enough for a workout, which I appreciated, and the next morning, I found myself in the makeshift gym in the larger outer room of the warehouse.

I wrapped my hands with Knight's hand wraps and tried not to huff the pear grove scent that lingered on them.

I did check to see how many he had and was pleased to find there were quite a few. They were a bit big to stuff in my bra, but I could come back later.

I lost myself in the workout. I'd had no nightmares in Kyan's arms, waking instead to the scent of fresh storms, and for the first time in my life, I was *trying* to conjure my monsters back with every hit to the punching bag.

I was falling too hard.

To Kyan, but also Knight and Zed. I couldn't stop myself, and with heat creeping up, my hormones were haywire. I needed to get them under control and find a way out of this.

The problem was, with every minute that passed, my will to

fight this was waning, and every inch I crept closer to heat, logic died in the face of hormones.

I'd lost track of how long I'd been at it, throwing my fear at the bag relentlessly, when I noticed I wasn't alone—aside from Lucy, who was curled up and napping in the coiled battle rope. But Zed was also leaning against the metal frame that most of the heavy-duty equipment was attached to, watching me with folded arms.

I dropped my fists, narrowing my eyes. "Do… you want something?"

He was silent for a long moment, and I wondered how long he'd been watching. I'd been so focused I'd barely looked around in a while.

"Come here," he said mildly.

I bit my lip, debating whether it was worth arguing. He didn't move, though, and I crossed toward him.

"What?" I asked.

He lifted a hand, flashing a small black box and miniature key. "Battery change."

"Ah. Right. Wouldn't want that to die. Then the Omega, who you don't want and doesn't want to be here, might get away."

He snorted, stepping toward me and reaching up to my neck. I shut my eyes, ignoring the little leap of my heart as his skin touched mine, or how each breath I took was filled with snow santal.

I waited, absolutely still, as he switched the battery on the collar, trying to ignore how much I wasn't at all affronted by the damned device.

"You still box?" he asked quietly.

I glanced down to my wrapped fists, then up at him silently.

"I can't imagine my brother supported the hobby more than your father did," he said as he withdrew his touch, holding the old battery.

I cocked my head, considering that. Knight had taken me on a few kickboxing dates when they were courting me, and I'd loved it. My father had supported teaching me how to use a blade for self-defence, but nothing as 'uncouth' as 'throwing fists or feet' as he'd called it. Leave the fighting to the Alphas.

I smiled coldly. "I took it back up after he dumped me."

It wasn't a lie. Both boxing and kickboxing were something I'd claimed back after I'd fled. Zed ran his tongue along his teeth, not moving, and clearly not done.

"What do you really want?" I asked.

"I'm wondering why it seems, all of a sudden, as if you do want to be here."

"What about my escape attempts seemed ungenuine to you?"

His jaw clenched as he stepped toward me. "You're getting very close to Kyan."

"I'm close to heat." I turned back to the punching bag in dismissal.

"You can't fuck with his head like that—"

"I'm not—" I spun back to him but cut off, scowling. He was too close. Those ice-blue eyes were staring down at me in challenge. "He's not making it easy." I waved at the gym. "Why do you think I'm out here?"

I was praying that I could cool off steaming hormones. I knew I couldn't get any closer than I had. I'd woken in their scents this morning, Kyan's arms around my waist, nightmares a million miles away. I was starting to believe in this safety—and I couldn't afford to.

Zed wrinkled his nose but didn't argue.

I should take a step back. We were too close, and it was doing things to me. Zed lifted his hand as if he wanted to cup my cheek, but caught himself.

"*You're* keeping me here," I said quietly. "You're responsible for leashing Kyan. I can't turn off being an Omega."

"And yet you could just... turn off being our scent match."

I broke his gaze.

I had to step away.

Last time I'd been this close to Knight I'd made an idiot of myself.

Zed returned his hand to my neck, cupping the collar, and his touch was like a shock from the damned thing itself. Every hair on my body stood on end, my blood running hot.

I hated the way my hormones had latched onto this collar. I'd been running from these Alphas for so long, knowing a future with them couldn't ever be, but they were defying that even when I couldn't. It was wrong because the threat remained, regardless of which of us broke Ace's rule.

"He wants to keep you," Zed said quietly. "Believes you want that, too."

I blinked up at him, throat dry, all responses dying in my mind as I tumbled into his eyes. He took one step closer, so close I felt his body brush mine as his hand closed tighter around my neck.

Instincts wiped my brain blank, my fists closing in his shirt.

I stared up at him.

Alpha...

Holy. Shit.

I was losing it. The panic was a faint echo, but I managed to try to take a step away. His grip tightened, holding me in place, and a faint whine rose in my chest.

Was I *panting*?

When had his hand found my waist?

My gaze dropped to where his lips were drawn in a snarl. It was all I could do not to tilt my neck to him like I had Knight, but fighting that took everything out of me.

Bite...

He was my Alpha—pack lead. His bite would claim me more

than this collar. His pupils blew, grip at my waist punishing as he dragged me closer.

He would.

He *had* to.

There was nothing more right in the world.

Then his hand was gone, and I was in freefall, heart dropping like a stone as his touch faded.

He took one step away, then another.

Ice speared my veins, panic creeping in.

Don't cry.

His expression was hard. "Hurts, doesn't it?" The quiet words were more empty than cruel. If anything, there was an agony in his eyes that matched mine.

He took a final step backward before turning and leaving me to hold back tears.

It took a while before I had the courage to walk back into the living room. I quickly made for Zed's shower—he'd told me I could use his since the cell didn't have warm water.

The shock collar was waterproof, at the least, but when I was finished, I wasn't sure what to do.

I settled on the couch beside Kyan, a part of me wanting to flee back to the cell so I didn't have to see any of them tonight. Zed was seated cross-legged with his laptop on the armchair not far off. I didn't dare meet his eyes.

"So." Knight dropped onto the coach beside me, either missing it entirely, or reading the tension in the room and not caring. "Why Ace?"

An horrible tension hit the room, which, by Knight's expression, was entirely his intent.

"Knight..." Zed looked sour.

"Nah. If she's gonna come back in here and start playing

Desperate fucking Housewife all of a sudden, we aren't so conveniently skipping the big questions."

They were staring at me, every one of them on edge for what I might say. I bit my lip, not meeting any of their eyes.

"Ace is..." I paused, trailing off for a moment, then shrugged. "He's not like any Alpha I've ever met."

Not a lie.

Zed's expression became stiff as he stared at me.

"Let's get it all straight, though," Knight went on. "You chose Ace over your own mates and then cheated on him two years later. Doesn't make much sense except for one thing."

I watched him curiously. That, I knew, was what people believed—that Ace had shown me mercy when he'd kicked me from the Brotherhood for cheating on him. "And what is that?" I asked. They'd had years to mull it over and probably a million ideas of why I was the scent match from hell. I'd done the same at the start, kept up at night wondering what they must believe.

"He found his scent match, and it was a bit of karma for you. Did you think he was going to reject his match, like you had for him?"

I stared at Knight, working through that.

Thistle was Ace's scent match.

I knew her. She was... a sister, in a way, a haunted mirror of myself, but her reflection had cracked long ago.

A sister who'd never had what I had, because while I had scent matches to fight for, hers had been from hell itself.

"Something like that," I replied quietly. "He was more interested in her when she arrived."

That was the truth. For a short time, she'd ripped the spotlight from me. I remember being relieved because Ace had a new fixation. Except she'd broken so quickly. Ace became bored, and he'd returned. I'd been left hollow at my own anger—that she couldn't have lasted longer, when I still fought.

What a vile thing to be angry about.

There had been times when I'd tried to comfort her—slipping into her rooms at night when I could get away with it. I would find her trapped in her own nightmares, and I would burrow beneath the covers at her side and hold her hand. Sometimes, she would drag me close, clinging to me like the last raft at sea, but I never knew if it helped or not. Her scent would sometimes seem more shattered by the time I left.

"I lasted a year with her there," I said with a shrug. The story helped me cover the truth they couldn't know.

It *had* been a year that Thistle had been there before I got away.

In that time, she'd broken in every way.

I'd seen her kill on his command—guards, friends, and even her own blood. In heats, she begged for him. I knew, because he made me watch so I could see what I could have if I would only cave.

Ace had a pack, if for no other reason than politics and control. His pack mates were two Alphas across different Brotherhood factions in other states. None outranked him, so they would visit for her heat, yet were banned from touching her until she'd asked for him first.

I'd *hated* seeing that more than anything else. Seeing her become nothing before him. Seeing her give up that last piece no one else should own as she begged for the man who'd destroyed her.

And she'd taught me a lesson more valuable than anything else: when bored, Ace became more cruel and creative than ever. Breaking for him was far from the end. And in that, Thistle had given me the greatest gift, even if she'd never meant to.

I met Knight's eyes, seeing disgust in them.

Right.

I was playing callous cheating bitch. It was important, since I had to stop them getting attached, and the story was working itself out so easily in Knight's head. Still, I didn't glance up at Kyan, at my side. He'd been quiet, hand hovering near my arm, as if he wanted to comfort me.

I forced a smile to my face. "I'm not big on sharing."

Zed snorted.

"Do you miss it?" I asked.

"What?"

"The Brotherhood." I was more curious about that than I would admit. How many times had Ace bragged to me that I knew him better than even his brother did? That he'd worn a mask for years, for Zed, even for his father—leaving me to take the fall with such ease when I had rejected them.

As sick as Ace was, I was grateful for that part. If Zed, Knight, or Kyan had suspected anything else, they might have come for me.

And if they had, they would have died.

But was there a forgotten future Zed had lost when he'd been exiled? A vision he'd had for the gang he'd once been destined to run.

There was a pause, and the look on his face told me he was trying to figure out why I was asking him about that. Eventually, he shrugged. "At first."

Knight glanced at me. "From what we heard, Ace turned it into—"

"Something my dad would be proud of," Zed put in. I could see the bitterness on his face.

"You would have done things differently?" I asked.

Zed shrugged, making a non-committal sound.

I already knew the answer, though. I knew Zed's heart. I knew he'd wanted to drag the Brotherhood back from the edge of the cliff his father had pushed them to.

He might have been able to, as well.

Ace, though? He'd made his father's legacy look like child's play. The gang was more brutal than it had ever been, eating their own and using fear to stay on top.

"Right. So what?" Knight asked. "Now you've been alone for years and you run into us again…"

I snorted, tapping on my collar. "I want to leave, remember? Don't act like I'm pining over you."

"You are, Sweet Oasis." Kyan pulled me into his arms. "I proved that the other night for everyone to see."

I snorted. "A good fuck does *not* constitute—"

"Shh," Kyan murmured, pressing his fingers to my lips. "Or I'll have to prove it again. You're not blushing nearly enough."

I was now just hearing the possessive rumble of a growl in his chest. Before I could stop myself, I'd sunk into the crook of his arm, finding it hard to fight my desperation for the way he felt, those old scars still closing with every touch.

Knight got to his feet, though, and I didn't miss the dark expression on his face as he exited the room to the larger open room beyond.

I hugged my knees to my chest, watching the boxing for a while longer before I made my decision. I got to my feet, crossing to Knight's room, and knocked on the door gently.

When there was no reply, I knocked again, unlatching the door and peering in. Knight was at his desk, but his eyes caught me the moment the door opened. He ripped his headset off, crossing to me in an instant. "I don't want you getting your scent all up in my fucking room."

"I don't have to come in."

"What do you want?"

"It's about Kyan," I said.

Knight glared at me. "What about him?"

"You're... together?" I asked.

"He'll have your neck if he hears you saying that." Knight snorted.

"You aren't?"

"No Princess. I like to punish him when he's a brat."

I frowned. He was protective of Kyan, beyond regular pack mates. "What happened with him after I left?" I asked. "I have to know." I thought maybe, I already did, but a guess wasn't enough.

Knight froze, glaring at me. Then he opened his mouth and shut it.

"You *have* to?" He looked bitter.

"It's... it's important to me."

"Bit late for that, isn't it?" he asked.

I waited, balling my fists at my side and bracing.

Finally, Knight unclenched his jaw. "Meeting you fucked with his brain chemistry, Glade. He wasn't stable to start with."

I nodded. I knew that. Kyan's family had resorted to barbaric methods to make him what he was—wanting a son who would make a name for them in the Brotherhood. Every Alpha instinct had been dialled up, pushed on, honed in, burning away everything else.

"What did you think would happen?" Knight asked.

I swallowed, having no answer to that. There had been no plan. Just a prayer that Zed and Knight would be enough.

And they had been, but maybe that was a closer call than even I knew.

"And when I... I left?" It was a question I didn't want to ask, and yet... I had to know.

"When you *rejected* us," Knight corrected coldly. "I'll tell you, not because you deserve to know, but because I hope you have some fucking decency left, and you'll stop screwing with his brain."

I stared at him, throat suddenly dry.

It was bad. I knew from Knight's fury.

There was a long, long silence before he spoke. "Found him on the roof of his dad's house, gun to his head."

What?

It felt like the very earth came to a halt as I stared up into Knight's eyes. I didn't know what I'd expected, but that wasn't it.

Somehow, I'd imagined that if things had become difficult, they would have got ahead of it.

But that...

Bile rose in my throat.

That wasn't just a close call. It sounded like there had been seconds between... Between a world with and without him in it.

The world spun. I didn't know when I'd reached the door to the outer warehouse, but I was staggering through it. I needed air.

I needed to be as far from their scents as I could get.

26

I found her out back of the warehouse.

There was a little collection of chairs and a table that subbed in like a pseudo patio, even if it was on rough concrete and half the chairs were rusted.

The parameters of the collar reached just a bit beyond, since fresh air wasn't a bad idea on the tail end of a rut.

Glade was seated on the concrete, back against the wall, eyes red as she hugged her knees to her chest. She got to her feet when she saw me, wringing her hands and wiping tears from her eyes like it might mean I didn't notice.

"You... all right?" I asked awkwardly.

She stared at me, chewing on her lip like she wasn't sure what to say.

"You don't have to stay out here," I said. "Kyan's out." He'd panicked when Knight told us what he'd said, and fucked right off. "Probably won't be back until early tomorrow morning."

He'd be... well, doing whatever he did when he needed to destress. For me, that looked like the training fields across town, turning anxiety into corded muscle, but Kyan was all over the map when it came to coping.

I closed the distance between us, cocking my head and folding my arms. "You... care." It wasn't a question. I wish it was, but it wasn't.

She didn't meet my eyes, tucking a lock of her long dark hair behind her ear. Her scent was so fucking distracting. We really needed to get her on scent blockers while she was around.

"I'm not a total bitch," she muttered, at last.

I could see that.

Was I *surprised*?

I wasn't sure.

"He's okay. Now, I mean."

"What happens when I'm gone?" she asked. "I shouldn't have..." She swallowed, searching for words.

"Have let him fuck you suspended over the whole damn warehouse for us all to see?"

She spluttered a laugh, wiping her eyes aggressively.

"Far as I could tell, he wasn't really asking."

Her smile was weak, chin quivering. Damn. She was way more distraught than I'd imagined she'd be.

I'd forgotten how unbelievably cute she was when she was vulnerable. And... well, as much as I didn't want to admit it, *caring*. So far we'd seen smoking hot mafia princess, but this was bringing back other memories.

"There needs to be a plan f-for when I..." She trailed off, struggling to find the words. "I can't stay here forever—"

She cut off at my low growl, eyes wide as she glanced up at me.

I blinked, realising my hand had jumped to her neck.

"You..." I cleared my throat, trying to ground myself. "You have to stop saying that."

Why?

It was the truth.

A low, white hot fury boiled in my blood at the thought.

No.

No, it *wasn't* the truth. She was ours. Then and now.

Forever.

Reality began to fade: of what she'd done, what we'd paid for that, of who she'd chosen over me. It was all slipping away like water down a drain.

Instead, all I could see was her. My mate, with tears on her cheeks, glittering from the sun above, all because she was afraid for Kyan.

And she was talking about leaving.

Never.

She was ours.

"Zed..." She frowned up at me, eyes darting between mine. "I think..."

Oh.

Shit.

I'd been so focused on Knight, I hadn't even considered...

Hormones burst like firecrackers in my blood. The warehouse, the patio set, the blue sky above, it all vanished. All I could see were bright brown eyes as my sanity fell away for a rut the likes of which I'd never felt.

KNIGHT

Holy shit.

Zed had devolved in a matter of seconds. One moment the bond was normal, then he'd gone completely primal. Kyan, of course, out and mid-tantrum, had locked the bond down completely.

Would he even notice?

I found the two of them outside. Zed had Glade against the wall, fist around her throat and collar.

He was fighting with himself as they stared at each other, the last dregs of sanity holding him still, even as he trapped her.

"Zed!" I grabbed him, ripping him back from her. He let out a snarl, throwing his weight against me for a moment, then catching himself.

Dammit.

There would be no redirecting. His snow santal was icy and primal. He truly was one hair away from a full-blown rut.

And Glade? She was... well, damn she was turned on, pupils blown, dark cardamom leaching into the air around her like an aphrodisiac.

Shit...

"Zed!" I spat. "Get it together. You're going to regret this."

His chest heaved as he stared from me to Glade.

Was he present enough to answer?

Could I pull him back?

He was staring at her exactly like a rutting Alpha could be expected to stare at an Omega. A scent matched Omega. Currently perfuming up the fucking space with need.

This was a mess. We still despised her for what she'd done, no matter what breaks in the clouds she occasionally offered.

I seized him, giving him a shake. "You *cannot* go into a rut and hate-fuck your mate after you put a shock collar around her neck."

Zed's answering snarl was a little worrying, and Glade's lips parted. For a second I swore she was going to argue.

She better fucking not.

"Leave," I said. "Slowly. Back out." I nodded at the door to the warehouse. The collar meant that was the only direction she could go.

I had to get Zed out of here. Now. I had to get him to the cages. A boxing ring. Anything.

"But—" Glade began.

"I'm taking him out," I said.

"Knight, you can't."

"Why?" I glared back at her.

"You can't drive like that," she hissed.

"Like *what?*"

But I knew. Her scent, his hormones, the surge of primal energy through the bond. It was... goddammit.

We couldn't *both* rut right now.

Not with her here.

"I don't..." *Fuck*, it was hard to think. "There's a place... in walking distance."

"No!" She sounded stunned. "What if you run into people on the way? An Omega—"

"Oh, *now* you're getting protective?" I snarled. I had felt the reaction from Zed at the mention of another Omega, he tried to rip from my grip, eyes wild. I dragged him back another step.

"What do you usually do with Kyan?"

"Collar, we brawl in there, and I fuck him real good, obviously," I said. "But I'm not fucking Zed—!" I cut off my own sentence as I saw the look in her eyes.

"*No.*"

Absolutely not.

Absolutely fucking not.

But she was so turned on I could scent the slick between her thighs. Zed could too. I knew it. He was trying so hard, shaking with the effort of letting me hold him back.

But if Zed took her right now, there was no way I wouldn't rut. No way in fucking hell. Even the idea of it was making my brain go foggy.

"There's two of us," I said. And Kyan was gone. Two rutting Alphas alone with an Omega?

"Uh… huh…?" Her pupils were blown as she looked between me and Zed.

For fuck's sake.

Zed let out a low, wounded sound, shifting toward her again.

But… she didn't… I frowned. She didn't mind?

Wanted us to, even?

I mean.

It made sense. One obvious way to get through a rut…

No, no, no.

Worst idea on the goddamned planet.

She seemed to see the conclusion I was drawing as I kept Zed back, and a little whine of irritation rose in her chest. It sounded like an angry chirp, and it made me rock fucking hard in an instant. Zed's breathing became heavier. Her gaze snapped to me, seeing the effect the sound had, and her eyes narrowed, the little downturn of a pout appearing on her lips.

She took a step back, then another, one heel through the warehouse door.

Oh… no.

"Glade!" I snarled. *"Don't—!"*

Fuck.

She did *possibly* the most bratty thing I'd ever witnessed—and the one sure-fire action that would set off a rut that teetered on the edge of detonation.

Our Omega turned and ran.

27

I sat on the Las Vegas Monorail among dozens of tourists, elevator music playing in my ears. It was actual, real elevator music, which was very relaxing. Relaxing was what I needed right now. I loved sitting on this rail, going backward and forward as much as I wanted.

I *could* get a day pass but I hadn't. I'd taken three rides so far, and each had been charged as a single ride. Last time, they'd locked the card for suspicious activity, so this time I'd brought three backups. All under Knight's name.

Fucking prick was gonna get one hell of a bill. The full ride only took fifteen minutes, and I'd be doing this until I felt better. How fucking *dare* Knight tell Glade my shit.

He had no right, and now she was more likely to panic.

That wasn't why I'd left, though.

I needed time to prepare. I needed time to come up with a good enough mask so that she wasn't scared when I finally brought it up to her. I had to find a way to play it off, to make it not that bad.

I paused, feeling a little flare from the bond. I narrowed my eyes, tugging an earbud from my ear and peeking into it as the elevator music faded.

Oh.

There was a legit tornado going on in there—a complete mess.

Was Zed...?

Uh... *Both* of them?

Ha.

I grinned. Fucking idiots.

Glade was about to get one hell of a treat.

Hmm... this was a good thing.

Definitely.

I put my earbuds back in, letting the elevator music soothe my anxiety as I locked the bond back down.

The rail ran until the early hours of the morning. By the time I got back, they'd all be one happy family.

28

The loud *crash* at my back signalled one of the Alphas on my tail.

I wouldn't get far, even as I sprinted toward the huge warehouse and toward the living room at top speed. A low growl rose across the huge warehouse and I heard thundering footsteps behind me.

Thrill lit my veins, a strange freedom I'd never felt.

I shrieked as a fist closed in my hair and a body crashed into mine. I didn't know how I got there, but I was on the hard concrete, pinned by a fist with a huge weight above me as another ripped at my pants.

I writhed beneath Zed's grip, but next thing, the weight was gone with a vicious snarl.

Spinning on my back, I saw Knight tossing Zed to the side, blown pupils fixed on me. I scrambled back, a desperate whine in my throat.

I wanted them to chase me and catch me.

I couldn't explain it. I just needed it.

Turning, I tried to scramble to my feet, but Knight was on me in an instant. Unlike Zed, Knight didn't falter when Zed's weight crashed into him. I was pinned, while Zed tried to throw him off me. I caught a glimpse of the fight. Of Zed catching Knight by the throat, and Knight using all his strength to shove him back.

Without much warning at all, my leggings were a non-issue, there was a sharp sting as my underwear was torn off without a thought, and I let out a whimper of shock as Knight impaled me.

Zed was picking himself back up as Knight began to fuck me mercilessly, cock already soaked with the obscene amount of slick I'd produced.

Fuck.

I could see Zed from where I was pinned, assessing us in a split second, clearly trying to figure out what he could do. There was a raging erection in his jeans, but it was freed quickly as he crashed to the ground beside me, grabbing me by the hair.

Stars burst in my vision as bliss began to seep into my blood.

I had a split second to prepare before he claimed my throat with as much brutality as Knight, whose grip was punishing at my hips as he slammed into my cunt over and over.

Instincts took over, and I went limp in their grip, letting them use me however they needed. The remaining breath was slammed from my lungs as Zed claimed my throat, wild eyes burning with passion.

His knot was swollen already, pressing against my lips every time he fucked me as Knight dragged me over his length. The only time I fought was when Knight's fist closed on the lace top. My T-shirt was gone, so that was the last thing protecting my scars.

A terrified whimper rose in my chest as I arched my back, giving myself to him while I made a silent plea for him to listen. He released the top, leaving it in place, as he slammed back into me. My eyes rolled back as an orgasm swept me away.

Zed held his cock deep in my throat so I could swallow down his seed.

I clung to him as he dragged me up and carried me through the doors and into the main living area. He pinned me on the couch, ice-blue eyes blazing with frenzy as he drove into me like Knight had, erection already back.

I moaned, arching against him as he fucked me so hard the world spun. He growled as he neared his climax and I let out a whimper as his knot stretched me out. He locked in, rutting me into the couch until I cried out.

Knight was there, standing above me, base of his shaft in his grip as he watched me finish, then he grabbed Zed by the arm, easily manoeuvring us so I was on top, trapped against Zed as Knight seized me by the hair and shoved me down against Zed's chest.

A whine slipped out as I felt the tip of his cock against my backdoor, but my instincts had taken over, demanding I relax and let them do what they needed.

It was going to fucking hurt, but I wanted Knight to be as rough with me as he was with Kyan. We had, before.

He knew what I liked.

There were only three Alphas in the world that knew, and two were here now.

His tip stretched me open without prep, my own slick making the entrance easier, and I panted as Knight drove his length right into me.

I whined, tears stinging my eyes as I cried out, another orgasm surging through my veins as Knight caged me in and fucked me like a rag doll.

"More," I pleaded. "Alpha..."

Every fucking movement he made rocked me against Zed, who was buried deep in my core. Knight growled, fist closing against my neck and holding me against him at my plea. I was dizzy with lust, caught between pain that set my veins alight and the pleasure of Zed's knot locked within me. The sounds I was making were as primal as theirs.

I felt so full, every instinct alight with joy as I was consumed by another orgasm.

The fog of the main rut cleared quickly.

The brutal and continuously competitive sex brought them some lucidity after only a few hours.

Still, in the throes of hormones, that didn't mean it was over. They still needed a hell of a lot to get this out of their system.

I ached, my body used to the very extent that it could be, but all I could feel was a wild high, the touch starved creature within me, humming with contentment.

"Present for him, beautiful," Zed said, as Knight's hand brushed my hips. I didn't hesitate, so dazed with lust that I was on my knees, arching my back in seconds as I lowered my cheek to the bed. At some point, we'd reached Zed's bedroom. "Good girl," he purred, as Knight nudged against my entrance slowly enough that I arched further, wriggling back and desperate.

Okay, so...fuck...

Zed was in front of me, hand in my hair, and now lucid enough to be fascinated by my expressions as Knight slipped in further.

And he'd started to be nice.

It wasn't that praise *didn't* turn me on, I just didn't think I could handle it. Not if I didn't want to burst into tears and weep in their arms while they rutted, and I had no intention of doing that. We needed to keep this mean and filthy. Plus, I had as much of a degradation kink as praise, so we could keep it to that.

I moaned as Knight filled me, nails digging into Zed's chest as

I found his eyes. "I left you in the dirt," I breathed, letting a smile curve my lips. "And you still need me, just like you did before."

His lips drew in a snarl, a flash of hatred in his eyes.

Just like I was hoping, he shifted, then dragged my lips to his cock and fucked my throat mercilessly as Knight claimed me from behind.

29

ZED

She was so fucking hot, breasts half spilling from the lace top she wore—one I didn't dare touch. She was desperate for us, though, pupils blown, eyes crossing with pleasure when we pushed her over the edge, and she tumbled from that cliff over and over and over, never seeming to get sick of us rutting her into oblivion.

I didn't know how many hours we'd been at it when Knight returned enough to feel lucid in the bond. He was the same as me, though, not free enough of the rut to have the self-control to stop. Not when she was like this for us.

A siren designed to turn our brains to mulch.

And she didn't seem to want to risk catching feelings, because she kept *taunting* us. She was being a cunt and... well; it wasn't making me want to fuck her *less*.

Quite the opposite.

I didn't know how many times my cock had found new life at this point. The rut left the cycle endless. She was presenting beneath me, my cock at her entrance, and I found the self-control to wait, hands lingering on her hips.

She let out a little whine of impatience.

"Beg," I growled.

Her breath caught, and she pressed her cheek to the sheets, rich brown eye taking me in, something furious in it.

"Zed!" she whined.

"Beg."

A moment passed, and she wriggled against me, trying to edge back over my cock. I held her still.

"Please," she said at last.

I growled, appreciation for hearing that making me even harder. "Please, what?" I pushed.

"Please, fuck me."

I almost came from her words alone, and how tight she was as I drove into her. Now I was lucid, the reality was setting in, and maybe it was fucked up, but hearing her beg for me was more than I could handle. "You walked away from us and look at you now, Little Devil," I breathed.

"Fuck you." She struggled beneath me, a snarl in her throat, but I felt the way she clenched around me. She was reacting to what I was saying. I let her writhe a bit, pulling out and flipping her on her back before driving back into her cunt. My hand closed around her neck where the collar remained. "Begging for my knot like a desperate little fuck doll."

I wasn't expecting how instantly she came from those words, whole body seizing over my length as she cried out.

Fuck.

I gritted my teeth and it took everything in me not to finish with her.

"You came so fast I didn't even get to knot you this time," I growled, leaning close, twisting her nipple roughly.

She let out a derisive snarl, her hand closing around my neck.

"I don't even think you care which hole I knot, as long as I'm using you," I breathed, pulling out and using the tip of my cock to stretch out her other hole.

Her chest heaved, generous breasts pressing against the lace that was supposed to be holding them in.

"Or am I wrong?" I asked, hand at her throat shifting up enough that I caught her chin, forcing her to look at me.

There was a long silence between us, and a bead of sweat trickled down her cheek.

"Are you going to make me ask again?"

"Please, fuck me, Alpha," she whispered, pupils still fully dilated as she shifted against my tip.

"Good girl," I growled, driving into her, feeling her tense at the initial shock before she relaxed around me.

"You want my knot, Baby?"

"Yes," she whined.

It was pure heaven, feeling her tight little hole stretch around the girth of my knot. I went slow, watching the way her teeth caught her lip, expression tensing as I made her feel every inch of me. And then I was in, rocking into her, feeling her tremble at the pressure.

Knight, I realised, was watching from the bathroom door, leaning against it, arms folded and a dark look on his face. He kept doing that, like he wanted to dip out. At the sound she made when I entered her, though, he gripped the base of his cock, an irritated expression on his face as he stroked his length.

He was far enough past his rut that he seemed happy to occasionally watch.

I wasn't. Not yet.

"You're such a good little fuck doll, Glade," I breathed in her ear, cupping the collar at her neck. "Maybe I'll keep you forever, after all, so I can use these sweet holes whenever I want."

She gripped me, another shuddering orgasm tearing through her as her nails dug into my flesh.

GLADE

At my side, Zed's eyelids drooped shut, and within half a minute he was out like a light. Once he woke up, I was sure the rut would have passed entirely.

I glanced up to Knight, who was propped up slightly by pillows at his back, but dropped my eyes before I met his, fixing my gaze on the beautiful deep brown rippling muscles across his chest.

We were connected, which eased so much within me, but now that the hormones were fading, I think I wanted to pass out as fast as Zed had.

I didn't, though.

Knight cleared his throat, and I jumped slightly as I felt his hand brush my waist. "I'm going to, uh..." He seemed to be searching for the word. "I'm going to... just hold you for a bit."

I looked up this time, unsure of what I'd find.

There was something faintly disconcerting in his gaze as his hands closed around my waist and he readjusted us.

"Hold me?" I asked, unsure exactly what he was getting at.

"It would be very rude to treat a girl like that and not... not um..." He didn't seem to be able to finish. Instead, he readjusted his sitting position so he was more upright, and my head easily tucked just beneath his chin.

I frowned, still not getting it, until his arms wrapped around me in one of his bear hugs, and a low rumble of a purr began in his chest.

Tears suddenly burned my eyes and I shoved them back, wrapping my arms around him and burying my face in his chest. I inhaled the low notes of pear grove, cool and sweet, lodging itself in the back of my throat.

We'd just gone through a rut together, one that had been neither gentle, nor kind. I'd left him and his pack mates, had put

Kyan on the edge of a roof with a gun in his hand, and still, he was holding me.

I love you.

The words whispered in my mind, over and over, desperate for freedom yet caged by shadows more frightening than any light they might bring me, even for a few brilliant seconds.

So I sank into his embrace, bit down on the tears and tried to claim this, even if there could be no more.

Of course, Knight made it all but impossible.

For an age, we lay like that, until his knot released me. And when it had, he shifted, lifting me to my feet.

What was he doing?

I watched as he crossed the room and put on a pair of underwear and sweatpants. He returned to me, handing me my underwear and waiting for me to put it on. He didn't meet my eyes as he drew me up in his arms and carried me to the bathroom, setting me gently on the counter.

Oh...

Okay.

I mean, if it was what he wanted, I'd sit through this quietly. I had sort of baited them into the fuck. And rut.

I was silent as he ran the tap and grabbed a cloth from beneath the sink. Then he stood before me, running it beneath my eyes and over my forehead, warming it when it got too cool. Then, when he was done with the cloth, he grabbed a bottle of lavender moisturiser and set it on the counter at my side.

It became too much when he sank to his knees before me.

"Knight, you don't have to—"

I cut off at his low growl, which he stifled just a little too late. He shut his eyes with a deep sigh, pressing his forehead against my shins and hiding his eyes for a long moment.

A long silence passed, and slowly he leaned back, touching

firm around my legs as he worked the moisturiser into my skin, not saying a word.

He didn't meet my eyes, but he was tense, as though waiting for another protest.

I didn't give him one.

"Kyan must be spoiled," I said quietly, needing to find something to break the strange serenity between us.

"Kyan refuses this," Knight replied, voice too flat.

I swallowed.

"Oh."

Damn.

Why was this so hard?

When he was done, he stood, rinsing his hands off in the sink and then returning to me. His knuckle brushed my chin as if he wanted me to look up at him, but I couldn't. Instead, I stared really hard at his abs, cursing the burning in my eyes.

Don't cry.

Don't fucking cry.

A hot tear splashed to my thigh, and I felt the shift in the air, the stiffness to the knuckle beneath my chin.

"I'm near heat," I whispered. "It's not..." I took a shaky breath. "It doesn't mean anything."

"Okay."

He was going to leave now, which was good because I think I was going to cry a hell of a lot more.

To my frustration, he didn't. "You're sick."

"Sick?" Finally, I glanced up, frowning. "What do you mean?"

"You told Zed you use drugs through heats."

I nodded.

"All of them?" he asked. "Were there any that you didn't?"

I frowned, trying to read his expression as I blinked away my tears.

"You're touch-starved, Glade," he said. "I looked it up."

My heart took flight in my veins, offsetting every ounce of peace he'd brought me in the last few minutes. "Looked... *what* up?"

"Why we're drawn to you *all* the time. Why it feels so..." He looked around, searching for the word. "*Right*, when we touch you."

"We're mates," I said, forcing a smile through a few more escaped tears.

"It wasn't like this before." He shook his head. "Not even close. You said you used drugs through all your heats, but were there any that you didn't?"

"You mean, did I skip the drugs and find a pack—?"

"No." Knight was firm. "I mean, have you had heats where you didn't have drugs or Alphas to get you through?"

My breath caught at the question, and I fought to keep my expression straight, pleading with the tears to stop.

So many... Over and over for years...

"No drugs or Alphas?" I asked, as if the question was insane, but my forced smile ached and sickness twisted my stomach. "Who would do that?"

"*...You can make it stop, Omega. One word from you, and this will all be over...*"

Knight was staring at me, though, gaze fixed as though he was processing every inch of my features, searching for a lie—one he'd find with ease if I couldn't pull myself together.

"Tell me the truth." The words were low, but his Alpha bark seized me. I clamped a hand over my mouth in shock, just managing to halt the words before they tumbled out. I slipped from the counter, eyes wide with shock, but the power of the bark was already fading.

"Glade—" He cut off, looking almost horrified at himself.

"This was a mistake," I whispered.

"What?"

"This was a mistake!" I could feel panic constricting my throat as I reached for the necklace—no. *Collar.* "Take it off."

"Glade—"

"Take it off me!"

Zed was there at the bathroom door, ice-blue eyes wide. "What's happening?"

"You said I could choose." My fingers were tight around the collar, the world blurring with tears. "I want the room. Take me back to the room."

"Why—?"

"Take me back!" The world was shutting down around me. I couldn't look at Knight as my feet hit the ground, and I stumbled toward Zed.

He caught me, frowning, but all I could see were his eyes: ice-blue, just like Ace's. I clung to that, needing to find my steel, even as tears fell from my eyes, making my vision swim as I repeated the only words I knew to say.

"Take me back."

30

"*Tell me, Omega.*"

I woke to another nightmare, as predictable as it was frightening. His breath tickled my neck. A monster in the flesh and made of smoke all at the same time.

"Have you failed at last?" Ace asked. "Failed to protect your mates for what? A rut?" His laugh was low. "That's all it took to make you crack? Disappointing that in the end you're as weak as your designation."

I shut my eyes.

"Tell me," he whispered again.

My fingers fumbled for the collar at my neck, the one that was no longer there. Why did I want it suddenly? As if it might offer me protection.

Last night, it had.

But now... Knight had realised the truth.

What did it mean?

"I don't like being made to wait..." My nightmare sounded

harsh, the slightest edge of ice to his tone that told me I was in danger.

His question echoed, a dare in my terrified mind.

And I was scared of so much more now. Scared of what they would do if they learned. Of what I would do if it mattered to them that I'd suffered all these years.

I could go out there and admit it all. Could take a risk...

No one had found us yet. Maybe... was it possible they never would?

Ace's finger traced my back, through my shirt, drawing across scarred lines we both knew by heart.

"You ran from me, Omega. You didn't listen," Ace whispered. "You're mine, and you will never escape me—"

"No." I shook my head.

"No?" He let out the faintest breath of a laugh. "No, what? You won't tell me?"

My breath caught.

...Tell me who you belong to...

I took a breath, hot tears burning my eyes. I was ready, at last, to stop being afraid of roses.

"Myself," I whispered. It was the only way forward. My hands shook, fists balled as I hugged myself, terrified of what my nightmare would do as I fought it at last. "Not you. Not them." My voice shook as I found words that freed me at last. "I belong to me."

ZED

I'd slammed the door in Knight's face, fury from the rut leaving me unable to talk to him.

It was irrational, but I was pissed.

Glade had been settled with us, happy and curled up between us on the bed. Whatever Knight had done, it had turned her on us.

My Omega.

This possessive tantrum would pass with the rut.

Still, I tossed and turned in bed for ages, almost getting up when I heard Knight turning on the TV outside. Given that the only instinct that popped into my head with that was decking him, I decided to stay put. I was completely irrational, and the hormones needed to take their course.

It didn't help that I was drowned in flashes from the rut. Of her beneath me, begging for me, lips parted as she shook with an orgasm, but perhaps more than that were the brief flashes of twilight between fucks. When she and I were locked together, and she drew me close. I'd spotted brief moments of anxiousness, as if she wasn't sure she should. But then my purr would rumble to life and she would melt, letting me hold her close, unlocking a piece of me that hadn't seen daylight in years.

Then I remembered what she'd said, the way she'd taunted us, and I found a way to dig up a little bitterness, though that need for vengeance was more fragile than ever.

I couldn't believe the first time I'd had a fuck in all these years had been with the only Omega I'd ever dreamed of. In a goddamned rut.

Finally, I heard more movement outside of my bedroom, and poked my head out of my door to find Kyan standing at the kitchen table, picking up the collar. "What's this doing here?"

Knight was leaning in the doorway that led out of the warehouse, tugging earphones from his ears.

It was four a.m., but maybe he was just as wound up as I was. He didn't look tired, like he'd hadn't slept despite the hour. Kyan glanced from the collar to me when no one answered. "I thought you guys were rutting?"

"We are—were," I said. "Kind of still, but it's mostly passed."

"Yeh…" Kyan said. "Banging an Omega for ten hours straight will do that to you…"

Ten hours?

But it was four a.m., and we'd only quit a few hours ago.

Well, *fuck* me.

"Where were you?" Knight demanded of Kyan.

"Clearing my head," he said. He seemed calmer than earlier, but his expression was a bit tight. "Where's Glade?"

"She's..." I looked at the cell, frowning. "She's in the room."

"Why?" Kyan asked, affronted.

"Something's wrong," Knight growled. "She's lying about something."

"No shit." I turned on him. "We know that. We didn't put a collar around her neck because she's trustworthy."

Knight was tense, though. "Nothing adds up, not even a little. We keep treating her like she's a freeloading bitch who left us for a better chance—"

"Because she did—" I began, but Knight cut me off. We couldn't just forget that because we'd had sex with her.

"Then why is she trying to get away from us?"

"What do you mean?" I asked.

"Ace kicked her out. He's not an option anymore. We're literally offering her protection, and all she wants to do is escape."

"Wait." I held my hand up. "That's what I was saying the other night, and you were telling me it was bull—"

"And then I told her about Kyan," Knight snarled. "I thought she was going to throw up—"

"Now you've changed your mind because she cares if her mate *literally* kills himself, that doesn't mean—"

"She's touch-starved," Knight interrupted.

I froze, and a strange silence followed his words.

"What does that mean, exactly?" I asked at last.

"I think she's had heats without drugs or Alphas. I think that's why it's different when we touch her."

I frowned. *"Different?"*

But I knew what he meant. There was a comfort to any moment my skin brushed hers, like... well actually, like there was a sickness that needed fixing.

"Why would any Omega choose to have heats without drugs or Alphas?" I asked, something incredulous in my voice.

But it took about one second. One beat before my smile vanished, and the blood drained from my face.

"They... wouldn't." Kyan's voice was low. "Not by choice."

My heart hammered in my chest. It was... frightening how easily puzzle pieces slotted into place the moment you removed Glade from the equation. I could see the shadow that lurked behind, just as likely a culprit. A shadow that had haunted me for so long...

No...

But she had been larger than life, so close to us, so convincing and devastating that never once had I been able to consider anything else. Not when it would be dangerous—for Kyan, for the pack—to pine over what ifs, to chase the impossible dream that maybe, just maybe, Glade wasn't the villain. When, even now, even after we'd met her again, she'd never convinced us of anything else.

Except in the brief cluster of seconds, looking at me with eyes so loving, desperate for something more, cocooned in a wound I could touch but not see, as if every instinct in my bones had been trying to tell me since the first moment we'd met her.

That maybe she never had been.

I stared at Knight.

Something *was* wrong. Really, really wrong...

It was like a fly at the edge of my vision, right there, yet every time I turned, it vanished. "Tell me..." I cleared my throat, staring at Knight. "Tell me you were about to go on a walk at four in the morning." I worked to keep my voice steady.

"What?" Knight asked.

"Kyan just got in. You were about to go out."

"No," Knight said slowly. "I just got back. Already went on a walk."

I shook my head, lips parting. "Then who...?"

And then I saw it, the fly just out of reach. The thing that didn't fit.

My eyes fell on the TV, finally realising what was playing. Not a show I'd ever seen Knight pick in his life.

One I'd seen a thousand times, though. The World Series of Poker had been a staple in my house. Always running whenever it went on, something my father loved... My father, perhaps, but also—I backed toward Glade's room, heart in my throat.

"She needs space," Knight growled after me, but I ignored him, running to the door, fumbling with the lock and ripping it open.

I froze, terror spiking my blood with pure adrenaline.

The bathroom door was open, revealing the room beyond. The mattress was empty.

Glade was gone.

On the floor in the middle of the room were four face-down playing cards beside a single rose.

31

My dreams were restless. Drugged sleep held me under like an anchor. Roses and redwood surrounded me, sending me into a panic each time I surfaced, but like a cruel trick, my sleep was clear of nightmares at last; I didn't dream of Ace at all. Instead, I was drawn back to a much more distant memory.

I was reading on a bench in the garden of my father's manor when an Alpha took a seat at my side.

I'd looked up, inhaling the entrancing scent of snow santal, and found myself tumbling head first into ice-blue eyes. He had fewer tattoos back then, but the spindle-thin crown along the edge of his jaw was an arrogant nod to his heritage.

"You're…?" I blinked.

Zed Maverick.

A son of the head of the Brotherhood—a gang we were on the edge of an all-out war with.

And he was my scent match.

Dread seized me as I stared at him, walls closing in. My pulse was erratic, the obscene attraction I had to this Alpha making me want to run.

I was finally out of time.

My whole life had been a series of decisions others had made for me. Reared to be a perfect offering by a family that considered me nothing more than a tool.

But *this...?*

I'd always been afraid of a scent match. I'd always known that however powerless I felt, it would be nothing in the face of fated mates. My independence was further stripped from me until I was left with no choices at all.

My family was careful who I was exposed to, hoping I'd match an ally that was appropriate.

I'd just turned eighteen, and I'd even held out the sad hope that my father would choose a pack for me before I matched one, so that my future wasn't pre-ordained two fold. I don't know why it was worse, but a political scent match gave validity to the control he already had.

This match, though, it was... unexpected.

I frowned.

Why was he here?

He must have known.

"Does your father—?" I began, but he cut me off.

"We've said nothing."

"Then how did *you* know?"

He draped an elbow on the back of the bench, leaning back and fixing me with a curious gaze. "Three nights ago, my pack mate was sent to kill you."

There was one long beat, and then I reacted on instinct, blade from my thigh in my fist. I caught his wrist with my other hand as he flinched, twisting it and keeping my way open. I ended up on top of him, my knife pressed to the left side of his neck, switching my grip from his hand to his hair and tugging his neck back.

"Why are you here?"

A rather unexpected smile crept onto his mouth, so beautiful it set my heart fluttering. "That's up to you."

I didn't move.

There were two options with an enemy scent match.

Alliance or murder.

"If I was here to kill you, we wouldn't be speaking," he offered, like that made things better.

My eyes darted around the nearby hedges where my father's guards usually lurked.

I saw no one.

"They won't wake for a while," Zed added.

I tensed as I felt the brush of his hands at my waist. My eyes darted between his, hormones surging.

"A prince for a princess?" Zed asked. "Maybe, one day, a king for a queen."

That, I'd expected. He was suggesting flipping the script. Alliance from war. Scent-matched betrothals changed things.

"But only if she wants it."

Those words drew me up. "If I... *what?*"

Was he messing with me?

"Unstack the odds," he said. "I don't want this to be about politics."

I almost laughed. "Isn't it?"

"This is about a scent match," he said coolly. "The moment they find out, they'll strip every choice from us—from you."

I almost dropped the knife as he spoke words he could have pulled from my own heart.

"What are you saying?"

"I want you to choose us because you want us. My pack. My family."

His family?

The way he said that was like nothing I'd ever heard before—not from Alphas like him.

"You want…?" I frowned, the words so foreign to me it was hard to process them. "What?"

"Let us court you before anyone learns. If you don't want us, we'll never tell."

The knife slipped further as I tried to find a lie in his pretty blue eyes, but even his scent, a beautiful winter forest, was serene, as if saying these words was a weight off his chest.

"Why would you do that?"

The Brotherhood were the underdogs in the brewing discord, and my family was known for honouring fate. For him, this was an opportunity like no other.

"I love my pack, but *we* were chosen for each other—*they* were chosen for me. I don't want that happening again." He tilted his head. "You're the last choice we get to make. I want you to fall for us first."

I blinked, still struggling to process what his words meant. "A scent match means it's already been decided," I said. And besides, *who* would be mad enough to reject a scent match?

"I don't see it that way." Zed grinned. "If you *could* walk away, doesn't that make the choice all the more… powerful?"

And Zed had kept his word.

For four months, the Maverick pack met me in secret. And the freedom they'd offered me was like nothing I'd ever experienced.

It had been the sweetest time of my life. Where I learned to slip from my father's careful watch and tumble into their arms. Knight had taken me on dates to the movies like we were just normal people, with popcorn and jump scares. I'd found a gift in the garden, a set of earrings, each a delicate crown with a diamond stud. Once, I'd got away for the day, and we'd driven to the Grand Canyon and stayed so long my father almost sent out a search. As things became more dangerous, they became all the more exciting. Kyan had visited me, knocking on my balcony with flowers like something from a movie, so I'd learned how to sneak into their home and surprise them in their rooms.

I'd fallen harder for them than I ever thought possible.

I'd fallen for them in a little bubble of paradise, a courting of my dreams, without my parents' oversight, without the world knowing.

32

I'd never caught up quicker to my reality than I did when my eyes opened in this locked room. I'd had years to prepare, years of false starts. The scent of roses was the first thing in my senses every time I woke, even if, for every other time, it had faded.

All, so that this time, when I opened my eyes and the roses were real, I could breathe. So that I could find the courage to push myself up and look around at the room with dark wallpaper, a standing mirror in the corner, and a vacant red velvet armchair beside a fireplace.

So I could hold the tears in, one shaky breath at a time, as if a numb blanket of snow settled over my mind.

This was the fate always destined to find me, and in a way it was a painful relief.

All those nightmares *had* been for something.

I waited, seated on the edge of the bed, hands clasped in my lap. Finally, when too many minutes passed in foreboding silence, and the door opened, I held my head high and faced the monster who had caught up to me at last.

Ace Maverick was everything I remembered.

A few years had added sharper angles to his lean face. He was twenty-seven now. Far too young to have the power he had, or the know-how to wield it the way he did, but Ace wasn't anyone's idea of normal.

Not by any metric.

He leaned against the frame of the door, frighteningly familiar, from his pale face and ice-blue eyes to his memorable motions. Like the way he carefully picked a stray piece of midnight hair from his vision as he examined me.

Ace would never fit in with normal people. He moved, talked, and acted differently, as if social conventions didn't apply, or were perhaps never learned in the first place.

It made him unnerving to be around, even after you'd learned to translate his strange mannerisms. His intimacy with silence, I hated most, because it never had a translation. It could as easily indicate dissatisfaction as it could apathy, and there was never a clue. Not until he spoke, and then he chose words carefully, so you knew in a second if you'd made a mistake.

And by then, it was far too late.

What my nightmares had forgotten was the way every fight and flight instinct misfired when I was in his presence, right down to the heart of what made me an Omega. The predator before me was a member of his designation like no one I'd ever met. An Alpha with ice-cold instincts that set me on edge with every movement he made. There were things in this world that he wanted, claimed, and never forgot, and there was nothing more frightening than knowing I was one of them.

It was why, even with years between us, I'd still been a stranger to a full night's sleep.

I fought to steady my expression as he drank in the sight of me from the doorway, one thumb caught casually in his pocket as if he were examining wall decor at a dinner party. I noticed a piece of red fabric tucked over his arm and felt a faint sense of foreboding.

Finally, he stepped in, shutting the door behind him.

I glanced at it, but even if it wasn't locked, he would have men outside, waiting to catch me if I ran. He took a seat on the armchair, a loose smile on his face as he crossed his legs, eyes expectant.

"I've been so bored."

I bit my tongue on the thousand questions I needed to ask.

No nightmare could have concocted the situation I was in, because my nightmares would never have accounted for my mates bringing me into their home.

What had happened to them?

I shoved the terror and question away, knowing I needed to wait.

I held the silence, meeting his eyes in challenge. I needed more from him before I asked.

"Three years was far longer than I'd imagined you'd be gone."

I took a steadying breath. "How long *did* you imagine?" I asked, needing to know where he was at.

Was he here to talk, or to torture me?

"Weeks, perhaps," he replied. "I underestimated you."

A very slight offer of vulnerability, no matter how insincere, but he was at his most unhinged when at his most prideful, so I dared push that. "I would have thought losing me in the first place would make that difficult."

His underestimation was the only reason I'd managed to escape.

When he'd made me the promise that he would hunt me until the end of time—the final game—it had left me hopeless. It was in the wake of my hopelessness that my chance had appeared. I hadn't realised quite how intently he watched me, not until it waned. He believed I had broken, and I think, perhaps, I was. Just not completely.

Ace tilted his head. "*If* your escape had been entirely unexpected, then yes."

I stared at him, a lump caught in my throat.

What?

"You were getting dull. I thought it was low risk, giving you a chance at freedom, and then, when I got you back, it would all be better." He spoke flatly, as if stating the obvious.

He'd... done it on purpose?

He could be lying to save face, but it was a dangerous assumption to make.

My mind flashed back to the day I'd escaped. Rex Sterling, a member of his pack who lived in another state, messed up a cartel deal. Ace had left in a rage to fix it.

I'd become familiar with the few guards remaining with me, including one I'd long since learned had a hidden cocaine stash for particularly long shifts. Ace didn't let me nest, but that didn't stop me entirely. My nest had been the tiny space beneath my dresser where I collected a dozen different items that might help me escape—or survive. From it, I'd pulled the small bag of laced cocaine I'd slipped from a bad stash when Ace had taken me to a drug meeting that went south. It was easy to swap the drugs. With fewer guards than he'd ever left me with before—and one collapsed, I'd escaped.

Ace had a half-smile on his face. "You proved more elusive than I imagined."

I kept my mouth shut, stifling the wave of sickness as I considered that even my freedom had been something he'd planned for.

Ace rested his chin on his fist, still watching me unblinkingly. "Ask, Omega. It's not a secret that you care about them."

Goosebumps lit my skin at the mention of my mates. I swallowed. My voice was rough. "They were *not* protecting me."

He smiled, and like everything else about him, it was slow and calculated as if he were discovering more reasons for it along the way. "That's not the question," he taunted.

I bit my tongue, breath still caught in my chest.

He rolled his eyes as the silence dragged on. "The answer to your question is no. The only thing I touched in that miserable warehouse was already mine."

My mates were safe?

He… hadn't taken them?

Why?

A thousand wound coils loosened in my chest, and it took more to keep my expression neutral than anything before it.

"You're rusty," he murmured. "You used to be smarter with what to keep and what to give."

It was one of his old mantras. *Hide behind lies I know are lies, and you won't have any tells left that I haven't found.*

It's why I never lied unless I could be completely sure he'd never know. I'd never met a person more fascinated with learning to read people than Ace.

"I like a fair game and good players, more than I like claiming secrets. Don't disappoint me after all this time."

I didn't answer for a long time, breaking that down. He lived in his own little mind palace, speaking in ways that barely made sense half the time, and yet never was it meaningless to him.

This one didn't take me long to decipher.

Play the game better, or I'll get bored.

And there was nothing more frightening in this world than that.

"I brought you a dress." He lifted the red fabric on his arm. Of course, he had, with his compulsion to control every detail. "I can't wait to see you in it."

He draped the red, floral-patterned silk across the bed at his side, and tilted his head minutely toward it. It might as well have been an Alpha command for the amount of choice it left me.

Nausea turned my stomach, and I tried to bury it as I steeled myself. I had to find out what was going on, and I wouldn't get that by fighting. I would get that by stepping into the next game he wanted to play, in the hopes I could survive it long enough to get what I needed.

Ace was so... everywhere that a memory as simple as this, choosing my dress, at times, caused night-long battles with insomnia. I would relive it again and again: he would bring me an outfit and take a seat as I dressed, his gaze never drifting as he watched me turn myself into a creature to please him.

But this was not the hill to die on.

I took the dress, swallowed pride and fear, and slipped from the bed, facing him as I shrugged the shoulder of my shirt off.

As I tugged off my leggings, I tried to find the person I'd been before. The one with armour built for this. But she'd died a death at the High Roller, and then been buried six feet under when I'd met my mates again. There was a tremor in my hand as I lifted the gown. No longer the old me who would have been made of stone right now.

I hated the feel of his eyes across my bare skin.

The cool silk of the fabric brushed up my legs as I drew it up, knowing before it slipped into place upon my body, what kind of dress it would be.

The back was low, dipping to my tailbone and leaving on display the scars I desperately wanted to hide.

"Do you like it?" he asked as I adjusted the sleeve and it all fell into place.

I took a breath, glancing down at the silk that clung to my skin.

"Don't answer before you see," he said quietly.

He reminded me of my own father sometimes, who looked down on others with such disdain he felt the need to correct them before anything had even happened.

I followed his glance back to the mirror, then took one small step backward, knowing what he was asking for. I balled my fists to keep myself steady as I turned my back on him and showed my scars. The woman in the mirror blurred.

Don't cry.

I gritted my teeth as his scent rose in the air, controlled, but thick, redwood and rose sharp with every breath I took.

"Stay."

He got to his feet, approaching me so he could see in the mirror, too. My skin prickled with disgust as he took a closer look, and I finally got a hold of my tears.

"When is your next heat?" he asked, close enough for his breath to brush my temple.

I dropped my eyes, calculating my options. Risk a lie? Was he testing me? Was it something else he knew?

He knew about the High Roller.

"Within the month."

"How have you been managing them?" he asked, and there was something dangerous in his gaze.

I was suddenly grateful for my refusal of Travis' offer to become more than a bartender at the High Roller. The look in Ace's eyes told me that those clients would be vanishing from the streets.

"Drugs."

"Three years?" Ace asked, peering down at me curiously. "Three, since you've had a true heat?"

"I've never had a true heat," I whispered, glad my voice was steady, even if it was thick.

He smiled. "What do you think, Omega? Will you finally choose me over those scars?"

He used touch just as carefully as words, leaving it with a weight designed to frighten. I'd never seen him use touch for anything else.

He'd told me once that he thought his touch was worth too much to be offered easily. I believed *he* believed that.

I suddenly regretted not going on that date Leisha had set up and not letting someone in—*anyone*—just once. So the ghost of him wasn't the only memory joining the brush of his knuckle along the scars of my back.

The fact remained, I'd never felt Ace's touch without something terrible following.

So it was hard not to shiver as his bright blue eyes held mine, and his other hand wrapped around me, holding my chin steady as his palm flattened against my back and he dipped his chin lower, jaw brushing my hair line.

Rose and redwood seeped into the air and I couldn't fight the choked sob in my chest as he scent marked me.

I'm not his.

I'm not his.

His eyes glinted with delight as he got a reaction out of me.

"Do you like it?" he asked, firmer this time, like he wanted to know what I would say if forced.

I swallowed, finally seeing the woman before me. Truly. In floral red silk, held like a trophy by an Alpha who thought he owned me.

I'm not his.

My words slipped through gritted teeth. "I would hate the most beautiful dress in the world, if it was you giving it to me."

"Well." He flashed a smile. "I think you look stunning, Omega." He traced lines across scars he was too familiar with as I held myself still on a knife's edge. "Perfect bait."

"Bait?" My blood went cold, eyes snapping back to his. "You said..." I took a breath, world spinning. "You said you left them."

"I did," he replied. He dropped his hand from my chin, settling instead on my waist ever so delicately. "You claimed they weren't trying to protect you."

"They weren't."

"I'd like to discover for myself if you're lying."

"What?" I turned, staring up at him, finding more of my sanity as his touch on my scars vanished.

"I made them an offer."

"What does that mean?"

"I gave them a chance for everything they should want—if your story holds up—or..." He tilted his head, riveted by my reaction. "Or they could save you."

"No."

"You think they'll come, then?"

"They're..." I swallowed, trying to find a way out of this. "They're good," I whispered.

"Did you tell them that you ran from me?" he asked.

"I didn't tell them anything. They helped me get away one time, but they wouldn't let me go in case they needed leverage."

"The night my men almost caught you at the High Roller?" he asked.

"I would have used *any* pack."

"If your mates have truly accepted that it isn't their business to interfere with me or my property, then..." He stepped back, sitting on the edge of my bed. "...You have nothing to worry about." He reached into his breast pocket. "I left them a note. Four, actually."

In his hand, he split four playing cards to which I could only see the backs.

"Three queens. One ace. And all of them had a message."

I waited, heart pounding in my chest.

"On each, there was a location. All buildings that belong to me. I wrote that you would be at one of the three locations written on the queens. But, if they go to the fourth, they'll get life-time immunity from the Brotherhood and…" He shrugged. "One hundred grand. Give or take."

"And if they come for me?"

"You said they didn't care, and I've offered them all that they supposedly kidnapped you for, with extra on top."

"*What happens?*"

I knew, though.

"You'll be there, won't you?" he asked. "You'll see for yourself."

There was a long silence.

"You look so concerned," he murmured, delight dancing in his eyes. "Am I in for a show?"

A lie jumped to my lips, but this time I didn't dare speak it, seeing his curiosity to catch me hiding things from him again. I could never win, though, because my silence seemed to make him more pleased.

"You're coming back to me already, Omega," he said. "I knew…" He trailed off, eyes too intense as he caught himself, as if he were about to say something he didn't want to. My chest tightened, but instead of finishing, he lifted the four cards. "Choose one."

I stared at them. "Why?"

"You'll decide where we go."

"You said there were three places I might be."

"I did."

"Then what's the fourth?"

"The fourth is the same as their fourth. But choose the ace, and I'll replace that hundred grand with *three* six-foot graves."

"That's not…" My mind reeled, trying to find something to argue with. "It's not fair rules."

"Fair rules?" He laughed. "You ran, Omega. Right into their arms. I'm offering far more than they deserve."

He stood, cutting off any more argument.

I saw a flash of hatred in his eyes when he spoke. "You're mine, but I do not have you, not completely. I cannot forget that if your mates die, you will have no one left but me."

I caught another sob. "You could have killed them all this time."

"Do you want the truth?"

"No." My voice was bitter. Not that he cared.

"I don't know that you'll be a better toy once they're gone, or if you'll fade away."

I swallowed, trying to shove back my terror.

Of the future that was coming for me—one in which he owned every minute, every nightmare, every dream.

Of a world where the beating hearts of my mates might not echo somewhere in this world, even if further away than I would ever hear.

"But this way is fairest," Ace went on. "If they're truly... over you, well, seeing your face, that will be a reward on its own. But pick right, and it won't be so bad." He cocked his head. "Three locations. Three Alphas. Only one has to die. That, I think, will suffice."

I was trembling, nails digging into my palms as I tried to drag my eyes from him. *"Suffice?"* The word was faint and weak.

"I'll leave the others so that when I bring you home, you'll still fight me like you always have."

The world was going dark, blinders closing my vision. A fist crushed my windpipe, making it hard to breathe as Ace lifted the cards again.

"Choose," he said. "Or I'll choose the ace. And if they don't arrive, I'll hunt them while you watch."

I could fight him on this. Could sink to my knees and beg. I could swear to give him anything he wanted if he didn't do this.

And none of it would work.

He didn't want anything I had to offer because I'd handed it to him. He wanted to win it.

Was it possible that Kyan, Knight, and Zed would choose the ace?

Would they leave me behind?

I had never wanted them to hate me so badly.

Breath tight, I reached for a card, trying to contain the tremor in my fingers. But there was no hiding from this.

I didn't linger, knowing it wouldn't matter. Clenching my jaw, I picked a card.

I turned it in numb fingers.

"Seems two are safe," Ace murmured, as I stared in frightened shock at the picture in my hands. "For now."

The picture swam as I warred with tears until all I could see was the blurred reds of the queen of diamonds.

"Well." Ace stepped back and offered me his hand. "Shall we go?"

"Now?"

Like this?

Only... this dress could be designed for nothing else.

"Now, Omega. I'm dying to see what happens."

33

The trap was set.

I'd cycled through it a million times, trying to envision this end differently, but it never changed.

A heavy set of cuffs designed for Alphas chained my wrists, and a gag was tight around my mouth. Ace had picked the location for a spectacle. He lounged upon a wooden chair that almost looked like a throne, and I knelt before him, chained to a hook fixed to the wooden panels of a grand stage.

We were in a huge theatre, with curtains drawn to reveal a sea of empty red seats behind me. We weren't alone, though; I'd heard quiet footfalls from the balconies above. Silent watchers ready, I knew, to kill on Ace's command.

I was shivering from the cool metal on my wrists and the chill in the air. From shock.

My heart clenched as my mind ran into dead end after dead end, pure panic fraying the edges of my sanity as I fought with tears.

I'd rarely seen Ace so tense with thrill. He had chained me

here with deliberation. Anyone who stepped through the doors ahead and into the theatre would see the marks on my back. My hair was draped over my shoulder so they remained visible, a *part of the art*, he'd told me, which I knew was that threat that I would pay if I tried to shift it to cover the scars.

The scars that were a claim he could finally show to the pack I'd left for him.

"You'll see them first. They won't die straight away," Ace told me. "I *could* just have him shot, but where would be the fun in that?"

I stared at him, my mind working through that, then I turned desperately, the cuffs making it difficult. My eyes scanned the theatre, the rows of seats, searching for—

Then I spotted it, only just visible because I knew what I was looking for. The tiniest glimmer that didn't fit, the warm light that spilled from the stage, catching ever so slightly on something hair-thin.

A tripwire.

I couldn't see the setup, the device that would trigger the moment that wire snapped—but it could be anywhere.

"The poison your mates have a fascination with is broadly versatile. It's a neurotoxin. You can adjust the speed of paralysis before it finishes someone off. At its base, it should kill an Alpha in thirty minutes, but if I give them a little... help..." He tugged a little silver square from his pocket; it looked like it held a pill. "This will slow their death. They'll still be conscious, unable to move or speak as you cry over them. We could play a game if the other two decide to play the hero and get themselves caught—I'll free them if you make the first one suffer enough before he dies..."

I shook my head, a choked sound in my chest.

This couldn't be real.

They wouldn't come.

They would take the freedom and go...

"I can be merciful, Omega. When we leave, at least one will walk, just so you know the price if you leave me again." He smiled, his eyes too intent as he met my gaze.

It was rare for his scent to give him away. I'd never known an Alpha who could keep such tight control over it, but I caught the edge of pure thrill, an acid bitterness to his roses.

"And we start these games again," he said.

I turned back around the theatre, eyes wide, but when I looked at Ace again, he'd glanced down at his phone, a smile spreading on his lips.

"Someone is outside."

No...

I shook my head, adrenaline making the world around me spin.

He'd *won*.

I threw myself against the chains as the world swam through tears. I had to make him understand.

He didn't need to do this.

"I can only imagine what you're trying to tell me," he breathed, leaning down and gripping my chin. Tears tracked my cheeks.

He'd won.

I would never leave again.

But my pleas died at my gag and he let me go, leaning back with a cruel smile. "Which of your mates will die today?"

KYAN

The bond was tense and locked down.

I had an earpiece in to communicate with my brothers, but we hadn't spoken in a while.

I was in a dim hallway of a vast theatre, gun at the ready.

One of three locations.

My heart thundered in my chest, guilt setting me on edge. Ace had so much more intel than I'd realised.

She was alone.

Afraid.

My mate.

Just like I'd suspected, we'd found the traces of nesting in the cupboard beneath the sink in her bathroom. A bowl, my bracelet, and one of Zed's rings. A piece from each of us. The beginnings of a nest. Omegas didn't begin building a nest like that unless they felt safe.

And now... I'd failed her—left her to be taken from the place she should have been safe.

I had known, always, that I loved her, no matter the choice she'd made. She was my other half. A piece of me I couldn't leave behind, or hate, not like the others had.

I flinched as a voice crackled in the intercoms above.

"You know, she swore to me you wouldn't come for her..."

That was Ace.

This was it. She was here.

I shut my eyes, taking a deep breath before I readied my weapon, whole body tense as I edged up to a corner. Around it was a flight of stairs. I'd entered through the basement, and the main floor was above.

Ace's voice crackled overhead once more.

"...But she's always such a liar when it comes to matters of the heart."

We were on the back foot, and I wasn't used to it, but I couldn't get caught until I knew where she was. Gritting my teeth and knowing I would never leave this place without her, I took the steps to the floor above.

KNIGHT

I took the last few steps to the main floor, reaching a set of double doors.

She was here.

"Guys?" Kyan spoke in my earpiece. "I think..."

He trailed off as Ace spoke into the intercom above.

"You still have time to turn around and walk away."

The same voice echoed from Kyan's comm, too.

"He's playing with us," I growled.

"I have the same." That was Zed.

Fuck.

This was dangerous. Guns or not, one of us was walking into a trap. Maybe all of us. And yet, there was no choice. We were fighters, always had been. We had to hope that once it sprung, we'd be able to find a way out.

With her with us.

Kyan had gathered his whole stash of weapons. There was a gas mask clipped to my belt, and tubes of knockout gas in my pocket.

None of them would do us any good in most circumstances— not against guns in staked out locations, or places where they might be at risk of hurting her.

It didn't matter.

Taking a breath, I pushed the door open, slipping around it and into a huge, empty theatre lobby.

It was an old building with worn carpets, aged wooden beams, and dated chandeliers.

Each of the locations had been theatres all across Vegas. No one was more likely to be the right choice than the next. All easily staked out, meaning Ace would know if we didn't come alone.

And we'd had only hours—not nearly enough to make a better plan.

If we wanted a chance at getting her back, we had to take the bait.

I couldn't think about what would happen if we failed. About the fact that I'd been wrong all this time.

Ahead of me, in the silent lobby, there were two huge double doors. Beyond, I knew, was the theatre.

Beyond, I would find her.

"Last chance," Ace taunted above. *"Walk away and leave me to my prize."*

There were so many pieces of this puzzle we didn't have, but I knew now we'd made a mistake. She wasn't the enemy.

I would rather die than leave her behind.

ZED

I'd drawn the queen of diamonds, and it had led me to my mate.

I stepped through the doors into the vast theatre to find her. Beautiful and tragic, she was chained to a hook on the ground, straining to turn toward me. Before her, lounging in a chair like a king on a throne, was Ace.

My brother. Every hair on my body stood on end as I stepped in, not lowering my weapon.

Ace looked unarmed, but I wouldn't be fooled. My gaze darted to the side, but the lighting in the room was exclusive to the stage, and I couldn't see anything. I reached to my ear, pressing the button on my comms so it was open for my pack to hear.

"Brother." Ace's voice carried easily across the space as he spread his arms. In one hand, he held a black device—the microphone he'd been using to taunt us through the building's intercoms. "I hoped it would be you."

With another step, I took her in properly. She was gagged, and wore a red dress that dipped low upon her back, revealing... my heart tripped.

Her back was covered in scars. Old wounds she must have had for a long time. Deep enough I could see them from here. They seemed to form a deliberate pattern or shape. I took a step forward, unable to understand what it was, but Glade let out a wounded sound, throwing herself against the chains, eyes wide as she twisted desperately toward me.

She shook her head, tears tumbling down her cheeks.

It broke me seeing her like that. My pulse picked up, instincts threatening to steal me away, but I warred with them, knowing I needed to keep my head.

I knew the risk. I knew how vulnerable I was as I stepped out from beneath the balconies above and into the huge room.

Ace wouldn't be here alone.

But I had a gun trained on him, and he knew my aim was true.

"Name what you want." I forced my voice steady. "Let her go."

"What I want from *you*?" Ace laughed. "What could you possibly offer? The night our father called you into his study for the last time, you handed me all you would ever be worth."

I took another step, mind racing.

What did that mean?

"Three months?" My father was furious. "Three months since Kyan failed his assignment to kill Lily Romano. Since you convinced me to wait before taking action."

I stared at him, working through the answer I hadn't been prepared to give him. Lily was her birth name, but she was Glade to me. The name she'd chosen to hide her identity while we courted her. A name just for us.

"You waited three months to bring this truth to me?" my father asked. "You scent-matched her?"

I gritted my teeth, weighing my options, but he knew already. "We decided to..." *I faltered on the word 'court'. He wouldn't react well to that.* "To convince her to take our side."

"You... what?"

"She's ready to accept an offer of alliance."

"Accept...?" *He cocked his head, lips drawn in a flat line as he examined me, fury spiking in his eyes. I took a breath, cooling my nerves.*

That had been a mistake. I had to tread more carefully. "We need her father on board. Now, she can—"

"Need?" *my father asked.*

"If we want an alliance with the Romanos," *I said carefully. We did, but I'd hit a nerve. Joshua Maverick was a prideful man.*

"You think your own family is too weak for a war?"

"I want us to be as strong as we can be."

He sneered, getting to his feet. "And you believe we need a Romano whore's help for that?"

My anger flared at those words, but I bit my tongue, mind racing, searching for a way to calm him.

It was why I would never tell him the true plan. That I loved her—and she, us.

I realised as the red crept up his pale neck that it was too late. Far too late. "Go to your pack. Tonight, one of them will finish the job they should have finished three months ago."

My blood turned to ice. "You want us to kill our own scent match?"

"I didn't raise you to be soft." *His eyes were glacial, and his next words were like a knife to my heart.*

"Prove you're worthy of taking my place." Back in the theatre, Ace spoke, echoing the final words of my father before he'd left the room. *"See she's dead by the end of the night."*

He laughed coldly.

"You were there?" My throat was dry.

If Ace had overheard that conversation with my father, and then followed me, he would have known what happened next.

"I'd seen her sneaking into your room one night. I knew you were about to screw up, the way I'd been waiting for. And sure enough, you made sure *someone* was dead by the end of the night..." Ace grinned. "And all of it, the perfect gift for me. Father was dead and I caught Kyan with that poison. I had a tape that would have seen you all murdered by the Brotherhood for treason that very day."

My chest was tight as I looked from Ace, down to where Glade was chained. There were tears in her eyes as she stared back at me.

"I would have, too, until I realised there was one more thing of yours I could take."

No...

"Your mate..." He shifted his foot, tipping his boot to nudge her chin toward him. She twisted away, and I staggered another step toward her, a growl in my throat. "... More intelligent than her designation should ever allow for. She was visiting you that night, and she found out what I'd seen. She offered me a trade. If I spared you, she would choose me."

My stomach dropped, and I almost dropped my aim on him as I looked back to her, heart like a cold rock in my chest.

She *couldn't* have... but I saw sorrow crest her fear for just a moment as she met my eyes.

I heard a flicker of static in my ear, as if one of my brothers were going to speak, but nothing came through. Or I didn't process it as Ace went on, his voice faint beside the pounding blood in my ears.

"She would offset my claim, handing me just as much as that video would—my brother's own scent match—key to an alliance that would do nothing but bring us strength, walking away from destiny to kneel before his younger brother. And in exchange, I would destroy the evidence, show you mercy and banish you instead."

I'd... I'd handed him everything he needed to take her from me. Right down to the gift I'd given her—the chance to fall in love with us.

And she'd fallen so hard she'd done what no other Omega would have—not like an Omega bonded for alliance and nothing more.

She'd given everything for us.

And I'd... Bile burned my throat.

I'd believed, all these years, that she was the devil.

Ace continued, voice cruel. "I've never met a whore quite as stubborn. She never wanted me. Not really, but I'm not a *complete* monster. I won't claim an Omega who doesn't want me. I told her I *would* claim her, but only if she asked."

My gaze drifted to the scars.

What... *were* they?

"I don't think I've ever seen loyalty like hers. Heat after heat, she would suffer."

My gun had never trembled in my grip before, but it did now.

"I admit to taking it a little to heart. She was in heat, I was right there and still, she never asked..."

Another numb step down the central aisle, and I was halfway to the stage.

Glade threw herself against the chains, turning again, more frantic. Her eyes were wide and terrified, glittering with tears as she tried to scream *to* me. *For* me?

I didn't know.

But I was here. I would die before leaving without her. My gun was still trained on my brother as he spoke, but I dared not pull the trigger. Not until I could be sure she wouldn't pay.

"...Instead, she'd say the same three words, *over and over and over...*" Ace's voice dropped to something cold. "*...until I got sick of them.*"

He shifted his foot, catching the edge of the chains, dragging them toward him sharply enough that Glade was ripped toward him.

I finally understood.

The scars on her back were three carved words, and reading them made the earth come to a standstill.

They were our names, etched into her flesh.

Kyan.

Knight.

Zed.

34

"Consider this your last chance, Brother." Ace's voice was victorious. "Walk away and everything goes back to the way it was before."

The world was ending. It had to be.

Crying out was useless. With every terrified sound I made, Zed took another step. He hadn't taken his eyes from us, gun pointed at Ace, finger tense on a trigger he knew he couldn't pull.

"You have me," Zed snarled. "This is between us."

"Is it?" Ace laughed, but I couldn't hear what he said next. Not when every slow step carried Zed closer to that wire.

I couldn't watch this.

I wasn't strong enough, not after everything.

I loved him. I'd loved him more fiercely than even the day I'd met him. The Alpha the universe had chosen. A match of politics I'd always been afraid of. But he had become so much more than that—had given me a choice when I'd had none, and I'd fallen for him anyway.

I wouldn't watch him die.

The cuffs... they were made for Alphas, enough to capture my wrists, but they were loose. Agony seared my hands as I threw my weight against the chains with more desperation than I ever had before.

No...

Something hot and wet made the fight easier. I almost lost myself at the flash of pain in my thumb, but with a growl, I wrenched at it and I was free.

I couldn't wait—couldn't risk Ace stopping me as I threw myself across the stage, my desperate cry stifled behind my gag as I saw Zed take another step.

Too close.

The tripwire.

I almost lost my balance as I tumbled from the stage. I barely stifled my scream of pain as my broken hands caught my fall, but I was already shoving myself up.

My bare feet burned on rough carpet as I sprinted, heart in my throat. Ace hadn't stopped me. I didn't care what guns were pointed my way. Zed was only steps from death, eyes wide, taking them faster now I made for him.

"Glade!"

No!

I ran faster than I ever had in my life, ignoring the spinning world that blurred through desperate tears.

Two steps away.

The tripwire glinted again, like a strand of spiderweb in the morning light.

I would be too late.

After everything, I was going to watch him die.

One step—and he lifted his free arm, reaching for me, shock written on his face and the motion halted him.

I almost choked with relief.

I wouldn't be able to stop, but it didn't matter—I collided

with Zed, and he caught me. I felt a sharp pain pinch at my back —nothing compared to my wounded hands. But enough to know what had happened as the poison hit my bloodstream.

It didn't matter.

My hands, sticky with blood, fumbled for his face as I looked up at him, ice-blue eyes fixed on mine.

I love you...

Words I couldn't say as darkness crept in, but I was in the arms of the Alpha who'd given me a choice in a world that never had.

And this choice was mine, too.

To die surrounded, not by redwood and roses, but the cool mist of snow santal.

ZED

In my arms, Glade's eyes rolled back, and she went limp, her hands falling from my cheeks.

"N-no..." She couldn't be... I sank to my knees, turning her and trying to wake her. *"Glade?"*

Tears stung my eyes.

What had she done?

"What happened?" The faint static of Knight's voice was almost incomprehensible.

Her breathing was short and shallow... she was dying. But she couldn't—not now. She'd given everything for us, and I'd left her behind—left her to a monster.

"Come back, B-Baby." My words trembled as I cupped her cheek, devoid of warmth. "Wake up."

It couldn't end like this. When she thought I hated her.

"What the fuck is going on?" I felt Kyan's fear through the bond, could hear the sharpness of his voice through the earpiece.

"W-wake up." I shook her.

I heard footsteps, and my instincts misfired. My gun snapped up, pointing at Ace, who was walking toward me. Everything in me begged to pull the trigger.

It wouldn't be enough—a bullet wasn't enough. I needed to tear him apart piece by piece.

"I wouldn't..." Ace lifted a hand, and I paused, seeing two red dots appear on his palm, shivering back and forth. With a smile, he made a flicking motion toward me. My gaze jumped down to her, and my heart skipped a beat as I saw the target on her forehead.

The rich bronze of her skin was now sickly; her eyes were closed. But she hadn't been shot.

There was no blood. No... *anything* that would explain what had happened. The trembling fingers of my free hand searched her body desperately, trying to understand, until I found something below her left shoulder.

I pulled it free, staring at the tiny dart.

Poison...

My reluctant mind caught on.

This death was meant for me.

"Your pack's specialty, is it not?"

I looked up at him in shock, mind reeling as I tried to keep up. I *had* to keep up. She was dying. I couldn't kill him, not until I knew how.

"The same one...?" My voice was a faint rasp. Kyan would have an antidote.

If I could just get her out...

The red dot still hovered, a promise that at the slightest movement, this would all be over.

"I was always destined for this, Zed. To see you at my feet."

"Is it the same poison?" I asked again. They needed to know— Kyan did. If it was the one he'd used on my father, he'd have the antidote.

How much time did we have?

"Dad loved his poker, didn't he?" Ace went on, ignoring me, head cocked as he stared down at us. "The proof is in the game." His smile was wild. "What is the only card worth more than a king?"

He was mad.

Completely and utterly.

But Glade was running out of time. I needed to get her out. Plans spun and died, threats looming from every direction.

I clutched her close, like holding on would stop the poison.

I couldn't let her die.

"I loved playing with her, Zed. She changes even the best laid plans. Turns out a stolen scent match is worth even more than my own." He took another step, his knuckle tracing the gun I still held at him. As useless as it was. "I'm not ready for this to be over, not when she fought so hard." He closed the last step between us. "I'll give you one hour. Then I'm coming for all of you."

I couldn't process what he was saying. Did he mean—?

But the red dot vanished from Glade's forehead as Ace gripped my chin, forcing me to look up at him. His eyes danced with malice, his voice a low, predatory snarl.

"*Run.*"

35

ZED

They found me at least a block from the theatre. I hadn't known where I was going, just that I had to get away.

I was in an alley when they pulled up.

"Glade!" Kyan's voice was more broken than I'd ever heard.

"Poison." It was all I could say, unable to look away from her as Kyan cupped her cheek, tanned fingers shaking. Then he was dragging me into the back seat. He tried to take her, but I couldn't let her go.

The engine roared. Knight must be driving.

"You have the antidote?" I croaked. Where was it? He had to have it.

"I will."

It wasn't here?

"How long?"

"Working on it."

I ran my hand over her hair, watching her chest rise and fall, too fast, too shallow, but it moved. "Stay with me," I breathed.

Time was a blur as I held her in my arms. Kyan and Knight were talking. About what, I didn't know.

We had to get her a cure—had to get away.

That's all that mattered.

It felt like I blinked, and the engine had stopped. The sweet and woody scent of pear grove was right there. Knight was in the back with me. His hand brushed her cheek, and I felt him in the bond. A storm held at bay by a thread as if he was about to crack.

Like I had.

"Where's… Kyan?"

He was gone.

But he knew these poisons. He was the only one who could fix her.

"He'll be back."

Right. He'd just left. Going into a pharmacy, he'd said…

"He can… he can fix her?" I asked, voice hoarse.

"They're not over-the-counter meds. We'll have to cut and run the moment he's out. I'm sorting another ride now. Ace will have our plates."

That meant… I shook my head like I was trying to dislodge a fly. She was in my arms. My fingers had found the pulse on her wrist and it wasn't letting go.

Kyan was… he was robbing a pharmacy?

The image caught up to me. He'd been tugging a gun out, digging out a balaclava from the glove compartment.

"Why doesn't he… have the antidote?" I thought he would. Wouldn't he have brought it?

"Most of his drugs are back in the warehouse. It's not safe."

Okay. Right. There was no choice. It wasn't like the antidote was simple, but we had a plan. It would work—even when her pulse was so weak, breathing coming short and sharp.

It was wrong. All so wrong. I remember the first moment I'd

seen her, as she looked up at me from that bench in her father's garden.

I'd come to give her a choice, but I was forgetting why. She was the piece around which the world orbited, the most beautiful woman in the world, and I didn't know why I couldn't just claim her now.

But I'd learned why.

I'd learned why in the beauty of the smile I saw the first time when I'd earned it. The way the galaxy seemed to glitter in her eyes when she was filled with wonder. The heart stopping sound of her laugh, which I'd heard just briefly once more, up in Kyan's room when he'd taken her from me just days ago.

She made the world full of life and colour in a way it had never been before.

And I'd been stupid enough to believe it was all a lie. To believe that woman I'd fallen for, wasn't real.

"I was wrong, Baby," I whispered, stroking her hair. "I was wrong, and so fucking stupid, so just come back so I can tell you that."

But her skin was pale, and everything was wrong as she lay, limp in my arms.

"This is my fault."

"Not the time—"

"It's my brother... How did I not know?" I asked. "Why did I believe she... she left us?"

"Because she's the smartest person we've ever met, and that's what she wanted you to think."

I took her hand in mine. It wasn't warm enough.

One of her nails had snapped, I realised. I don't know why I couldn't take my eyes from it. Each was long, silver and mani-cured—except one, which was lilac. That was something she'd chosen to go and have done, even living by herself. Why hadn't I noticed before?

But now, one was snapped.

Had it broken today? Or when she was with us?

An Omega who deserved everything—the whole fucking world, and I'd locked her in a fucking cell.

"I'll get it fixed," I whispered, running my finger over the broken silver piece. I'd take her myself. I would fix everything. "Just wake up."

My finger traced her wrist, waiting for the pulse.

My jaw clenched, a surge of white hot fear hit my veins. "Her pulse..." Where was it?

Was I imagining it?

"Knight."

He was reaching over already, fingers finding her throat, brows drawn. "She's... fine. She has to be."

"Knight, I c-can't feel it."

His breathing was tight as he pressed deeper.

"No, no, no..." I stroked her cheek. "Baby, no, you've gotta wait a bit longer. Kyan's coming, all right?"

But... her pulse should be there. Panic gripped me as I looked up at Knight. "What do we do?"

This wasn't supposed to happen. There was a plan.

We were waiting for Kyan. He was a mad genius. He'd fix her, then I'd spend the rest of my life making it up to her. I would take her to get her nails done every day if she wanted.

She couldn't leave now. Not like this. Not because of me.

"Glade..." I shook her.

"Zed..." I'd never heard Knight like that. "Zed, move."

"Why?"

The pulse was gone, but *I* must be numb, that was all. I was so numb I couldn't feel it.

"Lay her straight."

What?

Knight was trying to take her from me. I didn't understand. Kyan was coming back. She'd live. I'd get on my knees and tell her... what? I was sorry? As if that covered it.

That was so stupid. She'd tell me it was stupid, too.

I stared at her, realising her breaths had stopped.

"Glade."

Her scent had changed, curdling cream, spice of cardamom turning stale in the air.

"Move." Knight grabbed my arm, his terror turning the bond to lava. "She needs CPR. She isn't going to—"

My sanity cracked, the feral side that made me an Alpha burning me alive. I didn't know what made me do it. Not when I should have moved and let Knight take over.

My fingers were weaving through her hair beyond my control as I lifted her.

"Zed—!" But Knight cut off as my teeth sank into her neck.

My offer of a bond burst to life in an abyss, leaving me frozen and more vulnerable and alone than I'd ever felt.

Glade?

I felt like I was calling into the void after her. If I offered a bond, she had to accept it to join, but Glade had chosen our pack long ago. She'd chosen us the day she'd given everything for our protection.

Don't leave me.

Not now.

She was drifting away, fading into nothingness. She needed an anchor. Something to hold on to.

Please, don't leave me.

GLADE

I was... nowhere.

Fading so fast, clinging to the only silver lining—death on my own terms.

But there was so much grief. So much terror that it was over and he'd won. What he'd taken was forever; I would never be with them the way I'd dreamed...

This couldn't be it.

The doors were closing, and I... I wasn't done.

I felt the rustle of life, leaves blowing in an icy wind, and ahead, the flicking warm light through a cabin window between santals strained beneath heavy snow.

Zed...?

I could feel him reaching out, trying to drag me back.

For one brief second, I hesitated; I shied back, even as everyone I loved waited ahead, an offer of everything I'd ever begged the universe for.

But if I crossed that threshold, would I bring with me the curse I carried?

Die with it, a voice whispered. *Let go, and take your nightmare with you.*

But then the ghost of that nightmare would be the only companion I'd ever had.

They had each other, while I had no one.

And I was so, so scared.

I didn't want to die alone.

So I did what I never should have, and I stepped toward the offer that was reaching back for me.

ZED

I don't know what it was—a strength of body or soul that the bond gave—but she came back. A flutter of life like a bird's wings in the darkness, the touch, feather light, but hers.

My Glade, holding on.

I choked in shock, breaking and curling over her, shaking as I clutched her, afraid to lift my teeth away as if it might remove the hand to which she held.

I didn't know how long I remained trembling, with the faintest thread between us.

Then there was movement. Her arm shifted, and autumn persimmon tickled my senses as I clung to her.

The engine started, and from the edge of my vision I saw a needle being threaded into a vein. His hands still shook, and he took a breath, steadying himself.

Kyan was back. He was saying something. To me or Knight, I didn't know.

"Distributes to the local hospital... Need to get out of here before..."

I didn't catch the rest, feeling the strength of her pulse pick up, and with it, my sanity began seeping back in.

She was alive.

Somehow.

"You can let her go."

I didn't want to move. She was alive, but what if... What if I let go and she fell, tumbling back into that abyss? Something told me if that happened, she'd never come back.

"The atropine is working. She's going to live, but there's more. You have to let go."

Finally, I drew back, a low wounded sound in my chest as I did, terrified of what might happen.

Kyan's hand cupped the back of my neck.

"She's going to live."

He would never say that if it wasn't true...

Uncurling and drawing back was like cracking a clay cast that surrounded me.

I made myself move, finally hearing the roar of the truck's engine, seeing the flashing Vegas lights passing us by, tasting the tang of iron on my tongue, and... It was the only thing that freed me truly. The soft, cool tones of cream cardamom in the air.

Her scent.

Clear.

True.

As beautiful as it was the first time I'd sat on that bench beside her all those years ago.

36

Glade was going to live.

That had been all that mattered ten minutes ago, but now the other problems were crashing in. The hour Ace had given us was almost up.

Zed was AWOL in the bond. Not that I fucking blamed him, but we had to drop the truck. Not because Ace was on our tail, but because Kyan had just robbed a pharmacy. He was good, leaving the only one who'd seen him unconscious, so there'd be a delay before the police got there, but we didn't have forever.

"I'll get us a car. You get us a destination," I said as I pulled into a grimy parking lot behind a seedy strip mall with the scent of old cigarettes heavy in the air. Kyan had already used his RF detector to make sure there were no tracking devices we didn't know about.

It would have to do.

We'd found them, but I was still shaking from the sight of it. Zed had been holding her, fingerprints of blood covering his face, staining his white hair. Glade lay limp in his arms, her dress as red as the blood that covered them.

I was on the verge of breaking, and Kyan was, too, but one look at them and we'd both known. Not now.

They needed us.

It was night, which helped, and we'd reached them before someone had noticed them.

Kyan hauled the black bag from the truck. He had shoved everything we needed into it since we'd have to ditch it.

I opened the door to the back seat, helping Zed carry her out without hurting her.

Zed clutched her to his chest, clearly trying to focus. "If the warehouse is compromised, we don't know what else he's got on us."

"I know."

Kyan appeared at our side, bag slung over his back as he nodded in the direction of the street. Beyond was a park. We could wait there safely for a while. Our phones were switched off, but he was already activating a burner and tossing it to me before getting another for himself.

I shot a text off instantly, knowing the numbers I needed from memory. I had a friend who could get us a clean ride and deal with the truck without too much trouble. We weren't short on contacts with skills for shit like this.

"I have an idea," Kyan was saying. "The place she was working at—the High Roller—I did a check on the staff. She wasn't the only Omega on the run."

"What does that—?"

"Just—" He waved a hand. "—give me a moment." He stared at the burner phone, eyes darting back and forth as he tried to pull up a memory. Then he was dialling a number and lifting it to his ear as we walked.

There was a long moment in which Zed and I watched him.

He muttered a curse, and I heard the faint tone that meant the call hadn't gone through.

"She's ditched it…"

"What?"

"Glade's not the only one who ran into trouble recently."

He was already pulling up his browser and doing a search. "I'm pretty sure one of the Alphas she took off with wouldn't risk dropping all his phones. Too much business on the line…" He dialled another number, and this time, I heard it ring.

"Forbes?" Kyan asked. I did a double take at the name. Forbes was a well known mob family.

"Who is this?" A voice asked as Kyan put it on speaker.

"Is Annika with you?"

There was a long silence, but he didn't hang up.

"Tell her I'm with Glade," Kyan added. There was pause, and then a softer voice on the line.

"Who is this?"

"Is this Annika?" Kyan asked.

There was another pause. "How did you find me?"

"I'm uh…" I saw his eyes drift to her, then dart away. I felt a freefall in the bond, a moment of complete and utter collapse. Instead, I focused on the faded patches of paint across the asphalt, taking in a deep breath.

He swallowed, glancing at me for a moment as I cupped his neck. His eyes met mine, and I felt him steady. "I'm Glade's mate. She's in trouble. We need a bit of help."

"Her… mate?" She asked, something suspicious in her voice. "What kind of trouble?"

"The kind that needs a safe house off the radar of… everyone. Mafia, Brotherhood. We can't be found."

"Hold on."

There was another silence, and we heard pieces of a discussion.

"...Safe house...?" That was the first voice. "...Get my father involved, he can get off our asses about not going to him before..."

Finally, Annika was back on the line. "I'll send you an address. Give me a few minutes. Can I text this number?"

"Yes."

"Glade, is she alright?"

"She will be."

"If you need anything else, let me know."

"Thanks."

"Why her?" I asked, as he hung up, and we stopped at a bench. I think it was best to keep him talking. Talking and doing things.

Zed didn't take the bench, choosing the grass instead, settling with her still cradled in his arms.

I took a steadying breath.

I had to hold on. For all of them, just like Kyan was fighting to do.

"Another on-the-run Omega—ex-Cavanaugh I'm pretty sure?" Kyan rooted around in the bag before producing a knife, rag and a jacket. "But the guys she just took off with are well connected. If she's anything like our mafia princess, they'll be eating out of her palm."

"How many in-hiding Omegas does the High Roller have?" I asked, as Kyan cut the rag into strips. It was easier to keep talking as I stared at the blood glistening along her skin.

He narrowed his eyes, counting silently on his finger before giving up and shrugging. "The manager really knows how to advertise."

I snorted, though the sound was devoid of real humour.

Kyan knelt beside Zed and began to wrap Glade's hands. We'd

need to treat the wounds, but stopping the bleeding for now would have to do.

Glade's bare feet brushed stems of grass. In the dark night, her crimson dress was like something from a fairytale. Both she and Zed looked haunted. There was dried blood on his face and hair, prints where her hands had cupped his cheeks.

I gritted my teeth, clinging to my shock. It was the only thing keeping my horror at bay. Each line I'd heard through my comms, each taunt from Ace. It had been a blow to my foundation, threatening full collapse.

We were wrong about everything...

And we weren't out of the woods yet.

"Is... there a plan?" Zed asked, as Kyan draped the jacket over her, and I wondered if he'd processed any of the conversation before now. "Or are we spending the night here?"

I dragged my gaze to him, clearing my throat.

I checked my phone again and wasn't surprised to see a reply.

"Jesse'll deal with the truck—owes me a favour. Dropping us off a ride, too. If Kyan gets an address, we won't be here long."

37

We were safe for now.

I'd been right on the money; Annika's mob guy had come through.

The empty mansion, owned by the Forbes family, was far beyond Ace's clutches. Zed still hadn't let her go, and he was carrying her as we stepped through grand doors into a huge home with beautifully kept gardens that stretched for miles around. It was like something from a movie as Zed stepped in with her still in his arms, like a princess stolen from the jaws of a dragon.

With every rise and fall of her chest, my muscles loosened. Her long, dark waves swayed with each step Zed took, and one arm hung limply. As I watched, one crimson drop of blood slipped from the rag I'd tied around her hands.

There was a haunting serenity to her right now, to the silence from the space she'd carved out in the bond.

She was my storm, and these were her few moments of calm before she woke. She was safe, and it was on the back of her own work and friends, not because of me.

I'd missed things I should never have missed, and Glade had paid the price.

I almost lost her forever...

I shoved the thought back as Knight, who was ahead, led us into a grand room with a four-poster pack-sized bed. Zed set her down as I tugged off my backpack, which held the collections of weapons, including the same poison that was surging through her system.

I'd brought poison, but no antidote?

Arrogant.

Stupid.

It wasn't my proudest moment, holding a pharmacist at gunpoint, but she had been so close to death.

It was something I'd always believed of the Brotherhood: they weren't able to conceive of a threat unless it was a gun pointed in their face.

And then I'd done the same.

I shut my eyes, grabbing out what I needed before fetching Zed a drink of water. He was fragments of an Alpha, surfacing here and there, made of nothing but agony. Knight was the same, if not as bad, but Zed had seen the worst of it.

An age passed as I stared at them. The threat had passed, and I was left with them, gun tucked uselessly into my belt as I sat on the edge of the bed.

Knight left at some point.

Jesse had dropped us off a car and a shit ton of cash, and Knight was grabbing us essentials.

Zed was finally out cold, arm curled around Glade's waist as he slept at her side. I wouldn't admit to Knight that I'd slipped something into the water I'd given him. He was on the edge of mania, and he needed to rest. We couldn't afford another rut. Plus, now they were both asleep, I could take care of them properly.

They needed that, and so did I; insanity lurked, and I knew I was only a few moments of silence and inaction from ending up like Zed. Slowly, I got to my feet and went to gather what I needed before settling beside Glade.

I unwrapped the strips of cloth I'd placed on her hands. I couldn't look at anything but her skin, the scrapes along the edges of her palm and along the joint of her thumb. Skin ripped raw as she'd torn her own hands from the cuffs.

My pulse was erratic as I drew the cloth along those wounds, each one carrying a thousand flashes of her fear. Her desperation.

Her scent was as quiet as she was in the bond—the faintest trace of icy static in a cool storm wind.

Carefully, I wiped her other hand, cleaning the dried blood from the wounds beneath. I made the mistake of glancing up at her. Ashen face flecked with red, lips pale, dark bruising around her mouth and cheeks from the gag.

I hadn't been there for her.

How close?

I couldn't... I couldn't bear a world that had stolen her away.

Even when she wasn't with me, she was a storm in the distance, beautiful and alive; a power that never ended.

Until it had.

For one world-ending moment while I was in the pharmacy, I'd felt my Everstorm die; the other half of my heart swallowed into the void. The gun became a lead weight in my hand as the world drained of colour, and reality stopped making sense.

I was too late.

For the worst few seconds of my life, she was gone, and a whole bleak future began to unravel. I didn't know how I would survive it. Since the moment I'd met her, we were connected, as if, with every exhale of her lungs, I could draw breath, so without her I didn't know how to live. There were a thousand seconds before me, in a world she wasn't a part of, then a thousand after that, and I didn't know how to leave Knight…

I was lost.

Completely and utterly.

Except, with a bolt of brilliant energy, she'd come back. Not just to this world, but—beyond my wildest dreams—she was in the bond with us.

I took a deep breath, steadying myself as I rested her hand at her side, the wounds upon it now clean. I was still suspended between those two worlds—the one before me, and the one that had, for a brief moment, begun to take shape. Empty and bleak.

I swallowed my fear, wrapping the bandage gently and securing it.

Where was the basin?

That was next. I had to keep going. What if she woke like this?

With both hands done, I washed the blood away, smears of it upon her arms, neck, and face, but as I finished, my panic began clawing its way back up my throat.

My eyes snagged on Zed, whose arm was still curled around Glade's waist.

He was unconscious, but I felt his echo like a ghost in the bond, terrified and broken.

I blinked, tilting my head as I examined him. Knight wasn't the only member of the pack who continued to challenge the reality my father had tried to brand into my soul.

Zed had shattered into a million pieces today. I'd felt it in the bond, and heard it in the desperation of his voice as we'd been able to do nothing but listen through comms.

I had been taught to idolise him, born with Maverick blood— someone I might dream of one day being selected for as a pack mate. Zed was raised to be brutal and deadly, the pinnacle of what it meant to be an Alpha.

And he was in pieces. For us.

For her.

When we'd found those roses and cards—when we'd, at last, realised the truth—there hadn't been a moment where Zed had considered the offer of freedom and money. He had risked his life for his scent match, and when she'd fallen, he had fallen with her.

He didn't value himself more, as an Alpha. It was endlessly curious to me how far he'd distanced himself from the fathers who had raised us.

I dipped the cloth into the basin, shifting beside him. There was crusted blood across his face in the prints of thin fingers.

Glade's blood.

He didn't deserve to wake to that.

He flinched as the warm cloth touched his skin.

I closed my fist in his hair, ignoring his growl of panic, and wiped it off. One stroke at a time. I'd never realised, until now, how much I needed him as a pillar. Just like Knight.

So, I ignored his low sounds of distress, and rid him of every stain of blood, but for the fading pink in his silver hair.

Only, eventually, I was done with that, too.

I had to do more. I didn't know how to stop. Every time my skin brushed hers, her breathing would settle, but I hadn't done enough, not yet.

That dress was his. I didn't want her waking in it.

He would never touch her again, of that, I was sure.

I tugged my shirt off, scent marking it. The faintest trace of roses and redwood remained, but I would drown it. Lifting her gently, I used my knife to cut the dress free without moving her too much.

I was almost finished when my fingers brushed the scars on her back. She tensed, brow furrowing, her whine rising in the air between us.

I froze.

She was shaking, another panicked sound slipping from her.

"No... Sweet Oasis." My chest was tight, panic catching up as tears began leaking down her cheeks. "You're safe." With shaking fingers I drew the T-shirt down, leaning close and drawing my jaw along hers, scent marking her again.

Her tears hadn't stopped.

I knew what the scars were, now. I'd seen them when Zed had dragged her into the truck. That image would never leave me.

"She'd say the same three words, over and over and over..."

She'd called for us.

Her pack.

Her mates.

I broke, at last, my own tears blurring my vision as I trembled, throat tightening as I curled up at her side and held her tight.

I will never let you fall...

How many times had I promised her that?

But when my Omega had called for me, I hadn't been there.

38

I woke in a pack-sized bed, to find Glade in my arms.

For a very long time, I remained still, trying to process everything that had happened.

Knight was on her other side, and even asleep, his expression was drawn, one arm around her as if he didn't know what else to do. Kyan had been in here, too. His autumn persimmon scent hung heavy in the room.

I remained still, reality seeping in like spilled ink, turning the world dark, despite the light filtering through sheer curtains.

We were safe—I thought, anyway. I was groggy, and sleep came and went and time didn't make much sense.

I awoke properly at her distress. Knight had left now—it was just her and me, and she was restless. I drew her closer, instincts guiding me, even as I realised how little I deserved to be the one to do this.

My breathing relaxed as she did.

Was this real? Or was I dreaming again?

She was so fucking beautiful, so perfect. She deserved better.

I'd failed her.

The pack leader she should have had. The scent match who had let her take the fall... Shame washed over me, wave after wave, and my panic must have come through, because dark lashes fluttered open, and dazed eyes found me.

Her grip tightened as we stared at each other.

She blinked again, glancing around, frowning.

"What...?" Her voice was a low rasp as her eyes darted to the room around her. "Where am I?"

"Safe," I whispered.

I... thought so; their scents were in here. They had found safety while I was falling apart, and I needed her to believe in it. I knew safety wasn't something she'd ever been able to believe in before.

Her fists closed around my shirt as she drew closer, forehead resting on my chest as she shook.

She was crying, I realised, and I gently rested my hands on her waist.

"I promise."

"Your brother." She looked up, and my heart tripped at her look of desperation. At her fear. "Is he...?" She trailed off, expression cracking.

I struggled to find my voice. *"Glade—"*

"Is he alive?"

There was something caught in my throat as I tried to swallow. Finally, I nodded. "Yes."

I hadn't killed him. So far from it—I was alive on his whim.

The low whimper she let out shattered me again, and she curled up against me, shaking violently.

"It was..." She trailed off, voice so weak, but she didn't say any more.

"It's going to be okay." I ran my hand along her hair, needing her to know that. She shook her head, and when she looked back up at me, tears clouded her eyes.

"It was... another nightmare?" she whispered. "I can't..." Her hand drifted to her throat as though she couldn't breathe. "Please..." She sounded so brittle as she squeezed her eyes shut. With the next words, I felt her tremor, her nails digging into my chest. "I'll do... anything," she whispered. "Anything you want."

I paused, stumbling over those words.

"I will be anything you want," she said again, this time forcing herself to look up at me. "Just let them live."

My blood turned to ice as I stared at her, realising what her dazed eyes saw.

Not me at all.

Ace...

I shoved away from her, fear lighting my system as I staggered from the bed, and she tried to follow, stumbling the moment she got to her feet, but I was backing up. The moment I let her go, a piercing whine ripped from her chest and she collapsed, knees crashing to the carpet.

The sound was like a dagger to my heart, and my instincts went haywire.

She needed me...

I was torn between running, and reaching for her. Her scent rose in the air, dangerous, and she closed her hand around her throat, breaths short and sharp.

Brilliant chestnut eyes still glittered with tears, not fully here, I realised as she reached back out for me.

"P-Please," she begged. "I can't... I can't do it again."

Suddenly, Knight was there, dropping a tray of food on the bed and crashing to his knees before her.

"What happened?" he demanded.

I saw the way her body loosened at his touch.

That... that was what she needed.

Not me.

But she was fighting his grip, trying to reach for me, a vicious growl tearing from her throat as Knight tried to stop her.

I backed toward the door as Kyan arrived.

"No!" She was fighting Knight, eyes wild, dark cardamom, a feral haze in the air.

I all but scrambled into the hallway, colliding with a balcony railing. Terror closed like a fist around my heart, making it hard to breathe, but the moment I was gone, I heard her screams, each sound a vibration to my very bones.

KYAN

Glade was burning up. Feral, fractured scent clouding the air and threatening to turn my mind to mush.

"Her heat—!" Knight growled.

Knight didn't have to tell me. I was already tearing open the bag of supplies he'd grabbed when he was out.

Every fucking hormone drug you could get was in there, thank fuck. I found the shot I needed.

"Shh, shh, Princess, I got you."

Knight had trapped her in a bear hug. She was bundled amidst thick, muscled arms and loose, chaotic locs. His unnerved purr rumbled, barely doing a thing to settle her. She was still trying to fight him, and the cracked whimper escaping her chest with every breath sent splinters through my heart.

When I touched her arm, she flinched, chestnut eyes finding me, lips drawn back in a snarl, panic etched into each line of her face. Knight had his fist in her hair too, using his strength to keep her steady against his chest.

"I'm here, Oasis," I breathed. Something softened in her eyes as I cupped her cheek. I felt the static between us, and she stopped writhing against Knight, unable to take her eyes from me.

I dropped my hand slowly, finding her arm and holding it steady.

She frowned, head cocking slightly, eyes darting between mine as if she wasn't sure what I was doing.

Her whine broke my heart as I pressed the needle into her flesh. She flung her weight against Knight to no avail as I injected the drug.

"I'm sorry." My voice quaked at the betrayal in her gaze before her eyelids fluttered shut and she went limp in Knight's arms.

"What was it?" he asked.

"Suppressant." I swallowed. "Strongest kind. Should push it off for a while." They weren't like regular suppressants, they were much stronger, and terrible for hormone balance, but I couldn't risk it going any further. She'd also have to take it on a schedule. But if we gave her something lighter and her heat broke through, it would be too late for anything safe.

"He was waking up—coming in and out." Knight's doubt was flooding the bond. "I thought he'd need food. I didn't know he would let her go."

We'd realised she needed our touch. Without it, she was getting feverish. The stress of what she'd gone through was throwing her into heat. Between the hormones and the trauma, it wasn't surprising at all she was going feral before our eyes. The only thing that had settled her was our touch, and Zed had been impossible to pry from her until now.

"Kyan."

I swallowed, not taking my gaze from her, guilt swallowing me whole.

It was my fault.

Knight and Zed had both been here, and I couldn't sleep. I thought... It was so stupid. She needed me here, and I was...

fuck... Now I'd given her drugs that could make everything worse. What if I wasn't thinking straight? What if there were better options—?

My thoughts cut off as Knight reached out, grip firm on my chin as he forced me to look at him.

"It was the right call." His voice was rough. "You need to check on Zed. I have her."

Knowing there was no force on this earth that would pull Knight from Glade, I dared leave to find Zed outside the front doors, crouched on the steps that led up to the grand mansion, fingers digging into his scalp.

I sat down beside him.

A long, long time passed,

I didn't say anything.

I'd always been shit at comfort and feelings. But sometimes, when Knight was upset, I felt him calm in the bond when I sat near him, even if I didn't say anything. The bond was really useful for things like that.

Zed wiped his eyes with his sleeve and glanced at me.

I made sure to meet his eyes, and sure enough, the bitter edge to snow santal smoothed out a bit.

Good.

I was doing it right.

"Is she...?" He trailed off.

"Heat. I gave her drugs. Knight's taking care of her."

"I fucked up."

"You didn't know." She took touch-starved to another level. She needed one of us there at all times—I was anxious leaving her now, even knowing Knight wasn't going to let her go. But Zed was important, too.

There wasn't a piece of this family that we could neglect, and for the first time in my life, it was just me and Knight holding up the ship.

"I don't know how to do this," Zed said at last.

Hmmm.

Okay, I was in a little more trouble if he wanted to actually talk.

Still, he looked distracted, running fingers through his hair as he stared off into the beautiful gardens.

"You... never wavered," he said. "When I couldn't stop hating her, you never found a way to stop loving her."

No.

But we were just... different. When she rejected Zed and Knight—after they'd fallen in love with her so hard that she'd stolen the colour from every other inch of the world... Well, I think they had to hate her so they wouldn't hurt so much.

But for me, that would have been impossible.

She was my oasis. Rain clouds in unending drought. Not loving her just wasn't in my DNA. It was figuring out how to live without her... That had been the hard part.

"The night at the High Roller..." He asked. "You were the one who found her."

I cocked my head, considering where he was going with that.

"How much did you know?" he asked.

"I knew she was in trouble."

"You were watching her?"

"From the moment she left Ace. I just didn't know..." I frowned. I'd made a mistake. "I never wanted to take away the choice you gave her."

It was something Zed had offered that I couldn't have thought up, and I'd realised at the time, it was that choice that she needed most.

Only, it had blinded me to her pain.

Glade was my other half. Something burned so deep in my bones, sometimes it was as if I knew when she was near.

I think she did, too.

At first, when she'd escaped, I'd gone to her. Never showing myself, but waiting on a bench she would pass on her way home from the shops, or sit in the coffee shop beside her gym. I just needed to remind myself what it was like when I could breathe.

She was the static in the empty air, the silence before a roll of thunder, or the first, warm drop of an oncoming storm. And yet, that was also how I'd come to believe she didn't want us—even after Ace.

Because when I was near enough that I could take a breath, she'd run. Every time. As if she could feel me, too.

Now, I knew she *had* sensed me, but when she'd fled, it wasn't because she'd hated me at all. She was protecting me. She'd been on the run, always terrified that we'd pay the price if she turned to us.

It all made sense. Her aversion to us, her fear of getting close.

I hadn't seen it.

Everything else, but not that.

"How much do you know about my brother?" Zed asked, dragging me from my musings.

I met Zed's eyes, feeling something through the bond that I could relate to entirely.

"What do you want to know?"

"Anything you have." His jaw ticked as he looked back out across the neatly trimmed gardens. "I can't face her again. Not until I have something to give her."

39

How many times had I woken?

Sometimes, there was light filtering down from above—I'd lived a dream a thousand times. A bond I should never have had. But I knew when something was too good to be true.

But snow santal turned bitter, and Ace was there... I'd given up at last. I had tried to hand him everything, had begged him to take anything if it meant never seeing them in danger again.

Had I managed to?

Was Zed alive?

I hid from the surface, too afraid of what reality held.

I knew I would wake to his arms around my waist, teeth grazing my neck as he told me a truth I would never survive.

So I ran from it, trying not to wake, like I could push it off forever.

When I woke up next, I was crying.

I inhaled the cool pear grove, arms drawing me close as I tried to swim through the swamp of fatigue that still weighed me down.

I was in a bond. I could feel them there within a bundle of life tucked away in the back of my mind. How many times had I dreamed of this? Of what it would be like? Yet, I couldn't be... Everything around me was warm, uncomfortably so, but my mind was still so heavy, and I tumbled back into nothingness, afraid of the moment when the cool sweet scent of pear would turn to roses.

The next time I awoke, it was to a thunderstorm. To the cracks of lightning, the cool rain upon my skin. To a place safer than imagining.

I tried to dive back down, knowing this one, I couldn't bear to lose. Only, this time, I struggled to vanish. I could feel the slow breaths at my back, each rustle of his skin against mine like static electricity, promising safety.

I tried, and tried, and tried, but sleep didn't find me again, and the lightning storm never left, no matter how many seconds passed.

"Glade?"

That was Kyan's voice, a distant echo as I squeezed my eyes shut, panic gripping me, tightening my chest.

It wasn't possible.

A lightning storm rose in the air, worried and smothering as his purr stuttered out.

"I can't..." My words fractured. He was still there. Still holding me, peace in clouds, and rain, and rolling thunder. Was it... real?

His purr vibrated at my back. Ace would never purr for me like that.

I swallowed.

If this was real, then so was the bond. A whine of terror slipped out, and warm arms drew me closer. But this couldn't be happening. I couldn't undo this. When Ace caught up... I *couldn't* be theirs. He would never let it go.

How was I in this bond?

I had to have accepted it, hadn't I?

Yet... I thought I had.

I shivered, examining the connection open between me and these Alphas. I... I had accepted it in a moment of weakness.

"No..."

"Oasis..." Kyan's voice was a sweet whisper, and he drew me closer. "You're safe."

"I... I'm not." The words were thick with tears. I was shivering, both with shock and something else. My skin was hot. I reached up by instinct, placing my hand on his chest. It was bare, ridges of muscles beneath my touch.

I was so confused. Guilty, of both doing this to them, and...

"It's okay, Glade." His hands closed around my waist, and he shifted us, propping us up and drawing me onto his lap. I kept my eyes squeezed shut, pressing myself against him, feeling a rush of relief at every inch of my skin against his.

My loose hair brushed the side of my hand, and I felt a prickle of pain.

"Zed...?" I asked. I realised my voice was raw—much too raw, like I'd been screaming.

"He's alive," Kyan whispered into my temple. "You saved him."

My breath caught, a flood of relief surging through me, and I finally found the strength to open my eyes and look up into his.

Beautiful gems of jade.

Not ice-blue with a sweep of black hair.

And his scent that drowned out everything else in the whole world.

This was real.

All of it was.

"You almost went into heat," he murmured, palms gentle beneath my loose top, gently pressing against my waist. His every movement soothed me, making it easier to breathe. "I gave you suppressants to delay it. Not forever, but just for a bit."

I tried to keep up, but thinking still felt like swimming through mud.

Heat...?

That explained the discomfort. But it wasn't that bad right now, not with his skin against mine.

"This was a mistake." My voice cracked. "You're all in danger—"

"Shh..." Kyan drew my chin up, cutting off my argument as he pressed his lips to mine, catching me off guard before I could finish. A whimper rose in my chest, and my hands were desperate, clutching his cheeks despite the ache of my wounds. I drew him closer, every instinct demanding more, and the irate heat that was lurking faded at last.

When I found my strength enough to break it, breathing heavily as I looked between his eyes, he quirked a smile, tucking my hair behind my ear.

"Never ever apologise for being ours, Oasis."

"But—"

I cut off as he flipped us so I was on my back. He pressed his teeth to my neck as he buried me in a sea of soft pillows and blankets. Another sound vibrated through my body, but I didn't know if it was afraid or relieved.

He was here...

Ace had spent years conditioning me to be afraid, but my instincts... *they* told me this was right. He was... perfect. The east to my west, an unwavering absolute that fear could not unseat.

I let out a moan as his hands explored my body, goosebumps rippling along my skin, slick pooling between my thighs in seconds.

"Never apologise," he growled again, drawing back, eyes as bright as they were firm. "Keep trying and I'll have you shaking beneath me, begging me to stop, and I might just push you into that heat after all."

I caught my argument this time, unwilling to call his bluff—not that any of that sounded bad, but I... I didn't deserve that. Not right now. He didn't understand the weight of what I'd done to them—the endless depravity of the monster that now sought them. He drew back, head cocked, but I reached after him, shock echoing through my body as his contact vanished.

I was really broken.

He frowned, bundling me back up in his arms in a moment and drawing me against him, hands cupping my face tenderly as he ran his lips gently along my jaw and neck. "Let me take care of you," he breathed. "You're burning up. The meds can only do so much. If they're going to work, you need to relieve a little of this tension."

I opened my mouth to argue, but then his teeth caught my nipple and it was like a bolt of electricity through my nerves. I shifted, knowing my perfume was thick in the air.

"Good girl," he breathed, one hand firm in my hair, keeping me in place as he teased my nipple again, his other hand slipping beneath my panties. I was in an oversized T-shirt that smelled like all of them. He'd changed my clothes—or one of them had.

"I can't..." I tried to argue, but I couldn't fight him, low whines breaking free with each breath as he dipped two fingers into me, keeping pressure on my clit with his palm as he tugged at my nipple again.

"Since you're so argumentative, let me tell you how this is going to go." He leaned back so he could meet my dazed eyes as his fingers worked me.

It was almost embarrassing how quickly I melted beneath his touch, fingers biting into his bicep while I panted. "Knight, Zed, and me. We're yours. No arguments. No returns. You're our Omega. That means you're our queen."

It was almost cruel how soothing his words were, with his fingers curling right against my centre, working me with such ease as I stared into those glittering jade eyes. A cool, relieving orgasm rushed in so fast it was dizzying.

"That's right, Oasis," he breathed as I arched and he curled his fingers into me just right, letting me ride out the orgasm to its very end.

For a long, long moment I was still, breathless and speechless, unable to tear my gaze away as I let the surge of hormones pass. He was purring again, cupping my cheeks once more, as he watched me like he was looking for an argument.

"Is that clear?" he asked.

I could only stare at him.

"If it's not, I can send you off that cliff over and over until you understand."

"I..." I swallowed, voice caught in my throat. "I..."

Why couldn't I say it?

Kyan didn't pause, lowering himself between my thighs before I could protest, fingers slipping into me again, and I let out a gasp as his tongue found my clit, his tongue ring wiping my mind blank.

I let out a low moan, scrambling to remember what he'd asked. "I... I understand."

He drew back for a moment, jade eyes flashing. "Say it."

"I'm..." I gritted my teeth, stars bursting to life in my vision as his tongue ring brushed my clit again. "I'm yours."

"No, Baby, that's not what I said." He nipped the soft part of my inner thigh and I let out a squeak, but he'd already dragged his tongue up my centre again, fingers curling deep into my core.

I couldn't think straight, my mind already racing toward the edge of another climax. I whined as he sped up, slick pooling around his fingers as my body trembled with pleasure. Everything he'd asked of me, gone.

I cried out when I came, shaking violently as he dragged the climax out again until I was shuddering with bliss.

Then he was caging me in, fingers holding my chin as he forced me to look at him. "You're not ours," he growled, nipping my lip. "We're yours."

I stared at him, chest heaving in relief, the slightly too intense heat of my stomach dissipating already.

"I love you so much," he breathed, dragging me into his arms. "Until you feel better, you are never going to be alone."

Alone...?

I'd almost... been.

Forever.

Without him.

And now, I was in this grand bedroom, with sunlight filtering in, surrounded by cream wallpaper and a glittering chandelier of light above.

It didn't feel real.

"Glade, look at me," Kyan murmured, sitting down beside me. I blinked up at him. I would never get tired of those beautiful jade eyes. "He will never touch you again."

That promise was like a precious little flare, dancing to life, yet still, I couldn't go near its warmth.

"You don't..." My voice was choked. "You don't understand."

"I understand more than you know," he replied. My eyes snagged on his. "You think another Alpha could claim my mate, and I wouldn't watch his every move?"

I froze. "I don't understand."

"I've been with you, always," Kyan breathed. "My only mistake was thinking..." He frowned. "I thought you'd chosen to move on... I remember why you fell for us."

I shut my eyes, another tear leaking down my cheek.

A choice.

That's what Zed had offered, the thing I'd found irresistible. And it was, in the end, the thing that had kept him away.

Kyan didn't want to take that from me again.

"You never came looking for us," he said. "So I thought…" His gaze darted to the side, but I felt the bundle of nerves from him in this new connection.

He'd thought I didn't want him.

"I never wanted to hurt you," I said. "You couldn't be involved in this. If you've been watching, you know what he's like—"

"I wouldn't make this promise if I couldn't keep it," Kyan cut me off, drawing me closer. "He will never find you in your sleep, or take you from us; he will never touch you again."

I stared at him, trying to reject that promise, trying to keep it at bay before I tumbled headfirst into a feeling I couldn't afford.

"You aren't alone anymore." I felt his end of the bond open, and my heart clenched, chin quivering. "And you will never be alone again." He took a breath, drawing me closer, a low purr rumbling in his chest.

I broke, years and years of terror splintering me open as tears flooded my cheeks, soaking his shoulder.

"Take a chance on me, my Sweet Oasis. I will never let you fall."

40

By the time my tears cleared, Knight had appeared in the room with a tray of snacks and a thermos of what smelled like tea. He didn't say anything as he poured me a cup, but his eyes were more wary than I'd seen before.

"How long have I been out?" I asked, hugging the mug close to my chest.

"Three days," Kyan said.

I nodded, processing that. Three days since I'd been poisoned —since I'd almost died, and Zed had bonded me to save my life.

That, somehow, made everything better. As if, even three days away from Ace made it somehow possible I was… safe from him.

They knew everything, I realised.

Had they seen my scars? Of course they had. I'd been in that dress when Zed had come. The panic of knowing that might have consumed me, if I hadn't run headfirst into another question. "How did we get out?"

Ace had set it up. I couldn't imagine how Zed would have

found a way to safety. But Kyan had said he was, and I felt him in the bond. Alive, even if I didn't know where he was.

I glanced up at Kyan's silence. "What happened?"

"Ace let you go," he said quietly.

He glanced at my arm where his palm brushed as goosebumps rippled along my skin, enough that he noticed.

He'd... let Zed go? With me?

I shook my head. "There's a trick, Kyan, it can't be—"

"He said he was coming for us, but it's not going to happen." He was so firm as he brushed my cheek. "You're safe. We won't underestimate him again. Not ever."

I swallowed, trying to find a way to trust that as I took another sip of the tea, the taste of it settling me. English breakfast tea was one of Knight's comfort drinks. I'd forgotten that.

"Where are we now?" I asked, looking around.

It was impossible to miss how luxurious the room was—the complete opposite of the warehouse. The pack-sized four-poster bed had intricate carvings along the wood. The thick, velvet curtains hanging floor to ceiling were a royal red, and peeking past them was what looked like a grand window with gold gilding.

Despite all of that, I felt an ache in my chest that we were here, instead of back in the huge warehouse. Would we ever go back there? I was shocked, as the despair rose at the thought that the answer might be no.

"Your High Roller friends showed up," Knight said.

I looked at him sharply, completely taken aback by that.

"Annika. One of her Alphas set us up. Completely off the radar from anyone, Brotherhood or otherwise."

"Annika?" I asked. I wasn't the only Omega at the High Roller who kept to myself, but there was a sisterhood there, even if it was beneath the surface. She was fun and full of fire when she came out of her shell. We occasionally did a night on the town, and she had an Alpha bodyguard who I was pretty sure thought we never noticed when he stalked from the shadows.

Drunk Omegas *always* noticed.

And anyway, when had she got herself Alphas?

"Wait..." Panic gripped me all of a sudden. "Lucy—?"

"She's okay," Kyan cut me off. "Annika is out of town, but I managed to find someone to get her out. Guy I've crossed a few times—could rely on him to get her out safely—oh! I have pictures. Way too many."

He spent the next ten minutes showing me endless pictures and videos of Lucy, all of which made my breathing easier, until I realised what she was playing with. "Wait—is that a gun?"

Kyan scoffed. "She's with a Russian fixer, not a kitty-boarding school."

"Why is my cat with a Russian fixer?"

"She was a Brotherhood target," Kyan said defensively. "What the hell was I supposed to do?"

While Kyan distracted me with more pictures, I found myself drifting a little closer to Knight, who was still pretty quiet. I wanted him close, too, needing his skin on mine. Finally, as I was watching the fifth video of Lucy jumping for a set of keys, I dared reach out and catch his hand in mine.

I didn't look at him, pulse racing out of control, suddenly acutely aware my hormones were so fucked that if he pulled away, I might burst into tears.

Thankfully, he didn't.

Instead, he moved closer and I felt the comforting brush of his locs along my arm. I inhaled the fresh scent of pear grove, along with the trace of rose water I remembered he used in his hair.

"She's too fast for her size," Knight noted as Lucy scrambled after a tossed bottle cap, and visibly struggled to take a sharp left.

"Doesn't stop her," I replied, feeling an unexpected lightness in my chest.

Knight was still stiff, but I didn't think… Well, he didn't seem to *not* want me.

"Where is Zed?" I asked.

"Out," Kyan replied. "But he'll be back soon enough."

I nodded. It felt wrong, not having him here, but I did, at least, catch his scent of snow santal in the room. He *had* been here.

"Will you let me help you get cleaned up?" Knight asked, squeezing my hand. "I want…" He cleared his throat, and when I looked up at him, he didn't meet my eyes. "I think it would be best for you… the hormones, I mean, if his scent was gone."

I tensed at those words, hugging my tea closer, but nodded.

The faintest trace of Ace still lingered, not nearly as much as the other scents in this room, but my nerves were frayed by even the smallest hint of him.

Knight got up, vanishing into the bathroom, where I heard the taps of a bath turn on, and then he was back, offering a hand to me.

Gingerly, I took it, clutching him tight, easily tumbling into a strange comfort as he picked me up like I was a doll, letting me wrap my arms around his neck as he carried me into a grand bathroom. It was the size of my old room at the High Roller, with a massive tub. It reminded me of my father's manor; a place where I'd never wanted for anything. Or at least, that's what I'd been told, until I'd met the Maverick pack, and I realised how much I'd been missing.

A little piece of paradise amidst endless bleakness, making everything else less vibrant for it.

41

KNIGHT

Glade waited quietly in my arms as the bath ran, and I found myself lost. She'd just been smiling, watching a video of Lucy, and my brain couldn't manage it.

She'd almost died, and now she was smiling?

Her fingers wove gently through my locs, and the feeling of it elicited an unexpected purr from my chest. She picked through a few at the front until she found her favourite one—a set of two that had combined.

"They're so long now," she said. "I'm glad you still have them."

She'd always loved them. There were moments in the last few years when I'd considered getting rid of them. But they carried pieces of my life—memories that sometimes I wanted to rid myself of.

I never could do it.

There were so many pieces of that story that made me who I was; the Brotherhood, the grief of being betrayed by everyone I'd known. The grief of losing her, and then the aching weight in my heart when I'd almost lost Kyan, too. But, I'd held onto all of it, afraid of keeping it, but far more afraid of the person I'd be without it all, because it wasn't possible to cut away the bad without shutting my eyes to the pieces I'd found.

A family. Unexpectedly. Against all odds.

One that never had and never would turn its back on me.

And now, she could be a part of that, too.

In hindsight, our lives were littered with evidence that we'd never let her go, no matter what we'd told ourselves. Maybe that was what had pushed Zed to go to the High Roller that night.

We'd all known we weren't over her.

I reached down to the tub, which was more than full enough, and turned the taps off.

We'd drowned her in our scents, and still, traces of Ace remained. He'd scent-marked her. He must have, for the persistence of redwood and rose that still lingered.

I didn't want him anywhere near her.

Never again.

Her skin lost a little colour as she glanced down to the bath and back to me. "You're not going to leave, right?" she asked.

"If you want Kyan to help you, that's fine." She still wasn't well enough for one of us not to be there. She frowned, glancing between us, and I felt her little flutter of insecurity.

There was a pause as I tried to work that out, but through the bond, I could feel her nerves spiking.

Oh, shit.

She seemed on the verge of tears. "I can wait for him to be done," she said. "If you'd rather not—"

"No." I cleared my throat. Looking back up at her, I realised what was making her uncomfortable. "I want to help you, Princess. I just wasn't sure if you wanted me."

"I do," she whispered.

I was being stupid.

Her want for us had transcended consciousness, a want so fierce and deep that even on the brink of death, she'd accepted the offer of a bond. A bond that had saved her.

No, the question wasn't if she wanted us; it was if we could ever be worthy of a love that fierce.

Kyan was right about how wounded she was. Until this sickness had passed, we wouldn't let go of her. Not for a second.

"Do you want me to help you take this off, or can you manage it?"

Her eyes darted between mine, and for a moment, she was slipping away, dark cardamom turning unnaturally sharp.

"Glade," I breathed, needing to ground her. What was surfacing was feral and dangerous.

She took a breath, nails digging into my skin. "You... saw them?"

Her scars.

I knew, without having to ask. The ones that sent spikes of ice through my veins when I saw them, vile hatred grinding down the edges of my sanity to the feral Alpha below.

"They're yours, Glade," I said, drawing her up to look at me, not letting her miss a second of this. "You tell me what you need. If you want to talk about them, or not, I'm here. If you don't want us to, we'll never bring them up again, but I never want you thinking you have to be ashamed of them."

It took a while before she nodded.

I dropped my hand, checking the water, and when I straightened, she was tugging at the hem of her shirt.

I helped her out of it, not taking my hand from her waist the whole time, trying to keep my gaze from drifting where it certainly didn't deserve to drift right now.

She had been out for three days. Long enough that the bandages had come off the wounds along her hands and wrists. But the scabs were angry.

They'd leave her with more scars for life.

Scars she'd given herself to save Zed.

I steadied her as she stepped into the huge tub with jets rippling bubbles about, the water breaking over each perfect curve as she sank in. She'd turned toward me, and I wondered if it was for fear of revealing the scars again.

"Knight?" she asked, peering up at me.

"Yeah…" There was very little left in my brain as I stared down at her, though my instincts fired off in panic as I saw her dark brows bunch. A quiver returned to her lip, the hand still clutching my wrist becoming demanding.

She didn't need to ask; I just… I hadn't because… Actually, the reasons were foggy as I tugged my shirt and pants off, unsure about the boxers. But she all but growled at me when I tried to get in without removing them.

"I'm yours, Princess," I said, and her breathing settled as I sank into the water at her side. It was designed more like a hot tub than a bath, with jets and seats along the edges.

I had to remind myself how much she needed our touch to heal the wounds the suppressant had left behind.

That wasn't fair.

"We move at your pace, Glade. I'll be whatever you need."

"R-Really?" She blinked at me as if I'd just dropped a bomb on her. A frown creased her brow, and her cream cardamom scent was made of silk, wrapping me tight. In it was an edge of need and claim like I'd never felt before.

By the way she was chewing on her lip, eyes narrowed, I suddenly realised… Oh… Damn. With the hormones still raging, I think she'd taken my words in the opposite direction than I'd meant them…

Uh… she definitely had. She drew herself over me, droplets tumbling down glistening skin. My eyes were drawn down her neck to where her breasts were still free of the water as she stared down at me, knees on either side of my lap. Her dark hair made up two curtains, creating our own little world as I forced my gaze back up into her eyes. Her pupils were dilated, chest heaving, only she looked unsure, like instinct had guided her here, but now she'd stopped to think.

"Are you sure?" I asked.

She let out a little hiss, nails digging into my flesh. "Kyan said you're... mine..." She frowned, as if unsure whether it was a question or a statement, palm lifting from my chest and cupping my throat instead.

A growl of approval rumbled to life in my chest and the anxiety drained away a bit. "Of course I'm yours."

That wasn't a question.

For a moment, she was suspended between two halves of all she was. One, fragile and wounded, trying to hold herself together from years of darkness. The other, the queen who'd protected us, giving up everything to keep us safe—the Alphas she'd claimed, even when we hadn't known it.

She was the strongest person I'd ever met. Stubborn, resilient, fierce. And she'd shattered for us. The scars on her back were a testament to that. I knew what they meant. I wasn't foolish enough to find a claim within those marks—not one for which I could take credit.

Glade had fought through all of those heats to keep what was hers. We were hers because she'd chosen us, and it was that choice she'd never let him have. Not even in the face of agony.

It was why every touch of my skin against hers made me ache to draw her closer. It was why she was sick.

Plus, I was a little nervous to deny the latter half; a distant storm clouding the back of her eyes and reminding me that she was wounded, not weak—and Glade was pretty damned dangerous when fucked with.

"I'm yours forever, Princess," I said, leaning down and grazing my teeth along her forearm, where she still gripped my neck in a way that sent an unnatural amount of blood to my cock. That storm dissipated, her scent smoothing out as her lip caught in her teeth and she pressed me back with one hand. The other reached down, curling into a fist around my base.

Well. *Shit.*

She sank down over my length, a little whine rising in her chest that was so hot it made my blood turn to lava.

I groaned. She was so tight, even as she lifted that perfect body back up, right to the tip. My heart was pounding in my chest, and I couldn't move, desperate for her to claim me however she needed.

She slid closer, knees bumping against the tub wall as she sank back down, both arms now draping around my neck as she took me all the way to the knot, a dazed look in her eyes.

I growled, fingertips brushing her hips.

She let out another whine, squeezing me so tight I almost came then. She arched against me, round breasts glistening with water as she settled right over my knot, a look of bliss in her eyes.

"That's my girl," I breathed, returning my arms around her.

She was calm, at last, amidst the silence, and it was a long time before I spoke, knowing what I needed to say. Knowing it wasn't enough.

"I'm…" This didn't feel right. The word wasn't enough. "I'm so sorry we were never there." I was shaking, having gone through these words over and over in my mind, trying and failing to find a combination that was right. That she deserved. "Not one of us ever stopped loving you. We haven't been able to, no matter how much we…" I swallowed, not wanting to say it. To risk hurting her more.

"I know you hated me," she whispered. "I needed you to."

"I'll still never forgive myself for it."

A smile wobbled on her lips. "That would be really mopey of you."

I snorted, dragging her closer, arms winding around her waist as she sank against my chest. "I'm so sorry, Glade."

It felt hollow beside what she'd given us—beside what she *kept* giving.

The worst part was that I didn't know if we would have survived. If Ace had truly figured out what Kyan had done to Joshua Maverick, Zed's father, if he'd had proof, we would have been corpses that night. But she'd found the one path to save us, and taken it. Even though it had cost her everything.

"I forgive you," she whispered. "I did a long time ago."

I shut my eyes, chest aching. She should never have had to.

"Where's Zed?" she asked.

I frowned. I knew she had already asked that of Kyan. "He's... taking some space."

The fact was, I didn't know where he was, and Kyan wouldn't tell me—which meant he was likely doing something stupid.

"Does he not...?" I saw a flash of worry in her eyes.

I frowned, trying to work that out.

"Does he not what?"

She shrank, eyes darting around. Her pupils were still dilated, hormones clearly still raging in her system. "He's... he's my pack leader now. And I just..."

Her brows creased in the most heartbreaking frown. Her next words were as quiet as a wisp. "I haven't felt him in the bond... I thought he would have wanted to see me by now."

"No—Princess." I drew her chin up to look at me, shaking my head. "He wants you. He's just... So much happened. He's processing."

That didn't seem to settle her. "O-Okay."

"He was in here—he wouldn't leave your side."

A little relief flashed in her eyes as she processed that. "Then... why isn't he here now?"

She didn't remember. Hormones or drugs, or both, I wasn't sure, but I was glad she didn't. The image of her pleading with him, unable to let him go, screaming when I'd pulled her away, trying to give herself up over and over, it would never leave my mind.

"It's not because he doesn't want you—I promise. He wants you so much, but it's killing him, learning what you went through for us. It's worse for him. It's his pack, his brother—just give him time. And he was the one—" My breath caught. I could still feel the echo of Zed's grief like a twisting dagger in the heart. We'd all felt it, but he... he had seen it. "Me and Kyan will be here until then. We won't leave your side."

Slowly, she nodded, curling back up against my chest, and I drew her into a bear hug, my purr strong enough that it made the faintest little quakes upon the surface of the water. She was fragile right now, and there was only so much my words could do. She needed to see it from him herself.

"He'll be back, Glade, I promise."

42

"It's been too long. She's stressing. Where is he?" I demanded.

It had been four days since we'd escaped Ace, and over a day since she'd woken, yet Zed wasn't back. Glade was improving, albeit slowly.

This morning she'd woken up and slipped downstairs to get herself a glass of orange juice without either of us. We didn't want to leave her for extended periods, but it was early evening, and she'd dozed off to a movie in the bedroom. I felt safe enough dragging Kyan out to ask him what the fuck was going on with our pack leader.

I wouldn't do it in front of her since she didn't need to stress out more. She was on suppressants around the clock, had physical wounds that were still healing, and the lingering after-effects of how touch-starved she'd been—whatever they were—made her hormones erratic as fuck.

She didn't need to worry about Zed on top of that.

"He's working things out."

"I'm all for that, but she needs him, too."

"He... told me not to tell."

"Are you fucking joking?" I asked. "Our Omega nearly died. We don't have room to hide shit!" My fist closed around his throat as I pinned Kyan to the wall. "You're going to tell me."

"He'll be back soon—"

"Kyan." There was a snarl in my voice, primal instincts rising as they so often did with him. "Tell me what the fuck you know."

"Or what?" There was a challenge in his voice, one that always baited my Alpha. My instinct rose, a sneer curving my lips. But then, with a jolt of shock, it all tumbled off the edge of a cliff and I released him.

Insecurity gripped me.

Were things the same now?

What was between Glade and Kyan was special.

I wasn't sure.

Kyan's eyes flashed, darting between mine, and by the look on his face I might as well have struck him. With a snarl, he took advantage of my hesitation, twisting in my grip.

Pain split my chin as his elbow caught it, and I staggered back, tasting the tang of iron. He was on me in a second, his weight enough to send us crashing to the floor.

Shit.

He was pissed—a storm of fury in the bond. Fury that masked something else.

That was... good. I thought.

It *felt* good.

I shoved him off hard enough that he went sprawling to the side. He was pushing himself up by his palms, blood dripping from a cut lip, when I launched at him, getting my knee on his back to use my weight to keep him down.

"Fuck you!" he spat, using his full body to shove back up against me. There was something desperate in those words, and he off-balanced me enough to slip free. He moved faster than I could react, his knee smashing up into my side. I let out a hiss of pain as he staggered to his feet, fist closing in his hair before he could turn.

He grunted with the force of it as I rammed him against the wall.

I felt the fury falter through the bond, revealing what was beneath. He was panicked.

Damn.

I was still catching my breath, hip and chin aching from his blows.

The foundation of our relationship had never been words, and maybe that was fucked up, but that was all he could manage.

It wasn't like with Glade. He felt safe with her. He was the protector, playing the role he'd always been taught to.

That was the opposite of what we had.

Glade... She was his missing piece, but I realised she wasn't going to offer him more sanity—and he could push that sanity until he tumbled off into the abyss. I was the pull back, and the only one who ever had been that for him.

Kyan had been raised a monster, taught to fight and kill without blinking. What he'd never learned was how to ask for help. Anything his father considered weakness was burned away, pieces of him left to rot.

"You're going to get on your knees, Rat," I snarled. "And hope you can finish me before I choke you out."

I felt his flood of relief, my own nerves settling.

"Fucking make me." He flashed a wild grin, head turned so his cheek was crushed to the wall, a growl on his lips, but he tried to throw me off. Then I caught the faintest trace of dark cardamom, a sharp spike of lust in it even as it faded.

I didn't turn, a faint smile tugging at my lips as I leaned close. I tugged out the switchblade that hadn't left my pocket since we arrived. I flipped it open and pressed it to his neck, speaking only for him. "You're going to get on your knees and show our Omega how well you take me."

He froze, chest heaving against me.

I shifted back, loosening my grip on his wrist without moving the knife. My fist was still in his hair, knife lingering on the upper right side of his neck. I tilted it enough that he'd feel the pressure.

He reached up, fingers deftly undoing my belt.

It was hard not to turn my head. She must be watching through the crack in the door from the bedroom. How fucking bad did I want to see those blown pupils of hers watching as I claimed him.

I wasn't going to be nice about it, either.

Flipping the switch back, I tucked it into my pocket. I squeezed my swelling knot, pressing it between his lips without waiting for him to react to the missing weapon. He barely had a second to adjust before I'd driven my tip to the back of his tight throat.

Fuck.

The feeling of that tongue ring against my length was a sin. He was so hot, wild eyes fixed on mine as his fist balled in my jeans, his body seizing over my length as I choked him. I tilted his head so I had an even better angle, placed my forearm against the wall for balance, and fucked his bratty throat without mercy.

By the time I pulled back, his eyes were desperate.

I let him catch his breath for half a second before going again, knowing it would almost be worse for that. Again, I caught the edge of dark cream cardamom, a sharp edge of lust in the soft spice. I had to draw out again so I wouldn't finish. Kyan's pupils were blown, his eyes fixed on me, but I knew he could scent her too.

"Are you going to tell me where he went?"

He caught his lip in his teeth, but didn't answer.

I hadn't thought so.

This time I drove my shaft deeper, forcing him into just the right angle, so I could claim more of his throat. I held him there, feeling him shake, gritting my teeth at how good he felt. Finally, he seized, giving me the reward I was looking for. The low whine was desperate, something purely primal.

From the very first time I'd claimed him, that had been the sound that lit my veins. I'd felt him cave beneath me, an Alpha at my feet, pleading for air while I took my pleasure.

Another beat passed before I drew back, letting him gasp again, another whine slipping out.

"That's better, Rat. I love it when you choke on me."

I drove back in, and it didn't take long as I pinned him to the wall and drove into him at a brutal pace. The cardamom spiked again, and it took everything in me not to look over this time. She was wet for us, the scent of her slick filling the air.

I groaned as I finished, holding my knot right to Kyan's lips as I forced him to swallow every drop of me while our Omega watched.

43

Fuck me.

I hurried from the door, realising probably far too late that my perfume had gone off like a bomb.

Knight was stepping through it before I could figure out what to do with myself, and I could do nothing but stare up at him stupidly as he rounded on me.

"Princess." His voice was a low rumble.

My breath was sharp, and I was completely entranced by how dilated his pupils were. I don't know when he'd manoeuvred us, but my back suddenly touched the wall, and I was acutely aware of how... *everywhere* he was. He might be the chillest of the Maverick pack, but his Alpha instincts flipped on a dime, and right now, I wasn't sure if there was anything but hindbrain active behind those eyes.

"What are you doing, Princess?" he asked.

"I was watering—getting water for Lucy—for me. Coffee." Shit. It was the evening. "I'm..." I trailed off, unable to stop my eyes from dropping to the bulge in his pants. Already...? I mean...

There was a smoking hot arrogant smile on his face as he watched me fumble for words that didn't make sense. "Were you watching?" he asked, leaning close.

"No... Yes. Not on purpose."

So on purpose. Why was I even denying it? Would he be upset if I was?

Neither seemed to care that Zed and I had watched the first time... Oh... bad choice, remembering the way he'd pinned Kyan to the table.

I had to squeeze my thighs together.

The cool breeze of a lightning storm washed into the room, and I glanced over to see Kyan leaning against the doorframe, arms folded as he watched us with a mischievous look on his face.

The two remaining functioning brain cells officially crapped out as Knight took my chin between his thumb and forefinger, tilting my gaze back to him. "Lie to me, Princess, and I'll have to punish you."

I opened my mouth to tell him I had lied, then shut it.

No.

That would be the truth.

I narrowed my eyes. This was a really mean trick and I couldn't figure it out, so instead, I did the one thing that was always guaranteed to get me what I wanted.

I tugged my chin free and ducked beneath his arm, making a dash for it.

Knight's growl sounded behind me and a thrill lit my veins as he dived after me. A squeak of shock was squeezed from my lungs as he caught me in a full-body hug, lifting me with ease before crossing to the bed and tossing me down.

I barely had time to scramble away before Knight had me by the hair, fist closing in it and winding it tight. The ease with which Knight could manhandle me was obscenely hot. Before I knew it, he'd tugged my underwear down and cupped my heat, bowing over me.

"Did you lie to me, Princess?" He growled in my ear, fist still pinning me to the bed by my hair.

"No," I whined, wriggling against him desperately, and I knew he could feel how wet I was.

"Kyan's going to come over here and do what he's told, or you'll take the punishment for the both of you."

Kyan didn't need a threat. He dropped onto the bed and might as well have been rolling up non-existent sleeves for how ready he was. Knight released my hair, cupping my neck instead and dragging me up against his chest.

"You think you can take him like he took me?"

I whined, breathing coming sharp as Kyan got to his knees. Between Knight's locs that draped around us, I could see him freeing his cock.

Knight had always had a dominant streak and a filthy mouth, but there was something even more hot about it now I knew he'd made Kyan buckle for it, too.

Fuck, I was so turned on.

Knight shifted back and Kyan gripped my hair instead.

Knight dragged his teeth along my neck from behind, hand dropping between my thighs and pressing down on my clit.

"Brats put their tongue out when they're offered cock," Knight growled. "Or they'll watch their Alphas finish without them."

I slid my tongue out instantly as Kyan arched my neck. I met his eyes. He looked so hot, the tip of his tongue caught between his teeth as he watched Knight order me around.

"Good girl." Knight drew back, though he still caged my hips in as Kyan drove his length down my throat.

Kyan was as ruthless as I'd hoped he would be, and when he gave me a second of leeway, I gasped for air.

He barely let me catch my breath, pressing back in, and forcing a whine from my chest.

"Should he go easy on you, Princess? Or do liars get choked?" His hand tightened around my neck, and I almost came right then, stars bursting in my vision as Kyan held my lips against his knot.

"You're so fucking wet for us."

I tried to arch my back, presenting for him while Kyan fucked my throat ruthlessly, his grip on my hair tightening so he could thrust deeper.

"Do you deserve a knot, Princess?" Knight asked. Behind me, I felt him readjust, and then his fingers pressed against my entrance. "You want me?"

Kyan drew out enough to let me catch a breath. "Yes."

His fingers dipped in further and it felt so fucking good that I was shaking by the time Kyan returned to fucking my throat. I was helpless between them, and it was setting my nerves on fire. Knight began thrusting his fingers into me as I deep-throated Kyan, my eyes fixed on his. I moaned again as Knight sped up, and the sound was desperate.

But then Knight's touch was gone, and my whine sounded pathetic as Kyan dragged my lips all the way to his knot with a groan, and I felt him finish down my throat.

"Fuck, I missed how well you squeeze me," Kyan growled and didn't stop until I'd taken every last drop.

Catching my breath, I glanced over to see Knight had dropped onto the bed at the headboard, the topless image of sexy arrogance. "I want to see those perfect tits of yours when you crawl to me."

I didn't even fucking hesitate, my core still aching with need from the touch he'd withdrawn. I did what he asked, tugging my shirt off and crossing the distance between us.

"I want those sweet lips of yours to warm me up first," he

growled. "And present for Kyan; maybe if you're lucky, he'll fuck that needy cunt with his fingers while you get me ready."

My heart was racing as I adjusted myself, reaching for Knight's sweatpants and freeing his cock while I lifted my hips toward Kyan.

"You're beautiful, Oasis," I heard Kyan growl. Static leapt between us as he brushed my hips, grinding up against me.

I held Knight's eyes as I slid my tongue up his shaft, loving the low growl that rose in his chest, lips drawing in a snarl. I worked him slowly, never taking my eyes from him as Kyan gently pressed his finger into me from behind.

It wasn't enough.

Not even as I squeezed Knight's knot and slid his entire, massive length down my throat, holding his glittering midnight eyes the whole time.

"You want it filling up that tight cunt of yours?" Knight asked.

I drew back slowly, fighting more whines as Kyan added a second finger.

"Yes, Alpha," I said, when I slid his cock from my mouth, still squeezing his knot that was swelling so thick it was hard not to just jump him now.

"Face him," Knight said, a grin playing on his lips as he caught my gaze darting down to it. "He deserves to play with our sweet little fuck doll for taking me so well."

Kyan's jade eyes were dancing when I turned to him.

I adjusted myself over Knight, one palm on Kyan's chest, the other shifting his length so I could lower myself onto it. Knight held me still, though, hands on my hips, just the tip at my entrance. "Were you watching us?" he asked.

"Uh huh," I whined, fighting the grip he had on my hips that wasn't allowing me to sink over him any further. I was trembling with need.

"You perfumed—for the second time—watching me wreck Kyan?" Knight asked.

I could only nod, as Kyan squeezed my breasts and rolled my nipples between his fingers. I was practically seeing stars and Knight hadn't even entered me yet.

"And?" Knight asked.

"It was really... really hot." I whimpered as Kyan pinched both my nipples at the same time. "Please..." *Goddamn* it, I couldn't do this teasing anymore. "Fuck me like you fucked him."

I needed him. Slick was running down my thighs and over his length.

"She's asking so nicely," Kyan breathed, and I shuddered as his teeth caught my shoulder, one finger dipping to my clit again.

A snarl slipped out before I could catch it.

Kyan laughed, his hand closing around my throat. "Our perfect little brat."

My eyes rolled back as Knight dragged me down with a growl. Fuck.

I wasn't ready for what it felt like to be impaled by Knight—I didn't know if I ever *could* be.

"You're taking him so well," Kyan groaned. "So fucking beautiful."

Behind me, Knight, with a punishing grip on my hips, began driving into me ruthlessly.

I wasn't going to last, not as Kyan sped up on my clit. I felt so full with every one of Knight's thrusts, and it made my little Omega heart so fucking happy.

I let out a moan as I came apart between them, Kyan's tongue down my throat, his finger circling my clit as Knight drove all the way into me. I felt him climax an instant later as my body seized over him. I whined as I felt him fill me with his seed before stretching me out with his knot.

"I could watch you be a brat forever, Oasis," Kyan told me,

kissing me again as Knight adjusted us into a sitting position so I could be more comfortable while we were locked together.

It was so hard not to just be content, trapped between my Alphas. I wanted this to be forever. I shoved away the flutter of fear at that, desperate for the what-ifs of the future to fuck off.

Not now.

Not here.

This was mine—for a bit, at least.

Being surrounded by their scents made it so much easier, and, after Knight's knot had released me at last, I ended up curled beneath Kyan's arm amongst the pillows and blankets.

"How did... this—" I looked between them. "Start?" I asked curiously.

The Knight and Kyan relationship was new and somewhat unexpected.

Kyan's eyes flickered to Knight. Something cautious in them. Finally, he shrugged. "The night he... caught me on the roof."

Oh... My stomach twisted. "That must have been really... emotional."

Knight's bark of a laugh caught me off guard. "That's...a word," he said as he got to his feet and began collecting blankets and pillows from around the bed.

"A *word?*" What the fuck did that mean?

Was he going to put all the bedding around us? My heart got all warm at the thought of it. He was helping me nest?

"Don't worry, Oasis," Kyan growled, tugging me closer as Knight began tucking pillows around us. "Knight keeps all the romantic shit just for you. I'm not taking any of it."

I snorted.

It wasn't just how unexpectedly hot Kyan looked getting ruined, but it flipped every possessive Omega switch in my fucking body.

"I wasn't worried," I whispered, glancing up to Kyan. "I love that you love him." It's all I'd wanted. Every second I was gone from them.

They were my Alphas.

My pack.

My mates.

That was a need I'd learned was true, because I hadn't just wanted them to survive when I'd chosen Ace—I'd needed them to find happiness, even if I wasn't a part of it.

But Kyan had gone stiff at my words.

Knight, I realised, hadn't moved from where he was clutching a huge duvet in his arms, half turned from the two of us. Not since I'd spoken. There was something charged in the bond, a tension that hadn't been there before.

I glanced back to Kyan to see he was staring in Knight's direction.

I shrank. Unsure. He... did, though? This was what Kyan's love looked like—prickly and full of energy, like a cut live wire that was left to spark. Chaos in every direction, even if they looked like the wrong directions from the outside.

Kyan cleared his throat. "I... love everyone in my pack," he said at last.

For a second, as the words came from his mouth, I felt him shrink in the bond like he'd been burned. I felt a moment of sheer panic, complete insecurity, as if he was in freefall.

Very slowly, Knight draped the duvet over us, then sat down on my other side.

"But uh..." Kyan's voice was rough.

Fuck.

I'd definitely said something wrong. Knight had the faintest smile on his face as he settled in.

"Shut it, Street Rat, before you make it weird," he growled, tugging both me and Kyan into a huge bear hug, and I felt Kyan relax, a faint smile tugging on his lips, his anxiety dissipating.

44

Red and blue blinking lights flashed behind me.

Fuck...

Ah.

How fast had I been driving?

I found the closest place to pull over, my heart racing as I drew my car to a halt.

Without making any clear moves, I slipped the balaclava into the gap beside my seat and reached over, popping open the glove box to grab what I needed. I glanced at the bag on the passenger seat.

Nothing inside was visible.

I wore a toque, and my face had been washed. I shifted, catching a view of myself in the rearview mirror as I rolled the window down.

No blood.

Still, this could quickly turn into a complete fucking disaster, just when I was about to return to her with a gift.

We'd found a safe house, but we hadn't got a complete identity renewal. If my name got into the system... I couldn't afford any paper trail to where I was heading. Especially not less than twenty minutes from where Glade was.

The flashlight strobed across the back seat before blinding me.

"Licence and registration." The cop peered down at me, but I was already handing it to him.

"Do you know how fast you were going?" he asked, glancing over my paperwork.

I winced. "Too fast."

He looked from the paper to me, shifting the flashlight back to blinding. "What's the rush?"

"My... Omega. We almost broke up. I got her a gift. I wanted to get home and wasn't paying enough attention."

The cop's eyebrows rose as he considered me, and I sensed the tension diffuse just a little. "Scent match?"

"Yes, sir."

He glanced back down at the papers before flashing the light back into my passenger seat. "That the gift?"

I nodded, trying to keep my expression neutral.

"What's a good enough gift to make it up to a scent match?" he asked.

"Uh..." I glanced at the plastic bag, blood roaring in my ears. My trophies were in a box, which made the package look bulkier. That was good, because I'd be getting more than a ticket if he looked to see what was really in that bag. "Box of chocolates and pack tickets to a Swift concert." I almost winced at the stupidity of the lie.

"She's a Swiftie?" The cop chuckled. "Same as my daughter. Easy way to their heart—and those aren't easy to come by."

I shook my head.

"I'll let you off tonight, but take it slow on the way home."

I nodded. "Thank you, sir."

He handed me back the paperwork and took a step back. Thank fuck.

My chest loosened, until he paused, glancing back at me. "Where did you get the tickets?"

"Dodgy marketplace meetup. Why I'm out so late."

He snorted, tucking his flashlight away. "Well. Load them into those apps they have before you give them to her. Never know if it's a dud."

I nodded and found a weak apology.

I'd never been more on edge as I drove (really fucking slowly) back to the safe house. Or mansion. Or whatever it was that the Forbes family had set up for us. I couldn't afford to get a speeding ticket. Ace had the kind of resources to track us down if my name popped up on any databases.

Until the flashing lights, I'd been nothing but raging Alpha hormones and thrill, but I needed to get a grip. There was too much on the line.

I arrived safely and clear of the law, grabbing the bag from the car and making my way to the kitchen. I thought that was the best place.

It was the middle of the night, and I hadn't given any real consideration to how I wanted to present what I'd brought. I tugged the bag open, pulling out the box within and staring at it.

Shit.

Now the initial thrill had passed and my hormones were settling, I was second-guessing everything.

What the *fuck* had I been thinking?

This was a terrible idea. She was traumatised. Did she really need this in her life right now? I'd been in a state, completely focused on vengeance, furious instincts guiding me. I hadn't considered how it might come across...

I opened the box, still warring with the dumbass whispers that this was the perfect gift. Blood had dried against the cardboard, turning a faded brown. The blood from the two disembodied appendages I'd brought her.

Two fingers, each from a different Alpha.

Yup.

This was nuts.

Kyan had given me all the information I needed—and fuck knows where he'd got it, but it had allowed me to descend into a full-blown Alpha *episode*. I'd spent the last few days making the whole plan and then executing it. I had become a monster my own father would have been proud of.

And now I wanted to give her *fingers*?

But the tattoos between the knuckles, those marked their value to her.

Evidence of what it meant...

Revenge.

I couldn't help myself, drawing them out and laying them on the counter as if they could offer me confidence in the decision that was quickly turning sour. As I picked up the first, I flashed back to the moment I'd claimed it.

The Alpha was limp, head lolling weakly in the chair he was bound to. His death would be silent. He wouldn't feel fear, even though he should.

That fear would give me away—would alert Ace to what I was doing before I could carry out my plans in full.

I'd been quick to find him, and found no thrill in execution now that he was out cold. I fixed the obscene, gilded crown to his head, knowing the drugs in his system would keep him knocked out until morning. By then, he would be dead.

I stepped back, examining my work, taking a picture with my burner phone. It was a risk in itself, but I needed to remember the image Ace would also see.

I had two hours.

Two hours before the toxins on the metal crown would have burned through his skin and my brother would know what I'd done.

In the kitchen, I reached for the second finger.

Kill number two.

More depraved, a fall far further into a past I'd spent so long running from. But if reclaiming it meant protecting her, I would do it without hesitation.

This Alpha was tied up, and awake, low whines sounding from his chest.

He struggled weakly against bindings that tied him to the chair, the gag at his mouth stopping him from speaking. I was seated on the bed beside him, propped against the headboard, arm resting on my knee as I waited.

His terror seeped into the room, the scent of mist and oak souring with every passing second.

His death was inevitable; it was just a matter of time.

I tapped on my phone.

Ten minutes.

"There's no way Ace chose a pack with Alphas he couldn't trust to be as twisted as he was."

I'd found evidence of that.

"You use your own product for a quick fuck when you're bored," I said. "Doesn't seem to matter to you that you have a scent match with my brother back in Vegas."

There was no lack of money to be found in trafficking. The places Ace had extended an arm, branching the Brotherhood, were into territory that even my father hadn't dared venture.

And this Alpha. He was the key piece of that puzzle.

Cities away from Vegas, he ran trafficking operations that were now making the Brotherhood millions more. Ace had packed up for political gain.

The other, the one with a crown on his head that was slowly killing him, was the kingpin in a drug trafficking ring with reach halfway to Brazil.

Money and control.

"Though, I hear you return to your scent match for heats," I murmured. "Thistle?" I asked. "That's her name, right?"

An Omega unfortunate enough to match Alphas like these.

The Alpha struggled again, eyes wide and terrified. I'd given him a sedative, too, but that was working slowly. Slowly enough that he would know *what was happening.*

My phone blared an alarm through the hotel room, making the Alpha jump violently.

"Time's up," I said.

He let out a pitiful whimper through his gag, but I ignored it. The poisoned crown would be doing its job. Ace's first pack mate was minutes from death.

I got to my feet, stepping before the vile Alpha, who was slowly losing feeling in his whole body.

That wasn't how he would die, though.

I turned the playing card in my fingers.

Gripping his hair, I dragged his neck back, ripping the gag from him and ignoring the desperate plea.

I was, in that moment, the son my father had raised. Not the Alpha so desperate to pave the way to something better.

I pressed the card into his mouth and raised my gun to his lips, using the tip to drive it deep into his throat. Ignoring his shudders and weak attempts to choke it out, I forced it deeper, shoving it down until, when I pulled the handle back, I could barely see the edge of the crushed card jammed down his throat.

I stepped back, watching as the Alpha seized, eyes bugging out of his head as he fought his bindings.

I cocked my head, watching the whole time, waiting until the Alpha's last shudder died down and he went still. Just in time for my second alarm. The one marking the death of the first. The poisoned crown now rested upon the head of a corpse. Ace might be hiding out of sight, but he didn't take nearly as much care of the Alphas he'd bonded. Within minutes of each other, he would feel those deaths. The complete destruction of his pack bonds.

It was agonising, or so I heard.

Agonising, and just the start.

Before I left, I took my knife to his middle finger just like I had with the first. Then held the power button on the Alpha's phone, watching it flicker to life, traceable once more.

As I stepped from the hotel room, I let a card slip from my hand.

A king of diamonds with a message scrawled across it for his people to find.

"You come for my pack, I'll come for yours."

Both fingers lay on the marble kitchen countertop.

Both with a slim rose tattooed between the knuckles. Proof of who they were. These days, most of the Brotherhood had a rose tattooed on their wrist, but these two, they were elites. Ace was the only one, I'd heard, who didn't have the tattoo. He was arrogant enough to believe himself the representation of the rose, all by himself. Too much about my brother was rumour, though. He kept himself hidden away and protected, far more paranoid than even our father had been.

I stared at the fingers, cycling through the kill once more, I realized how fucking crazy this was.

I should have bought her Taylor Swift tickets.

Instead, I was giving her... *fingers?*

She didn't want something like that—something that tied me so definitively to my brother. I reached for them, absolutely sure I needed to bury them in the backyard (and prayed that no one would ever go digging), then froze.

Her scent was here.

Was I imagining it?

I turned, staring around the kitchen, searching for her. My eyes locked in on movement, just the faintest sway of hair between the crack in the kitchen door, as if she were stepping back.

"Glade?"

There was a long moment, then the door creaked open and a pair of chestnut eyes were peering through. My throat went bone dry, and I took a quick step in front of the counter where my trophies—fingers—were on full display.

Shit.

She slipped in, closing the door behind her as if she was worried there might be people listening in. The moment she entered, it was like the whole world vanished.

I couldn't take my eyes off her. From the glimmer in her eyes, to the red of her lips, and the blush climbing up the rich brown of her cheeks as we stared at one another.

Alive.

Well enough to be up by herself.

I didn't know why I was shocked. Between travel, planning, and execution, my trip had been five days. It hadn't felt like it, and the burner phone meant no texts or calls. I'd locked the bond down, too, but now I cracked it open, realising I'd been keeping her out.

I was met by a fierce ball of anxiety.

"You came back?" she asked.

"Of course I did." How could I ever stay away from her?

She took another step toward me, eyes so nervous that my chest tightened.

I hadn't expected how hard it would be to stand before her—

to truly face her after knowing what she'd given.

Raised on the harsh indoctrination of toxic Alpha rhetoric, I'd never learned to face a queen. A woman so fierce she'd stolen my chance at saving my pack—a chance I would have wasted—only to sacrifice herself instead. My father never taught me what to do in the face of a woman like Glade, because he would have turned tail or cut her down for challenging his idea of power.

Or tried to crush her into a cage smaller than her reflection left him. Just like Ace had tried to do, only to learn she would survive scars before she bent the knee to any Alpha.

But I needed to become self-taught quickly since she was here, living, breathing, and waiting for me to speak. Living and breathing in a bond that tied me to her forever. I couldn't watch her suffer another day with anything less than she deserved.

While I scrambled to figure out what an Alpha she deserved would say, she found her words first. With a shaky breath, eyes darting to the ceiling like she was trying to stop herself from crying, "Kyan said you bit me because I was dying."

Shit...

I took two more steps before halting myself.

I had. It was a moment that would never leave me. But I thought... well, she'd entered the bond—accepted us—but *of course* she had when the alternative was death. "I didn't want it to happen like that." My voice was rough.

Another two hesitant steps, and she was almost within reach. This close, I could see the different shades of brown flecking her glassy chestnut eyes.

"Oh..." The word was so broken as it tumbled from her mouth. Her fingers twisted together, each breath a little shaky. "I... uh... I get that..."

My mind was racing, half of it sinking in guilt, at the bond I'd believed she'd taken out of necessity, not the choice I'd always wanted her to have. The other half was ringing alarm bells that something was wrong.

I frowned, my voice still dry.

"I mean…" She looked confused. "It wasn't fair to you, to make you decide like—"

"No." I cut her off, what she was saying finally clicking.

Shit.

"I want you," I growled, my own hairs standing on end as I closed the gap between us, reaching for her face. "I want you in this pack more than anything in the world."

She should have been here this whole time.

Her expression crumpled, and I had to steady her.

"You were gone when I woke. I thought maybe you were angry, or—"

"I was angry," I breathed. "Not at you."

At the whole fucking world for what had happened to her.

At myself.

My voice was broken as I sank to my knees. "I'm so sorry." In that moment, I forgot everything in the world but what felt right. She deserved this. A real apology from me. I took her hands in mine, the edges scabbed from wounds she'd given herself to save me. "For everything you went through because I wasn't enough."

This was my pack.

My scent match.

I shut my eyes, feeling a wave of grief crash in, held at bay by rage and vengeance, blood and death, as if it made a difference to the agony she'd already suffered.

Her scent calmed, as if, somehow, I might have done something right.

"You protected us when I couldn't," I breathed. "I hated you for it, and I'm so… so sorry."

With tears glistening in her eyes, she was so fucking beautiful as she stared down at me. Dark cardamom settled further as she took her time processing my words.

"I want you to forgive me when... when I've earned it." I couldn't take anything less from her. I didn't know how.

She nodded, still a little unsure, but opened her mouth as if about to speak when her eyes flickered up, drifting around the room for only a moment before stopping behind me.

She went still, a frown on her face, and the world rushed in.

Oh...

I staggered to my feet, but she was already crossing toward the counter.

"Hold up—" I darted in front of her, but she tried to duck under me, eyes wide. I grabbed her. "Just—!"

"Are those—?"

"No."

"They're fingers!" Her voice was weak.

Ah, shit.

I let her go, since it was too late anyway, and she reached the counter, gripping it. There was a long silence as I tried to come up with the right way to say it, but she spun on me, chestnut eyes bright.

"That's..." Her breathing was tight, shock taking over her expression. "Those are... Wait. The roses... His pack?"

I nodded stupidly.

"They're dead?"

"Yeah."

"*You* killed them?"

"That... is what happened."

Was she angry? Afraid? Shocked? I couldn't tell.

"How did you know where they were?"

"Kyan had some... guesses."

All of which were correct. I was going to have to talk to him about that. He knew far more than he was letting on.

"It was a stupid plan. I don't know what I was—" I cut off. I'd reached out to put them back in the box, but she caught my wrist, a little growl in her chest.

Oh. All right then.

She was staring at them with strange curiosity, and her eyes looked funny.

Was I... witnessing possessive-Omega-Glade?

Damn.

I needed to get my head on straight. Wounded she might be, but she'd been raised in the Romano Mafia. She'd probably seen fingers before. Worse, even.

She reached out for them, and I blocked her. "You... *cannot* take them to the nest." Why had I said that? It would be ridiculous. She couldn't possibly want—

"Why not?" Her voice was high-pitched, her gaze furious.

Oh *god*.

Anywhere but the nest.

Why would she want that?

You were the fucking idiot who decided they were good trophy gifts from her new pack lead.

And she was an Omega.

A *mafia* Omega.

But Knight would string me up if I let her—and add my pinkies to the display.

I cleared my throat. "We have a no-dismembered-appendages in the nest rule."

"No, you don't." There was a definite hint of a brat rising in her voice.

I snorted. "We do *now*."

"You can't give me a gift this good and *not* let me take it to my nest."

"Oh... I really can."

I palmed the back of my neck, an unexpected flush rising. A

gift this good? I did puff up a little at that. Maybe I wasn't so stupid after all. "I'll wall mount them for you, set them in resin— I'll even make them into a necklace, but they aren't going anyplace where we're going to fuck you." Uh... That last part hadn't been the plan.

She did a double take, blown pupils suddenly holding mine with intensity.

We stared at each other for a long moment, then she lifted her hand, hovering toward the severed fingers while holding my eyes.

"Glade!"

They were supposed to be for looking at. She didn't need to touch them.

That was gross.

The most breathtaking smile lit up her face as her hand flashed toward them. I snarled, catching her wrist, then sweeping her over my shoulder to the cutest shrill squeak.

45

GLADE

Icrashed backward into a massive bed with very little dignity.

Zed was above me, caging me in, lips brushing my neck as I wrestled his shirt over his back.

I thought we were in a spare room. Not the main nest, which meant Zed had every intention of keeping me all to himself.

His gift, his fuck.

That was fair game.

He was careful where he touched, shifting around the scars on my back as he tugged my shirt off, and I moaned, lightning in my veins as he dragged me against him, lips brushing down my neck to my breasts.

I dragged him closer, nails digging into his skin.

Fuck, I needed him.

"Let me worship you, first."

He flipped us, tugging my panties down my thighs, and slipping down beneath me with ease. His fingers ran along my entrance, making me shudder as I found my balance.

"You're so fucking wet." His tongue found my centre, I shuddered, eyes rolling back as he drove his fingers into me.

My heart fluttered, peace and pleasure settling over me like a blanket as he dragged me down over him, free arm clamping around my hips. My breaths came faster as he shifted me so I could feel the pressure of his tongue drawing up my centre.

I shuddered, but he didn't let up, pushing me all the way to the edge. I moaned as my orgasm crashed into me, making me whine as he drove two fingers into me, dragging it out until I was a melted puddle on the bed.

Fuck.

He drew me back down, so I was straddling him as I tried to catch my breath, hormones resurging as I felt how hard he was beneath me. I removed my underwear entirely, and reached down, fumbling with his sweatpants. He tried to help, but I let out a growl, my hand closing around his throat, instincts sweeping me away almost entirely.

"You're mine."

He groaned as I said it, right as my hand closed around his cock and tugged it free. "Fuuckk, say that again, Little Devil," he breathed.

I adjusted myself, feeling slick wetting my thighs as I sank onto the tip of his cock, my hand still clamped around his throat. His pupils were blown, eyes fixed on mine and lip caught aggressively in his teeth as I lowered myself onto his length.

"I'm yours, forever, Glade," he breathed, and I had to catch myself for balance as he gripped my thighs and pressed up into me, making me see stars with how deep he drove.

I closed my hand tighter around his throat and his grip on my hips loosened just a little. Enough to give me control, and let me sink down over his length, a moan rising in my chest as I settled around his knot, letting it stretch me just a bit.

"You're so fucking pretty, using me like that," he growled.

I drew my hips back up, finding that perfect spot to ride him. Bliss was rising in my veins every time I took him all the way, a shiver rolling up my spine as I teased myself with his knot.

"Keep doing that..."

I loved the way his jaw clenched, muscles in his neck straining beneath where my palm was pressed as I lowered down on the edge of his knot, then held myself there. "Say you're mine," I growled.

"Forever yours, Little Devil," he breathed, thumb finding my clit as he drove up into me. "The only one I've ever been with."

Those words turned every nerve in my body alight, and I stretched myself over his knot with a groan of pleasure, my climax hitting at the same time I felt his hot seed spilling into my core.

Fuuckkkk.

I sagged against him, catching my breath as the bliss faded, my eyes locked with his. His fingers wove through my hair, and I hummed contentedly, curling up against him, loving how it felt to be locked against him and full, as a purr rumbled to life in his chest.

The high remained, even after the orgasm had passed.

My Alpha.

My pack lead.

And he'd destroyed one of the most precious things Ace had.

Kyan had promised me safety, and maybe, just maybe, I was starting to believe them.

"Is there a nest for you to bring them to?" he asked, and I glanced up at him.

"Not yet."

I swallowed. I hadn't found the right place to nest in this place. I didn't know if it was because it felt too much like the mansion I'd grown up in, or if I just needed to wait for my hormones to settle.

"There will be," he said.

I smiled, hugging him tighter.

We lay like that for a while in silence, but eventually, I propped myself up on his chest and peered up at him, far too curious. "Tell me how you did it?"

He grinned, rocking into me and making me squeak before his thumb began circling my clit lazily again. "You sure you want to know?"

"Tell me." That came out so much more demanding than I'd intended.

"You're so fucking hot." He clamped his grip on my hips so he could rut into me with his knot. "But I don't know—"

"Tell me!" I seized his hair, another growl rising in my throat even as my blood heated at the stimulation he was giving me.

His grin was dazzling. "I gave one a poisoned crown," he said. "And the other I left to choke on a card."

I tilted my head, catching my lip with my teeth as he rocked into me again. "A... card?"

"Mhmm."

I moaned as he maintained the rhythm, pushing me right to the edge, but his next words sent me tumbling into the bliss of my third orgasm.

"A queen of diamonds."

46

During the afternoon of the next day, I hopped up on the kitchen island to join Knight as he prepared for a movie night.

The mansion had a theatre room that we'd decided to take full advantage of. However, it seemed they didn't have a popcorn maker.

Kyan and Zed were in the theatre right now, squabbling over a movie list for the evening while Knight was cooking snacks and fully committing to microwaving a dozen bags of popcorn.

I couldn't help wondering if it had anything to do with one of our earliest dates, when his pack took me to the movies. Not a flashy date for most, but none of us had normal upbringings, and it had been the most exciting date I think I'd ever gone on at the time.

I grinned as Knight swapped one bag in for another and set the timer before sliding onto a barstool at my side.

"You feeling all right today?" he asked.

I nodded, though I couldn't catch my yawn. All the drugs made me sleepy at unexpected times.

"How are you doing with all the meds?" he asked.

I shrugged. "There are worse things." I had to take the suppressants throughout the day and night, but I had a vibrating alarm set for the midnight dose, so I didn't have to wake them up.

Missing a dose wasn't an option. Kyan seemed concerned that, if I did, I might slip into heat in an instant. I wasn't ready for that. Not yet.

Discussing my meds wasn't why I'd come. "About the other day…" Clasping my hands, so it wasn't so obvious how nervous I was. "I'm sorry if I said anything about you and Kyan, I mean, that I shouldn't have."

Knight glanced at me, a smile on the edge of his lips as he tugged the corner of the popcorn bag he'd just popped and picked a few out for himself. "Don't be, Princess. You didn't do anything wrong."

I nodded, but my chest didn't ease. It didn't feel that way. I hadn't known… I swallowed.

I didn't want to hurt any of them.

"I don't want to get in the way of anything."

"You won't." Knight stopped before me, dragging me to the edge of the counter so I was all but forced to tangle my legs around him as he cupped my cheek. "I promise."

"Okay." It was just so important that nothing changed because of me.

"I *know* Kyan," he said, seeming to see the conflict in my eyes. "Despite how rigid his father was, there's nothing complicated about him saying he loves you. You're the Omega he matched. The universe stamped its approval. It's safe for him. But with other things, he's still figuring out his way from the maze his father left him in. Wrong turns didn't just leave him lost, he was punished when he wasn't the perfect image of an Alpha, and he was young enough that he was still trying to make sense of the world. There's a lot of shame and fear, even if he doesn't want it. But what he can say doesn't change who he is—or what he feels."

I nodded, processing that.

"Does it... hurt?" I asked. "That he doesn't say it?"

Knight considered that for a long time, then shook his head. "I don't need Kyan tying himself in knots trying to figure out how to say shit I feel down the bond from him every day. I love him, and beyond that, no one owes me their healing. That part is his, and it will happen when it needs to."

I stared up at him, feeling his conviction and peace, and it unwound a piece of my soul, too. I was supposed to be their Omega, but I just felt... broken and worn thin. I'd been running for so long I didn't know if there was anything left but scars. Would he maybe have room for some of that for me, too?

Did I even deserve it?

"Besides," Knight murmured. "If he can believe in you for all these years, I can believe in him."

"I don't know how he did."

"You were always special to him."

I peered up at him, caught a little off guard by that.

"Zed and me, we're your mates, but Kyan?" Knight tilted his head, eyes curious. "You're two halves of the same whole."

I frowned, my mind clawing at the edges of a reality that had been whispering to me for a long time. It felt like there was something caught in my throat.

"We knew the moment he saw you," Knight said. "Felt it through the bond like a lightning bolt—and he came to life. It's why Zed locked it down—didn't let a soul find out who you were until he'd met you. Kyan came home that night—his mission failed—I swear, he was getting ready to kill us."

"To... what?" I asked, startled.

"He'd just fallen for our target—the Omega he was sent to

kill. We'd been chosen for Zed's pack—highest honour in the Brotherhood, but I didn't join this pack thinking it would be a family—that Zed would give a shit who we were. Not until that night." A faint trace of a smile curved Knight's lips. "Until then, Kyan... it was like he was just burning. Fire and ash, everything he'd been taught and nothing beneath. He'd never failed a mission in his life, but when he saw you, something happened, and I found out who Zed was that night."

I cocked my head. "How did you get the truth out of Kyan if he was worried you'd kill me?"

Knight grinned right as the microwave beeped. He crossed over to it and replaced the popcorn bag before returning to me. "Look. It was messy as fuck. Lot of guns being waved around, you know? Until Kyan had Zed with a knife to his neck and he told him he'd rather kill us all than see you die—and then Zed started laughing, because... well, he's just Kyan with a better mask on a good day, and he said there was no way in hell he would let you die, not when it was the first sign he'd ever had that our pack might be more than Brotherhood weapons."

I sat in silence, taking that in, trying to process it all.

"You brought him to life," Knight said quietly. "Before you, he was nothing. I know. I was in a bond with him."

"None of you ever told me that..."

"It wouldn't have been fair to put that on your shoulders. Would have swayed your choice—and the whole fucking point was your choice—it wouldn't have been fair to either of you any other way."

"And then I left..." My expression crumpled. "And he—he almost—"

"No." Knight's voice was rough, and he cupped my cheek, thumb brushing away the tear that had escaped. "You taught him what it meant to love, and then he learned to do it all by himself."

I swallowed, my chin still quivering.

"I saw that firsthand," Knight said. "He's not very good at talking about it, but he learned to love so damned much, he outdid the rest of us. He forgave you first, loved you because he wanted to—because he knew it was right."

"He needed you for that, too," I whispered. Without Knight... What he'd said about finding Kyan on a roof that day. I couldn't think about it. A world without Kyan in it would be cold, silent, and empty.

"You helped him learn to fly, Princess, I just made sure he didn't go face first into the sun."

I choked a half sob, half laugh, leaning into his palm.

"Is it... wrong, if my connection with Kyan is... different?" I asked.

Knight's chest rumbled with a laugh. "Your connection to all of us is different. The way I see it, you're both mine—and brats— so what's the difference?"

"And Zed?" I asked.

Knight snorted. "He's still got Maverick blood. We're all his. The closer we're tied, the easier it is for him to keep us all in his little pack box for show and tell."

I glanced up at him, a smile still stiff on my face. He seemed to see that, though, too.

"You can't worry about it anymore," he breathed. "Every-thing..." He trailed off, scrunching his nose all cute-like which meant he might be close to tears. "Everything after was inevitable. Soulmates on either side of a war. Kyan could no more kill you than you could have let him die. That's all there is to it."

47

I t was movie night.

We were all making an effort to help her settle in. She was having trouble, though. Every morning she woke in our arms less sick by the day, but it wasn't enough. She wouldn't admit it to any of us, but we all knew. The meds wouldn't stabilise her forever, and her heat was approaching quickly. She *should* be nesting.

She was so fucking perfect, curled up in my embrace on a huge couch facing a TV that spanned almost the entire wall. The Forbes mansion was nothing if not stacked.

It was evening, and we were watching a movie. I wasn't really focused on it, though.

I didn't know how to be, with thunder and lightning in my arms, the most beautiful scent on the planet.

My burner phone buzzed, and I glanced at it, then stifled a growl. Lev needed to leave off. It was getting ridiculous, and my instincts misfired every time I saw his name on my phone screen. Our last texts (not involving cat pictures) went something like:

. . .

> Lev: There are only three of you in that pack, right? Heat is going to be rough. Let me know if you need a fourth.

> Me: We can handle our Omega.

> Me: If your cell number ends up in one more cat picture, I'll fucking skin you.

I'd received nothing to that but a middle finger emoji.

And another Lucy video.

Prick.

"Kyan." Glade's whisper ripped me from my thoughts.

"Yeh?" I asked.

"We never talked about…" She frowned, chewing on her lip. The word was just for me, the sound of the movie drowning our voices from the others. "I mean. We don't have to, but… before everything happened with Ace…" She trailed off, like she didn't know how to say it.

I shifted so I was facing her.

I'd been so pissed at Knight for telling her that day, but a lot had happened since. It had put this all into perspective. And I know for a fact that they had been talking about sappy shit earlier because neither of them knew how to lock the bond down. Getting left behind wasn't on the agenda when it came to our omega.

I tucked her hair behind her ear. The action scene of the fantasy movie we were watching, drowning our words to the others.

"I almost… left…" I whispered. "Left you. Left Knight and Zed.

Left... everything." I felt the goosebumps rising on her skin at my words.

"It's okay," I said. "Knight taught me it was okay to love you even after what happened. He helped me see I was allowed to believe in you. No matter what."

And so I had.

And I still would.

It's why I knew this wasn't over. Not yet. Not even in this hidden mansion.

"You're the other half of me," I whispered. "I trust you. Life or death, truth or lies, there's nothing that can change what's between us. For me, the same one who turns the world is the same one who halts it." I swallowed. "I know love isn't supposed to be like that."

"Like what?"

"Like... Everything I am."

That's what people said, at least. But people who said that didn't understand what they had. For them, loving too hard might mean being left with nothing. That meant something came before. Loving Glade was the first time I thought I could have something for... me. Something I could claim, could nurture, could protect.

But after she'd left, after I'd almost given up, Knight had helped me learn the other half of that truth: I should never have burdened her with that.

It was why I couldn't do this without him, either. I was still pissed about the other day. How could he doubt, for a moment, how important they all were to me? *He* was to me? I'd always loved her. And... and him at the same time. If she was here or not, nothing changed.

That was the whole point.

My love for her didn't have to be conditional on her acceptance. It didn't have to mean she chose me, or was near me, or even wanted me. He'd taught me that it was okay to just... carry love. To have it with me, no matter what.

And when you learned that, love wasn't dangerous anymore.

"I love you, Glade," I whispered. "More than anything else in the world. I love you like..." I trailed off, not even knowing how to put words to it.

"Like... a soul match," she whispered, curling closer, chestnut eyes holding mine.

I'd heard the term before. It was rare, so much so that some people didn't believe it was real. But Glade had always smelled like a lightning storm to me, even when I knew it wasn't the same for my pack. It was something special. Something... different, just between the two of us.

She *was* my other half. I was drawn to her always, no matter how far apart we were, like magnets. A piece of me that had existed before I'd taken my first breath, and would remain tangled with my soul no matter what happened.

I pulled her closer. "Just like that," I breathed.

She leaned up, drawing my lips to hers, and the kiss was like its own lightning strike, static with every touch, her scent drowning me completely.

Until she drew back. Her smile was beautiful as her fingers slid down my arm. She found another bracelet on my wrist. There were only three left, now. Two, once she slid it off and put it on.

I smiled but it didn't feel right on my face. I waited for her scent to shift, but the change never came. Something was wrong.

I knew the truth.

She'd done it yesterday, too, stealing another of my bracelets off and putting it on—I could see it right now, beside the one she'd just taken—but it wasn't right.

I'd seen the look in her eye when she'd done it the first time— when she'd stolen one from me in the warehouse, thinking I didn't know—I remembered the way her scent had changed. But this time, it never changed.

She was faking nesting. For me. For us.

But it wasn't good enough.

I held her for a while longer—enough time that she wouldn't connect my departure with the bracelet—then made an excuse to go. She didn't seem suspicious, easily slipping into Knight's arms as I left.

It didn't take long for me to write the words as I sat alone on a barstool in the grand kitchen. But for an age, I held the letter I so desperately didn't want to send, signed at the bottom with a singular 'M'.

It was dangerous. Plans had changed so fast in the last little while, and I wanted more time. But time wasn't on our side, and we were running out of options.

Staying in this place carried more risk with every day that passed.

We'd failed her again, and her trust was shot. We couldn't survive like this—she didn't deserve it, not for one moment more than she needed to. And I had no idea how long we would be safe here.

Carefully, I tucked the letter into an envelope and sealed it.

Tomorrow, at last, I could tell my brothers the truth I'd been keeping all these years.

48

It had been over a week since we'd fled Ace.

That should have been enough time for me to start feeling safe, but I was struggling. It wasn't their fault. I actually didn't think I'd ever felt as happy as I did when I reached out and felt them in the bond with me.

But my instincts were haywire.

I didn't want them to know how much I was struggling; it would make them feel worse. I was waking in the night for doses of suppressants. When I first woke, Kyan had said it wouldn't be forever, and I knew he would want to discuss when I should decrease them.

I was grateful that he hadn't pushed it yet.

But my heat was a problem. While the suppressants were keeping my heat at bay, it shouldn't be interfering with my need to find a nest. To feel safe.

But no matter how hard I tried, I couldn't.

I'd been pretending, though, so that they wouldn't feel so bad, and I think it had helped them relax.

For the first time, I'd left the safe house.

Zed had taken me out to get my nails done, of all things. "Like I said on the phone, this one's broken," he'd told the lady at the front desk, holding my hand up. "Very serious. They need fixing."

I mean, he wasn't wrong. It had been on my radar.

The nail tech seemed to think it was the cutest thing in the world and asked him what colour he was getting.

He'd raised an eyebrow like that wasn't a hard dare, then asked the lady to give him black polish, adding, 'the shitty kind that's gonna chip'.

He'd stopped off for pizza on the way home, and then, when we got there, he'd set it down on the bench in the grand gardens and drew me into his lap.

I laced my arms around his neck, sinking against him and looking around at the place that was a reflection of the one in which we'd first met.

"I'm so... sorry, Glade," he whispered.

"I know."

"I'll never be able to say it enough. For everything I did, and said, and believed of you."

I drew back, tumbling into those pretty ice-blue eyes. The same shade as Ace's but with none of the cruelty.

"I lied to you," I whispered.

"There's no redos, but it's not going to happen again. Kyan promised, but I promise, too. We're going to protect you."

Sometimes, when I looked into his eyes, I saw a flutter of fear. A mirror of my own. A future we didn't know.

And maybe something else.

That day, Zed had got a taste of what it felt like to be helpless before Ace. It was something sinister, and it crept into your heart, lodging thorns so deep, making every shadow you ever glanced at loom larger than it had any right to.

I never wanted that for him. Not because I wouldn't wish that feeling on anyone, but because I didn't want him to spend his nights wondering how long I'd felt it for.

"I survived," I whispered. "And I wouldn't change…" My voice shook for a moment as I held his eyes. "I wouldn't change any of it."

Nothing.

Because, no matter what I'd suffered, I wouldn't trade that for their lives.

It was as freeing, as it was terrifying, realising that.

That I would do it again.

Not would. Will…

I shoved the cruel voice away, trying to believe in his promise.

We'd stayed on that garden bench for an hour, and he'd just held me while the pizza got cold, but I didn't mind.

I was going to believe him. I had to find a way or I would never nest, and I didn't know how I would survive this heat—I was far past the safe hormone balance levels for out-of-hospital sedation.

No.

This heat was going to find me, one way or another.

I woke to the vibration of Kyan's burner phone alarm, as silent as I could make it so the others wouldn't wake. I rolled over in the dark, eyelids heavy, feeling the weight of one of my alpha's arms around me.

This was always the tricky part—slipping out without waking them. It was Knight, tonight, and I tucked a pillow carefully beneath his arm and ducked away without too much trouble.

Zed was sleeping chaotically across the bed, and Kyan was buried beneath a pile of blankets and pillows. I made my way to the bathroom, shutting the door carefully behind me before I flipped the light switch.

I blearily cracked the drawer that held the bottle of suppressants, halfway to reaching in when I froze, my blood turning to ice.

It took a long, long time for me to gather the courage to reach into the drawer and pull out the playing card waiting for me.

It was happening again.

Again.

And again.

And I realised that it always would.

This week, I knew at last, was a gift. Nothing more, as I turned the ace of diamonds in my trembling hand, and read what was scrawled across the back.

Found you, Omega. You have an hour to get to the Gilded Lily Theatre without them.

You have one more chance to negotiate.

This time, you'll give me everything.

It'll be my name on your back.

49

For an hour, I sat curled up in the driver's seat of the black car I'd taken from the mansion. I was across the road from the large, deserted parking lot of a theatre. It was closed right now, though the doors, I knew, would be unlocked.

But I was running out of time as fast as I was running out of conviction. My fingers shook as I clutched my temple, nausea turning my stomach, a breath of desperation slipping out as I tried to gather myself.

I'd left them again, sleeping in our bed. I hadn't had much time to consider, knowing they could wake up any moment. But in the end, there was no choice.

Tears leaked down my cheeks, terror and hormones colliding like a storm.

"I don't..." My voice cracked as I hugged myself. "I don't want to leave..."

Knight had said it. The impossible. The inevitable. I'd protected them just like I always would have.

I'd done everything for them, and now...I was here again.

Because of it.

It wasn't fair.

Nothing was fair.

Anger warred with dread, knowing what was coming for me. The hopeless, all-encompassing knowledge that I had no choice. Not last time, not this time.

I had to find my conviction. I didn't want to give him this, too —and that made me so angry.

My family.

My pack.

A life I'd seen a glimpse of.

And it was over.

Trembling violently, I ripped the glove box open, searching through the car until I found a pen and a blank space on the back of the car insurance.

With tears wetting the paper, I found the words, and wrote. The letter I needed to write to Ace, even if he wouldn't see it.

Because they were for me.

For my mates.

So they would know the truth.

It took me half the hour I had left to find the right words, the right sentences, but finally, I was done, and my breaths were coming clearer, tears finally drying up.

Not because everything was okay.

But because I would survive with the choice I made.

And now they would know that, too.

At last, I sat on the broad stage, legs dangling over the edge in the dim emergency lights and exit signs that flickered dully.

It was quiet and cold in here, representative of what the rest of my life would look like.

They'd tried.

They'd done everything in their power, and I loved them for it. I loved them more than I ever had, and each minute I'd had with them was a gift I never thought I'd get.

But now it was over.

I hated the idea that I couldn't believe in them, but this was so far beyond that. This was about fear I'd been given over years, and I was so broken, no one could have taken that away from me.

And this was about love—the thing I would never trade. Everything Ace preyed on, and every vulnerability he would never have.

I wasn't weak for that, and neither were they. In the world in which we were raised, it took strength to love. It meant making dares of devils that would never stop chasing us.

"I will never let you fall."

Kyan's promise sounded in my head. I had fallen for it, and I would never regret doing that.

Time ticked slowly on, and I knew he would be here soon.

Dust motes floated eerily in the cold air around me, and goosebumps pricked my open skin. I was suddenly so grateful for my pretence at nesting. Right now, I wore Zed's T-shirt, one of Kyan's bracelets on my wrist, and a lone bead I'd stolen from Knight's locs. He only had three, and in my pocket was the one with the blade of grass.

Ace would take them from me, but I knew that.

I didn't bring them to keep, I brought them for strength. My final nest.

The seats stretched out before me, red fabric staring back for row after row, like an audience of ghosts.

I had a gift this time.

I could see them all, a picture of a family—one that loved each other even without me there. And it gave me all I needed to do, what I'd never been strong enough to do before.

My mates would try to find me, but even that was impossible.

Ace would make sure of it, but if I gave him everything he wanted, then maybe—just maybe—that would be all he took from them.

And eventually, they would go on.

They'd done it once, and now I knew they could do it again.

I shut my eyes.

Ace could take and take and take in this world, but behind every curtain, he would find nothing but dust and ash. He would lose, in the end, because he could never have what they did.

The only thing that truly mattered.

At last, I heard the creak of a door to my left, coming in from the side of the stage.

I didn't look up.

I'd written my letter to Ace. I'd given every part of myself to those words, and they were lodged in my soul, my comfort.

There is no justice in power, but there is consequence. It asks for nothing but depravity, but it never comes free. We are all condemned to lives of our own making.

I've made my choice.

You've made yours.

Footsteps echoed upon wooden floorboards, nearing slowly. My fists balled in my shirt, and I swallowed.

This was it.

The beginning. The end. And I was so fucking scared, so I clung to those words, trying to find peace in hopelessness.

There is no loophole, or escape. You will forever settle for less of what makes us the best we can be, or mangle your own mind in order to convince yourself otherwise.

When you steal what should never be stolen, you become a more pitiable creature than you so desperately wish you could make me. There is no power that will allow you to claim what gives me my strength.

The footsteps to my left came to a halt, feet away.

Still, I hadn't moved.

My mates would read it, too. To reach the end and maybe, just maybe, find peace.

You can take me from all that I love, but you will never take them from me.

And in that,

you will never truly win.

"A promise is a promise." The voice echoed across the theatre, and my breath caught, head snapping up in shock as I looked back to the figure standing on the wing of the stage. As I'd expected, I found myself looking into ice-blue eyes.

Only, it was the ice-blue eyes of the wrong Maverick.

50

Footsteps sounded ahead.

Ace drew up in the centre of the room as his eyes fell on me.

I wasn't who he was expecting and I could see the briefest flicker of surprise on his face.

My chest loosened. If he was here, then Zed would be with Glade.

That was the plan. I'd sworn to her she would never face him again, not on his terms. And I would keep that promise.

I would face the man who had been hunting her. A coward who chased only when it was safe, cloaked in paranoia, always hiding out of reach. Until now.

"Kyan?" he asked. "Are you here to take your Omega's place? Or are you under the delusion that you might save her?"

I watched him step into the grand theatre, shifting my foot as he crossed the threshold, my heel silently catching the switch at my feet.

Ace grinned. "I thought you might have learned from my

brother exactly how much she suffers from such..." He grimaced as if the word was distasteful. *"Heroism."*

I didn't move, eyes tracking the guns in their hands. The two thugs behind him had me in their sights even if Ace's gun remained at his waist.

"You only got this far because of Mirage," I said.

Ace paused, teeth catching his tongue as he grinned. "You think you're ahead of me because you know the name of one informant?"

"Mirage is one of your most valued informants," I replied easily. "The one who refuses electronic communication because the information he traffics is too sensitive to risk interception."

Ace paused his approach, eyes fixed on me as the two thugs at his back scanned the room. They would see nothing of threat, though.

"He gave you the tip on Novikov movements, Andretti Brother vendettas, the locations of Brotherhood traitors fleeing Nevada, and Glade's whereabouts when she was at the High Roller."

Ace cocked his head, eyes narrowed as he stared at me. "You intercepted my source?" he asked. "So what—?"

"I didn't intercept him."

I'd watched Glade since the moment we'd been banished, but it hadn't been until she'd fled Ace after years with him that everything had changed. Then, I'd been able to track her properly. To watch over her and make sure she was safe. I'd learned that he was after her, despite the lie he let slip to others about her cheating.

That was when this had begun.

Yet still, fleeing him did not mean she wanted us—that was the mistake I would carry forever. But I'd long decided I loved her no matter what. I'd tracked her movements, tripping up Ace's men when they got too close. I was her protection, no matter if she wanted our pack or not.

She was my soul match, and I'd protected her until I couldn't anymore.

The Brotherhood, however, weren't easy targets, and Ace Maverick, even less so. So I'd created a persona to gain a foothold with the gang I knew was hunting her.

There was a long, long pause. *"You're* Mirage?" Ace asked, finally catching on. "You gave up your own mate?"

"I gave up her location after I knew your men were about to find her." One already had, so I made sure the Brotherhood members chasing her got the intel from me first. But that was when I knew Mirage wasn't enough anymore, because the Brotherhood wouldn't quit. "I told your men what nights she worked at the High Roller, and when Cassian Forbes was visiting, taking the attention of club security."

All so that I could monitor everything. I'd known the night they would strike, and I'd baited Zed into taking us there to confront her. To take it into my own hands—something I'd never wanted to force on her.

But even with the protections against the Brotherhood I'd been building for years, I had underestimated Ace's reach.

This time, though. This *was* the last time. And the last fear my Oasis would ever have to face when it came to Ace.

"And you gave up your own location tonight?"

Yes.

The true nature of how far Ace would go—not just make her an enemy of the Brotherhood, but target her himself, or of how much pain she had caused—I'd known that for a week.

A week, to find a way to face him, once and for all—while keeping my promise to her. As arrogant and unattached as Ace might act, he believed he had a claim on her, and sure enough, with her heat approaching, he turned his efforts to ten.

Of course, she was the final piece. The bait that would make him trip up.

It was only a matter of time before he found us. So I'd given us up and waited, knowing Ace was nothing, if not predictable. Even more so, since Zed had killed his pack. I could see the instability in his eyes right now, in the slight edge to his scent.

And sure enough, he'd sent someone in to leave her a note. I'd found it and written a new location for her. One Zed would be at right now, ready to take her to safety, while I dealt with Ace.

My only regret was that he hadn't come to take her himself today, like he had in the warehouse, so Glade had to go through one more day of terror.

But this wouldn't take long.

"She's mine, Ace," I said. "She was never yours."

"You think it matters? I'll take you tonight, and when I catch up to her and those pathetic packmates, I'll make her put a bullet in your skull."

The men behind him shifted, on high alert for an order as they kept their weapons trained on me. But they were waiting for a reaction that wouldn't come.

"Every letter I sent to you was laced with poison," I told him. "A poison deadly even to the strongest Alpha without a trace."

Ace's lips curved in a smile. "Poison?" he asked. "The same you used to kill my father, I'm sure?"

"The only mistake I made that night was not realising you'd found out." I didn't know it at the time, but Glade paid the price.

That last piece of the puzzle was the greatest mistake I'd ever made: believing her rejection of us was her choice.

"Pathetic." Ace snorted.

"It's the Brotherhood's greatest weakness—your greatest weakness. You only see a threat if it's the barrel of a gun pointing in your face."

I got to my feet slowly, watching the way the guns shifted with the movement.

"If you poisoned the letters," Ace sneered, spreading his arms.

"You did a shit job." He glanced around with a wild grin. "I'm still here."

At Ace's side, his guard coughed, one hand withdrawing from his gun to clutch his throat.

Scentless and odourless, the poison was already beginning to seep into the room. It had been for a while now. Ace's eyes flicked to the side for a moment, not quite leaving me entirely.

On his other side, there was an awful choking sound and the other guard also seized his throat, weapon clattering to the floor. It didn't take more than a few seconds before both men were on their knees, wheezing for breath they would never find again.

"I wasn't trying to kill you," I said quietly as Ace turned back to me, and I saw the first flicker of something unsure shadow his features. Ace was paranoid, keeping his locations secret, with constant guards. No alpha that paranoid would allow himself to be killed the same way as his father. So no letter I'd sent had a *traceable* amount of the toxin filling the air. "I wanted to make sure you have the same thing I have."

I stepped toward him and he reached for his gun at last.

His hand trembled at the movement and he swayed. I'd dosed him for years, never needing more than a traceable amount. Not enough for *full* immunity—not like I'd built. But enough that, with the flood of odourless, scentless gas that was spilling by the gallon into the room, he *would* survive.

He coughed, staggering a step back, eyes suddenly wide. *"Why?"*

I caught him easily, disarming him and tossing his gun away as I took his chin and forced him to look at me. "I knew, if I ever came for you, revenge wouldn't be for me..." He tried to fight my grip, shaking to the bone, the faintest drop of blood beading his eyes. "And death," I said, as his eyes rolled back and he went limp. "Would be far too kind for what you did to her."

51

ZED

"I d-don't understand." Glade was in shock as she got to her feet, staring at me across the stage.

"He's not here."

I took a step toward her, but she stumbled away from me, eyes wide, hands up. Her cream cardamom scent was edged with a panic I recognised. "H-he left a card. He knew where we were."

I took another step and she edged back again. But I'd seen enough of my Omega protecting us.

Never again.

"Stay." My Alpha bark was softer than most, but enough to still her as she teetered on the edge of feral.

I closed the distance before she could fight it, holding her terrified eyes the whole time.

"You're safe," I said, drawing her into my arms. "I promise, Glade, he will never come for you again."

She crumpled against me, her small frame trembling. I picked her up, letting her wind her arms around my neck and draw me tightly as I carried her back to the car.

She'd left the keys in the ignition, and it pained me to pry her from my arms long enough to drive us to the location Kyan had set up. It was Dezhurov's territory—one of Kyan's contacts—and he knew we would be waiting here. We would be safe until I got the call I needed.

Kyan had filled us in on everything the day before. Just in time for us to keep up.

And while I hated it when he kept things from us, this time... This time, he'd come with a solution to everything.

Finally, a way to take control back.

Glade still hadn't spoken, and I glanced at her as I pulled the car to a stop behind a huge building. She was seated with her hands clasped in her lap, her glossy black hair tumbled in loose waves to her thighs, swaying with the braking of the car, even when her eyes were fixed, staring at the dash.

She was in shock.

I'd read the letter, found it left on the seat of the car after she'd abandoned it. Perhaps she'd written it in the faint hope that, if we read it, we might be able to let her go.

Never.

I climbed over the centre console, and drew her into my arms once more, hating how much she was still shivering. Hating any moment the world made her seem so small.

"All those years ago, I promised you a choice," I breathed. "And then I left you behind. We're never going to do that again. Fuck the letter," I whispered. "We're going to give you everything. It is your turn for justice, Glade."

KNIGHT

It took hours to ensure everything was contained enough for us to meet up with Glade and Zed. While Kyan and I dragged Ace back to the warehouse, it wasn't safe for her yet.

First things first, we chained an unconscious Ace in the cell and slammed the door shut.

I was still fucking reeling.

Yesterday, Kyan had briefed us, giving just enough time to pivot.

My job was to be his backup. Since the theatre incident, Kyan paid guys to install heat sensors around every building he knew of that Ace owned. It was a quick, barely detectable job, and while not a guarantee, it let us know Glade was safe and if Kyan would need backup.

The hardest part was the price she had to pay. If Ace had found our safe house, we had to assume he was monitoring it too. Kyan made sure the car had no bugs, but Glade had to leave. Kyan had dared to slip out earlier, but we couldn't risk the whole pack missing in case it would draw too much suspicion.

So, Zed and I were forced to wait and pretend to be asleep before leaving to catch up with her. We didn't believe—if Ace was still watching our house at that point—he would notice Kyan's absence.

Then Zed went to her, while I arrived at Kyan's location in time to be his backup if needed.

Kyan's last trick had been screwing with the quality of Ace's security cameras enough that he wouldn't notice anything amiss about the hooded figure who entered the building Glade was supposed to arrive at. We didn't need much, just enough to blur the image so it could be mistaken as her.

Then he'd wandered right on in, dropping pressurised canisters rigged to puncture at the push of a button.

Kyan may not have known Glade was being blackmailed into choosing Ace, but it was still pretty fucking clear he'd been fantasising about killing the Alpha who'd taken his mate for a long time, regardless of whether he intended to respect her autonomy.

While he pulled out his laptop and executed his long-awaited plan with intensity, there wasn't much for me to do but wait. Of course, like the mad fucking genius he was, he'd planned everything, right down to doorstep deliveries. So I was able to spend my time putting together the brand-new pack bed he'd ordered, while he updated me with things like: "Jesse tapped into some of their communications. Whole lot of them are scrambling." or "Henderson warehouse is dead already, my eyes are saying they're jumping ship."

And finally, the best news of all: "The whole Brotherhood is cracking way faster than I planned for. I think they were way more shaky since Ace lost his pack."

"Good."

Un-fucking-surprising, really.

Ace ran the Brotherhood on threats and fear. There was no loyalty left, and as fast as it had risen, it had fallen, ready to crack at the slightest pressure.

All we needed to know was that there wasn't anyone with a vendetta that a few of Kyan's connections couldn't handle. For a few weeks, he'd organise around the clock eyes on the warehouse. Even then, it was unlikely—his biggest concerns had been Ace's pack mates, but Zed had already handled them.

Finally, when the sun was rising, Kyan got the all clear, and the others were safe to return.

The bed, by now, was sorted, as was the sea of pillows Kyan had slowly been accumulating since we'd first kidnapped her. I'd set it all up in the main living room. We would figure out a proper nest for later—for now, with her hormones, we needed it ready.

I wished Lucy was here, too, but Lev was having a pretty busy evening, so I hadn't pushed that one.

And finally, after a strained few hours, Glade entered the warehouse with Zed at her side. She was tense, as if on high alert, and it broke my heart, seeing her like that.

That last part—the trauma we couldn't save her from, had

taken its toll. Her eyes were still blank with shock as she watched us approach.

I reached her and drew her into a hug. She clutched me, far too fragile.

How afraid had she been?

Kyan was next, and he held her in his arms for a long time. He might be feral about catching Ace, but letting her believe, even for a moment, that we'd failed her, had broken him, too.

"I have a gift for you," Kyan told her, when he drew back.

She just stared at him, but didn't argue when he led her through to the living room.

He opened the cell door, and she froze.

His scent of roses and redwoods was impossible to miss.

Kyan didn't push her, and it took a long time before she stepped into that doorway.

She vanished in the bond when she caught sight of him, just... slipped away for a moment.

A long, long time passed, and then finally, she looked up at Kyan.

"It's over?" she asked.

"It's over, Oasis. He's never going to hurt you again."

52

The cell door closed and something deep within me rattled the cage of my shock, demanding to be let out.

A breath.

I think... I could take a breath.

As if it was the first I'd ever taken.

And finally, something soared free in my chest as I stepped back into my pack's living room. My home. Ace was chained up *in my home.*

And of course, with that, like a monster waiting to pounce, the dam broke, the meds failed, and my heat crashed in.

That sense of freedom I'd just felt dissolved instantly for terror. It was hard to explain why, exactly. This was the heat I'd been waiting for, for years. It was more than that.

All I knew was that I was going to lose my mind, and I was terrified.

"Oasis."

I shook my head, realising too late that I couldn't have heat without my scars. Until now, they'd been so gentle with them, avoiding them, and never making me feel pressure to reveal my back.

But... I couldn't breathe. The world was going dim, as sharp pains speared my stomach.

A pain I'd felt a thousand times before.

"Shhh, Princess, I've got you." Pear grove felt like a cool breeze, and strong arms were lifting me. I looked up into beautiful midnight eyes, knowing he could feel me trembling.

My voice shook. "I d-don't know how to do this."

My scars hurt almost as much as the heat spikes. Each line upon my back was open again, and tears were tracking my face as he guided me down to the huge pack bed, hands still at my sides. Not enough, and yet, I didn't know how to ask for more.

"However you need us, remember," Knight whispered. I nodded, though I didn't know if I believed it. But he made Kyan feel safe.

"Can I touch you?" he asked.

Touch me...?

He was.

But, I think he meant, like... for heat. During heat...

Ace's hands closed around my throat as he held me still.

"Ask, Omega."

I squeezed my eyes shut, pain rising like an ocean tide, and I knew it would drown me.

It would drown me, and so would he.

My breaths were short and sharp. Pear grove was tangled with roses. But my mind tripped over that, trying to figure it out.

Which was a nightmare? Which was a dream? They were never both there at the same time.

Only... right now, they were.

I nodded, a hiccup caught between sobs.

I don't remember what I was saying yes to. Not until his touch brushed my skin like ice melting against a furnace, and I shuddered, leaning into it, needing more. His purr rumbled through me as I leaned against his chest, his skin cooling mine.

He was here.

"Knight."

How many times had I whispered his name? How many times had the pain that sliced across my back still been nothing to the heat I was fighting?

But this time, when I said his name, he answered.

"I've got you, Princess."

The breath I took was long and shuddering, like it had been trapped for an eternity, and then I was clutching him, low, desperate whines in my chest and I forced my eyes open.

"You're h-here." My voice was choked as he blurred in tears. Sharp jaw, dark eyes, long locs that brushed my skin, pear grove, as real as the roses that lingered in the distance, finally marking this reality as the real one.

"I'm here."

I shifted over him, a low moan of pain slipping out. Now the nightmare was behind me—now, reality was crashing in. I... I needed him.

My nails dug against his skin.

"I'm here, Glade," he said again, easily shifting me. "I'm here and I'm never going anywhere ever again."

Our bodies connected, and I reacted on nothing but instinct, taking his hand and dragging it backwards as I tilted my head.

"I love you," I whispered, freeing words that had been caught in my soul for far too long.

He let out a low, rumbling growl, following my guidance without hesitation. I sank lower. He completed me as I took his knot and soothed my heat for the first time in my life. His hand circled my waist, trailing up my back until he found his name among my scars, his other tangled in my hair, holding me still as his teeth found my neck.

"I love you, too."

I soaked that in and realised how safe I felt.

More safe than I'd ever felt in my life. And then my eyes fluttered open, sticking on tears that had finally stopped.

The others...

As if they could feel it through the bond, Zed and Kyan were at my side. I was crying again as their scents tangled with Knights.

"I love you." I was sobbing like a baby, reaching for them.

"I love you too, Little Devil," Zed breathed, his lips finding mine.

Kyan was there, wrapping his arms around me from behind, and the muscled ridges of his chest, a massive wall of Alpha skin soothing the warmth of my skin.

"You already know how much I love you," Kyan breathed, teeth grazing my arm. "My Sweet Oasis."

It was over. Ace was caught, and my heat was here, and I had the Alphas I loved.

Kyan had promised me I would never have to face Ace again, and he'd done it. Somehow, he'd managed it.

Once the sweetness was out of the way and Knight's knot released me, full heat collided with me like a freight train.

Actually, a freight train might have been kinder.

I was in a daze.

Tears were a distant memory; surges of hormones that incinerated every rational thought left to man. Or Omega.

Or whatever.

All I knew was that I needed my Alphas like a fire needed oxygen.

Like a desert needed rain.

Like a... I didn't know where I was going with that. All I *really* knew was that I was caught between Knight, who had a firm grip on my wrist and hip from behind, and Zed who was before me.

And I was *still* pissed because Kyan hadn't figured out where to stick his dick yet.

I think I growled at him—over Zed's length, which I had just taken down my throat with a whine. Zed dragged me back, fist in my hair as if trying to figure out what was wrong, and I stared up at him in utter, dazed shock.

What the *fuck* did he think he was doing?

"I think she wanted more, not less," Kyan snorted, squeezing my breast.

I *almost* fought Knight's grip on my hips to launch at him, but then I'd be down to zero dicks—and besides, if I killed them all, I was really fucked. I let out a snarl at Zed's impish grin, but he did drag me back to his cock, which settled my temper.

Woah.

I mean.

I knew heats were wild, but... fuck.

ZED

After years of being touch-starved, Glade's heat was off the charts. She was a fucking cyclone of hormones, which was either the hottest or the most frightening thing I'd ever seen.

Apparently, an Omega in heat could be managed by exactly how many knotted-peni in the room they believed were eligible for fucking. The problem was, Glade was so insanely *gone,* that she was on the edge of hallucinating. For a particularly worrying stretch, her temperature had soared. She'd been whimpering in distress no matter how many ways we'd fucked her, eyes fixed on one of the dusty windows.

Luckily, Knight clued in before we had to call an ambulance. He crossed the room, picked up one of my thrift shop plant holders on the windowsill (which, I realised, looked faintly phallic) and tossed it in the trash, where it shattered.

In hindsight, it was obvious he should have thrown a blanket over it instead, because at the destruction of what she'd clearly long considered a potential suitor, she lost it. With a shriek of rage, she tried to dive from the bed. Thankfully, Kyan pinned her down and knotted her before she could reach a gun, which dialled down the threat from *furious mafia-Omega murder* to *possible pouty dismemberment*.

For the next half an hour, Knight couldn't come near us without her snarling at him. Problem was, despite the attempted kill, he was still an eligible peen, and thus, had to brave it when her temperature started soaring again.

When she had him pinned beneath her, hand closed around his neck with what might be a genuine (if mildly adorable) attempt at strangulation, it was to mount him with disconcerting aggression. I'd never seen an Omega murderously take a knot before, but now I could add it to the list of kinks I didn't know I had.

Luckily, Knight agreed, because I don't think I'd ever felt him so turned on down the bond.

GLADE

I don't know how long I'd been in heat when the faintest semblance of normal consciousness returned.

It had to be more than a day, at least.

There were significantly more open cans of energy drinks and snacks littering the room as I looked around.

I think we'd fucked, like, all over the place.

There were some really odd memories floating in...

I sat bolt upright in shock.

"What is it, Little Devil?" Zed, who was currently knotted in me, blinked drowsy eyes open.

"Was there another Alpha?" I tried not to sound so wounded.

"Oh..." Kyan chuckled, sitting up beside me and tucking my hair behind my ear, his expression telling me he was surprised I was talking. Well... actually, he probably was given how out of it I'd been. "There was until Knight killed him."

I scanned the chaotic mess of blankets and pillows until I saw Knight, who was frozen mid-stride on his way back to the bed, mug of steaming tea halfway to his lips.

"You... killed him?" I asked.

He narrowed his eyes, something wary in his gaze. "So what if I did?"

I breathed a sigh of relief that made Knight relax.

He set the tea on the side table and dropped down at my back. "You decided you don't want another Alpha?" he asked.

In response, I lowered myself against Zed's chest, wriggling back against his knot, the sensation making my eyes roll.

"You're more than enough," I said, tilting my head and keeping one eye on Knight and his beautiful, beautiful bare torso of thick muscles.

"Glad you've come around," he purred, his hand squeezing my ass hard enough to make me squeak.

"Come around?" I asked, as he pressed his tip and stretched me out. I didn't need prep at this point.

"I think you tried to shoot him, Little Devil," Zed chuckled, his hand in my hair as Knight's cock pressed into me an inch.

"I did not—" I let out a groan as he filled me with one thrust, scrambling against Zed's chest for a moment to adjust to the sensation, little moans of pleasure slipping out as I felt his knot rock against my hole.

Kyan cupped my neck, and I pushed myself from Zed's chest on instinct as Knight gripped my hips and began pumping into me properly.

"It was cute and vicious," Kyan told me with a grin, going for what I wanted and un-tucking his cock from his sweats.

My tongue was already out, eyes dazed as Knight sent me racing toward the millionth orgasm of the heat.

Right as Kyan gave me what I wanted, making me feel completely fucking full of Alpha, I did what I think I'd been doing for every other orgasm before it.

It took one last check of the air, finding a strange comfort in the distant, souring scent of roses.

The next wave of heat was a lot more conscious, and a lot more enjoyable.

I don't think I'd slept yet, but I got the feeling my Alphas would need to soon. I was, at least, ready to start letting them tag out.

And eventually, after what might have been another day, my eyelids fluttered closed. I might have passed out—it was hard to tell, but Zed's voice woke me.

"Do you think we should deal with..." His voice trailed off. "I can move him out of here—" His words cut off at my whine.

No...

I knew who they were talking about. They would go in and out of the cell occasionally—making sure he was alive, I thought —and the scent of roses and redwood would seep out.

"You... want him here, Baby?" Zed asked me, cupping my cheek and helping me focus on him. I nodded my head, a little panicked.

The scent was grounding. He didn't understand; if Ace was gone, he could be anywhere. Redwood and roses would follow me into any heat I had. But this time, I didn't have to be afraid. It wasn't haunting me in nightmares, it was tangible; something I could cross the room and open the door and see for myself, chains and all.

"Okay," Zed breathed. "If you don't want him gone, he stays."

Good.

Okay... I nodded, realising I was humming happily, as I sank back against Kyan's chest and adjusted myself over his length, feeling him shift inside me to keep at bay the warmth that threatened from a distance. A pain I'd become too familiar with.

But I didn't need to be afraid.

My Alphas were here.

This was their home, which meant it was now mine, but it still needed fixing up. There were pieces of this place tangled in my fears.

In their rejection of me.

I had forgiven them, but Ace... he was the root of every fear remaining. Every moment of pain I'd suffered, every lie I'd been forced to make them believe.

So he had to stay chained in the next room, mine—just as he'd once believed I was his.

When I let him go, I could let go of all of it. Let go of everything that was stopping this place from becoming my home.

But I could choose when that was. This game was mine to play, and there was one more reason I wasn't done with him yet. Every time I caught his scent, it was more agonised than before.

A rut, I realised.

In response to a heat he could feel. Vicious and overwhelming from years of agony and drugs—a heat he had created.

I smiled, shifting again over Kyan's length, letting out a little breath of satisfaction as he held my hips, drawing me closer.

53

The first wave of heat came to an end at last.

Two days.

Two fucking days just for wave one.

My dick was sore. I didn't even know that was a thing that could happen to Alphas.

I mean, it didn't matter. There was no part of me that cared how much my dick ached, not when we were taking care of her like we were.

I was the one on Ace duty right now. I would keep him alive until she said otherwise—even if only just.

It was as I was making the final adjustments of the bindings, I'd just returned to myself, when I heard the buzz of my phone.

A smile crossed my face as I checked it.

My delivery was here—at fucking last.

The others might not have noticed, but I had—I'd been looking for it. Sure enough, there were times, over the last days, when Glade had stared toward the cell, something longing in her expression.

I'd even caught her slipping from the pack bed and hovering at the door, lip caught in her teeth as she clutched the doorknob, like she was daring herself to go in.

I knew what it was she needed.

"What the fuck are you doing?" Knight growled, as I stepped back into the living room, arms bundled with a massive bouquet of roses, the scent choking up my lungs unpleasantly. But I would sacrifice anything for my Oasis.

Glade, who'd been dozing in Zed's arms, happily settled on his knot, snapped to attention immediately, eyes wide as she stared over at me.

Luckily, Zed seemed to have deflated, because the speed at which she bolted from him told me she might not have cared either way. She rushed over to me, eyes wide, stopping at Knight, whose arm she grabbed as if for support.

She was so cute, peering around him like I would bite, one of our massively oversized T-shirts covering her to the mid-thighs.

"Are you fucking mad?" Knight demanded.

"It's a gift," I said. "A... first heat gift."

Was that a thing?

If it wasn't, it should be.

But Glade was staring at the bouquet, eyes glassy and fixed on it like a cat. I thought she might even follow it around the room if I moved it.

"Is this what you need, Oasis?" I asked.

The sweetest sound of desperate need rose in her chest as she stumbled from Knight—who tried to reach out to grab her just too late—and drew up before me.

Oh... boy, if I thought she'd been feral before.

Her eyes were wide, and she was shifting around the bouquet like a curious mouse, occasionally lifting a hand as if she was going to take it, then drawing back with a frown.

Finally, she settled on closing her fist in my shirt and dragging me across the room. I shot both Knight, and a very confused-looking Zed (who was rubbing his eyes of sleep) a huge grin before Glade had marched us to the cell door.

54

"**W**hat in the ever-loving fuck is she doing?" Zed appeared at the door to the cell.

"She's... nesting," I said flatly.

Because there was no other way to describe the behaviour I was watching right now. Glade was taking every mat, pillow, and blanket Kyan was handing to her, and arranging them slowly in the cell.

"I mean... are we going to be able to move it?" Zed asked. He hadn't spoken quietly enough. Glade went tense, her furious gaze snapping to him in a moment as she plumped a pillow in the corner.

It would be a lot more cute if she weren't a foot away from the rutting, out-of-pack, evil Alpha chained to the wall.

I snorted. "That's a no."

Fucking Kyan.

Goddammit.

But it had worked—of course. Our Omega was truly, properly, nesting at last.

In the cell we'd kept *her* in. Still holding the Alpha we'd caught for her—which I was beginning to suspect was a pivotal feature to its conception.

But a nest made in heat was a thousand times more likely to stick than one begun any other week of the month.

Well, I supposed we'd done up a lot worse than the cell. We could make it respectable. Aside from Ace. But that was just temporary, right? She didn't expect to keep him locked up in here forever.

He was gagged and chained and temporarily unconscious—which I was sure had taken a hell of a cocktail since he'd long gone into a rut. He was also in close proximity with an Omega in heat—one who hadn't touched him, all while his body was still processing the vicious poison he'd inhaled.

Even from here, I could see the way his body trembled, pent-up energy with nowhere to go. Energy that, when he woke, would be eating him alive, and with every one of her movements, every new wave of her scent in the air, it would get more painful.

Of course, that had been a good thing, until she'd decided he was a nesting ornament.

Now I was just concerned.

Should we encourage this?

Once she was done with the pillows, blankets, and mats, she settled at Kyan's side, crossing her legs and facing Ace.

I noticed that there was a semi-circle of un-pillowed concrete floor around where he was chained. As if it were the most normal thing in the world, Glade took the bouquet of roses from where Kyan had laid it down, and got to phase two of *Glade nest making*.

One by one, she plucked the petals of the roses and tossed them onto the concrete before Ace. Her scent eased, the need shifting to something peaceful, even if she was definitely still in heat.

It took a while, and none of us moved. Despite the insanity of it all, I could watch my girl nest all day.

Finally, the last petal had fallen, and there was barely a spot on the concrete around Ace that wasn't covered in rose corpses. She tugged one of the stems from the bouquet, staring at it in a dazed way for a moment before frowning. She looked up at Kyan, but he was already producing a knife from his belt.

The frown smoothed out as she got to work, shaving every thorn from the stems and letting them scatter over the rose petals.

She was left with a bundle of thornless, green and white, shaved stems. Those, she gathered up and placed carefully in the corner before turning back to the nest and scouring it again. I thought we might be done, but she frowned.

Kyan followed her, drawing her close and cupping her face. "You're getting hot, Oasis. Let me take care of you?"

She let out a frustrated little chirp, shoving him away, distress on her face.

"What's wrong?" he asked.

She pouted, which was the cutest thing I'd ever seen, even if the look of reproach in her eyes was enough to set me on edge.

Whatever it was, I would fix it.

But her heat-dazed, chestnut eyes were fixed on Zed, not any of us.

"Ah... *Fuck*." Zed let out a breath, running his fingers through his hair.

"What?" Kyan asked, accusation in his eyes.

Zed looked between her, and the Alpha still limp in his chains, then sighed. "Fine. Fucking fine." He turned tail, and before he vanished to his room, I heard him mutter something about, 'lucky I already sorted the resin'.

55

This was all seriously fucked up, and also so damned hot. Knight looked ready to blow a fuse when Zed returned with two severed fingers. They were treated and set in resin, and she scrambled toward him, seizing them from him in an instant.

Right.

Those were definitely rose tattoos.

Ha.

What a fucking gift.

She set them carefully down on either side of Ace, the most content sound rising in her chest as she stepped back to examine it.

"There you go, Baby," Zed breathed, dragging her close. "I broke my rule for you."

I grinned.

Now. Now we were really set.

Pillows and blankets, check.

The scents of her pack, check.

A pool of dying rose petals and thorns, check.

The drugged body of her enemy, chained to the wall, check.

And the last touch, dismembered fingers: Zed's gift to her.

I glanced at Knight with a grin. Pear grove was a nice scent and definitely shouldn't be able to give off violence, but I had the distinct impression that he was ready to take both me and Zed out back and finish us off for encouraging this behaviour.

How was he so goddamned sane?

He'd been raised Brotherhood, just like the rest of us. And her heat hormones were like a drug. She was my girl, and if this is what she wanted, who were we to argue?

She turned to me, pupils blown, lips parted. Now everything was in place, I could practically see the heat sweep her away.

Wave number two.

My brain lagged.

Glade didn't want to leave the new nest, and I didn't have a problem with that at all.

Apparently, screwing our Omega in front of an out-of-pack Alpha wasn't Knight's thing, and that was fine.

She had passed the most intense stage of heat, and we didn't know how long this was going to last, so maybe it was best if he went and passed out.

Ace was awake and I could almost feel his agony in the air, the furious growls slipping from him with every breath.

It seemed to do nothing but spur Glade on.

She was trapped between me and Zed. Her hands and cheek pressed to his chest, dark waves sticking to the sheen of sweat on her cheeks, bright eyes fixed on Ace as I drove into her.

He was losing it, pupils constricted, snarls tearing from his chest as he watched. The rut wouldn't allow pride to hide the claim he so desperately wanted. Ace's mask was cracking, and beneath was nothing but weakness and obsession.

I tilted her hips so I could drive deeper, and I felt Zed speed up his circling of her clit.

She moaned, shuddering with an orgasm, which sent Ace into a frenzy, and—in response—drew her climax out longer.

"You're so fucking perfect," I breathed in her ear as she melted against us.

Zed seemed to have maxed out his desire to be around his brother because he dipped out, saying something about ordering food.

Good.

I wanted some private time with my Omega.

I could fuck her in front of this piece of trash all day—and I thought she'd let me. It wasn't just thrilling for her; it was cathartic, as if the insanity of it all was healing pieces of her soul that had broken over equal and opposite insanity.

I understood that.

So I worshipped her until the room was a lightning storm with no roses, until her eyes were dazed and her lips curled up in a smile, her fingers tangling in my hair as I made her climax so many times even her heat-hazed body was done.

And then I pinned her to the mats and knotted her to his snarls and insanity as he suffered just a fraction of the pain he'd made her feel.

Finally, when I'd held her against me and let her recover, and our bodies were no longer connected, I drew her up to her knees to face him, pressing my chest to her back so she knew she wasn't alone. She was shivering with exhaustion, but my hand closed around her neck as I held her still.

Her breathing hitched as my knuckle brushed her back, and she shivered as static danced between us. I felt her rush of anticipation as I trailed my lips down her neck, below her shoulder blade.

Through the bond, I felt a fissure down something that had been entombing her for too long.

I lowered my free hand, running it down her arm and then her wrist, taking her hand in mine, my thumb grazing the scars she had there, too.

There was another fissure, and this time cracks webbed outward as my lips drew down to the mangled marks upon her back. Ridges that marked pain as much as they marked a choice she'd made so that one day this tomb could break and inside there might still be life.

Goosebumps rippled along her skin as my lips traced the marks.

Zed.

Knight.

And finally, my name.

As I sank my teeth into that mark, I felt the tomb shatter at last.

ZED

Glade didn't know I'd woken when she slipped from my arms in the middle of the night.

Of course I'd woken. I would never allow her to be stolen from me again—especially not with his scent lingering.

She'd never asked us to get rid of it, no matter how deep into her heat she was.

Right now she wore the sheer gown we'd stolen from the High Roller. It shifted over her body like liquid gold, barely hiding anything beneath, but she didn't seem to mind as she vanished into the cell.

I was silent, following her. Instincts telling me whatever this was, I shouldn't interrupt it.

Ace was on his knees, hands tied behind his back. There was a trail of blood down his chin from where he'd fought the gag so hard it had rubbed his skin raw.

I felt nothing for him: no pity, no kinship.

The only emotion that stirred as I watched her approach him was the faintest itching of envy that I wouldn't get to be the one that dealt with him. That was the Alpha part of me, demanding retribution, demanding to see this problem solved with my bare hands, but I would stifle it.

It was hers.

She'd earned it.

His head was bowed, the rise and fall of his chest the only indication that he was still alive. When she stopped before him, though, I saw him shudder. He was still in the rut and his scent held the agony he felt. Bitter thorns of roses rolled from him in waves.

Slowly, he looked up as if he couldn't stop himself, constricted pupils, gaze trailing every inch of her body, breaths becoming deeper. Her scent was thick in the air, the trailing end of her heat turning it into a siren's call.

A rutting Alpha, and a touch-starved Omega who'd gone through the most intense heat I'd ever heard of.

He must be in agony.

When she reached down and brushed his chin, the faintest whine rose in his chest, his breathing picking up.

The smile that lit up her face was beautiful, and through the bond, I felt it. A moment of pure freedom as she looked down at him.

"It's almost disappointing, watching you break so fast."

Carefully, she sank to the floor before him, tilting her head slightly, regarding him like she might a toy. Her pupils were still so wide, the heat and instincts burning strong.

"Are you still here?" she asked.

I couldn't take my eyes away as she wove her fingers through his hair, dragging his neck back. He let out another pathetic whimper at her touch, though it was quickly followed by a growl.

Her laugh was light as she drew herself up so she was looking down at him, her nose an inch from his, her free hand cupping his cheek and stroking her thumb along it. I felt her enjoyment as more shuddering, pained noises tore from him with every exhale.

"I won your game," she whispered, just loud enough for me to hear. "And all the games you made me play."

His lips drew back in a snarl, something more aware in his blue eyes. Glade lowered herself, and I frowned, unsure what she was doing until she stopped beside his neck. With one hand holding his hair taut, she pressed her teeth to his neck.

The sound he made was pure madness, and he tried to struggle from her grip. All she did was pull him tighter, and I watched the blood trickle down his neck where her teeth dug in.

When she drew away, there was a smear of that crimson on her cheek, and her eyes danced with delight.

Then she reached for the box waiting at his side.

Crossing her legs, she unscrewed the cap from a bottle. I knew Kyan had told her what all the drugs in that box did. I watched as she crushed one of the pills between her fingers, then reached toward Ace. He fought harder this time, eyes wild, but the bindings held, and Glade was easily able to smear the powder across the bite she'd left.

I wondered what it was that she'd chosen.

"I'm done with you," she whispered. "I won, but choosing to kill you now? That wouldn't be fair." She stood, but Ace was limp now, breathing short and sharp, head lolling. "That choice isn't mine."

56

There was one last thing to be done.

Ace was limp, his body unmoving, resting on the blankets of a large bed. The scent in here was neither mine nor his, but we both recognised it.

Everything was in place. The poison was in his blood—and just like it should have killed me, it would kill him if not stopped.

But true to my word, I wouldn't be the one to decide.

I slid onto the bed where he lay and straddled him, fingers digging into his chin and making him look up at me. "I've done to you once, what you've done to me over and over again," I whispered. "But my turn is almost over."

Almost being the key word.

I watched with satisfaction as his eyes darted between mine. The slightest, faintest sound came from his chest as I hooked his arm over my shoulder and hauled him onto his back.

Ace had tortured and hurt so many people in his life. But there were two I'd seen him keep and scar. So when I drew my blade out and drew lines across his flesh, like he had enjoyed doing to me, I made sure to leave space.

His whole frame shuddered beneath me, low, useless whines slipping out as a trail of crimson dripped down pale skin. When I drew back, I was finished.

I didn't need more.

What I left was the simple, singular line symbol for Omega. For me, and every other he'd tried to crush.

"How did it feel, Alpha?" I whispered, mirroring a question he'd asked me a million times before. "Are you ready to beg?"

Beneath me, I felt just the slightest hitch in his breathing, but he could do no more. I grabbed his hair and dragged his neck back viciously before I pressed my lips to his. I don't know if it was sick, truly. All I knew was the way it made me feel like I was alive as I felt him helpless beneath me. Every instinct purred, almost making me wish it wasn't over so soon.

At my kiss, a low growl rose in his chest, but there was no true threat in it. I caught his tongue between my teeth and bit down until I tasted the tang of iron. I scooped the pill from my cheek and pressed it into his. The drug would do nothing to me, but for him—the moment it hit his bloodstream, it would take effect.

"The guards are gone," I breathed when I leaned back at last, releasing his chin and cupping his neck instead. My hair pooled around us, creating a silent world where it was just me and wide, ice-blue eyes that had, for so long, been my nightmare. "There's no one here but you, and her—not for as far as the property reaches, and there are hours and hours between now, and when this poison will finally end you. That drug will slow your death. You'll still be conscious, unable to move or speak."

That was the pill. The same drug he'd threatened on Zed. To torture him while I watched.

What came next for Ace, I didn't need to watch.

It wasn't mine. A gift from me to her, and the faint hope that it might give her the same closure I'd already claimed.

"What do you think?" I asked. "She could speed up your death—even save you if she wanted to."

I felt a smile curve my lips even at the idea, and leaned close once more, drawing my chin along his, leaving my scent so she would know where the gift came from.

"Do you think she will?" I asked as I drew back. "Because if I were you, I would pray to choke on my own blood before I was found."

Ace's eyes were wide, darting between mine with nothing but pure terror as I let him go at last. "Someone will be here tomorrow to deal with your body. If there's anything left of it."

He couldn't move, couldn't speak. He couldn't do anything as I slipped from the bed and over to where Kyan waited for me.

I was almost through the door that led to the ground floor when I heard the faintest footsteps in the distance. I glanced back just in time to see the figure appear around the corner. Slender and timid, with long, straight dark hair that hung to her waist. Her eyes were just as haunted as I remembered. But Thistle went absolutely still as she caught sight of the helpless figure of the Alpha on the bed.

Drugged and helpless.

The scent match who had broken her.

EPILOGUE ONE

"Lucy had *kittens*?"

My voice was a high-pitched squeak.

One more surprise, they'd told me. *One more fucking surprise.*

And I really hadn't known what to expect, because the word 'surprise' in this pack could mean getting a manicure, being gifted the blood of my enemies, or tiny little hairless creatures all stumbling around my Lucy's nest.

It did, I supposed, explain why she'd been so territorial about the cupboard since we got her back.

Poor thing was in a rush to find a comfortable place to give birth.

Zed, who, along with Knight, had been happily crossed legged watching the kittens amble about, looked up to us.

"You know," I said. "I'm calling Elena. She was obsessed with Lucy. I'm sure she wants a kitten."

"She's the one with connections with Lev," Kyan said absently. "I think…"

I blinked at that. "Why would Elena be involved with a Russian fixer?"

"Nah. Irish mob, from what I can tell, but Lev works with them."

Hold on. Irish—"What?"

I'd always known Annika was like me—seeing how she interacted with the world was a bit like looking in a mirror—but Elena? She was timid and a total hot-mess, in a cute-omega way. How had she ended up with the Irish mob?

"Packed up. Or kidnapped. Hard to tell with the mob. Probably... both?"

"Uh..." He really was stalking my High Roller life. "Wait. Can you contact her pack? Only thing better than getting a kitten is getting a surprise kitten."

Kyan shrugged. "I think so."

Well.

I didn't care what her alphas said. I'd be dropping a kitten at her doorstep.

EPILOGUE TWO

GLADE

I fixed my diamond studs onto my ears, taking a breath and checking myself once more in the dressing room mirror.

I pushed open the door and made my way to the second-floor bar just before open. Only, I stopped in my tracks at the obscenely handsome image of Zed Maverick in a dark, well fitted suit, leaning arrogantly against the bar. Which was odd, because it was still fifteen minutes until open.

Uh. My eyes narrowed. That was *my* bar. I hadn't been here in months. Why was he touching my bar before me? He grinned as he adjusted his cuffs, looking me up and down dramatically as if he hadn't driven me here in this outfit.

"What the hell are you doing?" I asked. He'd offered to drop me off, not come in.

"I got a job," he declared.

"You *what?*" I asked.

"I get paid to follow you around." He looked so fucking pleased with himself as he adjusted his collar. I narrowed my eyes. Ah. Shit. That was one of the security outfits.

"No way that's your job."

"Travis doesn't really care what I do, as long as there's the same number of bartending omegas at the end of the night as there was at the start. Apparently, a load of you have gone *missing* recently"—he cleared his throat.—"can't *imagine* why. But he's paying for extra shadows."

"You're joking."

"I certainly am not."

"And he didn't mind the face tattoos?" I asked, a little surprised at that.

"I like to think they look rather classy with the uniform," Zed said, affronted.

"He's right, you know." That was Tallow's voice behind me. I spun to see him sliding onto a barstool, but he'd only got halfway on before I'd thrown my arms around him.

"Damn, the scent match thawed you a little, Ice Queen." He chuckled, drawing me into a hug back. And to my relief, I didn't even flinch as his hand brushed the fabric over my scars.

"You know?"

"Well. None of us did until Roger spilled."

Ah. Right. Nothing stayed secret that long at the High Roller.

I let Tallow fill me in on the rest of the drama I'd missed while I got ready for the shift.

It had taken a while, after my heat, to recover. Not just from the heat, but from everything. One thing in my life I realised I'd loved was the High Roller.

But my first shift back was different.

I found it easier to talk to the patrons, Tallow, and Jade, who was back with her own pack, who seemed head over heels for her.

True to his word, Zed dogged me all night. He was quite good at keeping out of the clients' way, though he'd have to work on his facial expressions when packs hit on me, because that was just part of the job.

When I slipped into the passenger seat for the ride home, I noticed Zed giving me a funny look.

"What?"

"Nothing."

"What?"

"You were just... glowing in there."

I snorted. "My cheeks hurt."

"Yeh, I don't think I've seen you smile that much in my life—I didn't even know you could, Little Devil."

When we got home, I was still smiling, clutching Zed's hand as we walked through the main warehouse, where the huge graffiti wall had the words 'Sweet Oasis' with a crown beside it.

Both Kyan and Knight were waiting in my nest with snacks, and a movie running. My new nest was the old cell, but the guys had insisted on knocking a wall down and expanding it.

And renovating it.

And getting hot water to the shower—finally. But *no one* touched the little box of dead rose stems that sat on my vanity.

I tugged off my dress and heels, slipping into an oversized nest T-Shirt with all their scents on it, and burrowed beneath the piles of blankets until I was cuddled up between all three of my alphas. And of course, just like she always did at the scent of the full pack together, Lucy came rushing in, trampled over Knight, Kyan, and Zed, to curl up at my side.

"How was the evening?" Knight asked.

"Amazing."

"And you?" Knight prodded Zed. I was leaning forward in bed like a kid at Christmas, enjoying the sight of him unbuttoning his uniform, as Kyan tugged me into his arms.

"I missed you," he breathed. I giggled.

"Well," Zed said. "I learned that Glade is very proficient at pouring drinks."

"Really?" Knight asked.

"And the flirting?" Kyan had a grin on his face.

"Flirting?" I asked.

"We have bets."

"On what?"

"How long Zed will last at a job where he has to watch other alphas flirt with you."

"Turns out I think our omega is infinitely more sexy when the whole world gets to see..." He dropped down right between me and Kyan, dragging me against his chest, teeth grazing my neck. "...But not touch."

His palm brushed the claim along my back. The one with his name.

I loved it when he did that.

I was theirs, and they were mine.

A new page.

A new life.

I felt his hand brush my back, running along scars I now knew would never haunt me again, because for the first time in a long while, I could try for a little normal. Popcorn, and movies, and dates beneath the stars, and—

"Forever and always, Oasis," Kyan breathed. "You're our queen."

THE END

READ THISTLE'S STORY NEXT IN PSYCHO ALPHAS: PART ONE

THISTLE'S STORY
KNOX
ROGUE
MARIE MACKAY
PSYCHO
ALPHAS
THISTLE
BUNNY
DARK. DERANGED. UNHINGED.

AFTERWORD

Or check out the rest of the High Roller Omegas!
Queen of Hearts by Sarah Blue—Elena's book (if you want yet
more kidnapping, mafia and a kitty-loving Omega)
Queen of Spades by Jillian West—Annika's book (If you want
some more mafia, psycho Alphas and more soul matches)
Queen of Clubs by Alisha Williams—Jade's book (if you're feeling
rockstar Alphas and some more steamy MM)

MORE FROM ME?

Want to hear from me more? My newsletter has art, goodies (free
novellas and bonus content), ARC ops, as well as signed copy and
special edition opportunities! *Sign up at Mariemackay.com for all
my bonus stuff!*

Want more of my stuff and don't know where to start? *Did
you like...?*

- **The bully and rejection but with a bigger grovel?**
  Read Sweetheart *(This one also has a clinically
  psychopathic love interest, so if that sounds good—run!)*

- **The enemies to lovers + an omega who fights for her pack even before they learn she's on their side?** Read Havoc K!lled her Alpha
- **The *crazy* fun pack dynamics, Kyan-level *obsession*, but with a little more dark romance thrown in (dub/non con)?** Read Shattered Omega
- **Want more MM and *more* omegas?** Read Forget Me Knot for a double omega pack!
- *For all my book links, go to Mariemackay.com*